AF444848

F. R. E. KINNEY

Wind Dreamed

Copyright © 2026 by F. R. E. Kinney

All rights reserved. No part of this publication may be reproduced, stored, or transmitted in any form or by any means, electronic, mechanical, photocopying, recording, scanning, or otherwise without written permission from the publisher. It is illegal to copy this book, post it to a website, or distribute it by any other means without permission.

This novel is entirely a work of fiction. The names, characters, and incidents portrayed in it are the work of the author's imagination. Any resemblance to actual persons, living or dead, events, or localities is entirely coincidental.

F. R. E. Kinney asserts the moral right to be identified as the author of this work.

Imputing this work or any parts of it, including any amount of the text and any art or images on the cover or inside the book, into an AI without the express, written, and signed permission of the copyright holder is ILLEGAL.

First edition

ISBN: 979-8-9991498-2-4

Editing by Sarah Hemmi
Cover art by Em Kinney

This book was professionally typeset on Reedsy.
Find out more at reedsy.com

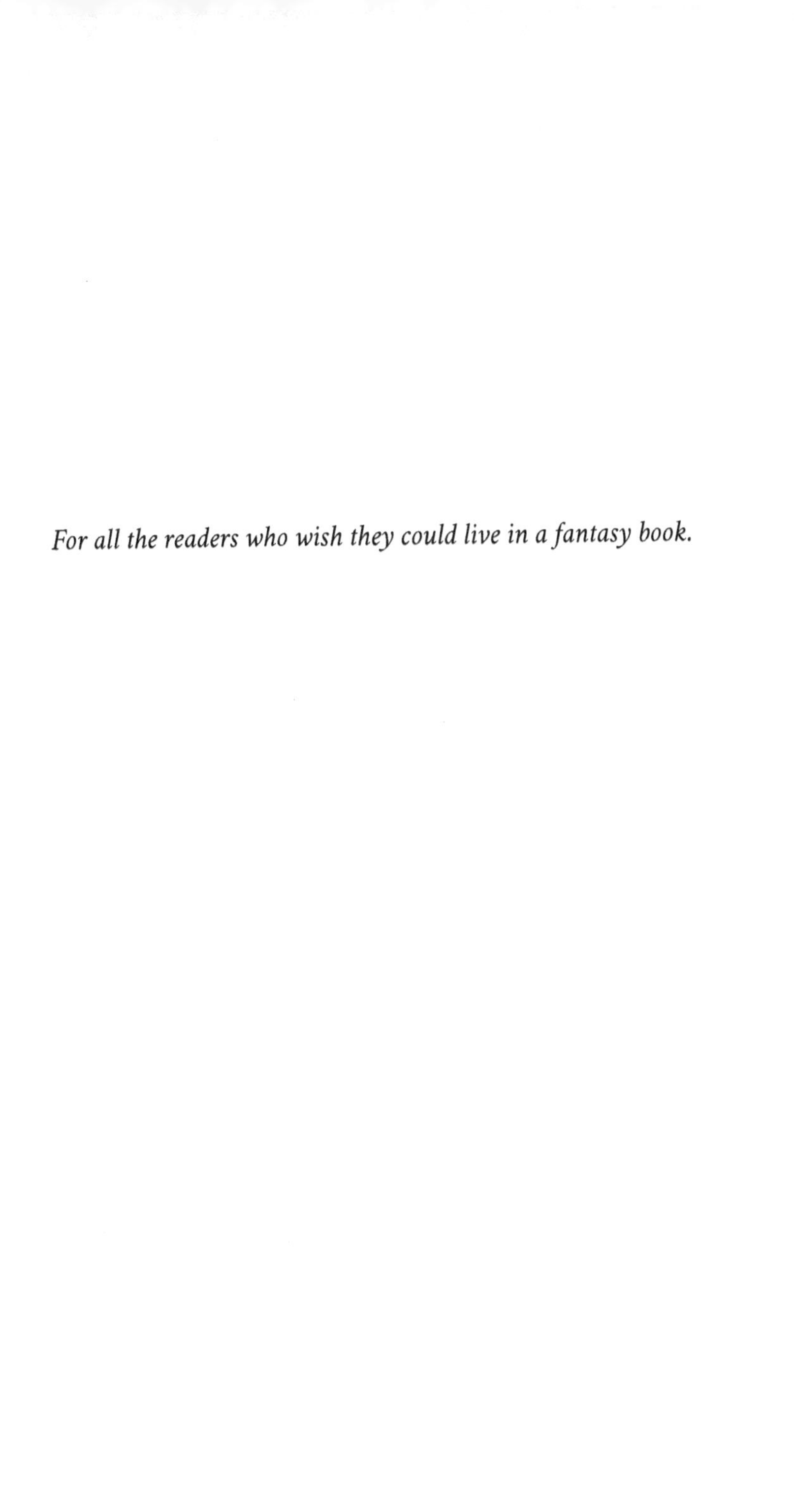

For all the readers who wish they could live in a fantasy book.

Trigger Warnings

This book contains depictions of physical injuries/assault
and kidnappings that may be upsetting to some readers.
Read at your own discretion.

1

One

The bed itched.

Beds weren't supposed to do that. They were supposed to be soft and inviting, coaxing you into slumber. Even in my half-awake state where thoughts blurred at the edges, I knew you weren't supposed to wake up with the desire to scratch your skin off.

My eyes cracked open and found... a field of grass.

Well, that answered one question. And spawned dozens more. Not the least of which being, how did I go from sleeping in my bed in my dorm room to sleeping outside?

I sat up, surprised that I wasn't sore in a dozen different places from sleeping on the ground. My hand patted the spot I'd been lying. It was remarkably soft. The ground had more give to it than expected and the grass was fluffy. Smoothing my fingers through the delicate blades, I marveled at how mattress-like it felt. It still tickled my hands, but otherwise, it was incredibly comfortable.

The sun-dappled field extended for several yards, inter-rupted periodically by patches of colorful wildflowers, until it dead-ended at a line of trees so thick, I couldn't see more than a couple feet past them. Though that probably had more to do with my missing glasses—things got really blurry without them. Big, leafy bushes obscured the ground under the tree branches.

I frowned as I pushed to my feet and turned. The forest surrounded the sunny meadow in which I stood with no clear path in or out. I patted the maroon tank top and white shorts I'd gone to sleep in last night. Nothing felt out of place. There were no aching wounds to indicate illegal organ harvesting or other abusive acts.

But *someone* had taken me from my bed last night. They must have drugged me too, since I couldn't recall the trip here. I definitely didn't sleep that deeply.

I started toward the edge of the field. The trees didn't look like the same kind from the forest that surrounded Mortorous Academy, but maybe this was just a different part that I'd never seen before. Or maybe they just looked different in the sunlight, which rarely pierced the ever-present cloud cover.

That had to be it. Someone was playing a joke on me, knocking me out and leaving me in the middle of the forest to find my way back to Mortorous Academy on my own.

I could name a few people who would think this sort of thing would be funny and ignore the danger it put me in. Nina Regine had been gunning for Sylvan Ravena for months, and as Sylvan's best friend, I must have also ended up in the crosshairs. Nina lived on the second floor of the girls' dormitory with most of her annoying little friends, like I did. Maybe my roommate or I had accidentally left the door unlocked, and they saw their chance. It all made sense.

Nina usually limited her bullying to snide comments and gossip. But at this point I wouldn't put anything past her. The girl had some serious issues.

I was more concerned with how I was supposed to get back to school. I could worry about Nina and whoever she'd coerced into helping her once I was safely back on campus. There had to be a path through the trees that I would catch sight of if I was close enough that I didn't need my glasses to see it.

"Wren Mentis."

The voice was barely more than a whisper, but I whipped around fast enough to give myself vertigo. Nothing. Just a breeze blowing through the meadow. I turned back to the forest. This prank was way out of line. I'd have to talk to my parents about it once I got back. They would be furious that this was allowed to happen under the school's watch.

"Wren." The whisper was right in my ear.

I jumped and whirled again. Still nothing.

The wind picked up. The fluffy grass whipped around my bare feet and ankles, making them itch. Flower petals blew off their stems and swirled in the air at the center of the meadow.

With one hand held up to ward off the flying plant bits, I took a step toward the strange series of gusts that converged above the spot where I'd awoken. They seemed to blow in five directions at once, radiating from a common center. My eyes widened as little steams of light flowed from that center to fully outline the wind's shape into something almost human.

"Wren." My name came from the strange weather phenomenon, whispered on the wind.

All the breath rushed out of my lungs. After going to school at Mortorous Academy for almost three years, I was used to seeing images of our mascot: the Boneman, a giant skeleton with the hornless skull of an antelope that had grown sharp, wolfish teeth.

I was also familiar with the mascot of our rival school, Animos Prep. I hadn't seen as much of it, and the costume didn't do it nearly enough justice. But the creature made of wind and light that called my name couldn't be anything other than the Wind Whisperer.

While the Boneman was an omen of death, the Wind Whisperer was a spirit of life, the opposite of him in all ways. But both creatures were just urban legends the school boards had turned into figureheads that the students could rally around for school spirit.

I had to be dreaming.

It made more sense than someone sneaking into my room, drugging me, and dumping me in the middle of the forest somewhere with the Wind Whisperer. Even the cruelest students at Mortorous Academy wouldn't do something like that. Right? Like me, most of them didn't truly believe the Wind Whisperer existed.

"You are awake, Wren."

The Wind Whisperer drifted across the grass and stopped right in front of me. It seemed to shrink, coalescing into a more rigid human shape. It didn't have eyes or a mouth or any other facial features, but it had a head. I did my best to look where its eyes should have been.

I squinted against the breezes wafting off its insubstantial body. "Uh, how do you know my name?"

The bright, eight-foot figure inclined its head. "I know the name of everyone who dreams."

A sigh of relief escaped me. "So, I *am* dreaming."

"No, you are very awake. This is all real." It waved a wispy hand at the meadow.

I certainly felt awake. Maybe it was a hallucination. I'd had one too many late nights reading books in bed and finally snapped. Mom always warned me things like this could happen to people who didn't get enough sleep.

"It is natural to be in denial when faced with the divine. People like to think they know how the world works and become rather distressed when they discover they are wrong." The words might have been intended to reassure me, but they sounded much more condescending.

"Ok, but you're…"

"What? An urban legend? A god of times long since lost? A counterfeit Aurora Borealis?"

I cringed. That's how I had described the Wind Whisperer to Sylvan a few weeks ago. Either this *was* all in my head, or the thing before me was the real Wind Whisperer. It couldn't have known what I said about it otherwise.

It raised a windy hand to my cheek. I expected the touch to be cold, but it felt like a warm summer breeze. "I know this is hard for you to comprehend. If we had the time, I would have approached you in a far more gradual and gentle way."

My brows furrowed. "If we had the time?"

It nodded. "You have come across information that is a threat to the world in which I live."

I laughed. "Unless something in one of those books I've been reading is true, I don't know any more about you than anyone else."

"But you have discovered the identity of your friend."

"My friend?"

"Sylvan Ravena. You have evidence that she is not who you thought she was."

My mouth opened to ask what it meant before the realization hit me. Sylvan had asked me to help her find her birth parents. She told me she'd been taken from them as a baby and only recently escaped her captors. I'd agreed, of course. Partially because I wanted my friend back after nearly losing her over some guy, and partially because the hunt sounded like something out of one of the books I loved to read.

We'd sent in a DNA test kit and hoped for the best. Last night, I'd gotten an email with the results.

It claimed Sylvan's parents had died.

Three hundred years ago.

I'd examined the gene map myself, and it matched the bodies of two people that had been excavated from the remains of an old inn buried under a rockslide centuries ago.

I'd stared at the results for an hour, perplexed beyond measure, before deciding that I needed to take a step back and read to clear my head. I had had no idea what I was going to tell Sylvan. I had had half a mind to march to her room and demand to know the secret to her immortality or search her room for her time machine.

But I had fallen asleep while reading. And woken up here. This wasn't a dream.

"So, the test results were real?" I breathed.

"Alarmingly," the Wind Whisperer replied gravely as it removed its hand from my face. "Usually, the Boneman has better control over his children."

"The Boneman? The Boneman is real too?" I'd gone to Mortorous Academy for all three years of my high school career, and a giant skeleton had been wandering around that close to campus? And Sylvan was one of his children, one of his Bone Touched?

Mind. Blown.

"All the gods are real, but you humans are not supposed to know that."

"Why not?"

I had always dreamed of finding out there was more to the world than we thought. I'd read books, watched movies, and wished I could be one of those characters that discovered they had dormant magical powers or found a portal to another world. And now that dream was coming true.

The Wind Whisperer folded its wispy hands in front of itself. "Because then we would have to disappear. The power humans have cultivated for themselves would be used to hunt us and our demigods, to take the magic we have by force, or at least try. Should the world discover that we exist, fear and greed would overtake reason, and we would have to abandon our sacred posts. Humans would be on their own, and they would not do well without our help."

I rolled my eyes. "You don't give us enough credit. We'd be fine."

"Can an ordinary human capture the lost spirits of the dead without getting themselves killed? Can an ordinary human slip into the dreams of other humans to influence their subconscious thought patterns? Can an ordinary human see into the future and avert imminent disasters before they occur?"

"Well—"

"No. They cannot."

I pursed my lips and clenched my fists. "I found you out.

So, you brought me out here to…what? Kill me before I can spill everything to everyone?"

I hadn't even found everything out. Until the Wind Whisperer told me, I'd thought the DNA results might have been a mistake. Would I have done enough of my own research to find out that they weren't? Probably. Would I have interrogated Sylvan about it until she told me everything? Probably. But I might not have. The Wind Whisperer just assumed I would and kidnapped me anyway.

And now it was here to silence me. My fists clenched tighter. If it thought I was going to go quietly, it had another thing coming. I had no idea how I was supposed to fight a creature that was made of light and wind, but I would certainly try.

The Wind Whisperer reared back as if I had slapped it. I wasn't sure if I could even touch it. It wasn't like it had a physical body other than the bits of flower petals and leaves swirling through the winds making up its figure. "I do not kill people. Neither does the Boneman. I am here to offer you a choice."

Why did I get the feeling it wasn't going to be much of a choice? Wasn't that how these kinds of things worked in stories?

"You know that Sylvan Ravena is Bone Touched. You know that the Boneman and I exist. You cannot be allowed to rejoin human society as you are now. So, you can either leave, go into exile, and live the rest of your life without ever seeing or speaking to another person again. Or you can join our world."

My arms crossed. "What do you mean *join your world*?"

"You would become a demigod."

My eyes went wide. I had to fight to keep my mouth from dropping open. That was pretty much everything I had dreamed of ever since I first read a fantasy book.

"You would have to be my demigod. The Boneman has an extremely specific way of picking his children, and Time..." The Wind Whisperer fell silent for a moment. "Time cannot be trusted with such delicate matters. So, that leaves me."

I'd barely heard of this *Time* that the Wind Whisperer spoke of, but when a mythical being told you something wasn't trustworthy, chances were they were either right or untrustworthy themselves. I didn't want to consider the latter.

"What's the catch?" There was always a catch in these situations, a dark side for the moon, a tail for the head of every coin, a double edge for every sword.

"You can no longer attend Mortorous Academy. You must transfer to Animos Prep and learn how to use your powers with my other demigods."

I had friends and a life at Mortorous. Sylvan was the first friend I'd made that I truly thought would last longer than a year. But... "You have other demigods at Animos?"

"Five of them. They will help guide you through the process since you will be starting later than usual."

I wasn't worried about that. I'd always done well in school and whatever else I put my mind to. Using magic was an extracurricular I would be more than happy to practice. And if there were others like me, I could make friends with them. I would miss Sylvan, but I could visit her on the weekends, right? And there was always texting.

I would definitely need to talk to her about all this demigod stuff. Even with the explanation the Wind Whisperer gave,

I couldn't believe she hadn't told me *anything* about it. And what about her parents? I had to tell her the truth about them.

But that could wait until I cleared the record with the god hovering in front of me.

"That doesn't sound too bad. What powers do I get?"

The Wind Whisperer laughed in a way that reminded me of leaves rustling in a gust of springtime air. "You will be a dream walker."

That sounded really cool, much better than living the rest of my life alone. "Ok. Then I agree to be your demigod."

The Wind Whisperer tilted its head. "Just like that? You do not need more time to think it over?"

"I'm sure." I stepped back and opened my arms wide. "Imbue me with your magic!"

It chuckled. "Very well, if you are certain. I need you to take three deep breaths for me."

I lowered my arms and gulped down a breath. I was a bit overly excited. I probably needed to calm down before the Wind Whisperer did its thing.

I blew out all the air and inhaled again. I hoped this wouldn't be painful. The Wind Whisperer should have told me if it was. That should be on the list of catches to being a demigod.

I exhaled and drew one last breath. Then again, what would a creature made of air know about pain? It had touched me earlier, but had it been able to feel me?

I emptied my lungs and opened my mouth to ask what happened next.

I didn't get the chance.

The Wind Whisperer dove at me in a rush of warm air. I didn't even have time to flinch back before it spiraled into a single thin column of wind and gusted into my mouth, up my nose. I gasped at the feeling of fresh air filling my throat without me actually breathing. That drew the Wind Whisperer in faster until it disappeared completely into my body.

My lungs felt fuller than they ever had before, like they might burst. I dropped to my hands and knees and coughed. Little wisps of light escaped my lips but got sucked right back in when I gasped for breath.

The Wind Whisperer was *in* my lungs. There was a god inside of me.

"What are you doing?" I choked while my body struggled to expel the Wind Whisperer.

"Imbuing you with my magic." The response whispered out of my own lips as I breathed out. "That is what you wanted, is it not?"

"You didn't tell me this was what you had to do," I choked.

"You did not ask."

My voice turned hoarse from all the coughing. If I did much more, I'd make myself throw up. "I knew there was a price to pay."

"You will get used to it in a moment. And once you absorb enough of my power, I will come out. I dislike staying in small spaces for long."

I rolled onto my back and focused on calming my breathing. I tried to distract myself by remembering the plot of the last episode of *Tournament of Crowns* I'd watched. It took longer than I would have preferred, but my lungs finally started working the way they were supposed to.

"How long is this going to take?" I asked in a scratchy voice.

"A few months at most," came the soft reply from somewhere in my respiratory system.

I sat up suddenly. "A few months!" The movement sent me into a coughing fit again.

"These things take time. Until then, you will be safe in this meadow. The bushes near the trees have edible berries, the stream down the hill has potable water, and nothing will come to eat you in the night as long as you stay out of the woods."

"So, not only do I have to live with you inside of my lungs for weeks, I have to survive out in the wilderness without electricity or running water?"

"The time will pass faster than you think."

I doubted that. Without a single book to read or movie to watch, I might as well start starving myself now. *Weeks* without anything to do. Torture. This was the catch, the other side of the coin.

It's better than spending your whole life in the middle of nowhere with no one to talk to. I told myself. I could go days without talking to anyone as long as I had a good book, but I was still human. I still wanted company.

At least I had the deity that had taken up residence in my lungs to keep me entertained. And after that I would have five new friends who would teach me how to use my new magic.

It was a fairytale dream come true.

Surely, I could wait a few months to have everything I'd ever wanted in life. The Wind Whisperer sounded optimistic about the timeline. I could probably find *something* to do.

What would Fare, the main character from one of my favorite books, *A Tear of Rage and Chaos*, do?

Probably figure out how to make a bow and arrows out of

a tree branch and some woven plant fibers with nothing but a sharp rock and some perseverance. I wasn't that bored yet, but I could file that idea away for later. If I felt like it.

"Wind Whisperer?" I asked as I lay back down on the squishy grass.

"Yes, Wren?" it breathed from inside my mouth.

"Do you know any good stories?"

It laughed and shifted around. I gasped and clutched my ribs at the strange sensation.

"I have lived for hundreds of thousands of years and seen every age of man. I could tell you stories until you died of old age, and we would only get through half of them."

I grinned. This definitely wouldn't be as bad as I thought it was going to be if I had my own audiobook living in my chest.

"Prove it."

2

Two

The bench outside the Animos Prep admin office was so much more comfortable than the one outside the Mortorous Academy office. For one thing, it had a pastel yellow cushion tied at the corners to the arms and back of the bench. It also leaned back some, which provided so much more back support than a rigid, upright model.

I tapped the toes of my sneakers against the marble floors and wondered how much it had cost to make them rainbow colored. Before, I would have thought such a thing would look tacky, but the ombre had been executed surprisingly well. The walls were an eclectic mix of murals, mostly scenes from nature, with a few abstract portraits sprinkled in. Whatever artist the school had commissioned to paint it was very talented.

The whole school was a riot of color. At Mortorous Academy, there was one uniform for the boys, a long-sleeved white button-down shirt and black slacks, and one for the girls, a long-sleeved white button-down shirt and a black skirt. Here the students wore a rainbow of pastel colors. They could wear skirts or pants, long-sleeved or short-sleeved shirts, and any color or combination of colors they wanted.

I'd been given a pale red short-sleeved button-down shirt and pants, but the admin told me they would provide me with all the color options in all the style combinations. The freedom was unexpected from a private boarding school but more than welcome. There had definitely been days back at Mortorous that I'd felt more like wearing pants than a skirt, especially in the cold months when we had only been allowed to put on white leggings to keep warm. It was better than nothing, but still not as good as a pair of pants.

"Wren Mentis?"

I looked up at a group of students who had approached from the opposite side of the bench. They wore all the colors of the rainbow except red.

"Nice to meet you," said a dark-skinned girl in yellow. She extended a hand. "I'm Imena."

I took her hand, expecting her to just shake. Instead, she pulled me off the bench and into a tight hug.

"Oh! Hi." It took me a second to get over my shock and hug her back. "Uh, nice to meet you."

She pulled back, bracing her hands on my shoulders. "Sorry. We're a pretty touchy-feely group. I forget it can take some getting used to." She spun me around to face the others. "This is everyone. Everyone, this is Wren. She's our new roommate."

The other four murmured greetings.

"Roommate?" I asked Imena. "All of you share a room?"

"Not exactly," answered a tall girl in blue. "But we'll get to that in a minute." She swooped in close and grasped my hand in both of hers. Her bright blue high ponytail swung close enough to brush my nose. "It's so nice to have another Wind Dreamed since Imena and Almos are going to be graduating in a couple months."

So, these were the other demigods the Wind Whisperer had told me about. At a glance, they all seemed normal, but there was a sense of peace radiating off them that normal people just didn't have. Like you could trust them with anything, and they would never betray you.

These were my new friends.

"Are we going to show her around, or did you want to hold her hand some more, Lorien?" A girl with bright green dip dyed hair and a pastel green uniform smirked. "Imena might start getting jealous."

Imena braced an elbow on my shoulder and leaned on me. "How do you know we weren't planning on asking her to join us tonight?"

Heat flooded my face. A tense laugh bubbled out of my chest. "Sorry, but I don't swing that way."

"Don't worry." Imena dropped her elbow to pat my shoulder. "I'm just joking. Lorien and I are exclusive."

"It's too early in the morning for this," grumbled a boy in purple. "Can we get moving? I skipped my morning coffee to be here." He started toward the open double doors that led into the school proper.

"Don't mind Reve. He's always this grumpy," whispered Lorien. "It's worse when he hasn't eaten or gotten his daily overdose of caffeine though."

I smiled. "Noted." My dad was the same.

"Let's get you familiar with the campus before he disappears into some dark hole."

I followed the group through the doors, repeating their

names and the colors of their uniforms in my head to remember them. *Imena, yellow. Lorien, blue. Reve, purple.*

I paused at the sight of their mascot statue. It was in the same place that Mortorous Academy kept theirs, a dais in an alcove facing the doors. But this statue wasn't just a bunch of pieces of painted plastic.

It was a life-sized blown glass sculpture. Most of it was clear, so you could see a distorted version of the wildflower mural painted on the wall behind it. But there were threads of color running along its nebulous limbs too, just like the lights flowing through the Wind Whisperer in real life. Despite it still having no eyes, it seemed to stare at me as I stared at it.

"Beautiful, isn't it?" the girl in green said, bringing up the rear of the group. "Supposedly the first Wind Dreamed to come to school here made it."

"It's a work of art." The whole school seemed to be.

We started walking again. "Yeah, that's kind of our thing here at Animos Prep. You won't find any conventional societal molds here. It's one of the big selling points when they bring prospective students through. We produce a lot of artists, musicians, creative writers. You name an art form, and we have someone in that field out there making a name for themselves after graduating from this school."

I chewed my lower lip. "So, this is an art school?" I wasn't sure how an academic like me would do in this kind of place.

The girl laughed. "No, but the environment encourages creativity so much it's hard not to get sucked in and at least pick up a new hobby or two. You should see all the clubs they have. I mean, have you ever heard of a school that has a stuffed animal sewing club?"

I twirled the end of my braid around a finger. "Can't say

that I have, but it sounds interesting. If you're into that kind of thing, of course."

"Can't say that I am, but if you are this is the place for you. I'm Frida, by the way." She offered me her hand.

I took it. "Wren." *Frida, green.*

She shook and let go instead of trying to drag me into a hug. "I know. I've been looking forward to getting a new Wind Dreamed, so I won't be the newest one anymore."

"Thanks?" It didn't feel like a compliment, but she said it with enough enthusiasm that it couldn't have been intended as an insult.

"It's not a bad thing to be new," she assured me. "There's just always that feeling of being slightly behind. Though maybe that's because this was my first time going to a private school. Anyway, it won't be a problem for you." She patted my back. "You're older and more adjusted, so you'll be fine. And if you aren't, that's what the rest of us are here for."

I smiled. "Thanks." They really were meant to be my friends.

The rest of the school was just as artsy as the foyer. Murals blended into each other with ease, like they were meant to be part of one big image. The floors glittered in their strange but beautiful rainbow colors. The classrooms had desks with padded chairs and more leg room than even someone as tall as Lorien could want.

The cafeteria had food that didn't taste like it had been taken out of the freezer and stuffed in the oven for a little too long. The library was so big and full of books. They practically called my name. I could hardly tear myself away to continue with the tour. All the buildings were made of cream-colored stone that was much more inviting than Mortorous's dark, gothic structures. And the campus was lush with flowering bushes, trees, and garden beds.

"And here is our dorm," announced Imena as we climbed up the steps to a six-story building that seemed to glow in the afternoon light. A covered porch full of couches and chairs wrapped around the front of the building.

"It's pretty big," I said. "Do all the students live in here?" It looked large enough to be co-ed.

"Yeah. We're on the top floor. Come on."

The first floor was the common room, just like in the dorms at Mortorous. It looked like someone had been indecisive about how the couches should look, though. There were a dozen different colors in a handful of shapes and shades. It felt like walking into a furniture store.

"Race you to the top!" Lorien called as she darted for a door off to the right.

Almos, the boy in orange, rolled his eyes. "She likes to take the stairs even though we live on the sixth floor."

Imena gestured at the two sets of elevator doors on the back wall. "She's gotten pretty good at making it up all the way without having to stop to catch her breath at each landing."

Almos waved a hand. "Maybe because she climbs them at least once a day. It's called working out. She used to cave and take the elevator the last couple of floors up when she first got it into her head to start doing that. And good thing too. You know what happens when a Wind Dreamed can't breathe."

I shuddered. The Wind Whisperer told me that we could die if we couldn't breathe. Because our magic was in our lungs and intertwined with our life forces, if we didn't have enough air to feed it, we'd be in big trouble. Unfortunately, that meant swimming was off the table.

"You don't give her enough credit." Imena rolled her eyes as we loaded into the elevator. She inserted a key at the bottom of the panel, turned it, and pushed a button labeled PH.

My eyebrows rose. "You have a penthouse? In a dormitory?"

Imena winked at me. "*We* have a penthouse."

Whoa.

The elevator rose. As soon as the doors started to open, Lorien lunged at us from the other side with a shriek. I was the only one who jumped back, nearly knocking Reve over. He grumbled something in annoyance under his breath, but the others were completely unbothered. Lorien cackled as she skipped off.

"That's mostly why she started climbing the stairs," Reve muttered. "You'll get used to it."

I quickly righted myself. "Uh-huh. I guess it's... fun for her?"

He shrugged and filed out with the others. "I guess." I could tell he really wasn't a people person despite his aura of calm. I wouldn't call myself a people person either, but he seemed like a downright hermit. He hadn't said much of anything during the tour to anyone besides that time he'd urged us to hurry up.

The room beyond the elevator distracted me from any further musings about the introvertedness of my companions. The common room downstairs had looked like a Frankenstein of colorful furniture pieces, but this room pulled off the multicolored look without appearing so hastily put together.

It looked like what I imagined the inside of a prism would. Different shades of paint blended into one another on the walls in a complete rainbow. The carpet and ceiling were a bright silvery white. Windows decorated half of the walls, letting in enough light that the overhead ones became unnecessary. The little suncatchers that hung from the blinds cast tiny rainbows over the walls and carpet. The furniture mirrored the walls. They were all the same style but came in different rainbow colors that matched the pastels of our uniforms.

There was a yellow armchair, an orange recliner, a green loveseat, one of the hanging chairs that looked like a blue egg made of whicker, and a puffy, red chair. Reve strode out of a swinging door with a mug in his hand and headed toward the purple sectional. I hadn't even seen him leave the room.

Almos grinned. "Wren, I'd like to be the first to say how excited we are that you're here, Wren."

"I already said I was excited to have her," Frida interjected.

Almos rolled his eyes. "You may be a little late to the game, but the Wind Whisperer chose you for a reason, so I'm sure you can pick everything up quick enough. It's really not hard once you put your mind to it."

That was two people who had mentioned I was behind.

"When do Wind Dreamed usually start practicing their magic?" I asked.

Reve turned sideways on his couch and stretched out his legs across the cushions. "They typically come in at the beginning of their first year, but we've had late arrivals before."

"Yeah, Reve arrived halfway through his first year and did just fine," Lorien chirped. "I'm sure you'll be a similar story."

I smiled. "I'm sure."

I'd been waiting my whole life for something fantastical like this to happen to me. I wasn't about to screw it up. Besides, I was good at all the things that mattered. I always had been. There might be a learning curve, but I had no doubts I would overcome it like I had with everything else.

I leaned forward. "So, when do we get started?"

"Tonight," Imena declared. "In the meantime, make yourself at home. The rest of us have to go to our afternoon classes, but feel free to explore. Your stuff should be in your room, so you can unpack. It's the first door on the left." She gestured at a hallway that snaked behind the elevator.

My stuff. I had never moved out of my dorm at Mortorous Academy. Someone else must have packed my things and brought them here.

"Who brought all my stuff? I didn't have time to get everything together." It couldn't have been my parents. I doubted they knew I wasn't at Mortorous anymore. I needed to call them and try to explain things without giving away the magical world that I had just become a part of.

Imena tilted her head. "You didn't?"

"The Wind Whisperer made me Wind Dreamed kind of suddenly." I didn't think it was a good idea to explain why I became a demigod. The others seemed to think I had been chosen, not forced into it. Even if I had technically decided to do it, it wasn't the same.

Almos shrugged. "It was probably someone from the school. They run the Wind Whisperer's errands sometimes."

I didn't want to think about some stranger rummaging through all my belongings. I said my goodbyes to the other Wind Dreamed and darted off to find my room, anxious to make sure nothing was missed.

My room wasn't hard to locate. The doors were color

coded too. The first one on the left was the same shade of red as my uniform.

I'd never thought of red as being my color before, certainly not such a light shade, but I was far too invested in the metaphor of us all being the different colors that made up white light to protest. Many parts but one body, and all that.

Throughout my life, making friends hadn't been the easiest thing to do. Between rapid digitalization and shrinking attention spans, fewer and fewer people were interested in the academic matters that I had been raised to value. Even at the private schools my parents sent me to, few people wanted to have study parties where they actually studied instead of swapping answers and looking up how to complete problems on their phones. Even fewer people were interested in reading for fun.

I'd always had a friend or two in school, but we'd never stayed friends for more than a year, never gotten close the way I wished I could be with someone.

But it seemed like that was about to change. Sure, I wasn't far from graduating, but these seemed like such genuine people, and the school felt so alive. I had high hopes.

My room was about the same size as the one I'd left behind at Mortorous Academy, but I had it all to myself instead of sharing it with a roommate. It had some basic furnishings— a bed against one wall with a nightstand next to it, a desk against another, a pair of closet doors. A stack of carboard boxes had been piled in the middle of the room with the words "Wren Penthouse" written on the sides of them.

I closed the door and ripped into the boxes. They held all my things from my dorm at Mortorous neatly sorted based on where they belonged. There was a large box for bedding, a smaller box for school supplies, and another for toiletries. I hoped a woman had packed that box.

Putting everything where it needed to go didn't take nearly as long as I thought it would, but I didn't have to work around a roommate this time. My bedding was bright blue instead of pastel red, but I could probably figure out how to get a hold of something more suited to my new role.

At the bottom of my backpack, which was also blue, I found my phone. I'd missed it during my weeks in the Wind Whisperer's field. The god had kept me reasonably entertained, but there was no substitute for reading from my eBook app with its virtual library of stories.

My notifications were surprisingly sparse, just a couple messages from my parents and a note from my eBook app that I'd missed a "buy one get one fifty percent off" sale last week.

I sighed. The things I did to live out my dreams of having magical powers.

My text thread with my parents had been completely deleted except for the messages I'd missed from them.

Don't worry, sweety. We've gotten all the paperwork and fees worked out. You're due to start at Animos Prep next week. Do you want any help moving? That was a text from my dad five days ago.

There was no reply from my end, but my mom had messaged as if there was. *Ok. Be careful. I know it's a long drive. You might want to take the Mortorous Academy magnet off your car in case someone tries to trash it. I know the school rivalry can get pretty intense.*

And that was it. Someone had managed to get into my phone and send my parents messages pretending to be me so they would know I wasn't at Mortorous anymore? Weird. Had it been the same person who packed up all my stuff and brought it here?

I wondered how the others had handled their parents when they became Wind Dreamed. Did they come from similar family situations? We couldn't all be the children of oil tycoons. That would be a little too on the nose, and a bit classist honestly.

And then there was the question of my car. Had someone brought it here? A little more digging in my backpack revealed that my keys were in the same place I always kept them. But nothing about this transition was normal.

I opened my door and went to go hunt down my car.

* * *

My sleek, green sedan was at Animos Prep, tucked away in a corner of the student parking garage. Lorien got really excited when I mentioned it over a takeout dinner in the living room where we all sat in the seats that matched our uniform colors. Apparently, only Reve had a car, but he rarely went anywhere and refused to take anyone with him unless it was an emergency.

"But now we can actually go into town and have some fun on the weekends!" Lorien squealed.

I grinned. "Definitely. When I was at Mortorous, I used to go into town all the time."

The room fell silent.

"You went to Mortorous Academy?" Lorien breathed.

They all stared at me like I'd turned into a giant spider. "Yeah. I know our schools have a rivalry and stuff but try not to hold that against me." I smiled tightly, trying to diffuse the sudden tension.

Frida shook her head. "We don't care about the rivalry. It's just…strange. Why would you become Wind Dreamed if you went to the Boneman's school?"

I shrugged. I really didn't want to get into all the drama with Sylvan's DNA test. They were already weirded out from knowing what school I went to before I became Wind Dreamed. I doubted they would be as welcoming if they realized I was only here because I had discovered their world on my own. They were probably here for legitimate reasons, while I had been bribed with magic to stay quiet.

"Do you like it better here?" Imena asked with a grin.

And just like that, the mood shifted to something much more lighthearted.

"It's certainly more colorful. Mortorous is all black and white. It's a nice aesthetic, but it can get kind of dull sometimes."

"I always thought their uniforms were dreary," Frida said. "They're just too rigid."

The others started in on the conversation, and I sat back, happy to let them talk without drawing too much attention to myself.

"So, do we start with the lessons now?" I asked as we cleaned up our takeout containers.

"Not quite." Imena wore a smile that promised trouble. "We have to go to sleep first."

I frowned. "We practice in the middle of the night?"

"How much did the Wind Whisperer tell you about what we do?" Almos asked.

"It said something about us being dream walkers." I had

made my own assumptions about what that meant but forgot to ask many questions. I was just glad to be part of something like this.

He smiled. "It's pretty exciting, lots of work, but exciting. The first step is to go to sleep. The rest will become apparent after that."

"If you say so." I was a little skeptical, but dream walking sounded like something better done while asleep anyway.

Everyone exchanged their goodnights as we retired to our rooms. Almos jumped in the shower in the bathroom at the end of the hall. Lorien followed Imena into her room, whispering and giggling until the door shut. I didn't see Reve go into his room but heard shuffling from the other side of his door.

"Don't be too nervous," Frida said as she passed me on her way to her room. "It can be a little disorienting at first, but you get used to it pretty quick."

"Thanks." I slipped into my new room and stared at the bed.

It looked just like the one in my Mortorous Academy dorm had, but everything was different. So far, the Wind Whisperer had delivered on its promises. The school was enchanting. The other Wind Dreamed were friendly. All that was missing was the magic.

I changed into the usual tank top and shorts that I wore to bed and snuggled under the blankets. Falling asleep was easier said than done. I'd had a full day but still buzzed with restless energy. Maybe it was all that time spent in the meadow, doing next to nothing, that made me ache for action. Maybe it was the urge to explore my new world more thoroughly.

I rolled onto my side and waited to calm down enough to

fall asleep.

3

Three

One moment I was lying in bed in complete darkness, trying to lose consciousness, and the next I was hovering in the air in a sea of swirling colors. I gasped and frantically searched for solid ground. There was none. Only ribbons of light gliding around me like snakes through water.

Some were thick and glowed so bright it was hard to make out the other ones around them. Some were thin and dim enough that I had to squint to see they were even there. They writhed around each other in a brilliant ball with me hovering in the center. The shifting pattern reminded me of the Wind Whisperer's strange but beautiful colors.

I reached out and touched one of the brighter ones. Instantly, the scenery changed. The lights disappeared. Ground materialized under my feet along with four walls and a ceiling. Figures with blurred edges moved around me in some kind of dance routine.

I ducked out of their way behind a curtain, a stage curtain. The usual darkness that obscured the audience from the performers' vision was gone. One girl, who didn't have fuzzy edges, was guided onto the stage. She looked incredibly nervous as she started to sing.

There was no reason for her to be. She hit every note perfectly, weaving a song together that had the hazy audience cheering for her. Her voice never wavered as she began to dance too. That took a considerable amount of talent and breath control. Then again, I was fairly sure this was a dream, so anything was possible.

Abruptly the lighting in the audience shifted to highlight a young boy in a dirty, oversized shirt. His features were indistinct like almost everyone else. Everyone except for the girl, who paused as she took notice of him.

"Find us." His voice was no more than a whisper, but it carried over the cheering crowd.

The girl frowned.

A hand landed on my shoulder and spun me around to face a young man who didn't have blurry edges either. "What are you doing here?"

"Uh, I just—"

The man dragged me farther backstage until our surroundings dissolved into a white expanse. "Get your own dream. I've already got this one taken care of."

I opened my mouth to ask what he meant, but he pushed me hard. I fell back with a grunt. When I looked up again, I was back in the ball of light.

What the heck was that? I struggled to right myself in the zero-gravity space.

"Wren." I turned to see the Wind Whisperer drifting toward me from the tangle of color.

"Please tell me you're going to explain what all of this is." I waved my arms at our surroundings, still wobbling without anything to ground me.

The Wind Whisperer put a hand on my arm to steady me. "My apologies for arriving late. There was a bit of a situation I had to attend to."

"Yeah, no problem. It's not like I was on the verge of panicking, because I have no idea where I am or what I'm doing here."

"There is no need to worry. You are perfectly safe here. Welcome to the Dream Realm. This is where you will develop the skills you need to do your Wind Dreamed duties." The Wind Whisperer floated over to the churning wall of light. "Each one of these colors is a dream. If a dream glows brighter, that means a Wind Dreamed is already in it, so you should not try to enter it too. Things get complicated when more than one Wind Dreamed is trying to influence a dream at the same time."

With my balance restored, I crossed my arms. "What do you mean, 'influence a dream'?"

The Wind Whisperer drifted back down in front of me. "As a Wind Dreamed, you are a dream walker. That means it is your job to enter the dreams of normal humans every night and send them the subliminal messages that will guide them to live their best lives instead of having your own dreams."

I grimaced. "That sounds... complicated." And I wouldn't have my own dreams anymore?

The Wind Whisperer nodded. "Depending on the dream, it can be. But I will be here with you for the next few weeks to walk you through some easier dreams and help you perfect your craft."

That didn't sound too bad. With the security net and

guidance the Wind Whisperer would provide, getting the hang of this dream walker stuff should be simple.

"Ok. How do I start?"

The Wind Whisperer took my hand, sending warm breezes coasting over my skin. "I think this one would be a good first dream for you." It touched a duller thread of pink light.

We got sucked into the dream the same way I'd been sucked into the other one. The light ball vanished, and my feet met ground. Houses and trees sprang up all around us. Vines and bushes popped into existence all over the place. It looked like we were standing in a neighborhood that had been left unattended for decades. Nature had started to reclaim the space. But the houses were still in good condition under leafy vines and behind flowering bushes.

The hazy outlines of people congregated on the front lawns. I started to back up out of their way, but the Wind Whisperer urged me forward. A large shadow passed overhead, followed by a joyful laugh.

"This one should speak to you," the Wind Whisperer murmured as the crowd around us cheered.

I shielded my eyes against the bright sun to look at the thing circling above us. It was a girl with giant, white-feathered wings. She glided through the sky like she was made to do so. Her edges weren't blurry like all the other people around us.

"That is our dreamer," the Wind Whisperer said. "The ones you can see clearest are always the ones doing the dreaming."

"This is a really nice dream she's having." I could remember having flying dreams myself. They were always my favorites.

"Yes. Now the work begins."

"What work?" I couldn't imagine this needed any fixing. Flying was a dream come true.

"Flying dreams usually signify a desire for freedom." The Wind Whisperer tugged me through the crowd as the girl swooped low over the street. "Combined with the applause, I would guess she is in need of some affirmation. She probably views herself as too ordinary and not good enough, so her subconscious is manifesting a way she can have what she wants. She is being hailed as some kind of hero."

"Wow. You got all that just from this?" I waved at the spectators.

"Not just this. It is a common condition. People these days are feeling the pressure and worrying they will not be able to handle it. I would wager a guess she is interested in nature too, given all the plants. My kind of girl." The Wind Whisperer combed its wispy fingers through the leaves of a nearby tree. "A lot of things manifest in the mind while it is unconscious."

"How am I supposed to add anything to the dream if there's so much to it already?" It seemed pretty complete to me.

"Your job as a Wind Dreamed is to help people process and rise above the things they want to get to the things they *need*."

"Looks like she has everything she needs already." I would love to live out this fantasy.

The Wind Whisperer sighed. "Because you are looking at it through the lens of what *you* want. You must think objectively. Analyze the dream and give it something more. For instance, she already has the freedom she craves with those wings. Why does she need the approval of her peers? She should be *free* from such a want."

"So, I should make her *rise above* it all?"

The Wind Whisperer didn't have a mouth, but I could hear the smile in its voice. "Exactly. Take her higher."

"But how do I do that?" I couldn't exactly fly over and pull the girl up myself.

"You just have to will it to happen. Really feel it and want it. See it in your mind's eye and make it happen." The Wind Whisperer leaned close, watching the girl over my shoulder.

"Ok."

I focused on the girl as she swooped around the street again. She should fly up in the clouds like the birds did. She didn't need to be tied to the ground anymore.

The girl started to soar upward.

"Good," the Wind Whisperer murmured. "Keep it up."

That was the idea. She had to keep going up until she couldn't hear the crowd below. Until she was in the sky.

All alone.

With no one to tell her they were proud of her or laugh with her or hold her when she was sad or talk about the last book she'd read.

The figure high in the sky suddenly dropped, diving back down. The crowd around us still applauded. The girl didn't seem to notice that she was plunging to her death. She probably wouldn't actually die since this was just a dream, but I doubted it would be a pleasant way to wake up.

"Bring her back up." The Wind Whisperer's voice was gentle but assertive.

All my concentration went into slowing her descent. I couldn't let her crash. I could still use this. I just had to make her swoop back up. Her momentum would carry her even higher into the sky than before.

Was that what she really needed, though?

The girl's wings opened wide, and she glided to a stop on the street. She looked around with a frown as the people around us fell silent and watched her. She took off running, then jumped into the air. But her wings were stiff, refusing to flap. She landed back on the ground and tried again with no success. The people around us started to fade out of existence one by one.

"What happened, Wren?" the Wind Whisperer asked softly.

"I don't know. It was going fine a minute ago." I willed the girl's wings to work. Nothing.

She stood in the middle of the street as the crowd slowly dissipated, leaving her alone with just me and the Wind Whisperer. Her wings drooped as she walked down the empty street. Everything turned grey.

"She wakes." The Wind Whisperer took my hand and pulled me away.

I followed it behind one of the houses but glanced back at the girl. Her image was fading away rapidly along with her surroundings, but from what I could still see of her sketchy outline, she looked like a fallen angel with her head lowered and her wings dragging on the ground.

The Wind Whisperer tugged me behind the house, and suddenly we were back in the Dream Realm.

My free hand clenched into a fist. "What went wrong? I did everything you told me to."

"Dream walking is about more than mechanically doing what you are told. You must believe in what you want to happen. Tell me, what were you thinking about when you were attempting to change the dream?" it asked as it released my hand.

I folded my arms. "I was thinking about making the girl fly higher."

"And?" the Wind Whisperer pressed.

"I… kept thinking about how alone she would be up there all by herself."

"How do you know she would have been all by herself? She might have gone all the way up to heaven and made friends with the angels. It was a dream. Anything could have happened, especially if you were there to guide her."

My gaze dropped to the nonexistent ground. "I'm sorry." I'd failed. My attempts to change the dream were useless. They were less than useless. They'd made it worse!

"There is nothing to apologize for. It was your first time. You cannot be perfect without any practice."

"But you said this one would be easy." I knew I was new to this. I knew I needed to put in the work, just like all the Wind Dreamed before me. But I'd failed so spectacularly. How could I have been that bad?

"I am not an ineffable god, Wren. You can never tell for sure how something will go until it is already happening."

I wasn't convinced. Everyone had been so confident that I would be able to do this, but I hadn't. I'd let them all down, myself included.

The Wind Whisperer cupped my cheek and guided my face up to look at it. "I still see promise in you. You will have many nights to work out the kinks and get used to this. For now, it is time for you to wake up. We will try again tomorrow night. I am sure you will do better now that you know what to expect."

I nodded halfheartedly. "Ok. I'll see you tomorrow night then."

"I will see you then, Wren." The Wind Whisperer leaned forward and pressed its forehead to mine.

4

Four

Sunlight poked through the window curtains when my eyes opened the next morning. That was another difference between Animos Prep and Mortorous Academy. Mortorous was located farther north and closer to the coast, where it was almost always humid and cloudy, often with strong chances of rain or fog. The days at Animos were the opposite, bright and sunny with a nice breeze that carried the scents of all the flowering plants straight to you.

The difference in weather helped ease the disappointment from the night before. It was easier to have a positive outlook when the weather was nice.

I kicked off the covers and got dressed in the first thing I pulled from my closet—another red uniform. Today was going to be my first day of classes. I might not have done so well with my magic lessons, but I had always been good at school. The other Wind Dreamed hadn't been there to witness my failure in the Dream Realm, but they would certainly see how academically accomplished I was. This was where I could prove myself until I got the hang of this whole demigod thing.

The others were already bustling around the living room, packing up supplies, and messing around with each other.

"Frida, did you steal my pencil sharpener?" Imena called as she riffled through her backpack.

"I didn't *steal* it. I *borrowed* it." A yellow piece of plastic flew across the room.

Imena caught it with shocking ease. "People usually ask when they borrow things from other people. Or at least tell them when they take them."

Frida threw her hands in the air. "I was in a rush to finish some homework last night! What do you want from me?"

Imena smiled and shook her head then noticed me. "Morning, chickpea. Sleep well?"

Lorien popped her head out of the swinging door. "How was your first dream walk?"

"A little rough," I admitted with a grimace. "But it could have been worse." At least the dreamer hadn't splatted in the middle of the street in front of all those people. I'd been able to help her that much.

Lorien leaned on the doorframe. "Don't worry about it. None of us got it right on our first time either. Dream walking is like nothing you've ever done before. It takes some getting used to."

My expression was tight. "Thanks." Maybe the problem had more to do with the dream itself and I would do better with a different one tonight.

Almos came up behind Lorien and nudged her out of the doorway. "Ready for your first day of school?"

"Yes." I had all my supplies in my backpack. Yesterday, the admin had given me a stack of textbooks and other reading material I would need for my classes. I had it all organized in the many pockets of my bag and was ready to go.

Reve drifted out of the swinging door next with a plate of biscuits in one hand and a mug of coffee in the other. He shoved the plate into my hands as he passed. I barely had time to grab it before he let go and continued on his way to his room without saying a word to anyone.

"Do we have our own kitchen?" I asked as I picked up one of the biscuits and took a bite. It was a little cooler than I usually preferred but tasted really good.

"Yeah, it's great." Almos stole a biscuit off my plate. "Reve has a treasure trove of family recipes that keep our stomachs happy and our tastebuds even happier."

My eyebrows rose. "*Reve* made these? Not that I don't think he could, but he doesn't seem like the type to get up early enough to make something from scratch."

"He usually mixes all the stuff up the night before, so all he has to do in the morning is heat up the oven and let it do the rest for him. Gives him plenty of time to drink his coffee and get ready before eating."

Lorien snatched a piece of Almos's stolen biscuit. "He says it's calming, but I've tried to help him before, and it only ever made me anxious. Some of the stuff he makes is really complicated, and he takes his cooking *very* seriously."

"Lorien doesn't have the patience for cooking or baking," Imena stage-whispered to me.

"Hey! You're supposed to be on my side." Lorien gave her a poke in the shoulder.

Imena leaned over to kiss Lorien on the cheek. "I'm always on your side, chickpea."

Frida cleared her throat pointedly. "Where did Reve go? I

thought he was ready."

"I'm here." Reve breezed out of the bedroom hallway toward the elevator. He'd traded his mug for a black backpack. "Let's go."

Everyone grabbed their bags and followed him, stuffing themselves into the elevator. All except Lorien, who called something about seeing us at the bottom and disappeared off to the left. I grabbed the last biscuit, set the plate down in my red chair, and scurried after the others.

It was a quiet ride down. Everyone was still waking up. Maybe we all needed coffee in the mornings. Or maybe they were all thinking about how their dream walking had gone last night. Hopefully, better than mine.

Would it be impolite to ask them about what they saw and did? It might help me do better tonight if I knew what kind of things to expect and how to react to them.

Before I could get up the courage to talk about it, the elevator opened on the busy common room. Students milled around, mostly heading toward the front doors, but some lounged on the couches, talking and laughing. It was so much more lively than the girls' dormitory at Mortorous Academy.

Unless Nina was throwing one of her infamous Friday night parties, spending time in the common room had been a solemn affair. Everyone acted like they had just come back from a funeral, all quiet and keeping to themselves. I'd heard plenty of noise from behind the closed doors of people's dorm rooms, though. Maybe they'd just wanted to keep up appearances in public.

"You're staring," Almos noticed as we spilled out into the throng.

I glanced up at him. "I'm used to a quieter common room."

He grinned. "I hope you're not too attached to silence. We like to see and hear each other living here."

I noticed. I should have expected it, since the school's mascot was the god of life and Mortorous's was the god of death, but I'd been to private boarding schools my whole life, and none of them had been like this. It was exciting but nerve-wracking. How could it be so different from everything I'd experienced before? Wasn't a school a school?

We split up once we got outside. Imena and Almos headed off to their fourth-year classrooms. Frida drifted off by herself, since she was the only first year. And Lorien and Reve escorted me to the third-year classrooms.

We had history first. I felt good walking in. I'd read up on history in my spare time. I preferred fantasy books, but the stories of how things had happened in the past still interested me. Lorien and Reve sat in the front. Not my usual spot in the classroom, but I could make do as long as I sat with people I already knew.

It made me wonder what Sylvan was doing at Mortorous. The thought suddenly struck me that I hadn't told her I moved schools, and it had been months since the Wind Whisperer took me from my dorm room. Was she sitting at her desk in the back of Dr. Shalm's English class next to Nick, wondering what had happened to me?

I reached for my phone to text her, but the bell rang. I wasn't sure how strict they were about phone usage during school hours here, but Mortorous had drilled an uncompromising "No Phones" rule into me. It was better to play it safe, so I left my phone in my pocket.

The professor's desk was still markedly empty, but everyone fell silent as if he stood right in front of us, ready to yell if anyone so much as sneezed. A minute passed, then two, three, five.

I glanced at Lorien. She smiled at me. I opened my mouth to ask what was going on, but Reve, who sat behind me, slapped a hand over my mouth. I grunted and tried to pull away.

"Nice try, Reve, but that's time!" a voice called from the back of the classroom.

I turned in my seat to see what I thought was a student stand up from the back row. Now that I looked at him, I could tell he was much older than any of the kids in the room. But he still wore a green uniform and had a matching backpack slung over one shoulder and a green cap on his head that hid most of his features unless he looked directly at you.

He grinned at me as he made his way up to the front of the classroom. "I hope you don't mind too much, but I always like to play a little game when we get new students to see how invested they are in this class. Most only last a minute or so before they get fidgety or try to leave, so congratulations on making it five times as far!"

"Your disguise was very thorough today, Professor Midrid," Lorien said.

"Thank you, Lorien. And everyone else too for indulging me." He bowed dramatically to the class at large.

I blinked in silent confusion. It was a test? And everyone had been in on it? What kind of class was this?

Professor Midrid rounded his desk, faced us, and planted his hands on the bright green wood. "First off, welcome, Wren. It's always nice to have a new face in class."

I gave him a smile that didn't quite reach my eyes.

"But since we've already lost so much time, we'll have to

skip the elaborate introductions. Who can tell me where we left off on Friday?"

Several people raised their hands with considerable enthusiasm. I'd never seen so many students get excited about history. So refreshing. It was usually just me who was eager to answer questions in class.

Professor Midrid called on a boy a couple rows back.

"We were talking about the last battle in the revolution," the boy declared.

Midrid clapped his hands together so loudly that I jumped. "Indeed, we were. That's exactly where we left off, thank you, Tom. So, now we're going to discuss something a little less exciting." He turned to the whiteboard, grabbed a marker and wrote in big, messy, capital letters: TREATIES. "The signing of treaties. What are treaties? Wren?"

"The documents that two parties, often countries, sign in order to end a usually violent dispute," I recited. He wasn't going to catch *me* off guard with questions.

"A peace agreement." Midrid wrote out the words under TREATIES. "A ceasefire, a trade or land negotiation, sometimes both, whatever makes both sides happy enough to stop sending their citizens to die on the front lines. This particular treaty was unique at the time it was signed."

He continued with a lecture on the nuances of the ending of the revolutionary war. I'd heard and read similar lessons before, but Professor Midrid had a way of explaining everything that would keep even the most disinterested student riveted. He told a story that he was invested in and believed everyone else should be too. Being the bookworm that I was, I thoroughly approved.

"And now for your homework." Professor Midrid handed

out a sheet of paper. "We've talked about the revolution for a couple weeks now, so you should all be familiar enough with it to do a project." There were none of the typical groans at the mention of a long-term homework assignment. "You are to rewrite history. Give me a compelling story full of action and diplomacy and whatever else you feel like tossing in there.

"Make it how *you* think the revolutionary war should have gone. This can include any of the events leading up to its declaration, but it must involve the signing of a treaty. The only things you cannot include are any magical or modern elements. Everything must be accurate for the times and include the mention of at least three of the major players in the war *outside* the actual part they played in history. With a two-thousand word minimum."

The bell rang just as Professor Midrid circled back behind his desk. Everyone packed up their stuff and moved toward the door, but Midrid called my name. I grabbed my things and went to his desk.

"I have no idea where you left off in your schooling. Do you think you know enough to complete this assignment?" he asked.

"I know enough." I usually studied ahead of time so that I knew what the teachers were talking about during the lectures. "I've never done an assignment like this before though."

He smiled. "If you know the source material, changing some of the events around should be easy. The war can end sooner and save lives, or you can add some battles if you think it should be longer. Change who wins and describe how that would impact us now. Focus on a handful of players. It's as simple as that. Just use your imagination."

I nodded, still a bit unsure. "Ok, but what if I think it's just fine the way it is?"

He waved a hand. "Then only change a few little things, but you must change something. If you need help brainstorming, you can talk to anyone in the class. If that still doesn't work, I can help you out. I know things at your last school were probably a little different, but I've heard some rumors about the quality of your transcripts, and you should do just fine. You probably just need a couple days to adjust, but I have high hopes for you."

"Thanks." I turned away and headed for the door.

I understood that he meant he knew I could handle the difference in curriculum, but his comment about having high hopes just put more pressure on me. I'd thought I would do fine the first time I dream walked, but that hadn't gone well at all. What if this was the same story? This project was like nothing I'd ever done before in or out of school.

"Everything ok?" Lorien asked as I emerged from the classroom. She was waiting against the wall. Reve was nowhere to be seen.

I mustered up a smile. "Yeah, he was just making sure I could complete the project since I'm new."

"If you have any trouble, any of us Wind Dreamed can give you some tips," Lorien said as we started walking off toward our next class. "Except maybe Frida. She's just a first year, so they've only covered basics about the revolution."

"Thanks." She was right. The Wind Dreamed *were* there for me. "Where did Reve go?"

"He has a different class. But the two of us are still together, so I decided to wait for you."

"I appreciate it. Do we have the same schedule all day?" I had thought such a thing would be impossible, but Nick and Sylvan had shared the exact same schedule back at Mortorous. It would be nice to have a friend to guide me through my day, especially when I still wasn't sure if it was safe to text Sylvan.

"No. We have different classes after this next one, but I think you share at least two more with Reve and one with Imena. And all the third years have lunch at the same time, so you, me, and Reve will be back together then."

I breathed a sigh of relief. That accounted for most of my classes. I could survive one without them.

5

Five

As it turned out, all of my classes followed the same strangely creative and interactive format as history. Even the advanced math course I took with Imena showed us how to solve complicated equations by doing arts and crafts of all things. We spent the whole class making origami of three-dimensional geometric shapes.

In English, we drew an abstract visual representation of what went on in each of the minds of the characters from a short story. In chemistry, we made models of different chemical compounds that could combine into new ones. Gym was all about dancing, an art form the coach claimed was good for simultaneously relieving stress and expressing yourself.

Everything baffled me. Where were the worksheets that just asked you to regurgitate facts? Where were the teachers who cared more about how their students' test scores reflected on them than whether the kids were actually learning the information?

I could handle that just fine. I'd *been* handling it perfectly since I'd first started going to school at five years old.

I thought I knew how academics worked, but all this hand-on stuff short-circuited my brain and left me with more homework than I'd ever had to worry about before. I was a reader and a bit of a history buff, but changing the course of events?

Assign me a five-page essay about the nuances of ancient pottery. Assign me a packet of formulas that I had to graph. Make me read a book and take a test over the material. Tell me to jog laps around the track for all of gym class. Give me routine and monotony.

I could do all that practical stuff. I had barely done arts and crafts since I was a kid, and I liked to read, but creative writing was never something in my wheelhouse. But there I sat in my room at my desk, staring down at the empty notebook paper that was supposed to have a draft of a new version of the revolutionary war on it.

I sighed and thumped my forehead on the desk. I still had my half-finished geometric origami, two more drawings of characters' minds, and my model of the process of forging steel to finish. The projects weren't due for a couple days, but I was used to turning assignments in way ahead of time.

My dad always used to say, "If you're early, you're on time. If you're on time, you're late. If you're late, don't even bother showing up." He would apply that principle to every aspect of his life and taught me to do the same. But how was I supposed to complete my homework early when it was in a completely different style than what I was used to?

As if summoned by my thoughts, my phone rang. The caller ID read "Dad." Mom would probably be on the line too. I gave myself the space between rings to take a deep breath to try to de-stress before I picked up the phone. They could always hear it in my voice when something was wrong.

"Hey, Dad." I injected happiness into my voice.

I hadn't seen or spoken to my parents since before I became Wind Dreamed. That in and of itself wasn't anything unusual. My parents were businesspeople who liked to stay as busy as possible. With me out of the house, they could be more committed to their jobs. They knew I could take care of myself, especially where school was concerned. And I didn't have to worry about obsessive parents butting in to check on me like I heard a lot of only children did.

His voice rang with his typical charm. "Hey, sweetie! How was your first day at your new school?"

"It was…different." I poked at the mess of crafting supplies on my desk. "But nothing I couldn't handle."

"Different how?" my mother's voice chimed in.

"It's a lot more creative. I was looking at the syllabuses for all my classes and there aren't any tests or quizzes scheduled at all. Just a bunch of different projects."

"Well, you've always been good at projects," she said. "So, this should be no trouble for you."

Yeah. No trouble whatsoever. "How are things at home?"

We lived about as far from both Mortorous Academy and Animos Prep as you could get while remaining inside state lines. So, visiting was a little tough even though I had my own car. I had mostly just gone home for the breaks between semesters and around the holidays. But if I got lucky, my parents would come visit during the weekend of my birthday.

"A little hectic," Dad answered. "There's some speculation that our income might not be doing so good over the next couple months because of an outbreak overseas."

"Well, we still have our rainy-day funds. So, we'll be ok, right?" We'd weathered storms like this before without any real problems. Overseeing an international business meant a lot of moving parts and a lot of potential issues, but my dad was good at anticipating and making the necessary changes to minimize damage.

"Yes, of course. We just have to move some things around and wait this out. Nothing we can't handle." My mother liked to say hopeful things three times for good luck whenever she was worried. That didn't necessarily mean anything, though. She worried about things easily.

"I know it's your first day, but have you made any new friends?" my dad asked. I tried not to read into his indiscreet change in subject.

"Yeah, actually." That was the one good thing to come out of transferring schools so far. "I met this really fun group of people. We all live on the same floor of the dorm building and eat together and even share some classes."

"That's great!" My mom sounded way too enthusiastic. "Are any of the boys cute?"

"*Mom*," I groaned. I was aware of how incredibly single I was and how much she wanted grandchildren one day. I didn't need her to keep bringing it up when I wasn't even an adult yet.

"What? You love romance in books. I just want you to find something like that in real life. You deserve that happiness."

I agreed, but it wasn't that simple. I'd tried with boys before, but it never worked out. They'd always been interested in someone else or just uninterested in me completely. Like Nick. Even before Sylvan had shown up, he'd never dated any of the girls at Mortorous. But then she had transferred in, and suddenly he only had eyes for her. That was the kind of love I wanted with someone.

I folded my arms as best I could while still holding the phone to my ear. "Well, I just got here, so nothing like that has happened."

"I'm sure you'll find someone soon. I can just feel it," my mom gushed. "You know, I met your father when I was about your age."

A soft knock came at the door. Lorien poked her head in, saw I was on the phone, and mouthed a quick "sorry" as she started to back out.

"Wait!" I hissed, angling the phone away from my mouth. "What is it?" I didn't need to hear the story of how my parents met for the hundredth time. Whatever Lorien came to say had to be more important.

Lorien scooted back into the room. "We were going to go down to the meadow to relax. I came to ask if you'd like to come with us, but you don't have to if you're busy."

I could really use some relaxation time, and if it was with the other Wind Dreamed, so much the better. Mom could reminisce about the good old days without me.

I tilted the phone back into place. "Hey, Mom, Dad. Sorry, but something just came up. I have to go."

"Oh, nothing's wrong, I hope." It was fascinating how quickly my mom's tone could change from wistful to anxious. "Does it have to do with your new schoolwork?"

"No, I'm just going to go spend time with my new friends," I assured her.

"Oh, good. You do that then. You should be out there having fun and being a kid, really enjoying your teenage years," she rattled on.

"Yeah, thanks for calling. I'll talk to you later."

"Bye, sweetie," my dad said. "Love you."

"Love you too." I hung up as soon as the words were out of my mouth.

Lorien raised her brows. "You hang up on your parents that easily?"

I shrugged and stuffed my phone in my pocket. "They have better things to do anyway. Apparently, some stuff has gone awry with their business overseas."

"They have a business overseas?" Lorien's eyes widened.

I stood. "Yeah. They own some land that ended up being part of a major oil reservoir. They originally wanted to build a summer home on it, but when foreign governments offer you tens of thousands of dollars to build oil rigs on your property and continue to pay royalties decades later, you can afford to build your summer home somewhere else."

"So, your family is rich?"

"We're…well off. I mean, you don't spend your life in private boarding schools if your family doesn't have the money to keep you there. I know Wind Dreamed get full ride scholarships if they need it, but for everyone else, it's pretty pricey to attend even just for a semester."

"Wow," Lorien breathed. "I guess I just assumed you were from a normal family."

"It is normal. For the most part. I hope this doesn't change how you see me." I knew how people reacted when they heard I had money. Even Sylvan had been a little starstruck when she'd learned.

She shook her head. "No, of course not. I mean, a little, but not in a bad way. I want to get to know you now that you're one of us, Wren."

I tucked my hands into my pockets. "Thanks. So, what is this about going to a meadow to relax? Should I bring my suntanning supplies?"

Lorien grinned. "Oh, no. Nothing like that. We… well, we just like to hang out back there, especially on school days. It helps us to unwind and be mentally ready for the next day."

"That sounds nice. Where is it?"

Lorien sidled up next to me and hooked an arm through mine. "It's behind the library. Come on. We'll show you."

The others were already waiting for us in the living room.

"About time you two showed up. We were about to leave without you," Almos said. Given that he was sunk so low in his chair that he looked in danger of being swallowed by it, I would never have guessed he had any plans to move at all. He looked more like he was ready to take a nap.

Lorien let go of my arm to kick him lightly in the shin, to which he just rolled his eyes. "Be nice. Wren was on a call with her parents."

"Excuses, excuses," Frida drawled.

Imena pushed her off the back of her love seat into the cushions. "You're here now, so let's go."

Frida scrambled to right herself and scurried after the rest of us into the elevator. Lorien joined us this time, cramming herself next to me.

"Tell me more about your family," she demanded with a grin big enough to split her face in half. "Do you have any siblings? Where do you live? Are you from this area?"

Imena put a hand on her shoulder. "Take it easy, Lorien. She can't answer your questions if you keep asking them all in a row like that."

Lorien settled down a bit, but she still vibrated with

curiosity. "Right, sorry."

"It's ok." People at Mortorous Academy didn't usually talk about their personal lives unless it involved some juicy gossip. "I don't have any siblings. My mom had some trouble birthing me, so my parents never tried to have another baby. My house is about a five-hour drive to the northeast. I was born and raised there while my parents built their business."

"Cool," Lorien breathed.

The elevator opened on the busy common room. We all shuffled out of the building and down toward the library.

Lorien fell back to walk beside me. "Sorry if I overwhelmed you with questions. I don't have any family, so I like to hear about everyone else's."

"No family? Then who raised you?"

"The foster care system."

I winced. "Oh. No offense. I just haven't heard many good things about it."

She shrugged. "It wasn't the most enjoyable experience. That's why it was so nice to get out of it when I became Wind Dreamed. Even though, technically the state has custody of me until I turn eighteen."

"I can imagine." It must have been rough growing up without parents or siblings. But getting adopted by a primordial god? It sounded like the premise of a book series I'd read back in my early school days.

Lorien folded her hands in front of her and gazed at everyone walking ahead of us. "It might sound cliché, but the Wind Dreamed have really become my family since I joined them."

"You certainly seem like a tightly knit group." Even Frida, who was the newest before I came, was included in everything, participated in all the banter, and seemed valued.

"*We*," Lorien corrected. "No matter what brought you here or where you came from, you're a part of this now. And no amount of money from your parents is going to change that any more than my lack of parents did."

My arms wrapped around my ribs. That was all I'd ever wanted.

Lorien looped an arm around my shoulders. "If you need a hug, you can just ask. We love giving hugs. Except Reve. Don't hug Reve unless you have a death wish."

I chuckled. "Yeah, he doesn't seem like the hugging type. But he didn't strike me as the baking type either."

Lorien shrugged. "Everyone has their stories. Maybe you'll get lucky, and he'll tell you his. It'll probably take a while though. His trust is hard-earned."

We circled behind the library and into the bushes and tall grasses that surrounded Animos Prep. Like Mortorous Academy, it sat on a large piece of mostly undeveloped land. But unlike Mortorous, it wasn't surrounded by the most obviously haunted forest in the world. There were trees, sure, but it was more of a lightly wooded area with lots of space for low-growing plant life. It looked more like the kind of place you'd find fairies than ghosts.

After a few minutes of navigating the wild plants, we emerged into a small meadow that reminded me of the one where I'd spent time with the Wind Whisperer while it made me Wind Dreamed. It wasn't as big and tree branches shaded most of it, but it had the same feeling to it, the same sense that this was a world untouched by human hands.

Reve and Imena sat down in the grass under the tree branches and stared out into the meadow. Lorien sat down next to Imena, taking her hand and resting it on her knee. Frida flounced down and patted the ground next to her for me to sit. Almos sat on my other side.

"So, what now?" I asked.

"We meditate," Almos said.

"Meditate?" As in sitting still and emptying your mind and doing nothing?

"Yeah, just close your eyes, relax your muscles, and let all your thoughts flow out of your head until you're just present in the moment. Before we help people process their thoughts and emotions in their dreams, we have to process our own. We have to ground ourselves. Hopefully, this will help you do better when you dream walk tonight."

I definitely needed all the help I could get when it came to dream walking. Meditating had always sounded like a boring waste of time. There was so much to do and never enough time. I didn't have even a few minutes to spare to sit and do nothing. But if it would help me dream walk, I would try it.

"Is there something specific I should do?" I had no idea how to start emptying my mind.

"You can pick a short inspirational quote to think about or a meditative chant. You can try a specific pattern of breathing. It's really up to you. You have to figure out what works for your own mind. There is no 'one size fits all' technique. Try closing your eyes, being quiet, and see what comes to you."

I sighed. Quiet. Right.

My eyes closed. My hands rested on my crossed legs. *Mind. Empty. Don't think about anything.*

It was much easier said than done. A lot of things had happened recently. I'd become a *demigod*. How much bigger of a life change could you ask for? But on top of all that,

I'd been picked up and tossed into a new school that didn't operate like any I'd ever attended before.

I could do this. I could do this. I could adapt and keep moving just like I always did. And I was only going to be here for a year plus the few months it would take to finish out this semester. I could do this.

But my back was starting to get sore. I slumped down. Now that I'd shifted positions, my hands didn't want to stay where I'd first put them. I tucked them closer to my stomach.

That didn't last long. I was sore again after only a few minutes. Sylvan liked to curl up into a ball. Maybe that would work for me. But I couldn't relax my arms properly while they were trying to keep my knees tucked to my chest.

Finally, I flopped down on my back and stared up at the light dancing through the tree branches. The others still sat with straight backs and crossed legs, looking more like a rainbow of statues than people.

How did they do it? My mind *would not* empty. My thoughts *would not* calm. All I could think about was the homework that I'd barely made any progress on since finishing the school day. So much to do, and I was lying here in the grass, not getting any of it done.

I couldn't think creatively, meditate, or dream walk. Some Wind Dreamed I was turning out to be.

I lay there with my thoughts until the others opened their eyes and started to get up.

Frida turned, saw me lying with the long grass tickling my face and grinned. "I wasn't into it my first time either, but it grows on you the more you do it."

"You guys really do this every weekday?" I groaned as I got to my feet.

"Not every weekday," Reve said. "Sometimes there are couples out here having picnics or students blasting music through speakers while they pick flowers. Things that ruin any attempt at meditation."

I chuckled. "I'm sure."

"But if you ever need to come on your own to be alone or meditate, don't hesitate to visit for as long as you need," Imena said. "It's a pretty nice place to do homework too as long as you don't need to haul out half a craft store's worth of supplies to do it."

I couldn't believe the admin had stocked my room with so much stuff like that, but it saved me from needing to go into town anytime I needed some obscure tool. I had a feeling I was going to need them quite often. I'd already needed a hot glue gun and more origami paper.

"I think I need a little more back support to concentrate on homework." I tended to do better with a desk in front of me and a chair, preferably with some kind of padding, under me.

Imena shrugged. "Well, if we get too loud in the penthouse, feel free to come here."

"Thanks." This place might be good for reading books as long as the weather stayed nice. I'd always wanted to try out the "girl reading a book under a big tree" look. At Mortorous, it was always too overcast or too rainy or too foggy or some other weather condition that ruined the atmosphere. Any book I might have taken outside would have gotten ruined too.

But as we made our way back to the dorms, I couldn't help thinking about how comfortable my chair in the penthouse living room looked. It was also perfect for reading. This place had so much bookish potential.

Night came too quickly for my liking. I was exhausted from the day I'd had and all the work I'd managed to get done. The history assignment was still untouched, but I'd found a video online that guided me through the steps of making the geometric origami, so I'd finished most of that. I figured the best approach to all these projects was to concentrate on one at a time, and after the day I'd had, I could only muster the energy to get what I considered the easiest one done. At least there were instructions that would tell me how to do it instead of me trying to fumble my way through and screwing up.

I lay in my bed, wishing I was still at dinner with the other Wind Dreamed instead of about to face the Wind Whisperer after my failure last night. The other demigods and the Wind Whisperer itself had tried to console me, but I couldn't help feeling that the last twenty-four hours had set the tone for my experience here at Animos Prep.

I prayed I was wrong, but who was I supposed to pray to if I was a demigod?

My eyes slid closed. There was no point in delaying the inevitable. Maybe the sooner I fell asleep, the sooner I could get this done and wake up. Maybe the Wind Whisperer would have mercy on me and let me have a break in between nights spent dream walking. Maybe I could have my own dream. I liked dreaming.

6

Six

As consciousness faded, the orb of light representing people's dreams swam into view. I stared at the undulating colors, now knowing not to touch any of them unless I wanted to get sucked into a dream. I wondered if the Wind Whisperer could find me if I was already inside a dream. It hadn't last night, but it also hadn't appeared until after I'd gotten pushed out of that other dream.

It had been another Wind Dreamed that threw me out. I hoped I hadn't messed up whatever work he was doing. I could barely handle ruining one dream.

The dream threads that made up the ball around me flexed inward, stretching, and pulling away into the shape of the Wind Whisperer.

"Good night, Wren," it breathed.

My brows furrowed. "Isn't that supposed to mean good-bye?"

The Wind Whisperer didn't really have a chin to lift, but it managed to anyway. "Why should 'good morning' and 'good afternoon' mean hello, but good night has to mean goodbye?"

I shrugged. "Maybe because most people aren't awake during the night. So, when you say good night, it's because you won't be seeing them until morning."

The Wind Whisperer tilted its head back farther to stick what would have been its nose in the air. "That is no excuse."

A smile tugged at my lips. "If you say so."

"Are you ready for your next dream walk?"

I sighed. Not really. "Yeah. What am I supposed to do tonight?"

That invisible smile surfaced in the Wind Whisperer's voice. "*That* is the fun part. You never know until you are in it."

Personally, I wouldn't call that fun, but I didn't argue as it took my hand and tugged me toward the wall of dreams. I braced myself for the shift in surroundings as it touched one of the ribbons of light.

A classroom grew up around us with desks sprouting from a filthy, tiled floor. I lifted my foot away as if it would get contaminated by the stains and bits of dirt. This was a dream space. My physical body wasn't affected by what happened here. I knew that, but the scene around me looked real enough to elicit a reaction. Were most schools this unhygienic?

The teacher's desk appeared out of nowhere in front of a big whiteboard. The desks filled with shadowy students, whose features didn't quite rise to the surface.

Now that I knew to look, I could pick out the one who dreamed. It was a girl in the second to last row. The boy in front of her was slightly less hazy around the edges than the others. The girl in front of him was the same way.

I pointed at the boy and the second girl. "Why are those two clearer? They aren't dreamers too, are they?" This was a strange new world I'd found myself in. Maybe sharing dreams wasn't out of the question. I'd read books where characters did that kind of thing.

The Wind Whisperer shook its head. "There is only ever one dreamer. This is a classic situation of narrowed vision involving the dreamer and two characters in the dream. We have the setting and a full cast, but the focus is these three. Think of the others like extras in a television show, there to fill seats but not participate."

"Ok. So, something is going to happen with these three and that will be what matters?"

"Exactly."

I beamed. Maybe I wouldn't be such a failure tonight after all.

"This is most likely a call-to-action dream." The Wind Whisperer drifted up behind the dreamer. "One of our two other characters is going to do something, and the dreamer will have to choose how to react. Once the first action is made, you must think quickly and decide how the rest of the dream should play out in order to maximize the message you want to send."

Quick critical thinking. No pressure.

I wove around the desks, careful not to touch anything in case it disrupted the dream. "Can the dreamer see me?"

"Not unless you want them to." The Wind Whisperer bent down to look the dreamer in the face. She didn't react. "You should not attempt that until you get the hang of dream walking, though. Revealing yourself to a dreamer can impact a dream in the best way or the worst way. Figure out how to handle the dreams before you try anything that drastic. And even then, it is not something to be done often. Wind

Dreamed influence dreams. They do not take them over."

I nodded to myself. I certainly didn't want to try such a delicate procedure before I'd successfully dream walked. But I would work up to it. Eventually, I would master the art of dream walking and go out into the world to do great things as a demigod, even if my magic was limited to what I could do inside a person's head while they were asleep.

I paused at the front of the room, so I could see any small thing that might happen. I had to get this dream right. Last night could be chalked up to beginner's bad luck. This would be different. It had to be.

The boy suddenly leaned forward. He didn't say any intelligible words to the hazy girl in front of him, but the atmosphere of the dream shifted. The hairs on my arms rose. All my attention was drawn to the boy who suddenly had the air of someone dangerous.

"This is it," the Wind Whisperer hissed. "Sometimes there are no obvious tells. It is simply a feeling. Based on the negative aura coming off this boy, the dreamer feels he should not be talking to that girl. What should your dreamer do about it?"

"Stop him."

The Wind Whisperer nodded sharply and gestured for me to put my words into action.

I willed the girl to get up, get between them, and stop whatever was about to happen. The world was full of boys who didn't care about women. It was up to us to put them in their place before they got it into their heads that it was ok to treat us like we weren't their equals. This girl had to take a stand.

This boy had put on a mask to make himself seem like

something he wasn't. She needed to knock it off.

The dreamer shot to her feet and stormed toward the shadowy girl to get her out of harm's way. But as she went, she brushed against the boy. It was a light touch. The boy's body barely moved.

His head moved a lot more though.

It rolled clean off his neck onto the floor at the dreamer's feet. Then the face fell off like a plastic mask, leaving a blank expanse of skin behind. The dreamer screamed. The face on the floor screamed. The girl the dreamer had been trying to save screamed. All the other students in their desks screamed, coming into slightly sharper focus as they became a more active part of the dream.

I screamed.

The Wind Whisperer clapped its wispy hands together louder than should be possible for a creature that was no more than wind and light. I was thrown backward. The classroom vanished with a snap. The dream ball reappeared. The Wind Whisperer materialized before me.

"What happened?" I panted as I struggled to right myself.

"You tell me. Something you did caused that to happen. The smallest thought from you about the situation in the dream can influence the outcome." I hated that the Wind Whisperer's tone wasn't angry or accusatory. It made me feel even more guilty. "I ended the dream before anything else could go wrong. A severed head is enough of an image to leave a dreamer with."

I stopped trying to get up. I had failed again. I'd failed so badly the Wind Whisperer had stopped the dream.

My fingers raked through my hair. "What is wrong with me?"

"You are still learning, Wren. The mind is a hard thing to master, even your own."

"What am I supposed to do?" I didn't do this. I didn't mess things up so badly.

"Get up and try again. You will never get better at things if you do not practice."

But I was supposed to be good at the things I put effort into. I had been my whole life. Why was I suddenly bad at everything I tried to do now? I couldn't meditate. I couldn't dream walk. I couldn't even do my schoolwork.

"This is only your second time. You cannot be perfect at everything before you even try it."

I scowled at the ceiling. "I have tried it. Twice now."

And I'd messed up both times. Maybe I wasn't meant to be Wind Dreamed. The Wind Whisperer said it wasn't infallible. So, maybe it was wrong when it said it saw potential in me. It wasn't like it had made me a demigod because it wanted to. It had been forced into this situation just like I had. Clearly, this was a mistake.

The Wind Whisperer, perhaps sensing the direction of my thoughts, oriented itself so that we were face to face. "I am not going to take away your powers just because you have made a few mistakes. The mind of every single living thing is different from every other living thing. They all need to hear different messages. It takes time to attune yourself to those frequencies, especially when you are more used to having the dreams yourself."

"How much time?"

"There is no rush. Sometimes a bad dream can be as meaningful as a good dream."

"I want to be good at this." I *had* to be good at this. This was my dream. I hadn't come all this way just to crash and burn.

"When you wake up, just try to live your day with an open mind. Think about things objectively. Practice mindfulness. Do some meditation."

"I suck at meditating." I tucked my knees to my chest.

"Most do the first time they try. You simply have to try again. Now, wake up."

7

Seven

My eyes opened. I groaned and rolled over, burying my face in my pillow. I wished I could smother myself with it. Why couldn't I do this? It was one thing after another.

Maybe I just needed to relax *my* way. I'd been at Animos Prep for a full two days, and I still hadn't gone to the library since the initial walkthrough during the tour. It was a straight-up crime. How could I call myself a bookworm?

When I opened my door, Reve was walking down the hall with a toothbrush in his mouth and his phone in his hand. He paused and looked at me with raised eyebrows that almost disappeared under the messy, dark hair that fell across his forehead.

I gave him a tentative smile. "I was just heading to the library. If the others ask, tell them not to wait for me."

Reve just stared at me like he thought he was still asleep and had dreamed me up with the toothbrush hanging out of his mouth. He was even less of a morning person than I'd thought.

"Ok, then. See you in class." I darted down the hall. There was no time to waste when the library was calling.

The morning air was cool and crisp. It snapped at my face while I walked as fast as humanly possible to the library. Why couldn't I have gotten a useful power when I became Wind Dreamed, like teleportation? My five-foot-two body was not built for speed.

I would be so good at teleporting. There was probably some quick and easy formula that I could memorize, and within days I would be popping in and out of all kinds of places.

But dream walking…

Dream walking was so subjective and so objective at the same time. It drove me insane. But that was why I was going to the library. I could regain a bit of my sanity by losing myself in a book.

The library at Mortorous Academy had shared the building with the English and history classrooms. But the library at Animos Prep had its own building that was almost as big as the combined one at Mortorous.

The bright, white facade was done up like an ancient temple. Carvings in low relief stood out along the walls, showing everything from epic battles to pious monks to landscapes and homes from every era of history. This was what every library in the world aspired to be: elegant, extravagant, exceptional.

I raced up the stairs, eager for the smell of ink on paper.

The inside was just as regal as the outside. The tall shelves and stone walls were softened by a thin, cream-colored carpet and squishy chairs and couches with end tables beside them. Paintings and pottery that looked hundreds of years old and were probably worth a fortune sat in niches and hung on walls. The books on the shelves were aligned perfectly with each other in order of height.

The whole library looked more like a museum than a casual space where you could study or read books. I had to say, I appreciated the structure. So much of what I'd seen at Animos Prep so far was abstract, lacking form and instead flowing seamlessly into everything around it. It was nice to know that at least one thing hadn't been turned into a work of art at this school. This place just held the art.

I drifted between the aisles formed by the bookshelves. The nearest sections were all about different kinds of art. Painting, sculpting, and drawing took up most of the space, but there were more obscure arts like body painting, tattooing, pottery spinning. More crafty things like knitting, sewing, and origami were present too. There were even nonvisual arts such as music composition, and even writing, which I'd never really thought of as art until now. Some books taught. Others discussed different artists. Still others laid out histories of the different crafts.

The staggering selection on the topic could only be expected from a school that valued the arts above all else, but it wasn't what I was looking for. I wanted the stories, the more improbable the better.

Though now that I knew gods and magic really did exist, finding something to pull me so far out of the known world that I could escape my own thoughts might be a challenge. A challenge I was eager to take on.

Unlike the challenge posed by all my homework projects. I shuddered at the amount of work I'd left undone. I should probably be trying to complete that instead, but finding a steady supply of books would always be at the top of my priority list. I could get through any hardship with enough reading material.

Speaking of which, I really needed to figure out if there was a good bookstore in town. But that could wait until the weekend. This library should suffice for now.

The fiction section was all the way in the back, but it did not disappoint. The number of shelves of fantasy novels alone was enough to rival the collection in the art section. I dove in with glee, hunting for titles on my To Be Read list, reading descriptions of stories I hadn't heard of, lovingly stroking the spines of books I'd read before as if they were old friends.

This was a bookworm's paradise. If only my backpack were big enough to carry all the ones I wanted to check out.

I had a sizable pile spilled across one of the study tables in the back of the library, trying to decide which ones to check out and which ones to put back on the shelves, when Imena found me.

She paused at the opposite end of my table. "What are you up to, chickpea?"

"At the moment? Trying to pick between a paranormal horror and a fantasy romance. Have you read either of these? Do you know which one is better?" I held up both books, so she could see the front covers.

Imena took the chair across from me. "Can't say that I have, sorry."

I lowered the books. "That's ok. I know not many people read these days. Even if you did read, we might not have the same preference in genres, and the book market is so oversaturated that even if we did, there's a good chance you wouldn't have read any of the books I'd read unless you were one of those readers that can go through fifty books in a month. I never understood where people like that get the time to do it." I had to force myself to stop rambling.

Imena shrugged. "I wouldn't know. I've dabbled in reading but never done anything quite that drastic."

I leaned forward. Dabbling in reading was better than not reading at all. Even if it was only for school, reading was reading. "What kind of books do you like?"

"I've found interesting books in all kinds of genres. What I pick up is more dependent on how I'm feeling at the time I'm wanting to read. Sometimes I'm in the mood for contemporary. Sometimes I'm in the mood for something more fantastical."

I smiled. "Well, if you need any book recommendations, I'm happy to oblige. Reading is kind of my thing."

Imena ran a hand over the cover of the book closest to her. "Really? I never would have guessed."

I chuckled, then gestured at the nearest shelves. "Is there something you're looking for?"

"Yeah, actually." She straightened. "You."

"Me?"

"Reve said you were upset when he saw you come out of your room."

"Upset? I'm not upset. I just wanted to come check out the library a little better. We barely poked our heads in during the tour you gave me a few days ago." I forced a smile.

Imena didn't look convinced. "Reve is usually right about these things. See, the longer you spend as a Wind Dreamed, the better you can tell how people are feeling, what they are lacking in their lives, what they dream of. Reve hasn't been Wind Dreamed as long as me and Almos, but so far, he's the best at figuring out the emotions of other people. No matter how deeply someone buries their feelings, he can dig them out. Including other Wind Dreamed." She raised her eyebrows meaningfully.

That was a little disturbing. "Well, I guess his radar is wrong for once, 'cause I feel fine."

"How did your dream walk go last night?"

Dang it.

"It was alright." Until heads started rolling. Literally.

"And your schoolwork?"

"It's going just fine." I hadn't failed any assignments, even if that was just because I hadn't turned any in yet.

She sighed and sat back in her chair. "You know we're here to help you, right, chickpea? That's why the Wind Whisperer sends a new Wind Dreamed here at least once every year. We're supposed to stick together, help, and learn from each other."

I went back to sorting through the books on the table. "Thanks, but I really am fine. I just need some time to practice and adjust, and I'll be a good Wind Dreamed like the rest of you."

Imena shook her head. "You aren't supposed to be like the rest of us. You're supposed to be yourself. The Wind Whisperer chooses people from all walks of life for a reason. We all have our own perspectives, our own advice to give. What advice do you have to give?"

Don't get your hopes up, because your dreams might come crashing down around you like a too-tall stack of books.

I doubted Imena wanted to hear any of that, so I just said, "I don't know."

"*My* advice to *you* is to find the message you want to send to everyone in the world and build from there. If you have more than one, you have more to work with. But it's ok to just focus on one too."

I pushed my glasses up my nose. That didn't make much sense, but so far nothing had, so it wasn't new. "Ok."

She got up and leaned across the table to pat my shoulder. "You're going to get it. You just have to be patient with yourself."

Patience wasn't something I could afford when my entire school career and my status as a demigod were at stake. I needed results now. Or at least noticeable improvement.

"Thanks, Imena," I managed to say.

"No problem. Like I said, that's what I'm here for." She picked up the book that she had touched earlier. "This one looks interesting. Have you read it?"

My smile was as genuine as they come when I said, "Yeah, it's really good. Lots of intrigue and suspense. The romantic subplot is pretty sweet too." I'd been considering rereading it.

"Great. Don't be late to class." She turned and disappeared between the bookshelves on her way to the circulation desk.

I tried not to be too disappointed by the conversation. It wasn't her fault she didn't understand.

By the time the bell rang to tell me there were five minutes until class started, I'd managed to narrow it down to three books. Three was the magic number, after all. All the best things came in threes in stories.

I didn't count the extra one for helping me with the history project.

I went to the counter to check out. The librarian lounged in a rolling chair behind it, her brown hair pulled back in a messy bun and glasses halfway down her nose. She was so engrossed in the book she was reading that I had to clear my throat to get her attention.

"Oh, hi. Sorry." She jumped to her feet, pushed her glasses up, and tossed the book face down on the counter. "I got a little carried away."

I waved off her apology. "I get it. Sometimes books suck me in, and I have a hard time climbing back out."

"A bookworm, huh? What are you looking to read right now?" Her gaze dropped to the books in my arms.

I set them on the counter. "Some fun fiction." Plus one.

She picked up each book and scanned the barcodes on the back with the speed of a cashier who'd been working at a grocery store too long. "*Creative Writing for Fools, Fifth Flight, Carnival,* and *Nightshade.* All great books. Whenever kids come in looking for something good to read, I usually end up recommending one of these three."

Thankfully she didn't comment on the writing book. "*Carnival* is one of my favorites. This is my third time rereading it."

The librarian raised her eyebrows. "You must be an even bigger bookworm than I thought. You know, I don't think we've met before. Are you new?"

I tried not to fidget. "Yeah. This is my first week here."

"It's lovely to meet you. I'm the librarian, Dr. Scribira." She held out a hand.

I shook it. "I'm Wren. It's nice to meet you."

"If you're as big of a bibliophile as it seems like you are, you should join the book club. We meet here every Tuesday morning in one of the study rooms." Dr. Scribira handed me a half sheet with the words "BOOK CLUB" in big, bold letters on the top and several smaller notes on the bottom about the meeting location, time, and date.

I'd been in the Mortorous Academy book club and a book club in Noxier, the town a few miles from the Mortorous campus, as well as a few online reading groups on social media. It could be hard to find someone to talk about books in this digital age, so I loved those spaces where people could gather and do just that.

"We usually have some pastries and other breakfast-type snacks and drinks. After all, what's a book club without food?" Dr. Scribira grinned.

"That sounds like fun."

I'd been so excited to have built in friends among the Wind Dreamed that I hadn't thought I'd need other communities. But with demigod duties not going well, I hungered for something completely separate from them to keep me from spiraling about the fact that I had yet to successfully dream walk. This sounded like the perfect opportunity to do just that.

"It's lots of fun," the librarian assured me as she pushed my books across the counter. "I hope you can make it next week."

I gathered up my books. "I'll do my best to." Nothing would be right with the world if I wasn't in a book club.

* * *

I made it to Professor Midrid's classroom just in time to beat the tardy bell. Lorien grinned at me. Reve was already focused on the whiteboard up front. I eyed him as I sat down. He glanced at me with a vacant expression. I tried to smile, but his gaze slid away as if he couldn't be bothered to waste time looking at me.

Maybe he was picking up on my caution towards him. If what Imena said was true, he could tell what people were feeling even if they tried to hide it. I'd never been the best at hiding my emotions, but I didn't think I was *that* bad at it.

What a set of powers for a demigod to have. Wind Dreamed could know what you were feeling and manipulate your dreams. Again, I wished I'd gotten more substantial powers. Didn't the Bone Touched get to move bones with their minds? Why couldn't we have gotten something cool like that?

"Where were you this morning?" Lorien asked once Professor Midrid finished his short lecture on the weeks immediately following the war and allowed us to work on our essays for the rest of class time. "You missed Reve's famous cinnamon roll pancakes."

Those did sound delicious, but my library time had done what it was meant to do. Even after my talk with Imena, I felt much more centered, like I could do this.

"I had to get some books to help with my projects." Hopefully, after educating myself on the craft of creative writing, I would really be able to do it.

"Oh, that's good. You can also ask us for help if you need to. Imena and Almos probably did this project or at least one similar to it when they were taking this class last year. And Reve and I have started on ours already."

So, I was already behind. Great. "I appreciate it, but hopefully I won't have to bother you."

"It wouldn't be a bother. We're all happy to help. After all, how are we supposed to rise if we don't help lift each other up?"

That was a nice message. I wondered if that was what

Imena was talking about when she said we all had advice we needed to share with the world. If not, it would at least make a good inspirational quote or a line in a book.

"Well, I'll read the book and let you know if I still have no idea what to do," I told her.

She nodded in satisfaction. I could have sworn I felt Reve's eyes on me. Did he know I was lying?

8

Eight

We spent the rest of the class working on our essays. I pulled out the book I had gotten from the library and started trying to understand some of the nuances of creating a story. My writing might sound a little juvenile, like a bad fanfiction, but it would be better than nothing. I put pencil to paper and made a vague outline before the bell rang to send us to the next class.

We were doing more origami in math and more drawing in English. I started to get into the groove of things by the end of each class. Maybe my attempt at meditation wasn't as epic of a failure as I thought. Or maybe I'd just needed a day to get the lay of the land. Everyone had been right. All I needed was a bit of time to adjust.

The dancing in gym was still tricky, but I chalked that up to not having been much of an athlete before now. I probably just needed to stretch more and practice the routine on my own time. I was getting the hang of everything else, so it was only a matter of time before I got this down too.

My confidence resurfaced with each new understanding

of the material.

At lunch, the cafeteria served the juiciest, most flavorful chicken and mashed potatoes. And dinner...

Reve really did know how to cook. I had no idea where he'd gotten steak, but I wasn't about to look a gift horse in the mouth.

"Didn't you have food like this at Mortorous Academy?" Almos asked as he watched me inhale my meal at the large, white dining table in the kitchen.

I didn't blame him. Usually, I took more care when eating, especially when I was with my parents—my mom was a stickler for ladylike behavior. But this food was too good to spend a second without a forkful in my mouth.

I snorted at Almos's question. "Absolutely not. It wasn't bad, but they didn't make it nearly as good as this."

"Did you meet any Bone Touched while you were at Mortorous?" Reve asked.

The table went quiet. Frida must have kicked Reve under the table, judging by their sudden movements, but he maintained eye contact with me.

"You don't have to answer that," Imena said. "We don't usually talk about the children of the other gods." She looked at Reve when she said that last part. Again, he didn't react, didn't look away. His stare was starting to unnerve me.

I set down my silverware. "It's ok. I did know a Bone Touched back at Mortorous. She was a good friend, actually."

Lorien straightened. "Was it Sylvan? She was so nice."

"How do you know if she was nice? She barely said a word," Reve interjected.

"You're one to talk about how much people say." Lorien stuck out her tongue.

I sat in stunned silence for a moment. "You know Sylvan?"

"We met her at the kickoff basketball game in the fall," Almos said.

"She seemed really skittish," Frida added. "She wanted our help."

I frowned. "Help with what?"

Sure, Sylvan had been quiet during the time I'd known her, but the only thing she'd ever asked for help with was finding her parents. Parents that were long since dead. I wondered if she knew about that now. Had she found the truth on her own? Either way, I couldn't imagine her asking a group of strangers to help her with something so personal.

Reve was right about how reserved she was. Even in those few weeks of friendship, she didn't share much about herself up until she made up the kidnapping story, which now that I thought about it, might not be so made up after all. The Wind Whisperer had kidnapped me when it offered to make me Wind Dreamed. Maybe the Boneman had a similar m.o.

"The dreams of others are not ours to share," Imena declared before Frida could answer me. "And we don't mess around with the Bone Touched. The children of the gods are supposed to mind their own business. Meddling in each other's lives is strictly prohibited unless we are given special permission by the gods themselves, which rarely happens, and only ever in extreme circumstances. I hope none of us are subjected to such situations."

I looked down at my food. I guess that meant I was supposed to keep my knowledge to myself.

Thunder rumbled outside. I glanced out the window at the back of the kitchen. All throughout the day, banks of fluffy clouds had occupied the sky. During our meditation in the field, it had been windy, but I wouldn't have thought that meant a full-on storm was coming. And yet, raindrops speckled the window, and the sky overhead was grey and ready to dump rain all over Animos Prep.

Lorien leaned back in her blue chair, threw her arms in the air, and crowed, "It's raining!"

Imena put a hand on her shoulder just as she started to jump out of her seat. "Finish your food first."

Lorien pouted a bit but quickly tucked into her dinner, eating faster than I'd ever seen a person eat before.

"What's so exciting about rain?" I asked.

At Mortorous Academy, it rained all the time. The ever-present cloud cover over the school had constantly threatened to open and drown any students that dawdled on their way to class.

Lorien stopped eating and stared at me with wide eyes and an open mouth. "What do you mean 'what's so exciting about rain'? Rain is amazing. It makes all the flowers bloom and the leaves on all the bushes and trees brighten up. It gives life! Not to mention it's fun to play in."

I raised an eyebrow. "Is that why you practically flew out of your seat? No offense, but I'm not that interested in getting soaking wet."

Lorien grinned a kind of wild grin that had the hairs on the back of my neck rising. "If you don't like playing in the rain, then you haven't been doing it right. But don't worry, we'll fix that today."

I glanced around the table. I wasn't sure if I was looking for answers or for help, but I got neither. Everyone was eating like they didn't have a care in the world.

"I don't know if—"

"Don't worry, I'll outfit you in the best rain gear money can buy. We're going to have a blast!" Lorien resumed stuffing her face.

I wasn't so sure about all that, but it didn't sound like she was going to give me a choice.

* * *

As soon as Lorien finished her food, she leaped from the table and ran to drag me out of my chair. "Come on! The rain won't last forever."

I couldn't have resisted even if I'd wanted to. Lorien pulled me out of the kitchen and down the hall with all the bedrooms. She opened the blue door and yanked me inside, closing the door behind us, and released me as she moved to the closet.

"My stuff will probably be a little big on you, but it will have to do since we don't have time to get you something that's your size." She rummaged through the clothes, tossing boots and coats and ponchos around.

I took the chance to glance around her room. The walls were the same bright shade of blue as her hair. Her bed and furniture were more of a blue-green color but still stuck to the theme. Multicolored fish and other sea creatures had been painted all over the place, on the walls, the closet doors, the desk, the bed frame, everywhere. It felt like I'd jumped into the ocean.

I couldn't help noticing that all the blue fish swam very close to yellow fish.

I ran my hands over one such pairing. "Did you paint these yourself?"

Lorien glanced over her shoulder and quickly turned back

around, but not before I caught the faint tinge of a blush on her cheeks. Her voice came out much softer than I was used to. "Imena helped."

"I wouldn't have thought we were allowed to do that. I mean they're really pretty, but if I ever did something like this in my dorm at Mortorous Academy, the dorm supervisors would have my head."

Lorien turned with a pair of rainbow umbrellas on her arm. "I don't know if the regular students are allowed to paint their dorms, but I wouldn't be surprised. I'm sure you've noticed that Animos encourages all kinds of creativity."

"Yeah, I have." It made the learning curve that much steeper for me.

"Here." Lorien handed me an armful of rain gear. "Put it on quick, so we can go."

It didn't take me long to slip into the raincoat and boots, but it might as well have taken an eternity for how much Lorien was rushing me.

"Come on, come on!" She bounced around the room.

"Aren't you going to get dressed?" She hadn't put on anything to protect against the rain.

She shook her head. "I don't need rain protection. Now, let's go."

Lorien grabbed my arm and hauled me out into the living room. To my surprise, Frida and Imena were standing by the elevator in their own boots and coats.

"Finally!" Frida punched the button to summon the elevator to take us down. "We were about to leave without you."

Imena rolled her eyes and hoisted her pastel yellow back-pack higher on her shoulder. What was in it? "No, we weren't."

"*You* weren't. *I* was." Frida stepped into the elevator.

"Where are the boys?" Lorien asked.

"Still getting dressed. You know Reve loves water as much as a cat does. They said not to wait for them, so let's go." Frida held the doors open for us.

Lorien didn't hesitate. Imena gestured for me to go ahead. After Reve had sent her to me in the library this morning, I wasn't inclined to wait for him, but I would have thought Almos would be worth delaying our time in the rain.

Apparently not.

Imena and I slipped into the elevator and Lorien punched the first-floor button hard enough that I worried she might have broken it. Or her knuckle. She tapped her foot impatiently the whole way down and practically wrenched the doors apart when they started to open into the common room.

Plenty of people occupied the mismatched chairs and couches, lounging around and enjoying the ambiance of the storm outside. Normally, I would be one of those people. Rainy weather was perfect for wrapping yourself up in a fluffy blanket with a warm drink and reading for hours and hours. And I had those books I had gotten from the library this morning waiting on my desk.

But the Wind Dreamed had other ideas.

There was a large porch made of white wood around the dorm with seating and firepits. It was the kind of space that would have looked more appropriate on a log cabin or an old house than on a six-story building. But I could see the appeal. It was like the common room extended outside.

Lorien didn't wait for the rest of us before she kicked off

her shoes and bounded out into the rain that had turned from a drizzle to a downpour, blue hair flying out behind her. She didn't flinch when the drops splattered against her face and ran down her skin. Her clothes were soaked in seconds, but she didn't seem to care. If anything, it made her more excited. She bounced around, jumping in puddles, catching raindrops on her tongue or in her hands.

I couldn't help smiling as I watched her. Her joy was infectious.

Frida trotted down the steps from the porch to join her. She was much more appropriately dressed in a coat and hat that repelled the rain but had removed her shoes too. Frida jumped in a puddle near Lorien, splashing water all over her legs. Lorien shrieked and jumped in the puddle right next to Frida, splashing her back.

Imena charged at the two of them with a cup she must have packed in her bag. She'd filled it with the water pouring off one of the gutters and tossed it at Frida and Lorien. They laughed and grabbed for the cup, chasing Imena through the trees that dotted the lawn in front of the dorm.

I grinned as I watched them.

"I'm surprised Lorien hasn't dragged you down there with them yet."

I jumped a little when Almos spoke from behind me. He and Reve had finally emerged. Almos had on a coat and boots. But Reve had a coat, boots, a large rain hat, a giant umbrella, and a plastic poncho. It took everything in me not to laugh at how ridiculous he looked.

"It's only a matter of time," said Reve. "She'll realize we're all here and demand we have a big water fight or something."

"Good thing you came prepared then." Almos bumped

Reve's shoulder with his.

Reve took a pointed step away from him. "I've been around long enough to know when Lorien is plotting to get me wet."

"Why does she like the rain so much?" I asked as we watched the girls continue to chase each other.

Almos shrugged. "She just does. Imena and I weren't exactly keen on running around in the rain at first either, but she wore us down."

"She wore *you* down," Reve corrected.

"Don't pretend you don't like feeling included." Almos looked at me. "Reve plays the recluse, but he enjoys doing things with the group even if he would never admit it out loud."

"Hmph," Reve replied.

It reminded me of Sylvan. She was always quiet and withdrawn, but she never said no to hanging out with me when we were friends back at Mortorous Academy. Speaking of Sylvan, I still hadn't texted her yet. I pulled out my phone.

Lorien jumped up on the porch, skidded to a halt in front of us, and shook like a dog. I flinched a little and covered my phone as large water droplets hit Almos and me. Reve stood a safe distance behind us.

"Come on! Now that everyone's here, we can really get this party started." Lorien grabbed my hands and pulled me down the stairs out into the rain.

I barely had time to shove my phone back in my pocket and brace myself before the rain hit my face and instantly started speckling my glasses with water. This was another reason why I wasn't a big fan of being out in the rain. It was hard to see when water streaked your vision.

Lorien didn't seem to notice. She towed me over to the

same puddle Frida had jumped in a few minutes ago and pushed me into it. I stumbled and waited for the gross feeling of water soaking my socks, making my shoes squishy. But I was wearing Lorien's tall rubber boots. My socks were protected.

I took a few experimental steps in the puddle. It was fun to watch the ripples. I gathered myself and jumped up. The water splashed around my legs. Some of it ended up on them. Even though the raincoat I'd borrowed from Lorien was long on me, it still only reached my knees, leaving several inches between where the hem ended and the top of my boots began.

Lorien whooped and jumped in next to me. I recoiled with a cry, but most of the water splashed harmlessly against my coat and boots. I laughed and stomped my foot, angling to hit Lorien with as much water as possible. She shrieked with delight.

Frida ran over and threw a cupful of water on both of us—she must have stolen the cup from Imena. Lorien and I recoiled before turning on her. She had the sense to run as she laughed.

We four girls ran around dousing each other with water, laughing and screaming, for a while. Almos joined in at one point, but Reve stayed safely under the protection of the porch or the trees with all his rain gear on and watched the chaos unfold. At times, it almost looked like he was smiling, but I couldn't get a good enough look before someone splashed me with water or pushed me to run from whoever had the cup.

I ran out of steam before the others did and leaned against the trunk of one of the trees. Thick drops of water still fell from their leaves, but it was better than staying out in the pouring rain. Not that it would have made that much difference. My hair was soaked along with any exposed skin. Some water had trickled under the collar of my raincoat, so the top of my shirt was wet too. And my glasses were more water than glass.

I took them off to clean them on a dry portion of my shirt when Reve approached me.

"Hi, Reve," I said. He had an intense look in his eye that made me a little nervous.

"What do you know about the Bone Touched?" he murmured when he got close enough that I could see the line where his dark brown irises met the black of his pupil.

That was unexpected. I leaned as far away as the tree behind me would allow. "Probably not any more than you do."

He stepped closer. "You spent years at their school, and you don't know anything about them?"

"I didn't know Bone Touched were anything more than a myth until a few months ago," I responded. What was with the sudden interrogation? We'd all been having fun a minute ago. Well, maybe Reve wasn't since he didn't like the rain, but that was no excuse to corner me like this. "And didn't Imena say we weren't supposed to talk about the Bone Touched?"

"Imena says a lot of things. I want to know what you know." He was starting to scare me a little. He stood too close. He wasn't taller than average, but I was lacking the inches that would keep him from towering over me. And even though he looked ridiculous in all his layers of rain gear, they also made him look bigger.

I shrugged, trying to keep my composure. "I just know that they're the Boneman's demigods and they have cool bone powers."

"That's it? You were friends with one, and she didn't say anything, didn't drop any hints?"

I threw up my hands. "What do you want from me, Reve? She was my friend, but she never said anything about being Bone Touched. I was a normal person back then, so she couldn't talk to me about it!" She *wouldn't* talk to me about it.

He straightened at the sharpness in my voice.

I took a deep breath. I needed to get along with these people, not alienate them. "I'm just as curious as you, but I don't have any answers. Apparently, I'm not supposed to anyway and neither are the rest of us. So, why do you want to know so badly?"

Reve stepped back like I'd pushed him. "Never mind." He turned and walked back toward the porch.

I watched him climb the stairs and disappear inside the common room. I could understand being fascinated by the Bone Touched, but I had no idea why he expected me to have insider knowledge. Until I'd woken up in the Wind Whisperer's field, I hadn't known this part of the world was real.

I wished I had. I wished Sylvan had told me she was Bone Touched. I wished she had let me into this world instead of inadvertently leading me to it and pushing me into becoming a demigod the way she did. Did she have any idea what happened to me? The Wind Whisperer had taken me from Mortorous Academy months ago. Was she worried?

I dug my phone out of my pocket and searched for her phone number to message her, hunching over the screen to protect it from the dripping tree overhead. I couldn't believe I kept forgetting to text her.

Sylvan was a demigod too—a different kind, but a demigod

all the same. And a new one at that. She'd only been at Mortorous Academy for a couple months before I'd left. Maybe she would have some advice for me. If nothing else, we could bond over our shared experience.

But I couldn't find her number in my list of contacts. When I typed in "Sylvan" in the contact search bar in my text message app, it said "No Results." Even my trash folder lacked any reference to her.

I scowled. My text history was clear of any of the messages I had sent or received from her. It was like she had vanished from the digital world. Had someone deleted her contact info the same way they had messaged my parents about transferring me to Animos Prep?

Disgusting.

Just because I was Wind Dreamed now didn't mean I had to cut all contact with my old friend, who I hadn't even known was Bone Touched. We could talk about other things besides being demigods. Sylvan might have some advice on how to handle this new kind of schoolwork. She was definitely more artistically inclined than me. Her drawing skills were next level.

Besides, if I couldn't contact her, I couldn't tell her she was actually three hundred years old. That felt like important information to have about yourself. And Sylvan clearly wanted to know more about the family she'd been taken from.

Had it been the Boneman who kidnapped her the way the Wind Whisperer had kidnapped me? Had she been trying to get away from him when she asked me to help her find her parents? What had the Boneman done when he found out what she was doing? I had gotten to become a demigod as my "punishment", but what happened to Sylvan? Was she ok?

Without the ability to text her, the only way I could find those answers was to drive to Mortorous Academy myself. But I couldn't abandon everything here. Not in the middle of the week, anyway. That might get both of us into even more trouble.

"What are you doing on your phone?" Lorien practically barreled into me as she ran over, just barely managing to skid to a stop in the slippery grass before colliding with me. "The rain is slowing down. We can't waste these last few minutes of it with our faces glued to our screens."

I mustered up a smile. "I think I'm all rained out. The boots you lent me are starting to hurt my feet a little." That was what happened when you wore shoes that were multiple sizes bigger than your feet.

Lorien's brows pulled together in concern. "Oh, I'm so sorry. I wasn't thinking about how that might be an issue for you. You should definitely go inside and get off your feet then." She glanced over her shoulder. "The rest of us will probably come back up to the penthouse once the rain stops, and it looks like Reve already went inside."

I wasn't sure how I felt about being in the penthouse alone with Reve after what had just happened, but I wasn't in the mood to keep jumping in puddles either.

"I'll just sit on the porch. The atmosphere is nice and watching you guys is almost as much fun as playing in the rain myself."

Lorien's face brightened with a smile. "Oh, I'm so glad you had a good time."

As much as I hated to admit it, she had been right about playing in the rain. As long as I didn't have to worry about soggy socks and shoes, it was great, almost like playing in the pool, but less wet. Which was rich considering how much water I squeezed out of my hair once I got back to the porch. Weird how you could feel more wet when you were out of the water than when you were in it.

I draped my wet coat over the railing, sat on one of the couches, and kicked off my shoes. I might have blamed the ill-fitting shoes for me bowing out of playing in the rain, but they hadn't been too bad. I'd figured out how to walk and run without rubbing the back of my heel on the inside too much. I was slower because of it, but it worked pretty well. Still, it felt good to free myself from them. Maybe I should have followed Lorien and Frida's lead and gone barefoot.

The rain only lasted another fifteen minutes. By the time I realized I couldn't see the other Wind Dreamed from where I sat, I was too comfortable to move, so I opened my phone and went to my eBook app. Fifteen minutes wasn't a lot of reading in my world, but it was something.

After the rain stopped, the girls kept messing around in the puddles and shaking the water from the trees on one another. Almos made his way over to me. He took off his raincoat and tossed it next to mine before sinking down next to me.

"So, did Lorien sell you on the joys of playing in the rain?" he asked.

I smiled faintly. "Yeah. She kind of did."

He nodded. "Good. It's nice to have your own hobbies and interests, but having something to do with other people is even better."

I glanced down at my phone and thought about Sylvan's deleted contact card. "Almos, are the Wind Dreamed not supposed to talk to the Bone Touched?"

He turned toward me. "There's nothing wrong with talking to them. We wouldn't have met Sylvan a few months ago if we weren't allowed to interact with each other at all."

"Then why was Imena so uptight about talking about them at dinner? I mean, she made it sound like it would be a bad thing if we knew anything about them or made friends with them."

Almos sighed and looked off in the direction of the girls. I wondered if his extra height let him see them better. My best view was through the wooden bars that made it seem like I was in jail. "There aren't any set-in-stone rules about how the different demigods can interact. The main goal is to avoid conflict. The Boneman and Wind Whisperer ensured our powers couldn't be used against each other when they first started creating demigods. They didn't want to hand us primordial magic without any bumpers to protect us."

I guess that made sense. People were given power all the time only for them to turn around and use it against others. I didn't want to think about what those kinds of people would do if they had demigod magic.

"Was it always like this, or did something happen that made the gods decide to put those parental locks on us?" I asked.

Almos shrugged. "I've never heard of it being any different, and trust me, demigods like to tell stories."

The question still remained. "So, it shouldn't be an issue that I'm friends with Sylvan, right?"

"I wouldn't think so, but I haven't heard of a Bone Touched and a Wind Dreamed being close friends like you and Sylvan. I've never heard of a Wind Dreamed who came from Mortorous Academy either. Usually, the Wind Whisperer makes us Wind Dreamed right before we enter high school, so there wouldn't be potential for crossover."

Well, that eliminated one person from the list of suspects who would have erased Sylvan from my phone. That still left Imena—I doubted that since she had been surprised that I wasn't the one to pack up my stuff—and any number of people from the administration. I didn't think the Wind Whisperer itself would have done something like this. It was much more communicative and didn't seem like the kind of person—person? creature? being?—to violate my privacy and cut me off from Sylvan this way.

It would have explained whatever problem it might have with me being friends with Sylvan and convinced me to delete her info from my phone instead. No, this was someone else. Someone whose identity I might never discover. It wasn't like I could run around campus demanding to know who messed with my phone.

Lorien chose that moment to jump up onto the porch with a grin the size of the moon. Frida and Imena followed her much less enthusiastically. They looked tired.

"This was so much fun. I'm glad you gave it a chance, Wren." Lorien wiped the water from her skin.

Imena tossed her a towel from her bag. "It's definitely a great way to get up and moving after a long day of sitting still in desks."

"And it tires you out, so you can fall asleep and start dream walking sooner." Frida slipped her flip-flops back on.

I was definitely ready to go inside and pass out in bed. So, I got up, fit my feet back into the boots I'd borrowed from Lorien, and headed inside with the others. I said a quick good night to everyone and headed for my room as soon as the elevator doors opened into the penthouse.

Thoughts about the separated demigods and Sylvan still floated in my head. But I tossed my phone on my bed and sank into my desk chair. There was nothing I could do about it now. I could try to find her at some sporting event where our schools played each other and get her number again then. But until that time, the only way I could contact her was if she contacted me first.

In the meantime… homework.

I was tired from running around with the other Wind Dreamed, but that didn't mean I could ignore the daunting workload.

More of my essay was done by the time the sun went down than I expected. Once again, the library had been my savior. I couldn't imagine how I would have done this before I'd read that book on creative writing. I'd also managed to finish the geometric origami. That only left those paintings for English.

I flopped down in bed after showering and changing clothes with a light feeling in my chest. Hopefully, all this newfound skill would carry into the dream realm where I would finally successfully dream walk.

9

Nine

I came to in the dream orb. Its threads of light bathed me in color. I did my best to turn in a circle without having any ground to push off of. The lack of gravity was disconcerting to say the least. But was this my real body in here? Or was I doing some form of astral projection to get into the dream world?

Everything felt real, but that didn't make it real. After all, dreams weren't real. They were just manifestations of your subconscious mind. And dream magic. Apparently.

"You seem to be in a good mood tonight." The Wind Whisperer appeared out of the tangle of dreams like it had the night before. Did that mean the wisps of color running through it were dreams? Was the Wind Whisperer itself *made* of dreams?

"Have a good day?" it continued, pulling me out of my thoughts.

"It was better than yesterday," I admitted. It had been right about giving myself time to adjust. "I think this is the night I'm going to get it right."

It laughed softly. "I certainly hope so. Let us see if we can find you the right dream."

It turned to survey the wall of light. An uncomfortably long moment of silence passed before it reached for my hand and took us into the golden ribbon of a dream.

The ground that sprang up under my feet was tiled. The four walls and elaborate decorations of a mansion's foyer unfolded from thin air. A ceiling with a crystal chandelier closed us in. Strangely, there were no people.

"This is interesting," the Wind Whisperer mused. "You do not often come across a mind that can hold a large dream world together like this. There is no dreamer in sight, not even a character, but this room is still in perfect form."

It drifted over to the walls, muttering about imagination and potential. I stepped out of the foyer into the long hall that opened into the living room and continued to the left to multiple sets of doors. The living room was empty of people but furnished with incredible care. It reminded me of my home. Whoever owned this place had money to spare.

A chorus of laughter echoed through the halls. I turned in time to see a group of younger teens run down the hall past me. Most of them were hazy dream characters, but I caught a glimpse of an in-focus arm and tuft of hair from the middle of the group.

Not willing to be put off the chase so soon, I charged after the kids. They disappeared through a pair of double doors that had massive windows with wooden blinds obscuring the view inside. I slowly cracked one of the doors open and peered in.

"We should be safe and sound here." I picked out the smiling boy who spoke, the one at the center of the kids, as the dreamer. "None of the adults will come back to the office." He looked older than the others and kind of familiar.

Down the hall, the doorbell rang. A shadowy couple emerged from the once empty living room and moved to answer the door. The Wind Whisperer drifted out of the foyer toward me as the sound of the door opening and people greeting each other warmly reached me from the front door.

"Any progress?" it asked.

"They're hiding from the adults, but not in a scared way. More like they're playing a game," I replied.

"Interesting. And you have located the dreamer?"

I scooted over to let it peek through the open door. "He's the one in the middle."

"Hm," the Wind Whisperer mused. "Seems that they are trying to avoid parental restrictions. Maybe this event was something that happened during this dreamer's life, and now they are imagining it in a different way, because they are unsatisfied with how things actually happened."

I nodded and looked into the office again. The kids were building forts out of couch cushions and pillows and blankets—not sure where they'd gotten those from since the room was noticeably without furniture other than wooden desks, chairs, and filing cabinets—but they made them look like war trenches instead of the usual boxy little shelters.

They all ducked down behind them and giggled. From my vantage point, I couldn't see what they were doing, so I pushed the door open farther and slipped inside. The Wind Whisperer followed. I got behind the trench lines and found the dreamer. He was holding the hand of a younger boy. The more I watched them, the more I picked up on the bond between them.

"They're siblings," I said.

"Very good." The Wind Whisperer sounded impressed. "I am glad you are able to pick up on that so quickly after only having experienced something like this in a dream once before."

I smiled. This night was off to a very good start. Then it hit me who the dreamer was.

"He's in one of my classes, I think." The only one that I didn't share with any of the other Wind Dreamed.

The Wind Whisperer looked at me sharply. "How well do you know him?"

I shrugged. "I don't even remember his name. I just remember that he sits next to me in my finance class. He seems nice enough, but I've been more focused on getting the hang of the work than meeting anyone besides the other Wind Dreamed."

The Wind Whisperer nodded. "I will have to be more careful next time."

I glanced at it out of the corner of my eye. "About what?"

"Wind Dreamed are not supposed to enter the dreams of people they know."

My brows rose. "Why not?"

"Because they cannot look at the contents of the dream objectively. Whether they realize it or not, their feelings about a person will change how they influence the dream. That must not happen. Besides, we cannot have Wind Dreamed walking into dreams where they might be one of the characters."

I chewed my lip. It would be incredibly awkward to see a blurry version of myself running around in someone else's head, doing things I might not normally do. Though it might be nice to know how a person felt about you deep down where they couldn't lie to themselves or to you.

"If I knew him better, would you take me out of the dream?" I asked.

"Absolutely."

I opened my mouth to ask another question when the door to the office opened. The kids behind their pillow walls went quiet. A large man stepped in and looked around. His eyes landed on the pillow fortress. The atmosphere shifted like it had the night before. The hairs on my arms stood up. This man was dangerous. The dreamer's little brother peered through a gap in the pillows. The man saw and smiled, beckoning him forward.

The little boy relaxed and stood up to go meet the man. The dreamer tried to grab him back, but his fingers fell just shy of his brother's arm.

I already knew what to do and willed the dreamer to get up and go after his brother. He stood. The man had taken the hand of the little boy and was leading him toward the door. The sense of danger increased. The man was going to take the boy away and never return him.

"Give him back," the dreamer ordered.

The man didn't even glance at him. The little brother turned, though. Even though the details of his face were fuzzy, an aura of uncertainty hovered around him.

"Let him go!" The dreamer chased after them, but seemed to slow, so that he could never quite catch up.

He continued to shout after them. The little boy kept glancing back uncertainly, but he didn't let go of the man's hand as the scene morphed into a grassy field that spread out as far as the eye could see. A few trees dotted the landscape, but it was mostly empty.

The sudden shift gave me vertigo. This was new.

"Do not let the change in scenery shake you," the Wind Whisperer urged. "The dream is still going. Adapt and respond."

The man was still walking with the boy out into the field. The dreamer chased after them in slow motion, shouting as they got farther and farther away.

I threw up my hands. "But what is this supposed to mean? The whole dream changed."

"The basic elements are the same. The problem is the same. There are just fewer obstacles in the man's way. No parents to step in. No crowd to witness the dreamer screaming for his little brother. Think. Act."

But I had no idea what to do. When I willed the dreamer to move faster, he just seemed to go slower. If I tried to slow the man, he just seemed to go faster. This was a nightmare, and not only was I powerless to stop it, I was stuck inside of it. This dream wasn't mine but it might as well have been for all the control I had over it.

Why did I have to spend the whole day struggling to understand how to do my schoolwork and then spend the whole night trying to sort through other people's dreams? I hadn't had a moment of rest since I got to Animos Prep. How was that fair?

"Wren?" the Wind Whisperer breathed. "You are not doing anything."

My hands fisted. "I'm tired."

"You are asleep."

"I'm tired of *this*." I waved an arm around me. "You said there weren't going to be catches to becoming a demigod."

Watching siblings get torn apart was a pretty big catch even if this was just a dream.

The Wind Whisperer turned to face me fully. "This is your sacred duty. Did you think you would only play around with your magic?"

"That's not fair. You didn't tell me *any* of this when we were in that meadow." I thrust a hand at the dreamer, who had tears streaming down his face now as he kept trying to get to his brother. "You were so incredibly vague."

"You did not ask for clarification."

"Are you serious?" I turned away, raking my hands through my hair. "How was I supposed to know? I was thrown into this world without any prior knowledge of how it worked, and you expected me to know all the right questions to ask and things to say?"

After reading so many fantasy books, I thought I knew how to avoid this kind of pitfall. Apparently not. I'd been tricked just like all those main characters I'd read about. And now I was trapped in this situation where I was doomed to fail at every turn. I ruined every dream I entered. What a useless demigod.

"You wanted this." I wished the Wind Whisperer would get angry and yell at me, throw me out of the dream, something. How could it be so calm about all of this?

"And it's a crime to want something for yourself? Do you know what my life has been like?"

All the isolation, the mocking words behind my back, the people I thought were my friends but who only wanted something from me and left when they didn't get it. Maybe I was being a bit of a brat, but I had at least developed a rhythm before I got sucked into this. Now, I was lost.

"It is my job to know everything about the hopes and dreams of all people," the Wind Whisperer replied. "But what you want is not always what you need."

"As if you would know. You're not even human."

I could have sworn it flinched a little. "I have spent thousands of years learning the intricacies of human life. You are working with a mere seventeen years."

"Then you should know you can't work a person all day every day and expect them to do anything productive. I can't even sleep to take a break now! I can't even dream!"

The Wind Whisperer watched me for a long moment. "You are enough, Wren."

It was my turn to flinch. "What is *that* supposed to mean?"

"I think it is time for you to wake up now."

Before I could retort, the dream folded in on itself, and I popped back into consciousness.

10

Ten

It was the middle of the night. I sat up in bed, tired but too angry to try to go back to sleep. What would be the point anyway? I couldn't sleep without going to the dream realm, and the Wind Whisperer had made it clear I wasn't allowed there anymore. At least for the rest of the night.

I threw off my blankets and made my way over to my desk. If I couldn't sleep, I should at least try to get some homework done. But after staring blankly at the mess of papers and crafting supplies all over my desk for twenty minutes without mustering the will to do any of it, I gave up.

Useless.

I poked my head out of my door. The penthouse was silent. It must have been too early even for Reve to be up making one of his delicious breakfasts for the rest of us.

There were a few of the cinnamon roll pancakes left over in the fridge, so I got those out and ate them. They were divine when microwaved, but I was willing to guess they had been even better yesterday morning when they were fresh.

I felt a little bad about eating and running, especially since this was my first weekend with the Wind Dreamed, but I couldn't bring myself to stay after the night I'd had. How was I supposed to look them in the eye when I couldn't get one thing about being Wind Dreamed right?

And I'd yelled at the Wind Whisperer about it. I'd yelled at a literal god.

Part of me was proud that I'd been able to say anything, but the other part regretted it. The Wind Whisperer had given me a chance, and while it hadn't been entirely forthcoming, I couldn't blame my failure on it. I hadn't been chosen because I would make a good Wind Dreamed. I'd been chosen because the gods needed me to sign a proverbial NDA about their existence.

I wouldn't have been surprised if the Wind Whisperer had appeared right then in front of me, taken my powers away, and dropped me off at a cabin in the middle of the woods where I would live out the rest of my life in solitude. I'd blown the only shot I had at not turning into an ancient spinster in the middle of nowhere. Maybe someone would start a cool urban legend about me being a witch at least.

I stuffed some supplies into my backpack and took the elevator down to the common room. It was dead quiet for the first time since I'd taken the tour of campus. Only a handful of lamps lit the space to keep people from running into furniture if they were crazy enough to be awake at this hour. The eerie atmosphere reminded me of Mortorous Academy, even though the colors were all wrong.

The air was a little chilly the way it was supposed to be on spring nights. Dressed in my own clothes instead of my pastel red Animos Prep uniform, I made my way to the parking lot where my car waited.

I hadn't driven it since before the Wind Whisperer kidnapped me. I hadn't needed to. Up until now, all the days I'd had after becoming Wind Dreamed were school days, and I'd been so entranced by the newness of Animos that I hadn't wanted to go anywhere else. But now, I needed to get out, find the nearest town, locate a bookstore, and do some shopping. The library wasn't enough to satisfy my need for escape today.

The address took its time popping up on the map in my phone, but as soon as it gave me a route, I took off through the parking lot, out onto the street, and toward the beckoning books.

It didn't take as long to get to Luxem, the city near Animos, as it did to get to Noxier from Mortorous. And Luxem wasn't a small town like Noxier. It was a whole city. I came upon it quickly. There was nothing but the dark blobs of trees and grass one minute. The next, buildings lit up like fireworks around me. It looked like the kind of place where you might have to worry about traffic when it wasn't the early hours of the morning.

Since it was still fully dark outside, only a handful of other cars were on the road, so getting to the bookstore was easy. Getting inside was not. Only bars and hospitals were open at this time of the night. Not bookstores. The parking lot was empty. The lights inside were off, except for a couple of emergency fluorescents.

I sighed. I would have gotten out to walk around if I didn't suspect that someone might mug me on the street. So, reading on my phone until opening time it was. I settled in and scrolled through my eBook library.

At eight in the morning, someone finally unlocked the doors. I sprang out of my car and jogged in. The comforting smell of paper and ink washed over me. I drifted through the aisles, letting my muscles relax and my mind wander.

There was a certain order to bookstores. They might each have different layouts, but all the fiction was always grouped together, with the fantasy and science fiction sections right next to each other—those were the best genres for escapism. This store wasn't any different. At least some things could be counted on to stay the same whether the closest school to them was grim and gothic or light and artistic.

I spent hours browsing titles, reading descriptions, and calculating how much the growing stack in my arms would cost. My parents wouldn't be bothered by a few new novels, but if I blew my bank account at a bookstore again, I would hear from them before the end of the day. Maybe I should do it anyway just for an excuse to talk to someone who hadn't been converted to the Animos Prep way of thinking.

And to check on how things were going with their business. Dad hadn't seemed worried, and Mom was trying not to sound like she was concerned, but she wasn't that good at it. She wasn't good at not worrying though. This would just mean that the two of them would be pouring all their time and energy into fixing the problem and I wouldn't hear from them for a while.

Probably several weeks.

I sighed.

My phone buzzed in my pocket. A message from Reve of all people popped up on the screen.

Where are you?

In town. I didn't feel like explaining. He'd been the one to rat me out to Imena yesterday morning. If I said anything about where I was, I had a feeling she or Almos would come after me again.

There was a moment of radio silence before he messaged back. *Where?*

I rolled my eyes and put my phone away. Today was about having Me Time. I didn't need anyone bothering me.

I had made my purchases and sat in the café that took up one corner of the bookstore when Reve appeared in front of me.

I straightened. "What are you doing here?"

He stared down at me with an expressionless face. "You ate my pancakes."

My brows furrowed. "I thought they were for everyone."

"They are for everyone. When we're eating *together*. You ate them alone."

"Sorry?"

He crossed his arms. "Why are you here?"

"I wanted to buy some books."

"You got books from the library yesterday morning."

I shook my head. I'd had enough of people arguing with me about how many unread books I had at any point in time to know he couldn't be convinced that I needed these new ones for the sake of my sanity. "How did you even find me? I didn't tell you where I went."

"You didn't need to." He sat down across from me at the little café table. "What's wrong with you?"

I stiffened. "Excuse me?" There was a lot wrong with me right now, but none of it was any of his business.

"I told the others to give me five minutes with you before they came in. You can talk to all of us, but I have a feeling that's not what you want. So, what's your problem?"

I picked up my books just in case I needed to make a run for it. "You're going to have to be more specific."

"You're struggling, but you haven't asked anyone for help, not even any of the teachers. You run off to your books and your stories and hope they can help you, but you completely ignore everyone around you."

My grip on my books tightened. "And you know all of this... how? Last I checked, I was doing fine in school."

"When we're in class, you look around at what everyone else is doing, then stare at your work for a full two minutes, before you start doing it."

I had hoped no one had noticed that. "It's called organizing my thoughts."

He refused to relent. "How is your dream walking going?"

My jaw tightened. "What do you want, Reve?"

He braced his forearms on the table and leaned toward me. "I want you to be honest with yourself and everyone around you."

I mirrored his posture. "Maybe you can show me how by being honest about how you found out where I was."

His voice was drier than a desert. "I took a wild guess."

I pushed away from the table and stood. "Well, it was nice talking to you, but I think I'm going to go now." I was completely done with his weirdness. You didn't interrogate people about their friends and their life and not give anything in return.

"You can't do everything on your own, Wren," he called over his shoulder. "We're supposed to be a team."

"You sure have a funny way of showing it," I snapped as I turned toward the door and ran straight into Lorien.

"There you are!" she exclaimed with a bright smile and gave me a quick hug as the others filed in around us. "Reve told us you went into town, and honestly, I was a little hurt that you didn't offer to take me too. This is my first time back in Luxem in ages."

"Sorry, but I have to go." I wound around her.

She followed me. "Can I ride with you?"

"No!" I snapped. She recoiled as if I'd slapped her. "I need some time to myself. Don't wait around for me."

When I passed by the large windows out front, I saw the others inside clustered around where Reve still sat at the café table with furrowed brows and pinched expressions. Of course, they were talking about me behind my back. Wasn't that what people always did? The moment you stopped playing by their rules and being useful to them, they turned on you.

It was fine. I should have known this wouldn't last. You couldn't make a group of highschoolers be friends, even ones who were demigods. It didn't matter. I would just go back to what always worked before.

Me. Myself. I.

And books. Always books.

I tooled around the city, stopping at restaurants when I was hungry and window shopping to my heart's content. I did my best to forget about the other Wind Dreamed and my failed attempts at being a good demigod. Eventually exhaustion drove me back to campus.

I felt like a thief sneaking up to the dorm. Instead of taking the elevator, which would announce my presence in the penthouse when it dinged open, I found the stairs that Lorien always took. It took two long stops to catch my breath between flights before I finally made it to the top floor.

I had to use my key to unlock the door, then shut it as quietly as possible. It was getting late, but I wasn't going to take any chances. This was a me day and it would stay that way if I had anything to say about it.

I had to cross through the living room to get to my room. It was empty except for, of course, Reve. He was stretched out across his couch with a plate of food that smelled like heaven in his lap. I paused at the edge of the living room when he looked up at me. He just raised his eyebrows. I raised mine back. He sighed and looked back down at his food.

I marched off to my room. There was no time for his nonsense. I had work to finish. I'd already turned in the geometric origami, but everything else was due on Monday, so I needed to get something done today. My essay still needed some editing, and my collection of paintings was missing a couple pieces.

My bed beckoned as I worked into the night, but I didn't want to go into the dream world before I'd assured myself that I had nothing to worry about other than my inability to dream walk properly.

Given how little sleep I'd gotten the night before, and how out of it I felt, I was surprised at how easily I completed the paintings. Maybe that was the trick to being creative all along. You had to get out of your head, not think about it too much, and just let it flow out of you.

The essay was not the same story. That required more brainwork, which meant that I was slower to get that finished, but I got it done before my eyelids gave out on me.

I forced myself to take a shower to wash off the long day I'd had before I fell into bed. Why did humans have to sleep to survive? Why couldn't I just stay up reading the whole night and be fine in the morning? Why did I have to go back to that place where I couldn't do anything right?

I stared at the ceiling. What if I stayed up all night anyway and went to sleep when the sun came up? There probably wouldn't be as many people dreaming during the day. And there was no school, so I could sleep as long as I wanted.

The only problem with that might be if I was expected to attend to the dreams of the people on the other side of the world where it was still night. Knowing my luck, I would be.

There was no winning.

I might as well try to get some sleep and see what happened. I wasn't hopeful, but maybe something I'd said had gotten through to the Wind Whisperer. Maybe it would just let me sleep tonight. Maybe I would have my own dream where a Wind Dreamed would try to send me subliminal messages about doing my "sacred duty."

Wouldn't that just make my day?

11

Eleven

There was nothing. It felt like I'd closed my eyes one second and opened them the next. But it was morning, and I had slept through the night. Did that mean the Wind Whisperer had let me have the night off? Or had I just been banned from dream walking?

Either way, I was glad for the reprieve.

The living room was empty when I passed through it on my way to the kitchen. Lorien and Frida looked up from their conversation at the kitchen table when I entered. I gave them a small smile. They gave me half-hearted smiles of their own and looked away.

Ok then.

I made myself some toast since Reve didn't want me eating his food anymore apparently. Imena and Almos came in. They sounded like they were in a heated conversation before they passed through the door but stopped when they saw me buttering my bread. They glanced from Frida and Lorien sitting silently at the table to me and back again before sitting down quietly too.

"Hi, Wren," Imena said in a careful tone like she thought I might storm out of kitchen like I had stormed out of the bookstore yesterday.

"Hi," I replied.

Everyone else just sat there, not doing anything, not saying anything.

And then Reve entered. He stopped the moment he walked through the door and stared at me. I stared back. He eyed the toast in my hands, looked back up at me, then glanced at the other Wind Dreamed all sitting at the table. I could only see part of Almos's profile, but his face moved as if he was having a silent conversation with Reve through facial expressions.

About me, no doubt.

Fine. If they didn't want me there, I wouldn't be there.

I took my toast and marched out. This was stupid. I couldn't believe I had thought this was a good idea. Every single book I read where something like this happened, the main character ended up regretting having their powers. That should have been my first indication that something about being a demigod was wrong.

The second was how much everything had changed. It didn't matter if I had gotten the hang of schoolwork. It didn't matter if the school was prettier, or the curriculum was what students needed to not burn out in school. I never should have left Mortorous Academy.

I packed a bag and took the elevator down. I didn't care if the other Wind Dreamed saw me this time. So much the better if they did. They would know that they didn't have to deal with me anymore.

My car stuttered when I turned the key the first time but started the second time. I drove out of there as fast as possible, narrowly avoiding hitting the other cars. Usually, it took four hours to get from Animos Prep to Mortorous Academy.

I made it in three.

The familiar dark clouds and rainy weather met me halfway. I rolled down the windows to let the humid air in. The smell took me back to a time when I thought the Boneman and the Wind Whisperer were just stories made up to keep people entertained and teach small children lessons.

Someone had taken over my old parking space, so I had to search for a new spot. The only open ones were at the very back of the lot, which meant I would have to walk all the way up to the front.

I didn't care as long as I could go back to the life I had enjoyed before this mess.

I left my stuff in the car and trudged through the lines of cars. Puddles splashed underfoot. Rain drops beaded across the tops and sides of the cars. I could imagine the rainy night that would have left this behind. It was the kind that I used to love reading during even if it meant I stayed up too late and was exhausted for school the next day.

The foyer was just as I remembered it: black and white and pristine. No murals, just trophy cases. No multicolored tiles on the floor. No cushions on the benches outside the admin office.

I stared at that empty bench as I pushed the door open.

The woman at the reception desk looked up with a smile. "How can I help you?"

It was the weekend, but there was always someone in the office in case there was a bureaucratic emergency. Not that the problem would get solved any sooner, but it was the thought that counted.

"I'd like to transfer to this school," I declared. "Well, transfer *back*. I was here, but I transferred to Animos Prep. Now, I want to come back."

"Ok." Her brows pinched. "I can print out the forms for you. Do you have a parent with you who can sign them?"

I cringed inwardly. "Not right now." I wasn't even sure if my parents were at home or off on some business trip. I hadn't heard from them since my first day at Animos.

"In that case, why don't you give me a good email address, and I'll send the paperwork to you, so you can print it out at home and fill it out with your parents? You can just scan it and email it back when you're done."

That would mean I'd have to tell my parents about all of this. Maybe I could forge their signatures. I'm not sure how they had signed paperwork to get me to Animos. They'd known I'd "wanted" to transfer, but who had gotten them to sign off on it? If anyone. Maybe they made special exceptions for demigods.

"Ok. Then I can come back?" I asked.

"Then you'll have to request that Animos Prep send us a copy of your transcripts, so we can place you in the appropriate classes."

That would take an eternity. "But I've only been gone for a few months. I can just come back to the classes I had before."

She shook her head. "That's still a few month's worth of work you've missed, and we're not familiar with the curriculum over there. We need those transcripts."

I sighed. "Ok." This was the best I was going to get for now.

Walking out of the office empty-handed wasn't the best feeling, but at least I'd started the process. It was better than nothing. I wasn't looking forward to talking to my parents about this though. They would get all worried about me and my grades and what had happened to make me want to switch schools for the second time this school year.

I had no idea what anyone had told them to justify me moving schools before, but I would have to come up with an excuse. I definitely couldn't tell them that I wanted to escape the god that had given me a cursed set of powers and was forcing me to use them even though I couldn't seem to do it right.

It was barely noon when I walked out of the front building. I wasn't about to make the drive back to Animos after only a few minutes. So, I strolled around the backside of the main building and started to wander campus. I couldn't get in most buildings since I no longer had a student ID to unlock the doors, but the main campus area wasn't fenced in, so I could wander to my heart's content. It was the closest I could get to being back here until the paperwork got processed.

I saw him before he saw me and stopped to stare.

In all the time I'd known him, Nicholas Ater had never neglected his appearance. His hair was always swept back. There was always a shine to his eyes. And he always stood up straight like he was about to walk across a stage in front of thousands of people to receive some kind of award.

But the Nick that walked—trudged—toward me was the opposite of that. He looked like he hadn't slept or brushed his hair. His eyes were fixed on the sidewalk, and his shoulders slumped. There was tension in his jaw and some indescribable heaviness in his gaze.

Most notably, he didn't have Sylvan with him. Had they broken up? Was that why he looked so dejected? I'd always suspected she should be wary of him. Had she finally seen what I had seen and ended things?

He finally looked up and noticed me staring. "Wren?" He frowned like he didn't believe I was really there.

My mouth was dry. "Hey, Nick."

He stepped forward. "Where have you been?" he demanded.

"I…" How much should I tell him? "I transferred schools."

"In the middle of the year? For no reason?" He sounded a bit frantic.

"Something came up."

He scowled. "Where do you go to school now?"

What was his problem? We hadn't even been friends for that long. We certainly hadn't been on speaking terms before I left. He'd been acting weird around Sylvan, and I had wanted no part of it. Especially after he had practically accused me of pushing her around.

I swallowed the lump in my throat. "Animos Prep."

The scowl vanished. His eyes widened. "Wren, did you…?" He leaned forward, studying my face.

I was about to back up when I felt it. Felt him. There was something different about him that I'd never noticed before, this strange simultaneous pushing and pulling sensation. I frowned as I met his gaze, craning my neck to look up at him. It reminded me of how it felt to be around the other Wind Dreamed. Except there was no pushing with them, only a pull like gravity dragging me into their circle. Like we all belonged to each other. This felt like…

My eyes widened. It suddenly made sense.

Sylvan and Nicholas had been inseparable. Even after he pulled some questionable stunts, she had forgiven him and stayed his friend. I hadn't understood at the time why she would be willing to overlook his red flags or why he seemed so attached to her. Sylvan had refused to say anything about it no matter how I pressed her.

But that had been because she couldn't tell me.

It was because she wasn't allowed to.

Because they were *both* Bone Touched.

They stuck together because they were the only ones of their kind in the school. And they couldn't tell me, because I was the outsider who wasn't allowed to know.

Nicholas must have seen the realization on my face, because he nodded.

I put a hand to my mouth. "This whole time?"

"Yeah."

"You and Sylvan?"

He tensed when I said her name. "Yeah. How did you become…?" He gestured from my head to my toes.

I took a deep breath. "Do you have time for lunch? I could really use some food. And a place to sit down. It's a long story."

"Of course."

We made our way to the little café tucked into the shadow of the library. It was the only place you could get food without having purchased a meal plan that was loaded onto your ID. It was also the *best* place to get food. The cafeteria was alright, but nothing beat the fresh pastries at the café. Except maybe Reve's cooking, but if I was leaving Animos Prep, I wouldn't get any more of that.

"Where is Sylvan? She should hear this too." I also had my own questions I wanted to ask her.

Nick's hands clenched into fists, and he looked away. "That's a long story too."

"She's not on campus?" Where else would she be? I couldn't imagine she'd gotten enough training to go hunt ghosts. She'd only been here a few months.

"No."

I chewed on my lip as we stepped inside.

I'd missed this place. It was a bit of softness on a campus where everything was black and white, literally and figuratively. As far as I knew, there wasn't a place at Animos that wasn't bathed in art. The library came close, but it was still full of artistic touches.

I ordered a handful of pastries and paid with my credit card. Nicholas was uncharacteristically quiet while we waited for our food. I wasn't nearly as comfortable with the silence and searched for something to say.

"How are classes going?"

Nick stood as still as a tree. "Good."

"Tilns is still strict?" We'd had his class together for history.

His voice was distant. "A little less so. He's excited about his first grandchild coming this winter."

My eyebrows rose. "Wow. I didn't know he had kids. I mean, it makes sense given his age. I just never saw him as the nurturing type."

A hint of humor sparked in his gaze. "Me neither. He probably raised his kids like they were in military school."

I snorted. "Yeah. That sounds about right."

We got our food and headed upstairs where there were fewer people to overhear our conversation. A pair of armchairs in the corner provided enough privacy if we scooted them closer together closer to the window.

Nicholas didn't waste time with pleasantries. "How did you become Wind Dreamed?" he asked as soon as we sat down.

I sifted through my bag of food. "I found out about Sylvan."

He straightened. "What do you mean you found out about her?"

"I found out she was Bone Touched. Well, not exactly. I found out she was a few hundred years old."

Nick's eyes went wide. "A few *hundred* years old?" He choked on the words.

I could hardly blame him. I'd be shocked if I found out my crush was centuries older than she looked too. I took a bite of a donut and chewed. "Let me start at the beginning. Sylvan asked me to help find her parents—"

"She wanted to find her parents?" Nick looked at me like I'd said Sylvan wanted to start a nuclear war.

"Are you going to keep interrupting?"

"Sorry." He sat back. "I'll try to hold my questions till the end."

"So, she wanted to find her parents. She told me she'd been kidnapped when she was little and couldn't remember them. There wasn't much we could do, but I paid to get a DNA test."

Nick massaged his face with both hands and groaned. "Why would she think that was a good idea?"

So much for holding his questions. I shrugged. "We sent it in, and I got the results back within a week. It said her gene sequence was a perfect combination of two people they found buried in a rockslide. The rockslide happened three hundred ago."

Nick stared at the ceiling through his fingers. "I always wondered how the Boneman picked us. Three hundred years..."

I plucked at the dough inside the donut. "Anyway, somehow the Boneman found out that I knew where Sylvan came from.

I went to bed in my dorm room one night and woke up in a field in the middle of nowhere the next morning. The Wind Whisperer gave me a choice between exile somewhere I could never speak to anyone again or becoming Wind Dreamed, because they couldn't have me talking to people about what I'd discovered. I chose the latter."

"Yeah, that's not much of a choice," Nick murmured. He lowered his hands and looked at me. "But if you're Wind Dreamed, what are you doing here? Aren't you supposed to be at Animos Prep?"

I rolled a bit of dough between my fingers. "I'm not very good at it."

"At being Wind Dreamed?"

"Yeah. I'm actually really bad at it, which sucks, because I've never been bad at anything I've truly put effort into. And I've always, *always* wanted to have magic and be a part of a world that was bigger than the one I lived in. But I've failed." My voice cracked, and I took a shaky breath. "So, I came back. If I can't be something new, I just have to go back to what I was. Maybe I can be Bone Touched instead."

Nick shook his head so hard it looked like it might fly off. "You don't want to be Bone Touched."

I frowned. "Why not?"

"Aside from the fact that you already belong to the Wind Whisperer and the gods absolutely *do not* interfere with each other's children, becoming Bone Touched is a very long, very *painful* process. It sounds like it took Sylvan *three hundred years* to do it. The Boneman only knows if that's the standard for the rest of us or if we take even longer." He shuddered. "I wouldn't wish that on anyone, especially not a friend."

A friend.

I grimaced. "I guess I owe you an apology."

He raised his brows. "For what?"

I kept picking at my donut. "Before I left, I passed judgement on you when I didn't know everything."

He gave me a distant smile. "It's ok. It's not like Sylvan or I could tell you. And in some ways, you were right. I moved too fast with her, but we figured things out eventually."

"What happened to her, Nick?" I asked softly.

His gaze fell to the floor. A grim smile twisted his lips. "You think *you* failed?"

My stomach clenched. "Nicholas, what happened?"

"The thing about being Bone Touched... our bones are our greatest strength and our greatest weakness. They hold our magic, but it's the magic that keeps us alive. So, when our bones break..."

Oh no. "And Sylvan?" My voice was no more than a strained whisper.

"I was supposed to be there. I got to her as fast as I could, but I didn't even see who it was."

"*Who?* Someone hurt her?"

He stared out the window. "I have my suspicions, but without any evidence, nothing will happen to them."

"Where is she now?" If he said she was dead...

"She's with the Boneman. At least, I hope she is."

I leaned toward him, gripping the arms of my chair with white knuckles. "You don't know?"

"I gave her to him when she got hurt, but I haven't heard anything since."

"You can't ask?"

He shook his head. "It doesn't work like that. You can't just summon the Boneman."

"Why not? I see the Wind Whisperer literally every night." Except last night, but I didn't want to think about those implications. "You aren't allowed to ask him how Sylvan is doing?"

He shrugged. "Different gods work in different ways."

I flopped back in my chair. "So, there's nothing we can do?"

"We can only wait."

I stuffed the rest of the donut in my mouth.

"What are you going to do?" Nicholas asked after a long moment.

My eyes fixed on the ceiling. "I don't know, but I can't stay at Animos. The other Wind Dreamed hate me. I can't dream walk. If I can't be Bone Touched, I guess I have to go live by myself and never talk to another human for the rest of my life." I wasn't keen on the idea, but the alternative hadn't worked out. So, what choice did I have?

"If that happens, I'll volunteer to bring you pastries and books." Nick gave me one of his old, melt-your-heart smiles.

I grinned back. "You still know all the right things to say."

His smile turned brittle as he looked out the window at the damp, dreary campus. "Old habits."

My gaze stayed pinned to him. "Do you love her? Sylvan?"

He stole a breath before replying. "Yeah, I think so. For all the good it did in keeping her safe."

"That wasn't your fault."

Nick shook his head. "If I had gotten out of the car with her instead of letting Mallor drop me off at the boys' dorm, it never would have happened."

I had no idea who Mallor was, but that didn't seem like the important part. "You did what you could. Maybe no news is good news. I mean, the Boneman probably would have told you if she was dead. Right?"

"Maybe." He didn't take his eyes from the view of campus.

"Regardless, I'm glad you were there for her and care about her." I looked out the window too and realized a sliver of the forest—the forest where Nick had given Sylvan to the Boneman—was visible between the tall gothic buildings. "She deserves someone who does."

"So do you, Wren." My gaze darted to him. "I couldn't reciprocate your feelings when you were here, but I hope you find someone who will."

My heart pounded in my throat. "What are you talking about?" I'd only ever told Sylvan about the massive crush I used to have on him. She must have said something to Nick. Though with the vast number of girls who wanted him, I guess it wouldn't have been hard to figure out.

"It's ok. It never changed what I thought of you. I still consider you a good friend."

I was pretty sure my face had caught fire. "Uh, thanks." I wanted to crawl in a hole and never come out.

"No problem. I'm actually glad you showed up, even if you aren't technically supposed to be here."

I stuffed my trash in my bag to distract myself. "Are you going to get in trouble because I'm here? With the Boneman, I mean." The woman in the office hadn't said anything about it, but maybe she hadn't known about... everything.

Nick waved an absent hand. "He hasn't bothered to show up in so long, it will be a wonder if he even notices you're here. He can't really blame me for it anyway, since you came on your own, and you can always claim ignorance. The gods usually stick to themselves, but it's harder to control each other's kids. They're supposed to leave disciplining them to their patron god. You know, the way parents aren't supposed to yell at kids that aren't their own."

I'd seen plenty of parents yell at kids that weren't their own, but usually those were in extreme circumstances. Nick didn't seem to think this counted.

"Thanks for talking with me." I stood, squeezing the little paper bag where I'd shoved all my trash like it was a stress ball.

"Thanks for coming. I hope everything works out with you and…" He waved a hand absently, searching for the right words. "The powers that be."

"Yeah." I chuckled nervously. "I hope Sylvan is ok."

"Me too. I'm trying not to assume the worst, but it gets hard sometimes. I miss her."

"I miss her too. If I'm not locked away in a cottage in the woods by the time our schools play each other again, would you like to meet at the event?"

A ghost of a smile danced across his face. "Yeah, sounds like fun. Good luck."

"Good luck." Leaving Nick sitting there by himself, staring out the window, felt like leaving us both more alone than we had been before.

I paused at the top of the stairs to glance back at him. With his disheveled appearance and the low lighting silhouetting him against the stormy clouds outside, he looked like a painting come to life. A heartsick prince awaiting the return of his princess. The library at Animos Prep was full of images like that. I wished I was a good enough artist to capture this scene.

12

Twelve

I took my time getting to the parking lot. Not wanting to run into anyone else I knew, I kept to the edges of campus where short stretches of open land led into the forest.

The Boneman's forest.

I had gone to this school for two and a half years, learned all the variations of all the stories about the Boneman, heard of students wandering into this forest at midnight when the moon was full in search of a giant skeleton with the skull of a hornless, wolf-like antelope, and never suspected that the mystical creature might actually exist.

All evidence had pointed toward the contrary. The kids who came back from the forest were either disappointed at not having found anything or had made up inconsistent stories about their journey. None of the teachers ever seemed to take the legends seriously when they came up in class. There were parties and mascot costumes and so many other times where the Boneman was made fun of or turned into something less than what he was. No one saw him or any evidence that he might exist, so they didn't take him seriously.

But if the god of death didn't want you to see him, you didn't see him. He let himself fade into jokes, cheap merchandise, and late-night hazing rituals. All while he was doing real work behind the scenes.

"I wonder…" I approached the misty trees.

They looked so ordinary, but if I focused, I could feel a faint sensation like the one that came from Nick. It was far more distant, which made it less noticeable, but it was still there.

My hands burrowed into my pockets as I walked in. Somehow the trees seemed aware of me. I could have sworn they leaned closer as I passed. Could they sense my magic the way I could sense theirs?

I reached out and laid a hand on the damp bark of the nearest trunk. A cloying fear permeated my senses. I yanked my hand back, but the feeling remained. I shouldn't have come here. The forest was mad at me now.

What are you doing here? The deep growling voice came from inside my mind.

I put my hands to my head. "What…?"

What are you doing here? The voice was louder, harsher.

I tried to cover my ears, but it echoed in my thoughts. "What's going on? Who's there?"

I turned in circles, seeking the source of the voice. For several rotations, I saw nothing out of the ordinary. Then suddenly…

There.

Amid the dark wood of the forest stood a white figure. My eyes went wide. I'd spent two and a half years seeing that figure depicted all over the Mortorous Academy campus. Students wandered among these trees for hours looking for what I had found in a matter of minutes.

The Boneman was even bigger than I had imagined. He moved with a slow, plodding gait as if he had never had to hurry for anything in all his life. He was the god of death, so he probably hadn't. There was no need to rush when your time would never end.

I took a step back as he steadily bore down on me.

Do not dare to run away, he hissed in my mind. His expression never changed, but the anger in his tone was unmistakable.

You come into my school, into my forest, and shrink away when you have to face the consequences of your actions? Is that the thanks I get for allowing you to become Wind Dreamed instead of locking you away somewhere you will never be able to tell anyone what you discovered?

"I thought the Wind Whisperer made that decision." My voice trembled as he towered over me. The statue in the main building didn't do him justice. Sure, it was spooky, but the Boneman oozed terror the way the Wind Dreamed radiated peace.

I wanted to offer you a choice despite your reckless actions.

"*My* reckless actions? How is it reckless to try to reunite a lost girl with her family?" Pervasive aura of fear or not, I refused to be blamed for a god's failure. I'd failed plenty lately, but trying to help Sylvan wasn't something I could bring myself to regret.

You had no idea what you were doing, and you knew that. It was a matter for an adult to handle. A member of the administration would never have allowed such a gross breach in our security.

As if Sylvan would have trusted any of them with something so important and personal. The admin were more concerned with running the school so it would look like the best in the country. They didn't really care about us.

My hands shook as I clenched them at my sides. "It's not fair to punish me. I didn't know any of this would happen." If I had, I never would have sent in that DNA test.

This is not only about you. His bones rattled as he moved close enough that I could have reached out and touched his rib cage. I fisted my hands so tightly my nails dug into my palms. *Those people you sent that test to started asking questions, informing colleagues. They wanted to take your friend, my child in for further testing.* The Boneman paused as if the thought pained him. *I had to ask a favor from Time.*

"Time?" The Wind Whisperer had mentioned something about a Time in the meadow when it offered to make me Wind Dreamed.

The god of time is not the kind of being you want to be indebted to. They are the most dangerous of the three of us. There is as much a chance that they will make the problem worse as there is that they will fix it. But the problem was too widespread to risk not asking Time for help.

"What did Time do?" If they were more powerful than the gods of life and death, what *could* they do?

They reset the minds of everyone involved in the incident. None of them remember a thing about it.

My eyes widened. What an intimidating power. But if they could erase memories… "Why didn't they do that to me?"

I never would have had to become Wind Dreamed. I could have stayed at Mortorous Academy until I graduated next year and not known that this side of the world existed. I never would have screwed up so badly. None of this would have happened.

The Boneman clenched his sharp teeth together. *Time refused.*

"Refused? Why?" I could have kept living my normal life without a care in the world.

I never would have thought the Boneman could roll his eyes since he didn't have any, but he did his best. *Time likes to play puppet master. I imagine they had their own reasons that they did not care to divulge. They refused to wipe your memory, so we had to deal with you ourselves.*

Despite the consuming fear emanating off the Boneman, I found myself laughing at the cruelty of the situation. Of course there was a way out of this that didn't end in my life being turned upside down, but someone had decided not to let me take it. That was just my luck, wasn't it?

You must leave this place, the Boneman said as if I weren't losing it in front of him. *You were not invited, and you have overstayed your welcome.*

"Take me back," I pleaded. "I can't be Wind Dreamed. I want to come back to Mortorous."

The Boneman tilted his hornless skull to the side. *You want to be Bone Touched?*

I nodded. "Please."

Have you failed your duties to your god so miserably?

I avoided his gaze. I had completely, epically failed, and it hurt. Especially when a primordial deity pointed it out.

The Boneman leaned down to look me in the eye. *You occupy my school, put my children at risk, accept our offer to become a demigod only to give up when you find out you do not have a natural talent for it, then have the audacity to try to become a different god's child?*

I swallowed hard. "I can't do it."

The Boneman straightened and turned away. *You are no longer my problem. Go back to your own school and your own god. I cannot give you what you want. Do not return to this place without an invitation again.*

Just like that, my last hope was dashed. I was stuck in this.

"What about Sylvan?" I called after the Boneman. "What would she want?"

The Boneman stopped and looked at me over his shoulder. *She is not involved in this.*

"She started this. Where is she?" If he wouldn't help me, the least he could do was tell me where my friend was and if she was ok. "Nick said she got *hurt*." My voice broke on the last word.

You have more than enough of your own concerns. Do not worry yourself about her.

"I just want to know if she's alive!" I shouted, taking a half step toward him.

The Boneman turned to fully face me. *Regardless of how things turned out, I am glad that she had a friend like you during her time at this school. I hope more people like you are there if she returns. Now. Go.* He walked off into the forest.

If she returns.

It didn't sound very optimistic, but that had to mean she wasn't dead yet. Right? "If" meant there was still a possibility she would be perfectly fine, or better enough to come back to school at least.

I heaved a breath and turned back the way I'd come. It would have to be enough, because that's all the Boneman was going to give me. He was right about overstaying my welcome. Despite yelling at him—the second time in as many days that I'd raised my voice at a god—I wasn't ready to push the limits of this whole "gods don't interfere with each other's children" thing.

Making my way back to the lot where I'd parked my car hours earlier was torturous. All my escape routes had turned out to be dead ends. The only thing left to do was return to Animos Prep and hope for the best. Not that hope had done much for me so far.

I took the whole four hours to get back to school. There was no reason to rush when I would be stuck there once I arrived. It was dark by the time I parked. I turned off the car and sat there for a long moment.

I was so tired. Not just physically, but mentally, emotionally. And I still had to go up and face the other Wind Dreamed before the night was over.

After the monochromatic colors of Mortorous Academy, the murals and ombre rainbows of the Animos Prep dorm common room were a refreshing sight. That was the only thing I would have changed about Mortorous. It needed some pops of color to take the edge off all that black and white. An accent color at least.

I got in the elevator, turned my key in the lock that would enable me to go to the penthouse, and sank down on the floor with my bag in my lap. What was I supposed to say to the others? How would I explain myself?

This wasn't my fault, but it wasn't theirs either. They didn't deserve to be stuck with someone who hadn't been chosen to be Wind Dreamed like they had, who couldn't get any part of being a demigod right. It wasn't fair to any of us.

The elevator doors opened, and I heaved myself to my feet.

They were already waiting for me. Everyone sat in their chairs and on their couches. They must have been having a conversation of their own, but their eyes fixed on me, and they fell silent as soon as I came into view.

My chest felt tight, but after the day I'd had, I didn't have the energy to try to avoid them.

I stepped off the elevator and stopped. I let my bag drop to the floor. "I can't do this."

No one said a word.

"I guess I thought I could because all I've ever wanted since I first listened to a story about magic was to have it. I thought I could do anything I put my mind to, but no matter how hard I try I can't dream walk. And I can't just stop being Wind Dreamed, so what am I supposed to do?"

"You keep trying," Imena said. "The Wind Whisperer chose you for a reason—"

I threw my head back and raked my fingers through my hair. They got stuck at the top of my braid. "No, it didn't! No one chose me. It was a mistake." I looked down at the floor. "I was friends with someone who was Bone Touched. She asked for my help with something, and long story short, I found out she was more than just a regular person. So, I had to be silenced."

I looked back at them. Lorien had a hand over her mouth. Frida's eyes were so wide they looked like a breeze would knock them out of her head.

Imena's normally dark skin had paled. "You weren't…"

"No. I wasn't *chosen*. I was never supposed to be Wind Dreamed. That's probably why I keep failing." I crossed my arms as tears swam in my eyes. "I'm sorry I lied to all of you. I'm sorry you thought I was a real Wind Dreamed. I'm not. I don't think I ever will be. I'm going to try to talk to the Wind Whisperer tonight, so I can get out of your hair as soon as—"

Lorien was out of her seat and across the room with her arms around me before I could finish. I staggered back from the force of her hug.

"I want you to stay in my hair," she whispered in my ear, voice shaking with tears.

"So do I." Imena hugged us both. "Even if it wasn't the original plan, the Wind Whisperer wouldn't have made you Wind Dreamed if it didn't see potential in you."

Almos joined. "You *are* a real Wind Dreamed, Wren."

Frida nearly knocked us over when she jumped over the back of her couch and embraced us. Everyone's head turned in Reve's direction. He sighed and got up from his sectional. The others parted to bring him into the group hug.

He rested his chin on my head. "You don't have to be perfect, Wren. You just have to keep trying."

I let the combined strength of the Wind Dreamed hold me up as tears streamed down my face. I wasn't going to pretend to understand how they could so easily overlook everything I'd just admitted, but I was glad for their support. Carrying everything myself for so long was hard. It felt good to share the burden with them if only for a moment.

"Have you eaten dinner yet?" Frida asked.

"No." I hadn't eaten anything since going to the café with Nick.

"Good, 'cause Reve promised us casserole tonight, but he's just been lazing around all evening." She poked him in the ribs.

He glared at her. "I don't have to cook anything if you're going to demand it so rudely. You can go ahead and make your own dinner."

"No, come on." She let go of us and grabbed Reve. "Wren

needs a good hot meal to cheer her up. Let's go."

"You better help this time," he growled as she dragged him toward the kitchen.

"Only if I get to use your fancy knives."

"Absolutely not."

The others let go of me.

"Go take your stuff to your room," Almos said. "Then come to the kitchen. Sundays are board game nights, and you don't get to skip that just because you think you're not really one of us."

I smiled. "Ok."

I went to my room, set my bag on the desk, and turned to leave. Almos stood in the hallway just outside my door.

"Hey, mind if I come in for a minute?"

I waved an inviting hand. "Sure."

He stepped over the threshold and glanced around my room. "Nice set up you've got here."

My room was still mostly an ocean blue instead of the red of my uniform. "Thanks."

Almos took a steadying breath and looked directly at me. "Are you ok?"

I opened my mouth to say that of course I was, that the group hug had made me feel all better, but that wasn't entirely true. There was still a raw part of me that felt exposed from admitting I hadn't become Wind Dreamed due to my own merit.

I settled on saying, "I don't know."

Almos nodded as if he had expected me to say exactly that. "You know, how you got here doesn't matter nearly as much as you might think it does."

I wasn't sure about that. The other Wind Dreamed were all

cut from the same multicolored cloth. But I was something foreign, stitched into their seamless pattern with hasty, haphazard stitches.

Maybe Almos sensed my thoughts, because he continued. "Now that you're here, you have all of us behind you. And even if you like to try to prove yourself by handling your problems on your own, I want you to know that you can come to me or Imena if you need anything. You're one of us, and we pull each other up no matter what brought us here."

My expression softened. "Thanks, Almos."

He smiled. "Anytime Wren. We're here for you." He cleared his throat. "Now, let's go get dinner before Reve yells at us."

13

Thirteen

The dinner was great, and the games were fun, but they were only a distraction. Lying in bed after everything wound down was torture. What was I supposed to say to the Wind Whisperer? Would I have the chance to say anything at all?

I barely noticed when I slipped into the dream realm. It didn't look the way I'd gotten used when I fell asleep. There were no ribbons of light, no zero gravity, just a big, black expanse of nothing stretched as far as I could see. My body had weight to it when I pushed myself up from where I lay on the floor. This didn't seem right at all.

"Hello?" I called into emptiness.

"Wren." The Wind Whisperer's soft voice echoed back.

It slowly trudged toward me. It *trudged*. It didn't float. Was the gravity of this place affecting it too? Its shape was more condensed, more human. The bands of light running through its wispy body were dimmer, which made it harder to see.

"You went where you were not invited." Its voice stayed quiet as if there was something with us in the dark that it didn't want to disturb.

My gaze dropped to my feet. Of course it would know about that. I didn't have any excuses, so I didn't offer any.

"What were you doing in the Boneman's territory?"

I forced myself to look at it. "I'm a completely useless Wind Dreamed. I can't get anything right. I thought if I couldn't be Wind Dreamed, I might be Bone Touched."

The Wind Whisperer's colors flared brighter. "You wish to not be my child anymore?"

I shook my head. "It's not that. I'm just tired of letting everyone down."

It tilted its head to the side. "Who do you think you are letting down?"

"You. The other Wind Dreamed. The people whose dreams I keep messing up. I'm not even supposed to be here. You did me a favor by letting me be a demigod instead of exiling me, and all I've done since then is fail at everything you asked me to do." It deserved better than me. Everyone did.

The Wind Whisperer drifted closer. "Wren, I would never have made you Wind Dreamed if I did not believe you could do this. I have had plenty of demigods struggle to get the hang of dream walking. It is not a simple procedure. It is an incredibly complicated, delicate process. That is why I am here instead of leaving you with a human teacher."

I crossed my arms. "Even with you here, I still can't do it."

The Wind Whisperer took my face in its hands, the flowing colors of its fingers so gentle against my skin. "Because you are so focused on doing it *right*. There is no right way or wrong way. There is only your way and someone else's way. That is the beauty of it. There is no single path, no one size fits all. Your only problem is that you have yet to develop the style of dream walking that is right *for you*."

"How am I supposed to find that if no one tells me what works?"

The Wind Whisperer dropped its hands, turned, and swiped them through the air. The ribbons of light in its arms stretched and clung to the empty blackness in a streaky rectangle. The colors bent and blended into an image of a girl running through a series of back alleys, jumping fences, and crouching down behind dumpsters before taking off running again.

I frowned. "What is this?"

"A dream."

As the girl ducked down again, I caught sight of distant figures with hazy edges chasing after her. And hovering cross-legged above everything, floating as if he were sitting on an invisible flying carpet, was Reve.

"How is he doing that?" I had no idea we could *fly* in dreams.

"He has had a lot of practice. Watch."

The girl pulled out a phone and dialed frantically, but Reve tilted his head, and the phone screen went dark. At the same time, the people chasing her shouted and turned in her direction.

"He's leading them to her on purpose?" I demanded. I knew he was a little strange, but this was downright evil.

The Wind Whisperer watched beside me. "Reve specializes in nightmares. I have not seen him give someone a happy dream in a long time."

"I thought we were supposed to send people messages through their dreams, not terrorize them."

"A nightmare can be just as, often *more*, impactful than a good dream. People remember the nightmares they have because the emotions are so intense. Reve uses that to his advantage." The Wind Whisperer swiped a hand through the dream image, scattering the colors. They pulled back together to form a new scene.

This time, Imena was front and center. She stared intently at a distant group of people and horses. One girl stood a little farther apart from the others. Her sharper edges gave her away as the dreamer. One of the boys separated from the group to approach the girl. His edges were shadowy but clearer than the others. I could actually make out most of his features, including his smile. I couldn't hear what he said to the dreamer, but she seemed to warm to him.

"Imena has been in a romantic mood since she and Lorien got together at the beginning of the school year, so she likes to focus on that when she dream walks." The Wind Whisperer touched the dream screen. The colors absorbed back into its arm. "Lorien prefers making happy dreams. Frida likes to tackle political issues and life goals. And Almos likes to jump headfirst into dreams and work with whatever is already there. Everyone has their own way of getting the job done."

I got the picture. "But how am I supposed to find *my* way?"

The Wind Whisperer sat on the ground. "Well, what things are important to you?"

I sat down too. "A lot of things."

It leaned forward arms braced on its knees. "Like what?"

"Like stories and friends and doing well in school."

"So, you value entertainment, companionship, and success."

I shrugged. That sounded about right.

"You can start by looking for opportunities to weave those things into dreams and go from there. It will take you some time to develop the style of dream walking that works best for you, but maybe it will help now that you know some of the techniques others use."

"I hope so." I would need some time to think this over, but that was what my waking hours were for, I supposed.

The Wind Whisperer tapped its hands on its lap. "Do you want to try again tonight?"

After the weekend I'd had, I didn't want to do anything but sleep. "I don't know if I can."

It nodded. "You can take this time to think things over. But I need you tomorrow night."

"Ok. I can try again then." I'd had two nights off. I could dream walk tomorrow. Or at least try.

"Then rest here." It glanced over its shoulder into the darkness. "I have some dreams to attend to. Good night, Wren." It clasped my face in its hands and kissed my forehead as best it could without a mouth. "I am proud of you no matter what happens."

I wasn't sure I deserved that since I had yet to do anything right. "Good night."

Its colors brightened, and it darted off into the dark. I sat there by myself, staring at my hands.

14

Fourteen

I stayed there in that empty dream world for an eternity. Maybe it was because I had a dream to work with, but I didn't think I'd ever spent this long in the dream realm before. It was really boring when all there was to do was sit on the ground and stare into black nothingness.

Eventually, I woke up. My eyes felt dry and sticky like I'd only been asleep for a couple hours instead of the whole night. As dull as it had been in the empty dream world, at least I hadn't been tired there.

I dragged myself out of bed. My body felt heavy as I got dressed and packed my bag for school.

Only Reve was in the kitchen when I got there. He wore a loose purple T-shirt and long black pajama pants. His hair was a mess that wasn't helped by the steam billowing from the stove he leaned over.

I'd had conflicting feelings about Reve for a while now, but Lorien had said he had a story. Maybe it had something to do with why he only gave people nightmares. Imena said he was good at detecting emotions—the other side of the Wind

Dreamed powers. If I couldn't dream walk, maybe I could do that instead.

"Morning, Reve." My voice was rough from sleep.

He grunted without turning around and grabbed the spatula from the spoon rest next to him.

I sat down at the table. "What are you making?"

He scooted over and held up a pan with a neatly folded omelet softly sizzling away in it, then turned back around and slid it out onto a plate near his elbow before reaching for a carton of eggs.

"Looks good. Do you want any help?"

His hand paused on the eggs. He looked at me over his shoulder. "Do you know how to make omelets?"

"Not really." I rarely had to cook for myself. At home we had a personal chef since my parents were always too busy to cook, and at Mortorous Academy, the most I'd had to do was pour pre-made batter into a waffle iron and wait for the timer to tell me it was done.

Reve stared at me for a long moment like he was searching my soul. Maybe he was reading my emotions. He crooked his finger, beckoning me to join him. I got up. He scooted over to make room for me. The heat radiating from the stove warmed my face.

"Take three eggs," Reve instructed.

I picked them out of the carton.

"Crack them in here." He tapped a small bowl of milk. "If you only like the whites like Almos does, put the yolks in there." He indicated an empty bowl on the other side of the stove.

Thankfully, I didn't have to worry about trying to figure out how to separate the yolks from the whites. I smacked the egg on the corner of the counter.

It exploded.

I shrieked and jumped back. Reve didn't panic. He just grabbed a roll of paper towels and tossed it to me.

"Sorry," I muttered as I ripped off several paper towels and soaked up the mess as best I could.

"It happens. That egg had a lot of thin spots on the shell, so it didn't take much to completely break it open." Reve grabbed his own egg and cracked it with one hand into a different milk bowl. "Start gentle."

"Right." I picked up the remaining eggs and cracked them much more carefully.

"Whisk them together." Reve handed me a whisk.

I followed his instructions, careful not to splash everything everywhere. "Imena says you're really good at sensing other people's feelings."

"Imena likes to give compliments."

Reve already had a second pan out and heated. He moved his own bowl of eggs and milk to the other side of the stove to use the new pan and tossed little pats of butter in the pans.

"Pour it on."

"All of it?"

"Yes. Now."

We poured our mixtures over the melted butter. They made delightful sizzling sounds.

Reve spread the goop around with a spatula. "Make sure the mixture covers the bottom of the pan evenly. You should have a pretty thin layer."

I followed his lead.

"Pick your filling." He gestured to a set of tiny glass bowls full of sliced meat, cheese, and other assorted foods. "Only put them on half and be quick about it."

I decorated my omelet with ham, cheese, and peppers. Behind us, the kitchen door creaked.

"Frida, I swear to the Wind Whisperer, if you're taking pictures of us, they better be deleted by the time I turn around," Reve growled. He pointed at the glass cover on the counter next to the stove. "Cover your omelet."

I did and glanced behind me in time to see Frida and Lorien quickly disappear behind the kitchen door. Despite my exhaustion and Reve's brusque instructions, I smiled. Had they gotten their pictures, or had they deleted them like Reve ordered? I kind of hoped they still had them.

"So, how do you do it? Sense thoughts, I mean."

"You don't. Wind Dreamed pick up on emotions, not thoughts. We can't read minds. Come prep your next one while these cook." Reve grabbed the milk from the fridge and poured some into my bowl.

"Don't you measure it?"

"Don't have to." Reve grabbed his eggs.

"I thought you always had to."

"Only if you can't tell just by looking at it." He cracked the eggs one by one with a single hand while the other reached for a cup of coffee sitting in the coffee maker.

I started carefully cracking my eggs. I wanted to jump right in and demand he teach me how to detect emotions. But he was being as difficult as ever.

"How do you sense emotions?"

"By practicing empathy."

"That's it?" How was I supposed to do that?

"No, you have to successfully dream walk a few times first." There went that option. "But you can't pick up on other people's feelings if you're always wrapped up in your own. To feel what others feel, you have to become an empath."

I chuckled. "By that logic, you're the biggest empath out of all of us."

Reve stopped whisking his eggs to look at me. "Yes."

My face burned. I turned away and frantically searched for a change in subject. "Where did you learn how to cook?"

Thankfully, he accepted the new topic of conversation. "My family."

I set aside my bowl of milk and eggs. "They like to cook?"

"They own a restaurant."

My eyes widened. "Oh, wow. What restaurant?"

"You wouldn't have heard of it." The clink of his bowl hitting the counter punctuated his statement.

"Try me." I wasn't very confident in my restaurant knowledge, but I wanted to know anyway.

"Chetraveau."

I nearly dropped my whisk. "Your family owns Chetraveau?"

"It's my last name." He sipped his coffee again and stared blankly at the covered omelets.

My mouth dropped open. "Why didn't you tell me sooner? That's like the classiest, most critically acclaimed restaurant in the country!"

He turned narrowed eyes on me. "Don't shout at me before I've finished at least one cup of coffee."

"Sorry," I said much more quietly. "It's my dad's favorite place to eat. We go for his birthday every year."

"Your family must have a lot of money to throw around."

"I imagine yours does too. My family can afford it, but I've seen the bill three people can wrack up. You could put a down payment on a car with that kind of money. I can only imagine how much that place makes in one day."

Reve turned back to the stove. "Uncover your omelet and fold it in half."

I grabbed the metal handle on the glass cover. Steam billowed up into my face. I reared back but still got a full blast right in the glasses and had to take them off to see what I was doing. Reve folded his omelet perfectly in half. Mine wasn't nearly as even. The fillings poked out on one side. I blamed my lack of glasses.

"Not bad for your first time." Reve handed me a plate. "Folding it is the hardest part."

"Thanks." I flopped my uneven omelet onto the plate.

"Want to try again?" Reve held the bowl of eggs out to me.

I stared at my crooked omelet. "I don't want to mess up someone else's food." I'd done enough messing up the last few days.

"You'll do better this time since you know what to expect." He offered me the eggs. "Besides, Frida deserves a messy breakfast for spying on us from the doorway."

"Hey!" Frida poked her head in.

Reve didn't turn around, but a faint smile twisted his lips. It was the first time I'd seen him smile. It was also the first time I'd heard him say something encouraging. It was so unexpected after how he had treated me up until now. It took me completely by surprise, but I liked this version of Reve much better than the one who interrogated me in a rainstorm or a bookstore.

"Ok." I took the eggs from him. "I'll make sure it's extra crooked then."

Frida muttered something I doubted I wanted to hear.

Based on Reve's broadening grin, he *had* heard.

In spite of the disappointing news that I wouldn't be able to read emotions until after I successfully dream walked, the omelets turned out delicious. Once the others finally got into the kitchen and sat at the table, they all gushed about them. I wasn't sure if they were piling it on so thick because Lorien and Frida had told them I helped, but it was nice to hear all the same.

"Did you get pictures of us?" I whispered to Frida.

She smirked. "Oh yeah."

"Send them to me, will you?"

"Naturally, but you have to send them back to me 'cause Reve is going to corner me before we leave for class and make me delete them."

"You got it."

After we left the penthouse, my energy tanked. Animos had an engaging atmosphere, but the last week had been so busy that I dreaded everything. The class I didn't have with any of the other Wind Dreamed was the worst.

It was a finance elective class. We had to do a partnered project on the stock market. I had liked the class so far because it was the only one that had more of the straightforward work that I was used to. But I didn't like working with other students. There was always a point where they figured out that I was smart enough to do the project on my own and stopped contributing.

It didn't help that I was paired with the boy whose dream I had messed up a few days ago. He scooted his desk closer to mine.

"Hi, I'm Richard. Most people just call me Rich though." He offered a hand.

My smile felt wobbly as I shook it. "I'm Wren. I don't have a nickname."

"That's ok. Do we want to divide and conquer? Or should we try to work through it together?"

"We can divide." I worked better when I could do a section by myself and just shove it into the presentation where it needed to go.

We worked out which topics we were going to research and what equations we had to work on pretty quickly and sat in awkward silence for a moment.

"You're new, right?" Rich asked.

"Yeah." I fiddled with my fingers in my lap.

"Where did you go to school before this?"

"Mortorous Academy."

He laughed. "Oh, wow. What made you transfer to your old school's worst enemy?"

"It was… a unique set of circumstances." I'd made enough trouble bringing people into this world of magic. I wasn't about to repeat my mistakes by telling him the details no matter how badly I wanted to make it up to him after I'd ruined his dream the other night. "I didn't really have a choice."

He winced. "I'm sorry. Are you liking it here at least?"

"It was a big change. Mortorous doesn't teach the way Animos does. It's way more… creative here."

Rich nodded. "Yeah, it took me a couple weeks to adjust after starting here when I was a first year. But I'm glad they run like this. I didn't like school at all before I got to Animos."

"I don't know. The other way was easy. I just memorized facts and spat them back out. Now, I have to actually work and do all this creative stuff. Not that it's not fun sometimes,

I just got used to doing it the traditional way."

"Well, I hope you unlock the right half of your brain and enjoy this, cause there's no place like Animos."

I smiled. "Yeah, at least the people here are nice. Not that there weren't nice people at Mortorous. It just felt like there were less of them."

"Yeah," he echoed.

I cleared my throat and looked away. I tried to tell myself I was only talking to him so much because I felt bad about what I had done in his dream and not because he was smiling at me, showing off a small dimple. No. It definitely had nothing to do with how he talked to me like I was already his friend even though we'd just officially met a few minutes ago. Or how nicely his glossy brown hair framed his face.

I really regretted messing up his dream. I didn't have any siblings myself, but you didn't shout that much and try that hard to get to someone unless you loved them a lot. And I hadn't been able to help him at all. If tonight didn't go better, if I wasn't able to successfully dream walk, I wasn't sure what I was supposed to do.

Those thoughts ran through my head as I sat at the lunch table with Reve and Lorien, who were deep in conversation about some sculpting project from their art class. I couldn't focus on what they were saying and ended up listening to the conversation of the girls sitting near us.

They were all trying to convince the shy-looking one closest to me that she needed to talk to her family and tell them to stop borrowing her stuff just because they couldn't find their own.

"This is the fourth time they've lost something that belongs to you," said a girl with straight, shoulder-length brown hair.

"It doesn't matter if they buy you new stuff if they keep taking your things without asking and forgetting where they put them. At that point, why don't they just buy their own stuff?"

"Because they never realize it's gone until they really need it. They don't have time to go and buy it for themselves," the first girl said.

The other girl waved a dismissive hand. "Then they can go without. Maybe then they'll learn to keep their belongings organized."

"You just need to stand up for yourself." The girl sitting next to the shy girl pointed her fork at her. "You should start forming these habits now, so that people aren't walking all over you later in life. 'Cause it's only going to get worse from here."

"Wren!" Lorien shouted my name at the same time Reve elbowed me.

"Sorry, what?" I mumbled, rubbing my ribs.

"I asked if you want to come meditate with us this afternoon, but maybe you'll just end up falling asleep." She grinned.

"Probably." I rubbed my eyes.

"Didn't sleep well last night?" she asked.

"She was in the dream void," Reve said.

I frowned. "The what?"

"The place the Wind Whisperer puts Wind Dreamed when they don't want to dream walk. It's like being in time out in the dream realm."

"Reve!" hissed Lorien. "Be nice to her. She's trying."

He stuffed an unconcerned bite of roast into his mouth. "I'll be nice when she isn't spying on me while I dream walk."

I rubbed my tired eyes. "That was the Wind Whisperer, not

me."

"You were watching though."

"How can you even tell when someone is watching you from the dream void?" Lorien asked.

Reve shrugged. "It's just a feeling, and I haven't been wrong about it yet."

Lorien rolled her eyes. "Show-off."

Time out in the dream realm. Wonderful. I really needed to do something right tonight.

15

Fifteen

L orien had been right. I ended up nodding off during meditation and nearly face-planted in the grass.

Imena laughed on our way back to the penthouse. "At least you were relaxed."

"I guess." I massaged my temples. "I haven't looked forward to sleeping this much since I pulled an all-nighter to read the new *A Flame in the Embers* book and then had to spend the whole next day in school."

"That'll happen when you spend a night in the dream void," Reve said. "Our minds don't rest unless they have dream walked."

"Seriously?" So, not only was I doomed to wander other people's dreams instead of enjoying my own for the rest of my life, but if I didn't, I would never get a full night's sleep again? What kind of torture was this?

Frida ran up from behind. "Are you going to help Reve cook again?"

"No, she's not. We're having leftovers tonight," Reve replied.

"What!" Frida squawked.

Reve appeared completely unruffled. "What do you mean 'what'? The fridge will explode if I try to stuff anymore containers into it."

Frida groaned. "But it's never as good when it's reheated. Everyone knows that. Almos, make him cook us something fresh." She dropped back to complain to the others.

"She's a spoiled child," Reve grumbled.

"Says the boy whose family owns the best restaurant in the country," I replied.

His voice turned ice-cold. "Don't you dare compare me to her just because I have money. We are nothing alike."

I bit my lip. "Sorry. I didn't mean it as an insult." I thought bantering back and forth was a thing Wind Dreamed did with each other. I thought after this morning, Reve and I were on good enough terms to do that with each other.

"It would take a lot more than that to insult me." The deadpan statement didn't sound like an acceptance of my apology, but it didn't sound like he was mad at me anymore either. Though I couldn't tell if I was supposed to say something in response. It was so hard to get a read on him. One minute he was teaching me how to make omelets, the next he put as much distance between us as possible.

My phone rang in my pocket. I dug it out to see "Mom" on the caller ID. I had fully expected not to hear from my parents for another three weeks at least.

Imena glanced at the screen. "You should probably take that."

"Yeah, I'll meet you back at the penthouse." She nodded as I veered off and answered the call. "Hi, Mom."

"Hey, Wren! How is everything going?" she chirped.

I crossed my arms. "It's alright. I'm starting to get the hang of this schoolwork."

"That's good. And you're still keeping up with those friends you've made?"

"Yes." If she was skipping through the pleasantries this fast, there had to be a specific reason she'd called me. "How are things at home?"

"Oh, they're great. Your father and I are traveling again for an emergency business trip. We'll be out of the country for a while, and the schedule for our trip is jam-packed, so you might not hear from us for a few days."

I found a tree to lean against. "What is the trip for?"

"We're looking into some new investments. We don't know all the details, but if it works out, all this nonsense with the outbreak overseas will mean nothing." She sounded confident.

"Ok. Good luck then. Not that you'll need it. Once Dad starts sweet-talking whoever you're meeting, the contract will be as good as signed."

She laughed. "Yes, he certainly has a way with words. I just wanted to make sure everything was ok on your end before we left. I know this is kind of sudden, but you understand, right?"

"Of course. You two go do whatever you need to do." They went on impromptu trips like this all the time. Sometimes it was legitimately a last-minute thing. Sometimes they just forgot to tell me until they were about to board the plane. They always made sure I "understood" before they left though.

I wasn't sure what there was to understand. I didn't even live at home, and it wasn't like I visited often. They didn't

156

owe me much. I was just their kid who was away at school for most of the year.

We'd lived that way for a while. It was easier for them not to worry about what to do with me when they had to travel. And it was easier for me to focus on my schoolwork and building myself up to inherit their business when I was older.

"Thank you, Wren. I'll let you know when we get back. Love you, bye."

"Love you too." The call disconnected half a second after the words left my mouth.

I stared at the blank screen for a moment. I understood. I really did. They were trying to maintain our lifestyle. But every once in a while, I wished it could be different and we could be together as a family during the whole year instead of just during winter and summer break.

I stuffed my phone back in my pocket and headed toward the penthouse. Everyone was in the kitchen when I got there. Containers sat open on the counters. The microwave hummed away. Lorien and Almos sat at the table with their food already warmed up and ready to eat in front of them. Reve scooped the last of the chicken from the night before onto a plate but glanced up when I entered. He stared at me for a moment before heading for the sink with his empty container.

What had he seen when he looked at me? What emotions had he read?

"Hey, chickpea," Imena called from where she stood at the microwave. "How'd your call with your mom go?"

Everyone's attention instantly fell on me.

I tried for a smile. "Good. She was just checking in."

Lorien propped her elbows on the table and rested her chin

in her hands. "Do your parents do that often?"

"Not usually." Only when something major happened in my life like transferring schools or if they were going on a business trip. "But I just started at a new school, so they want to make sure I'm settled."

"How nice." Lorien grinned like it was the sweetest thing in the world.

I found myself glancing at Reve. He was washing the chicken container in the sink, but he met my gaze and held it until I looked away.

What did he see when he did that? Imena had said he could sense emotions better than any of the rest of the Wind Dreamed. I couldn't shake the feeling he was using that ability whenever he stared at me like he just did. I wasn't sure I liked the idea of him or any of them reading me like a book.

Especially when I couldn't do the same with them yet. I had barely worked up the courage to bring it up this morning. A decent part of me regretted not insisting he teach me whether I'd successfully dream walked or not.

"Are you going to get your food? Cause I'm not going to wait if you're just going to stand there and talk," Frida announced as Imena took her plate out of the microwave and Frida practically threw hers in. You would have thought the girl hadn't eaten in days.

Imena shook her head. "You have no patience."

Frida stuck her nose in the air. "Hey, someone has to make sure things happen around here in a timely manner."

"*I* contribute to that more than you do, and you know how I feel about being under time constraints," Reve muttered.

Frida stuck her tongue out at him, but he either didn't see or chose to ignore her. I found myself smiling either way. Their dynamics seemed to clash more than they cooperated, but their back-and-forth was hilarious. Reve's dry tone reminded me so much of Sylvan. Except that sometimes I'd suspected Sylvan didn't know how her words would be received. Reve definitely did.

I ended up with spaghetti and meatballs. Our meal was accompanied mostly by scattered conversation about how everyone's day had gone. I only partially listened. My mind was more occupied by my looming dream walking appointment.

I still had no idea what to expect or how I would react. So far, every dream had been different. It made sense since every person was different, and even if I had visited the dreams of the same person on all three nights, chances were they wouldn't have the same dream three nights in a row.

If only there were some way to plan ahead. I could do just about anything if I had a plan of action to follow. But the dreams the Wind Whisperer took me into were completely random. They could be from people in different countries of different ages and demographics. How was I supposed to handle cultural differences like that? How was I supposed to handle any of this when I was so tired?

A knee bumped mine under the table. I glanced to my left, where Reve sat.

"You're overthinking," he murmured under the buzz of conversation between the other four. "Stay present."

He'd done it again, read me like a book. "I'm fine. I'm present."

He raised his glass to disguise the movement of his mouth. "You've been spaced out for most of the day. Are you worried about how tonight will go?"

I opened my mouth.

"Please don't lie to me."

My lips pursed. "Yes."

"You'll do great. You just need to use what you have."

"What do I have?" It felt like a whole lot of nothing.

"Your brain." He drained his cup.

"That doesn't help as much as you think it does."

He shrugged as he got up to get more water. "You'd be surprised."

I was still mulling over his words when I lay in bed later that evening, staring at my ceiling and wishing I knew what I was doing. If only it were that simple.

People talked about their problems all the time in real life, but in a dream, those problems were wrapped up in metaphors and allusions. I wished there was a way for the dreamers to just tell me their issues. Like a therapist. That girl in the cafeteria was so quick to talk to her friends about what was bothering her at lunch today. Why couldn't I just deal with that problem?

Hm.

Maybe I could. Her situation was so similar to that of one of the characters in *The Brutal Heir*. She had finally snapped at her family for all the little things they kept piling on top of her. As it turned out, they hadn't even realized how much pressure they were putting on her. They'd apologized and explained their behavior, and everything got better between all of them. Well, most of them. But what were the chances the girl from earlier had a sister who would try to duel her to the death?

If I could get into that girl's dream and recreate that scene, I might be able to successfully dream walk for the first time.

16

Sixteen

The dream realm appeared as it usually did. The rippling, circular walls of multicolored light pulsed around me. There was no sign of the dark dream void from the night before. The Wind Whisperer was already there, hovering beside me.

"Are you ready?" it asked.

"Yes, but I have a request to make first."

It tilted its head to the side. "What is it?"

I took a deep breath. "There's a specific dream I want to find."

"Wren." It sounded a bit sad. "You know you cannot go into the dreams of people you know in real life."

"But I don't know this person. I only saw them in passing at school. I've never actually met them. They were just talking about a problem they were having at home, and I have an idea about how to advise them if I can just get into their dream."

The Wind Whisperer crossed its wispy arms. "This is not how dream walking is usually done."

I drew myself up to my full height. "I know. I understand if you don't want me to, but I really think I can do it this time."

The Wind Whisperer considered me for a long time. "You are sure you can be unbiased?"

I perked up a bit. "Yes. I promise I'll only ask for this once. I just want to get my confidence up and do something right for once. Please."

The Wind Whisperer surveyed the mass of writhing dreams surrounding us. "Show me this person." It laid a cool, slightly insubstantial hand over my forehead. "Think of them."

I called to mind the girl I'd seen at lunch, dredging up as much as I could remember of how she looked and acted.

"Ah." The Wind Whisperer sighed. "I see."

It let go of my head and turned around, floating down nearly to the bottom of the dream orb to a thin ribbon of green light. I followed as best I could.

"There she is." The Wind Whisperer pointed at the green line with one hand and gripped my shoulder with the other. "Would you like to do the honors this time?"

I took a deep breath and touched the dream. As with all the other dreams, our surroundings rapidly changed. A room enclosed us. A dresser appeared against one wall. A bed and a nightstand solidified along another. A small bookshelf sat next to the nightstand. I resisted the urge to search the titles for ones I knew. That wasn't what we were here for.

People materialized in the room. Their edges were fuzzy, and their features were indistinct. Except for one.

I recognized her from the cafeteria instantly. In this dream, she had a nervous energy around her that set me on edge too.

The dream characters milled around the room, touching things and moving them, sometimes taking them and putting them in their pockets. The girl's distress increased the more they took, but she just stood there, watching them silently. As upset as it made me, I couldn't have asked for a better stage to put on my performance.

"This is your moment, Wren," the Wind Whisperer said. It backed up to give me space.

"Ok." I sighed.

I could do this. I'd read that scene in *The Brutal Heir* a dozen times. I could recreate it in my sleep—which I was literally about to do. I focused on the characters. They were my puppets. I hadn't had any luck doing anything with the dreamers themselves, but maybe these would be different. I made them stop what they were doing and turn toward the girl.

"You understand, right?"

I'm not sure which one of them spoke, but the words came from somewhere. They stared at the girl with undefined but expectant expressions. She stared back at them.

"Come on," I whispered. "Tell them how you actually feel. Quit torturing yourself just because you're afraid you might hurt them."

"*No.*" The word was quiet at first, but the girl repeated herself louder. "No. This isn't what I want. Why can't you see that?"

I willed the dream character's faces to become confused. "We thought you were fine with it."

Suddenly there were tears in her eyes. "I was never fine with this! You didn't think I was fine either. You just wanted me to be, because you didn't want to stop doing it."

The characters moved toward the girl. "We didn't mean to upset you."

She was fully crying now. The characters moved in to

comfort her. They started handing her the things they had taken and murmuring soft words of comfort and apology.

They still huddled together while the dream turned grey.

I released my control over the dream and looked back at the Wind Whisperer. "She's waking up." My scene wasn't finished. There was supposed to be a part where the characters talked about why they thought it was ok to borrow things without asking.

"It is ok." There was a smile in the Wind Whisperer's voice. "You have done enough."

"Are you sure? There might be time—"

It took my hand. "Come on. We do not want to be here when she wakes up."

The Wind Whisperer took me out the bedroom door, and we were back in the dream orb.

"Wait, what happens if we're still in the dream when she wakes up?" I asked as I gripped the Wind Whisperer's hand to keep from spinning out into the empty space.

"She fails to fully wake up. Her body thinks that she is asleep, but her brain is awake. It is a strange in-between state of sleep paralysis. You do not want to be stuck in a sleep paralysis dream. Trust me."

Based on what I'd heard of it from books I'd read and shows I'd watched, it didn't sound pleasant.

The Wind Whisperer released my hand. "You were right about going into that dream. You did quite well."

I smiled unsteadily, not entirely sure if I should believe it. "Are you sure? I had more I wanted to do."

The Wind Whisperer floated around in a circle, following the walls without quite touching them. "That is alright. Her waking up was a good sign. The unconscious mind is not built to handle strong emotions. That is why you wake up in the middle of nightmares when you feel the most fear. But the same can be true of happy dreams. I have seen people laugh themselves awake before."

"Wish I could see the dream that was powerful enough to do that." It sounded wonderful.

The Wind Whisperer nodded. "It was quite a scene, but you should focus on your victory. You have had your first successful dream walk!"

"Yeah." I could still hardly believe it. I'd been so worried about doing it right for so long that the accomplishment didn't feel real. I still felt on edge, like it would all get taken back at any moment and I'd be right back where I started.

"You should celebrate by making breakfast with Reve again. He quite enjoyed that."

I blinked, surprised partially by the statement and partially since this was the first time the Wind Whisperer brought up my relationships with the other Wind Dreamed. "He did?" He'd barely said anything beyond giving me instructions, and it had all been in the same monotone voice like he couldn't be bothered to put any emotion into the conversation.

But wouldn't the Wind Whisperer know best how its demigods felt?

"He has a unique way of processing and expressing things." The Wind Whisperer had spiraled its way up to the top of the dream orb. "But yes, he liked having the company and someone to teach. And you liked learning."

I had. I'd never thought of myself as the domestic type, but I guess learning anything scratched that itch in my brain to know more about the world. And I needed to ask him about sensing emotions.

The Wind Whisperer dropped down in front of me. "So, go have fun with him and everyone else. Tell them all about how well you did tonight. They will be almost as excited as you."

As much as I wanted to... "I don't have to do another dream tonight? That one was pretty short."

The Wind Whisperer waved its colorful hand. "No, no. You have done enough. I never expect new Wind Dreamed to take on more than one dream in a night. You can start doing that once you are more comfortable with dream walking, but for now, this is sufficient."

"Ok." I still wasn't sure, but I was glad to not have to do anything else.

The Wind Whisperer took my face in its hands and kissed my forehead. "Have a good day at school, Wren."

My smile was real this time. "Thanks."

17

Seventeen

The sun shone through my curtains when my eyes opened. All the residual exhaustion and stiffness I'd felt after waking up yesterday morning was gone. Actually, I didn't think I'd ever slept so well before. I felt like I could get up and run a marathon without breaking a sweat.

I threw off my covers and got dressed. So much energy buzzed under my skin I practically flew down the hall after getting dressed. Reve jumped when I burst into the kitchen. Almos and Imena, who sat at the table, looked up.

I darted over to where Reve stood at the counter and hugged him tight. "You were right. I just needed to use my brain."

"Uh-huh." He hugged me back gently, hesitantly, like I might explode.

I let go of him and backed up. "Sorry, you don't like hugs. I'm just… Last night went *really* well."

He turned back to the waffle maker in front of him. "It's fine."

"Oh." I'd expected a little more resistance from him, maybe

some disgust. The others made it seem like he would rather flay himself than hug people. "Ok."

"You can take some." Reve gestured at a plate stacked high with waffles sitting on the counter by his elbow. "The ones on the top should still be pretty warm. Syrup and toppings are on the table."

"You don't want help?" The Wind Whisperer said he liked cooking breakfast with me yesterday.

"We only have one waffle iron."

"Ok. Thanks." I dug out another plate from the cabinet and stacked a couple of waffles on it.

As I sat down, Almos and Imena stared at me like I had just resurrected the dead.

I raise my eyebrows. "What?"

Imena shook her head wordlessly.

Almos glanced at Reve and said under his breath, "I've never seen him hug someone of his own free will. Especially not when it's so sudden and unprovoked."

I snorted. "Unprovoked? You make it sound like I attacked him." Sure, I'd grabbed him when I'd been told he wasn't a fan of it, but he'd brushed off my apology.

Imena shrugged. "Sometimes that's how he reacts to being touched. He likes his space. It's nice to see him opening up and embracing the physical affection. Literally."

Almos poured blueberry syrup over his waffles. "Frida will be sad she missed it."

"Devastated." Imena piled a mountain of whipped cream on her breakfast. "Lorien too."

I couldn't imagine it being that big of a deal. Plenty of people didn't like to be touched. That didn't mean you had to make a spectacle out of it when they did enjoy it.

Maybe I was just starting to grow on Reve. He'd been patient with me yesterday when we made breakfast. He'd even told me some things about himself. Granted, I'd had to drag them out of him a bit, but that seemed to be the way he always operated.

He really was so much like Sylvan—quiet and touch-averse and expressing emotions in small ways.

"I'm glad your dream walking went well last night. It's nice to see you in such a good mood again," Almos said.

I smiled at my plate as I scooped fruit out of a bowl in the center of the table onto my waffles. "Yeah, I finally got it right."

"Got what right?" Frida asked as she and Lorien pushed into the kitchen.

"Dream walking," Almos answered. "Wren had a good night."

"Oh, yay!" Lorien threw her arms around me from behind and pinched my cheek. "I knew you could do it. I'm so proud."

I pulled my face out of her hand. "Thanks, Lorien."

"No wonder those dark circles under your eyes are gone," Frida said as Lorien let go of me to kiss Imena on the cheek. "You've looked tired since you first got here, and you don't anymore."

I frowned, unsure about how to interpret that statement. "Thanks?"

Frida patted me on the back as she made her way toward Reve and the stack of waffles. "No problem."

Imena leaned toward me once Lorien went to get food. "You didn't look that tired. You just looked like you were carrying the world on your shoulders."

I sighed. "It kind of felt like it." The transition had been difficult, but I felt so much more adjusted now, like I finally fit into my skin.

"Cheers to you, chickpea." Imena angled her glass of orange juice toward mine.

I bumped it with mine. "Cheers."

* * *

I ate quickly and managed to field Frida's interrogation when she demanded to know where I was going in such a rush so early in the morning.

Because it was Tuesday. Book club day.

The library was quiet so early in the morning. I would have wagered that most students were still trying to sleep. But after a night of good dream walking, I had enough energy to wrestle a bear. The librarian, Dr. Scribira, poked her head out of one of the meeting rooms along the wall of the library.

She smiled at me. "Ah, Wren! You made it after all."

I smiled back as I went to meet her. "It would be a shame for me to miss this."

"It's a shame for anyone to not appreciate books enough to join book club, but that's a rant for another day. Come in and meet everyone." She gestured for me to follow her back into the room.

It was about the size of a classroom, maybe a little smaller. Instead of desks, the room held three rows of wooden tables all set end to end so it looked more like three long tables than several shorter ones. Wooden chairs painted with the titles and cover images of popular and classic books provided plenty of seating.

There was a large projector screen at the front with an

image of a book I hadn't heard of glowing on it. On the corner of one of the back tables, an assortment of store-bought donuts and other little pastries sat next to a couple bottles of juice. Paper plates and plastic cups followed behind along with a stack of napkins.

A handful of people milled around or sat in little groups at the tables. They all looked tired but happy to be there.

"Help yourself to the food and drinks and grab our book for this week." Dr. Scribira waved an arm at the stack on a library cart that was partially hidden behind the door. "We'll start in about ten minutes."

I'd had my fill of Reve's wonderful waffles, so I didn't need any food. It couldn't possibly taste as good anyway. I picked up one of the books from the cart. It wasn't the same one on the screen. Maybe this was the book we were supposed to read for next week and the one on the screen was from last week. I chewed my lip. I wouldn't have any idea what they were talking about as they discussed this book. But that's what I got for joining in the middle of the year.

"Excuse me, sorry." Someone rushed past me in a blur. I only got a look at their face when they caught sight of me and paused. "Oh, good morning, Wren!"

It was Professor Midrid, my history teacher.

"Morning," I echoed.

"Are you joining the book club?" he asked.

I nodded.

He clapped his hands together. "Good! You've been here for a week at most and are already settling in and getting involved. It's nice to see young people be so well adjusted. I'm one of the sponsors for this club. Dr. Scribira is in charge of most of it, but they have to have a second teacher and a certain number of members if they need materials like free copies of the books to take home. School rules and all that."

I wouldn't have thought a school like Animos Prep, which encouraged creativity and thinking outside the box, would have regulations on how their creative clubs could operate, but I supposed they had to have some kind of guidelines. Letting students paint their dorms was one thing, but if it required the school's money, that was another matter entirely.

"I have to help with the presentation, but it's wonderful to have you here." Professor Midrid strode toward the front of the room where Dr. Scribira fiddled with the laptop connected to the projector.

I took a seat in the back. Even if I hadn't read the book we were going to talk about, I was determined to enjoy this time.

Half an hour and a spoiler-ridden presentation later, the meeting ended. I packed my new book away in my backpack and got up.

Dr. Scribira caught me on the way out. "What did you think of your first book club?"

"Well, it's not my first. I was in a book club at my previous school. But this was nice." It had followed a more predictable pattern than most of my classes and homework assignments had, discussing all kinds of symbolism and plot points and character arcs. Then again, I hadn't read the book, so maybe some of the things we talked about were more mind-blowing than I would have thought.

"I'm glad to hear it. You know, if you have any recommendations for books we should read, you can tell me or Professor Midrid, and we'll be happy to check them out and see if they would be a good fit for our club."

"What kind of books wouldn't be a good fit?" As someone

who was a fan of just about any kind of fiction, I couldn't see a problem with any of it.

She lifted a shoulder. "Well, it does have to be school-appropriate. We have some fourteen-year-olds in this club, and there's a significant difference in the kind of content they should be reading versus some of the content our eighteen-year-olds sometimes read both in adult content and heavier themes."

Of course.

"And we try to stay away from the big-name books. This club is more about encouraging people to read outside the box than follow the reading trends set by the publishing industry and the larger reading community."

Oh. "I guess that makes sense." Even if I was usually a fan of those big-name books. I would have plenty of time to read them outside of book club.

"We love unique books, so if you know of any, we'd love to check them out." Dr. Scribira waved. "Hope to see you next week." She retreated into the office behind the circulation desk.

Professor Midrid emerged from the room behind me. "What did you think? Will you be here next week?"

I followed him toward the library doors. "Probably. Books are kind of my thing."

"But creative writing isn't?" He held the door open for me.

I grimaced at the reminder of the project we'd just finished up for history. "I'm a reader. Not a writer."

Professor Midrid shrugged as we walked to his classroom. "I find that a lot of readers end up enjoying writing, especially if they've liked reading for a while."

"Not me. I just like consuming the stories, not creating

them. The revolution project was kind of fun, but I don't think I'm cut out for writing outside of school assignments."

"Well, if you change your mind and want to give it a try, we have a creative writing club that I also sponsor. It's very casual. We have prompts you can answer, or you can just work on whatever project you already have going. We meet on Wednesday afternoons."

"I didn't know teachers could run more than one club."

He stuck his hands in his pockets. "We can help run as many clubs as we want as long as our schedules allow it. Many of us are just as, if not *more,* artistically inclined than the students, so we like to be as involved as possible."

At Mortorous Academy there were plenty of extracurriculars. Most of them revolved around sports or academics, but there was an art club, a book club, and a theatre club. Those didn't get as much funding or interest. There was only ever one teacher covering each of them.

Most of the kids who were in those clubs didn't have an interest in making them a full-time hobby or career. Nearly everyone at Mortorous was focused on going into one branch of STEM or another and put any fine art endeavors on the backburner. It was a school for the practically minded.

Animos was the opposite.

It was all about dreaming and tapping into your creative talents and taking a chance on a career path most people would say wasn't realistic. But it was all encouraged, all accepted.

At Mortorous Academy, students mostly picked up books their classes required them to read. Book club attendance had been sparse to say the least. But here, we had filled a room with kids who wanted to read fiction instead of textbooks.

I might not have been that interested in most of the artsy clubs Animos offered, but I felt at home in a room full of bookworms.

"That sounds a lot nicer than most teachers elsewhere get," I said.

Professor Midrid nodded. "Yes, we're very lucky to have the opportunity to teach here. Several of us are artists that couldn't quite get enough traction to make our art a full-time career. But you know what they say, 'Those who can't do, teach.' It might sound a little sad, but this is the next best thing."

"What kind of art did you try to do before you became a teacher?"

He raised his eyebrows at me. "I thought it would be obvious. I wrote books. Still do, actually."

I bit my lip. Would this be too personal? "Could I read them sometime?"

Professor Midrid grinned at me. "I would love nothing more."

* * *

The string of creative projects as homework assignments continued. We were supposed to make a model for history, a drawing made with graphed equations in math, and a knitted book cover for English. I'd stopped questioning the curriculum since I'd more or less gotten the hang of it, but even though we were studying book preservation in English, I wasn't sure how making a book cover was relevant. I would need to stop by the library to pick up a book on how to knit during lunch.

Rich said hello when I sat down in finance.

"Hi," I replied.

He searched my face. "You look like you're in a good mood."

"I had a good night."

He raised an eyebrow.

"Of sleep. I slept well." I hoped my face wasn't too red. It felt like it was. It felt like it was on fire.

"Right. Well, I finished my part of the assignment, but I was hoping you could take a look at this equation. For some reason, the total doesn't seem right." He passed me a sheet of paper covered in numbers.

I scanned the equation he indicated. "You just forgot to distribute the exponent to one of the factors in the parentheses."

"Oh, thanks. I knew I'd forgotten something."

"No problem." I was fine with divvying up the workload, but I didn't want my grade in this class to suffer because of a simple mistake someone else made. "Everything else looks ok. You probably just messed up because it was the most complicated part of the problem." I'd made similar errors before and always got so mad at myself about it. "Next time, look over your work the morning of the day it's due, so you're not relying on work you did the night before when you were tired. It's saved me plenty of times."

He took the paper back and started reworking the problem. "Thanks. I usually get up at the last minute, though, so I don't know if I'd have time to look at it before class."

"I can't count the number of times I've done homework in my other classes or during lunch." It was much better than waiting to do it all after school and feeling too pressured to get all of it done.

"You didn't have friends to talk to?"

I stiffened. "I had plenty of friends." They just didn't have the same lunch period or had other friends they wanted to sit with.

Rich winced. "Sorry, I didn't mean it like that. I just like hanging out with friends at lunch instead of working if I can. It's a nice break from doing school stuff all day."

"Yeah," I muttered.

I had loved talking to Sylvan during lunch at Mortorous Academy, even if she hadn't said much back. She was always an amazing listener. She always gave me her full attention when I talked to her. With her silvery-white eyes it was kind of creepy if she stared for too long without saying anything, but it was nice to have someone who paid attention instead of just waiting for their turn to talk. I hoped she was ok.

"Did you finish your part of the homework?"

"Of course." I always did.

"Do you want me to turn it in, or do you want to turn it in?"

"I can do it."

We ended up being assigned a larger project where we had to pick several companies to "invest" in and follow their stock market stats over the last six months to see how our investments would have gone. And we had to do it with the partners we had for the homework.

"Guess we're stuck together again," Rich said. "We could visit the library sometime this week to work on it together. I would hate to mess up this project the way I almost did with the homework."

"Sure." I knew this setup. He would try to get me to do his share of the work or just goof off the whole time we were supposed to be doing the project. Fine. I could just tell the teacher that I had done all the work and see how he liked a big, fat zero. "When?"

"I'm not sure. I'm trying to plan some stuff with my parents coming to visit and getting together with friends this week too. Can I have your number so I can text you about it later?"

"Sure." So, this was his ploy. He would claim he was busy and not get the work done. Oldest trick in the book. I gave him my number as the bell rang. If nothing else, I could say I tried.

"Thanks, I'll text you."

Sure, you will. "Ok."

I wished I could be friends with Rich. He seemed nice. Not to mention the fact that he was pretty. But I'd seen this kind of thing go down too many times to get my hopes up.

* * *

"How was book club?" Lorien asked as she, Reve, and I sat in the cafeteria during lunch.

"Good. It was about what I expected." Even if I hadn't read that week's book and therefore had no idea what everyone was talking about.

She grinned as she buttered her baked potato. "Great. I was wondering when you would find a club to get involved in."

I wasn't sure if I would have even been in the right headspace for book club if I hadn't finally gotten a dream right. I loved my books, but even I couldn't concentrate on them if I didn't have enough sleep. Spending more than one night in the dream void would have kept me from doing anything but passing out during book club.

"So how did you finally do it?" Lorien asked.

I paused with a bite halfway to my mouth. "Do what?"

"Dream walk."

"It's going to sound really nerdy, but the dream reminded me of a scene in a book that I read. It ended well for the characters in that book, so I recreated it in the dream." I didn't think I should tell her that I had kind of cheated by already having a plan of action and requesting a specific dreamer.

"Huh. I've never heard of a Wind Dreamed doing something like that before." She drummed her fingers on the table. "Have you, Reve?"

He shook his head. "But it makes sense that you would. Novels are supposed to imitate life and give people a way to both escape from and cope with their problems, much like dreams do. I'd love to be there if this dreamer ever reads the book you based her dream off of, though. She might think she can see the future."

Lorien and I chuckled. If I ever ended up doing something like that again, I would have to change a few things to make sure I wasn't just regurgitating the plotlines of books and movies into people's heads. That felt a little like cheating too.

"Well, I'm glad to hear you're figuring out your style of dream walking." Lorien tossed an arm around my shoulders. "I'm sure you'll only get better from here."

"I hope so. But I have a question."

"Yeah?"

"If we're supposed to wake up energized from dream walking, why does Reve need to drink coffee in the mornings?"

Lorien went strangely silent. Her gaze darted to Reve.

"It's not just about the energy. Not entirely, anyway," he

said as he scooped out a bite of baked potato. "It's the only thing that covers up the taste of my meds."

I frowned. "You have to take meds?"

"Bipolar depression and anxiety don't go away on their own."

I almost choked on my own spit. That was the last thing I'd expected him to say. How was I supposed to respond to that?

He glanced up at me. "Please don't feel sorry for me. Pity only makes me angry."

"Sorry," I muttered and stared down at my tray of half-eaten food, suddenly not hungry.

"It's not something you need to worry about anyway. I've worked through it."

"It's still not something I want my friend to have to deal with," I mumbled.

He gave a small smile. "I appreciate that."

We finished the rest of our meal in silence.

After my last class, I was free to go back to the penthouse. I already had an idea about what to do for the model for history. It would involve a lot of tiny, torn-up pieces of tissue paper and a gallon of glue.

The elevator dinged open at the top floor of the dormitory, and I slipped out. Everyone was gathered in the living room on their respective pieces of furniture. And sitting in my pale red chair was a woman who looked like a supermodel had strutted out of the pages of a magazine.

Her long, blood red hair cascaded over her shoulders like a waterfall. Her bone structure looked like it could cut diamonds. And her russet eyes pinned me in place like a butterfly to a board. But the most distinctive thing about her was the all-too-familiar sense of being drawn toward her and driven away at the same time. Nicholas had had the same aura about him when I'd visited him at Mortorous Academy, which could only mean one thing.

"Wren." Imena stood. "This is Keres. The Boneman sent her to us."

18

Eighteen

"The Boneman?" Last I'd heard from the Boneman, he didn't want his Bone Touched anywhere near us Wind Dreamed. Or maybe he just didn't want them around me.

Keres smiled. "It's nice to meet you. I wish we could have made our introductions under better circumstances."

I glanced around at the others. Lorien had her gaze fixed on Keres like Keres might attack her if she looked away. Frida watched her with more interest than caution. Almos seemed relaxed except for the way his fingers kept tapping on the arms of his chair. Reve met my eyes and patted the couch cushion next to him for me to sit. I joined him, eyes darting between Keres and the other Wind Dreamed.

What was going on? What did Keres mean about meeting under better circumstances?

Imena took a seat in her chair, which she had pushed closer to Lorien's to hold her hand. "We're all here now. What's wrong?"

Keres didn't waste any time. "People have been disappearing in Luxem at an alarming rate. Just since the start of the weekend there have been three disappearances."

I hadn't heard anything about this, but I didn't really keep up with the news in the first place.

"While we appreciate the concern, isn't that a problem for the police?" Almos asked.

Keres nodded. "Dealing with the criminal is, yes. But if we're dealing with a serial killer, that's Bone Touched territory."

I frowned. "Why?" That still seemed like the kind of thing the law enforcement should handle.

Keres sighed. "It is a great shortcoming that the races of demigods must stay divided. I'm assuming you don't know much about the Bone Touched."

"You catch ghosts, don't you?" Reve asked in his blank monotone. "At least, that's what the Boneman does."

"That's the short version." Keres agreed. "Our job as Bone Touched is to hunt the spirits of the restless dead and bring them to the Boneman, so he can deliver them to the afterlife where they belong."

"So, if there's a serial killer in town..." I trailed off.

"Then there are bound to be some very angry ghosts showing up soon," Keres finished.

"I'm still not sure why that involves us," Imena said. "I assume the Wind Whisperer already gave you permission to be in Luxem. So, why wouldn't you just find the ghosts, take care of them, and go? What do we have to do with any of this?"

"The Wind Whisperer didn't just give me permission to be here. It begged the Boneman to send someone here to protect all of you."

Frida leaned forward. "Why would we need protection?"

"Ghosts are after one thing in the living world. Life. They believe the way to get it is to kill a demigod. The powers of the Bone Touched come from the magic inside the marrow of our bones." She got quiet. "A lot of us have fallen while fighting the dead and had that magic taken from inside of us. Ghosts with the power of a Bone Touched are incredibly difficult to capture. But feeding on the power of death is one thing. Feeding on the power of life is another. You all have that power."

Lorien seemed to shrink into the cushions around her. "So, they'll come after us?"

"Yes, and you are all at even greater risk because you won't be able to see them. Only Bone Touched can fully see a ghost."

We exchanged glances. I had encountered a ghost before. Back at Mortorous, Sylvan and I went into town one Saturday and were ambushed by one. I hadn't been able to see or hear it, but it wasn't after me. It wanted Sylvan.

I hadn't known it was after her Bone Touched magic at the time, nor had I thought to ask why it targeted her instead of one of the other people walking around that day. I was too freaked out. We'd barely escaped. Now, it all made sense.

"There are wards on this school that might help keep the ghosts at bay, but that's why I'm here. To keep you from being killed." Keres stood and dug around in the pocket of her black pants. "Obviously, I can't watch over all of you at once, especially when you're in your different classes, but these should help deter the ghosts if they make their way onto campus and find you."

She handed a little leather bag to each of us. We all immediately opened them. Reve dumped his out on the sectional between us. Small, sharp, white objects tumbled across the upholstery along with a necklace made of the same material.

"Are these... bones?" He asked as he picked up what looked like part of a finger.

"Yes, Bone Touched use them to capture spirits, since only a physical body can hold a soul." Keres pulled a handful of what looked like animal teeth from her other pocket and held them flat on her palm. We watched with wide eyes as the teeth rose into the air and melded together into a small knife. The handle lowered into her grasp.

"You don't have the power to manipulate bones like I can, so you'll have to wear them around your neck and carry them in your pockets. If any unseen force attacks you, do your best to stab it with the bones. That should make it back off and give you some time to run."

"And the necklaces?" Frida held her string of white beads up suspiciously.

"Your power comes from your lungs, doesn't it? The air you breathe?"

Imena nodded. The time the Wind Whisperer had spent inside our respiratory systems diffused its magic through our airways, and that's where it stayed. Based on what Keres had told us, it was the same thing with the bones of the Bone Touched.

"The ghosts will try to steal it. Keeping them away from your head and neck by wearing bones should make it harder for them to do so if they do overpower you."

"In case they kill us, you mean," Reve deadpanned. Leave it to him to be blunt.

Keres grimaced. "Yes. I would also recommend you don't

go anywhere alone, even just sleeping in a room by yourselves. Have someone, Wind Dreamed or not, with you at all times. Most ghosts are ambush predators that like to work in the shadows without an audience. Murder victims can be a little more unpredictable, but having someone around to help is always a good idea. I'm going to do some investigating of my own, and I'll let you know when I find something. But in the meantime, do what you can to protect yourselves from any of the dead."

"That's it?" Reve asked. "We're just supposed to arm ourselves and act like frightened rabbits, always looking over our shoulders until you catch the ghosts?"

"There isn't much else you can do," Keres said. "You're not Bone Touched, and you're being hunted by invisible creatures that don't need to eat or sleep and can pass through walls. All you can do is wait."

"We'll see." Reve got up and stalked to his bedroom.

Keres frowned as she watched him go. "Should I be worried about what he's going to do?"

Almos sighed and heaved himself out of his seat. "He should be fine, but I'll go talk to him."

Imena squeezed Lorien's hand and stood, pulling Lorien with her. "I would guess we're having leftovers again if Reve is in a mood like this. You're going to be staying here with us, right, Keres?"

Keres nodded. "I was sent to protect you, so that would be best if you can spare the space."

"Of course. We have an extra room. We just need to get some sheets on the bed and clean up a bit. Frida, Lorien, come help me with that, will you?"

Lorien let Imena pull her toward the bedrooms. Frida

groaned as if making a bed were the worst torture in the world but got up and followed the two into the bedroom hall.

That left me alone with Keres. I guess I was expected to entertain our guest until dinner time.

I gave her a hesitant smile. "So, what's it like being Bone Touched?"

Keres sank back down in my chair. "It's a lot, but it feels good to have a purpose. Plus, I get to travel the world, even if I have to fight the restless dead everywhere I go."

"Must be nice."

I wished I got to travel the world to do my Wind Dreamed job. Instead, I just traveled into people's dreams. I was so jealous of Sylvan and Nicholas. I wondered if Keres knew them. If she was running around the globe, maybe she hadn't, but if she'd heard something about Sylvan...

"I had a friend who was Bone Touched."

Keres sat forward. "Really? How did that happen? I thought our gods liked to keep us to themselves."

"I went to Mortorous Academy before I became Wind Dreamed. Actually, I only became Wind Dreamed because I found out that friend wasn't a normal person. Another mutual friend said something happened to her after I left. I haven't heard from her since, but maybe you have. Her name is Sylvan."

Keres's brows rose. "You were friends with Sylvan?"

I straightened. "You know her?"

A smile blossomed on Keres's face. "We've met a few times. She's pretty new to being Bone Touched, so I haven't had the chance to work closely with her much, but from what I've seen, she's quite the character."

"I heard she got hurt."

Keres's smile fell away. "Yeah. No one's heard anything about her since it happened about five months ago."

There went my hopes of finding out how Sylvan was doing. "So, you don't know anything? Not even if she's alive?"

Keres's face pinched with pity and pain. "I'm sorry. I wish I did. There isn't much precedent for her condition. Usually, if a Bone Touched gets hurt that badly, they die. But Sylvan was close enough to the Boneman's forest at the time that he managed to get ahold of her. I hope he's found a way to fix her back up, but like I said, this hasn't happened before, so I don't know."

I flopped back against the couch. Nicholas hadn't heard anything, and he was probably the closest to Sylvan. But he was also a Bone Touched in training, so I had hoped someone who'd been working actively for a while might know more. So much for that.

"Sylvan was a fighter though," Keres murmured. "I may not know her that well, but I could tell that much. If there's a way for her to come back, she will."

"I hope you're right." The more avenues of answers I exhausted, the more worried I got. I knew Sylvan was tough in her own way, and I wanted to trust in Keres's confidence in Sylvan too. But until I saw her alive and well, part of me would always be concerned for her.

Reve came bursting back into the living room and stopped dead when he saw me and Keres. His eyes darted between us, no doubt picking up on the emotional rollercoaster of a conversation we'd just had.

His gaze finally settled on me. "I need your help."

I sat up. "With what?"

"Dinner. I can't feed our guest leftovers on her first night here. Come help." He turned and disappeared into the kitchen without waiting for my response.

"Speaking of characters…" Keres watched the kitchen door swing open and shut and open and shut from the force with which Reve had shoved through it.

I pushed myself to my feet. "Yeah, he's not so bad once you get used to him though. Especially once you taste his cooking."

She smiled. "I look forward to it. Should I come help too?"

"Probably not. He can be a little…" I waved my hand around vaguely. There weren't really words for what Reve could be.

She stood. "Right. I'll just go see how my room preparations are going then."

"Good idea." I scampered into the kitchen before Reve could come back out and yell at me.

He already had a cutting board out and was chopping vegetables like he had a personal vendetta against them when I entered.

"You ok?" I asked, stopping a healthy distance away from him and his very sharp knife.

"Fine," he said.

"You're cutting those vegetables like they killed your parents."

"I always cut things up like this. You can't be timid about it, or it'll take twice as long to get the job done and the cuts won't be as clean."

Maybe, but there was something about the way the air around him felt, like it was charged and ready to strike lightning-quick. Was this what it was like to sense how other people felt? Or was I just picking up on his body language?

"Do you not want Keres here?" I asked as I cautiously

stepped closer.

He turned around and pointed with the knife at one of the cabinets. "Pull out the biggest pot that's in there and fill it three-quarters of the way with water."

I did as I was told. "Is it that she's Bone Touched? You interrogated me that night you found out I was friends with a Bone Touched before becoming Wind Dreamed."

"Put the pot on the stove and boil the water."

I got the feeling that every time he avoided one of my questions, the answer was yes.

"Do you not like the Bone Touched? Or is it the Boneman that you don't like?"

He whirled around and advanced on me with the knife still in his hand. I backed up until my back hit the refrigerator. He looked me up and down, the air buzzed with that angry feeling. I'd forgotten how much taller than me he was.

"What are you looking for, Wren?" he asked in a hushed voice. "Because I'm not a book you can just pick up and read."

I stood up as tall as I could, which only brought the top of my head level with his chin. "You're upset about Keres or the Bone Touched or something. Why is it that you can sense when I'm upset and call me out on it, but I can't do the same with you?"

His hand tightened on the knife. "I have boundaries."

"So do I. But you didn't ask about them before sending Imena to the library to talk to me that one morning or when you pressed me last night about why I was agitated."

"Because I knew deep down you wanted someone to talk to about your problems even if you're too stubborn to realize it yourself," he growled.

"Maybe I know you do too!"

He flinched back a step. That angry feeling faded from the air, replaced by something more contained, like he was turning his emotions inward. Without thinking, I stepped forward and wrapped my arms around him. Like this morning, he stiffened at my touch, but I didn't let go, just rested my cheek on his shoulder.

"I don't think you want to be alone any more than I do," I murmured.

A moment of tense silence passed before he reached up and put his free arm around me. "It's not anything you need to worry about, Wren. I have… complicated feelings about the Bone Touched and the Boneman, and having Keres here is dredging them up."

"You can try talking to her. She seems like she'd be willing to help clear the air," I said.

"She works for the Boneman. She might not tell me anything. She might just leave altogether," he muttered.

I shook my head as much as I could with my face plastered against his shoulder. "I don't think she'd do that. We were actually just talking about my friend from Mortorous who's Bone Touched before you asked for my help with dinner."

"Did she tell you anything helpful?"

I winced. "Not really, but that's just because she didn't know anything. Look, it couldn't hurt to try."

"I guess," he grumbled. A long moment of silence passed.

"I hope you find what you're looking for."

"Thanks." He rested his cheek against my temple. The atmosphere had softened to the point that I could almost forget that I would probably have a permanent imprint of his collarbone on my face.

"No way!" came a squeal from the kitchen doorway.

Reve and I let go of each other and whirled toward it. Frida stood halfway in, halfway out of the kitchen with her phone pointed at us. She dropped her arm as soon as she saw Reve's glare.

"Lorien! Imena!" she shouted as she darted out of the kitchen.

"Put the pasta in the water and don't let it boil over!" Reve called to me as he took off after her.

The door swung violently as they darted through it, and shouts came from the living room. I giggled, imagining Reve chasing Frida around the couches and chairs, as I opened the bag of spaghetti noodles and dumped them into the boiling water in the pot on the stove.

Living with these people was like living in a house with my family, except there were actually people here that interacted with each other on a daily basis. At home it was usually just me by myself while my parents worked in the office downstairs or went on business trips around the world and left me with the house staff. Sometimes they took me with them and called it a vacation, but we never went anywhere just for fun.

It was nice to have time and space to myself, but there was something about having five other people around who were willing to talk to me or help me with my homework or just mess around with each other that made the penthouse feel like home. Even if they were terrorizing each other.

Going home for the summer after spending a few months with these people would be quite the change. Maybe I could invite them over. I had no idea where any of them lived outside of school. Lorien didn't even have a family to go home to during the summer and holiday breaks. Maybe she could come live with me. We could go shopping together and hang out at the house…

I shook my head to clear the thoughts. Summer break was still weeks away. And she might have somewhere else to stay. I shouldn't get my hopes up by daydreaming about it, especially when I had pasta to tend to. Reve would kill me if I messed up his food.

As if my thoughts had summoned him, Reve strode back through the swinging kitchen door, holding a phone with a green case high above his head. Frida followed close behind, jumping to try to snatch it away from him.

"Give it back, you thief!" she demanded.

"Taking photos of someone without their permission is against the law." Reve had the phone on and was flipping through something on it, probably searching for pictures of us hugging.

"Reeeeve!" She drew out his name in a long groan. "You never let me have any fun. How am I supposed to remember the times you show affection if I don't have pictures of them?"

Reve glanced down at her. "Last I checked, you had a brain. Or at least a couple brain cells." He tossed the phone to her.

She fumbled to catch it and instantly started searching through it to see what he'd deleted. "Recluse."

"I don't care for paparazzi," he replied as he strode back to the stove to check on my work.

Frida hmphed as she sat down at the table, still absorbed in her phone. "Please, everyone wishes they were famous enough that people around the world cared what they were doing. How else are you supposed to be remembered and make an impact on the world?"

Reve just rolled his eyes as he picked up the pot full of

boiled spaghetti and carried it to the sink. "Wren, I need the strainer out of that top cabinet there." He pointed.

I darted over to the cabinet and grabbed a giant metal strainer from it. Reve took it from me and put it in the sink before pouring the contents of the pot into it. Steam plumed so thick it clung to my glasses instantly, even though I stepped back.

I removed my glasses and wiped them off on my shirt. "Last time we talked about sensing emotions, you said I had to dream walk successfully first."

Reve shook the last of the water out of the pasta. "I also said you had to practice empathy."

"Wasn't that what I was just doing with you?"

The corners of his mouth twitched. "I suppose."

"So, can you teach me how to do it?"

He paused and eyed me. "Why do you want to learn?"

"Because it's part of being Wind Dreamed." I was finally dream walking correctly, so now I should be able to detect feelings too. It felt like the natural progression of my magical studies.

Reve dumped the pasta back into the pot. "If you just want to do it because you're Wind Dreamed, you're going to find it a very hard skill to master. Even harder than dream walking."

"What do you mean?"

"Emotions are like cats. If you actively seek them out and try to interact with them, chances are they're going to avoid you. But if you sit quietly and let them come to you, they will. Pass me the vegetables."

I grabbed the cutting board full of diced food. "Ok, but what does that look like in practice?"

Reve scooped the vegetables into the pasta and poured

a mason jar full of pale red sauce over the mixture before stirring the whole thing. "It looks like focusing on the person rather than just their feelings. Look at me and reach out, but don't grab at my emotions or try to force them to show themselves."

I shook my head. "That doesn't make any sense."

Reve gave me a sidelong glance. "It's about being open, not demanding. Just try it."

I heaved a sigh. I still didn't really get it, but I wanted to learn badly enough to put up with Reve's strange instructions.

I watched Reve add spices to the pot in seemingly random amounts and tried to "reach" for his emotions. I stared for so long, it started to feel awkward.

"I don't feel anything." Except impatience.

"I told you wanting it made it hard to grasp."

I crossed my arms. "'Cause your instructions were so clear."

"There was nothing wrong with my instructions. You just haven't gotten far enough in your demigod journey to understand them."

I threw up my hands. "How am I supposed to learn if I'm not allowed to want to learn and I'm too new to know what your vague directions mean?"

Reve gave me another long side-eye. "This is why we don't have a teacher other than the Wind Whisperer. It's hard for people to teach each other about the inner workings of the mind. Especially when we're so stuck in our own heads." A flicker of something sparked around Reve. Something heavy but quick. It was almost like a color, but it wasn't visible. It was more of a...

"Do that again," I said.

He raised an eyebrow. "Do what again?"

"Get annoyed."

"I'm not annoyed." But there it was again. That second where there was something surrounding Reve other than air.

I pointed a triumphant finger at him. "Yes, you are. I can see it!"

He tilted his head at me and that feeling around him changed, lightening to an airy substance that curled around him.

"Now you're—" I paused. "I'm not sure, but the feeling shifted."

"You can really sense it? That quickly?" Reve sounded a bit impressed.

"I think so. I mean, I don't know what else it could be."

"Interesting."

I grinned. "I guess you're a better teacher than you thought."

"Maybe." He sounded like he wanted to voice a different theory, but he just turned back to the pot. "Come put away these spices."

Reve and I finished making dinner half an hour later. My feet hurt after standing for so long, but it was worth it to see everyone enjoy the food I'd helped make. Maybe that was why Reve did it. He liked the validation. I certainly couldn't fault him for that.

Keres devoured her food like she hadn't eaten in days. "This is so good. You eat like this every night?"

"Unless Reve is tired and makes us eat leftovers," Frida grumbled. I imagined she was still upset about having her little photoshoot deleted.

"I haven't eaten this well since I took time off to go on a cruise. Turns out ships aren't the best place for a Bone Touched to take a break, though."

Frida perked up. "Why not?"

"Ghosts like ships." Keres stabbed a piece of potato with a little too much force. "And there's nowhere to run on a ship. You just have to stand and fight."

"Oh," Frida said. "How many ghosts have you fought?"

Keres paused, eyes narrowed in concentration. "You know, after you hit twenty or so you stop keeping count."

"That many?" Frida's eyes were wide.

Keres shrugged. "It's part of the job."

"How long have you been Bone Touched?" Reve asked.

"Ok, don't interrogate her," Imena said. The air around her shimmered with warning.

I stared for a moment. This had to be what the others meant when they talked about sensing emotions. It was strange. It felt like I was seeing it, but there was nothing to see; hearing it, but there was nothing to hear. It wasn't even about the little tells and body language that everyone had. It was just all in their heads, but in my head too. Weird.

"I don't mind." Keres twirled her fork through her spaghetti. "It's nice to have people to talk to about this. You wouldn't believe how lonely it gets running around the world, chasing spirits. Sometimes we partner up to take on particularly powerful ghosts or ghosts that have grouped together, but we work alone more often than not."

"You don't ever visit your families?" Lorien asked.

Keres's fork froze. Her eyes slid up to meet Lorien's. "We don't have families besides each other."

Beside me, Reve's emotions buzzed in an impatient jumble around him so quickly that I couldn't read them.

"The Boneman only makes orphans Bone Touched?" Lorien pressed.

"No." Keres lifted her spaghetti to her mouth and took her time chewing it. I didn't like how she refused to look at any of us. "We just don't remember them. The Boneman takes all memories of our past lives so that all we remember is him and what we are."

Reve stood silently and left the table. His plate of half-eaten food stayed in front of his empty purple chair. The others stared after him. Keres didn't seem to notice, but I sensed the buzz of anxious curiosity around everyone else. Almos and Imena exchanged pointed looks, but neither of them got up to go after him. Frida tapped her fork against her food and glanced at Lorien, who bit her lip.

Alright then. Up to me, I supposed.

I got up and followed Reve. His purple door was at the end of the hallway on the left. I knocked gently. No response.

I knocked again. "Reve?"

Still nothing. I tried the doorknob, but it was locked.

"Reve!" I pressed my ear to the wood. Nothing made a sound on the other side of the door. I thumped my forehead against the purple paint. "If you want to come by my room later, I was planning on watching a movie on my laptop while I work on a project."

No sound.

"My door will be unlocked. You don't have to knock, just let yourself in." I toyed with the end of my braid. I hadn't known anyone with a history of diagnosed mental illness, at least not anyone who had told me. So, I wasn't sure how to handle Reve. Hopefully, the invitation was enough but not too much.

I made my way back to the kitchen, where Frida had started the conversation with Keres back up. They stopped when I walked through the door.

"He forgot about a project due tomorrow." I said it mostly for Keres's benefit. There was no way the others would buy it. They'd known Reve for too long, even if he hadn't told them about whatever might be bothering him.

"What I wouldn't give to only have to worry about procrastinating school projects," Keres said. "I hear the job of the Wind Dreamed is a lot less strenuous than the job of the Bone Touched."

Imena picked up the conversation. "Physically, yes, but it has its own challenges."

"I can imagine. Being a demigod never comes cheap."

I sat down and did my best to focus on finishing my dinner as fast as I could. I had no idea if Reve would take me up on my offer, but I didn't want to not be in my room if he did.

Frida managed to keep her inquiries to a minimum for the rest of dinner. Imena and Almos spearheaded the conversation with Keres as if they could prevent someone else from storming out of the kitchen and locking themselves in their room just by avoiding certain topics. Lorien was really quiet.

"Are you ok?" I quietly asked her at one point. She was usually the chipper one who wanted to talk to people. But maybe having a Bone Touched in the penthouse was affecting everyone in strange ways.

"Yeah, I'm just…" She fidgeted with her fingers. "This isn't the first time I've met a Bone Touched under bad circumstances."

"You mean Sylvan?"

"No, I mean someone else. It didn't end well for them." The implication that something terrible happened to the Bone

Touched she talked about agitated me, but I didn't think it wise to press her about it in front of everyone.

19

Nineteen

When dinner finished, we assigned roommates, so we wouldn't be alone if some hungry ghost came after us in the middle of the night. Lorien and Imena would stay together, obviously. Frida made a comment about them keeping quiet, so they wouldn't wake us up in the middle of the night. Lorien stuck out her tongue.

Frida and I would share my room. And Almos would be with Reve once he was ready to be around people again. Keres would be on her own since she knew how to fight ghosts and could actually see them.

"So." Frida turned to me as everyone dispersed. "I'll get my stuff and head over to your room?"

"Could you give me a couple hours? I have some homework I want to work on, and I don't want to get distracted if you're there. Not that you would be distracting on purpose, it's just a mentality thing if other people are in the room while I'm working, you know?" I hoped she couldn't tell that I was lying.

She shrugged. "No problem. I had some stuff I wanted to

get done anyway. We should leave our doors open if we're going to be alone though."

I nodded. "Good idea." There would already be someone else in my room if Reve accepted my invitation.

And there he was when I walked through the door. Reve sat in my desk chair in front of the window with the lights off, just staring out into the night beyond. There wasn't much to look at. My window overlooked the sidewalk between the dorm building and the admin building where all the teachers and staff lived. There were plants and trees below, but from six stories up you couldn't see much except the roof of the building next door and the sky.

"Hey, Reve," I said softly as I turned on the lights.

He didn't so much as twitch at the brightness.

"I'm glad you came."

He turned the chair slightly to the left, then back to the right, swinging it back and forth.

I went to the desk next to him and grabbed my laptop. "I'm gonna set up on the floor, so there's more room. You can sit with me if you'd like, or you can pull over your chair."

I couldn't pick up any emotion from him, like he was a rock.

I put everything I needed on the floor and flipped through the movies I had downloaded on my computer, settling on a comedic crime film. I did my best to not pay Reve much attention as I started on my model for history. He seemed to want to be left alone for the most part.

It only took him a couple minutes to get up and wander over. He sat on the floor with his back against the bed where he could see the laptop screen. I resisted the urge to smile. As if that might jinx it, and he'd get up and leave if he saw.

We sat in silence. Reve barely moved during the whole movie. I focused on my work. Using modeling clay wasn't as easy as I thought it would be, but after looking up some videos on my phone, I more or less got the hang of it. The little people I made wouldn't hold up under much criticism, but at least they looked like actual people and not bipedal blobs.

My phone buzzed on the ground halfway through the movie. An unknown number had messaged me.

Are you free Thursday evening?

I frowned as I picked it up. Who would be messaging me from an unknown number? I hardly dared to hope that Sylvan might have returned and wanted to meet up. I couldn't make the drive to Mortorous Academy on a school night, but if it meant seeing her in one piece, I would get to her as quickly as possible.

Sorry, came another message from the same number. *Is this Wren? It's Rich.*

Oh. Richard from my finance class. He said he would message me about getting together to work on the project for class sometime this week.

Hi, Rich. This is Wren. I think Thursday works for me. What time?

Right after school if you can. I have a baseball game that night, so whatever we can get done between school ending and the game would be a huge help.

Ok. Sounds good. I smiled to myself. Maybe this would work out after all.

"Who are you messaging?" Reve's voice, though quiet, made me jump.

I turned to see him staring at me with those impenetrably

dark eyes. "Just a classmate I have to do a project with." I bit my tongue once I heard how defensive I sounded. Why did I feel like I had to defend myself to him?

"Mm," he said and focused back on the movie.

I squinted at him, trying to read his emotions. They swam in a tight layer around him like a second skin. I couldn't quite figure any of them out. I guessed I hadn't gotten enough experience, or maybe he was trying to hide them from me. Could you do that? Imena made it sound like you couldn't if a Wind Dreamed was powerful enough.

My door opened. I paused the movie. Almos stuck his head in. "Wren, have you seen—? Oh, there you are, Reve."

Reve glanced up at Almos without moving his head.

Almos leaned his shoulder against my doorframe. "We're supposed to buddy up tonight since Keres said we shouldn't be alone. I looked in your room, but you weren't there. What are you doing in here?" He glanced between the two of us like he'd just caught us with our tongues in each other's mouths.

"Watching a movie," I replied, face rapidly heating.

"Cool." I couldn't help feeling like he wanted to say more, but he focused on Reve. "I'll just get my stuff and set up on the floor in your room. Unless you want to come to mine."

"We can stay in my room," Reve said as he focused back on the computer screen, clearly finished with the conversation.

"Alright. I'll see you whenever you're done in here then." Almos backed up and closed the door behind him.

I turned to Reve. "Are they going to think we're a couple now?"

His eyes didn't leave the paused screen of my laptop. "They know I'm asexual. They're probably just getting excited, because I'm spending time with you so soon after you got here."

"Oh." Why did his bluntness keep surprising me? "Why *are* you spending time with me? Not that I don't appreciate it, I'm just wondering what makes me an exception to the rule."

He shrugged. "You're different."

"Different? Different how?"

His gaze slid to me. "I don't feel like explaining."

I pursed my lips as I pressed play on the movie. "Ok then."

Reve left once the movie was over without a single word. Soon afterward, Frida breezed in carrying a bag, a rolled-up air mattress, and a little electric air pump. She closed the door behind her with her foot.

"How is Reve?" she asked as she unrolled the air mattress and plugged in the pump.

I pushed my desk chair back into place. Reve had left it in front of the window. "Heck if I know. I can't get a read on him."

She had to shout to be heard over the noise the air pump made once she turned it on. "Aren't you starting to get in touch with your powers? I started being able to sense people's emotions once I successfully dream walked."

"A little bit," I called back. "It's inconsistent though. And Reve was hard to read before."

Frida nodded. "You'll probably just pick up on strong emotions for a few days until you get more connected with the dreams you walk through and your own feelings. You should try meditating more. That seems to help me."

I sat down at the foot of my bed. "I'm not very good at that."

"It takes practice." Frida turned off the air and plugged the mattress up quickly. "You have to want it."

"Want what? To sit and do nothing for half an hour?"

Frida dug around in her bag and pulled out a set of sheets for the mattress. "To be at peace."

"But I do want to be at peace."

"Maybe, but you want to have a nice little list where you can check off each item and a guarantee that once you've done them all, you will be at peace. It's never that simple. Achieving peace is about letting go of your processes and your problems. It sneaks up on you until one day you're just in it, and you're not entirely sure how you got there."

My eyes narrowed. "Did you get that from a TV show?" The line sounded familiar.

Frida shrugged. "Maybe, but it's true. You can't force this, Wren."

I'd figured that much out with dream walking. It was only when I let myself be in the moment and focus on what was happening instead of the thousand other possibilities of how it could go that I'd managed to do it right.

Frida finished making her bed and wriggled under the covers. "Don't forget to wear your bone necklace. I don't want to have to sacrifice my sleep to save you from a ghost."

I snorted. With that kind of attitude, I would be the one saving her from a ghost.

20

Twenty

I hovered in the middle of the dream orb that night, contemplating everything that had happened that day. I went from tentatively elated that I'd dream walked correctly to tentatively afraid that a ghost might phase through the walls and try to choke the life and magic out of me. And that didn't even take into account all the drama with Reve.

"You have a lot on your mind tonight." The Wind Whisperer emerged from the wall of dreams and drifted over to me.

Understatement of the year. I turned toward it. "You really sent someone to protect us even though you didn't know if there were actually ghosts around?"

"Of course. Did you think I would not do everything in my power to protect my children?"

I shrugged. "I haven't known you for that long to say."

The Wind Whisperer was a god. It had big, world-changing, divine things to worry about. In all the mythology books I'd read, gods were usually less than caring toward their half-mortal children. So, it wouldn't have surprised me if the gods of this world had turned out to be similar. The Wind Whisperer had never been harsh, but driving me to work night after night wasn't exactly taking it easy on me.

"Well, we gods care for all of our children, whether they are new and still learning or long past the need for our supervision."

"But the Boneman sends the Bone Touched into danger all the time. That's kind of their whole job." At least from my understanding. Keres had said Bone Touched were killed by ghosts all the time.

The Wind Whisperer sighed in a way that sounded like breezes blowing through tall grasses. "We gods answer to the order of the universe. Humans were created to be what they are. To take one and give it even a fraction of our divine power requires that power to be used for its intended purpose. Dream walking is usually harmless for both parties. But the Boneman performs a task that is much more dangerous to humans, and he has to live with the consequences of his actions when one of his children dies in the name of that cause."

"So do the Bone Touched." I couldn't imagine Sylvan or Nicholas going out into the world and getting killed by a ghost. Their one chance at life would be squandered just because some god decided to "adopt" them.

"Their sacrifice is never in vain. They ensure a safer world for every living creature, especially other demigods."

"But their job is to catch ghosts, not criminals. How do we know someone will apprehend the person responsible for this? Is that Keres's job, or are we hoping the human police find the culprit?"

"Keres will be conducting an investigation of her own while

she is at the school, but if mortal law enforcement takes care of it, the same result is achieved. I asked the Boneman to send the best person suited for this job, so I trust that she will handle everything."

"Do you talk to the Boneman very often?" Life and death were opposites. The gods responsible for each certainly seemed that way, outwardly at least. I couldn't help being curious about their relationship.

The Wind Whisperer tilted its head. "Are you trying to distract me because you are nervous about dream walking, because you are looking for comfort in a stressful situation, or because you truly want to know?"

I chewed my lip. "All of them?"

It chuckled. "There is nothing to worry about. The Boneman sent the best. You can dream walk just as well as you did last night. And my relationship with my fellow gods is not something you need to be concerned about."

"Sorry." I'd kept my curiosity in check up until now, but I'd gotten too comfortable with the Wind Whisperer. Gods had boundaries too.

"There is nothing to be sorry about. It is only natural that you would be curious." The Wind Whisperer took my hand. "Now, let us find you a dream to walk through."

"I know I said I wouldn't ask you to take me to specific people's dreams again," I started as the Wind Whisperer pulled me toward the wall of dreams. "But is there any way I can look through the dreams of the people in the school or town to see if I can find any clue about who is kidnapping people?"

The Wind Whisperer put its free hand to what would have been its chin if it had a face. "Theoretically, you could as long as you do not enter the dreams of—"

"Of people I know. I know."

"This is not something I would recommend though. You are still quite new to this process. You have only just begun to learn how to influence dreams the way you want. I am not sure you would be able to pick up on any of the incredibly subtle clues that might point to our culprit. I say this with as much love and support as I can while still being realistic about the whole thing."

I sighed. "No, I get it. I just want to do something more than sit and wait for someone else to fix this problem. And you'll be in the dreams with me. You're a lot better at reading them than I am, so you might pick up on something I'd miss."

The Wind Whisperer lowered its head to look me in the eye. "Are you trying to flatter me into letting you have your way?"

"No, I'm trying to flatter you into helping me do the right thing. Isn't that what being Wind Dreamed is about? Helping people be the best version of themselves and encouraging them to do the right thing?"

The Wind Whisperer straightened. "I am unsure if I should be proud or offended that you are using my own lessons against me, but you have a point. I do not want to get your hopes up though. Reading dreams is not the same as reading minds. We might get lucky and stumble across something, but do not hold your breath."

"A small chance is better than no chance," I replied. "Let's go."

The Wind Whisperer surveyed the wall of dreams like it was a shelf full of books, and it was deciding which one to read. "This one should be interesting. She usually has vivid dreams." It touched a red ribbon of light.

Our surroundings changed rapidly. One moment we were in the dream orb, the next we stood in the middle of crowded festival grounds. Shadowy dream characters were everywhere, dozens and dozens of them. Stands selling snacks and cheap souvenirs were backed by rollercoasters and swinging rides that looked like the perfect place to lose your lunch.

I took it all in with wide eyes. "How are we supposed to find—?"

"There." The Wind Whisperer pointed to a non-hazy girl walking away from us through the crowd. Despite the amount of people here, she had a clear path through the throng. When it was your dream, everyone made way for you, I supposed.

"Come quickly before we lose her."

The Wind Whisperer floated up above everyone's heads and darted off toward the dreamer. I wound my way through the crush of bodies, wishing I had learned how to float above the scene the way I'd seen Reve do in that dream the Wind Whisperer had showed me during my time in the dream void. I willed myself to rise above the maze of dream characters the way I willed things to happen in the dream itself, but my feet stayed firmly on the ground.

I lost sight of the dreamer a few times, but the Wind Whisperer hovering over her head like a rainbow banner was more than enough for me to find her again. When I finally caught up, she had stopped by a fountain that was dyed a bright shade of red. She had just finished talking with someone and waved goodbye to them as they walked away. She had this flushed sort of aura around her like she'd accomplished something she was truly proud of. It tinted the whole dream in a warm, calm hue.

"How is it possible to be out of breath in a dream?" I panted once I finally had time to stop.

The Wind Whisperer shrugged. "I do not make the rules. The dreamer does. But you had better get ready. I think something is about to happen."

I focused on the dreamer. She stared at the fountain. It was deeper than most decorative fountains I'd seen in parks and places like this. The red color made the water look like a sparkling pond of liquid rubies. The dreamer looked up, glanced around, grinned, and dove right into the fountain.

I shrieked and threw out my hands as if I could stop her. But she was swimming like she wasn't surrounded by people who would be concerned that a person was splashing around in the fountain.

Maybe that was it. She just wanted to have a bit of fun after whatever she had accomplished and didn't care if anyone saw. I smiled. If she wanted fun, I could give her fun.

At my command, her legs melded together and grew large fins like a mermaid tail. The dreamer shot around the red fountain, propelled by the power of her new tail. I couldn't quite tell through the water, but I was reasonably sure she was smiling wide enough to hurt.

"An interesting choice," the Wind Whisperer said. "You are treating her instead of teaching her?"

I didn't take my eyes off the dreamer in case I lost focus. "She should have the space to celebrate every once in a while. If there's no positive reinforcement, what's to keep her going and doing the right thing?"

"Hm. I think you are starting to get the hang of this," the

Wind Whisperer murmured appreciatively.

I made sure everyone had their eyes averted, so there wouldn't be a massive panic caused by the sudden appearance of a mermaid in the fountain. This girl could have her fun. But what was she celebrating? Could it be the recent kidnappings? Was she the criminal we were looking for?

I didn't think so. Her joy felt too pure and lighthearted to be tied to anything so dastardly.

The girl popped out of the fountain. I had to be quick about returning her human legs and making sure she was miraculously dry as soon as she emerged from the water. She wasn't at all fatigued by her swim and darted off down a side path.

"Try to keep up, Wren." The Wind Whisperer followed through the air while I was left to navigate the crowd again.

When I caught up to them, the dreamer had gotten herself stuck amid some kind of tiny, model city that was probably supposed to be purely decorative. How she had gotten in the middle of it without crushing any of the tiny buildings, I didn't even want to know. She tiptoed along the streets, trying to keep from stepping on anything, but it was hard for her to keep her balance.

Fly.

I took inspiration from the first dream I'd ever tried to manipulate and gave the dreamer wings as she wobbled on her feet, losing her balance and pitching forward. Her wings caught her and sent her soaring over the little city. I circulated air under her to keep her from having to flap—one wingbeat and the model would be decimated. She flew so low over it. But it seemed to stretch farther and farther the longer she flew. It definitely hadn't been that big when I'd first found her towering over it.

She was almost out of sight when the dream started to turn grey. Thank goodness. I wasn't sure I could keep up with her if the dream lasted much longer. Who knew where she would have run off to next and if I would be able to think up a solution before she ruined something or drew attention to herself.

"Not bad," the Wind Whisperer said as it led me behind a cotton candy stand and back into the dream orb. "That was a pretty fast-paced dream. I am glad to see you could keep up."

I let my muscles relax as the zero gravity held me in place. "I would have lost her if you hadn't been hovering over her like a beacon."

The Wind Whisperer chuckled. "Some dreams are like that. They change faster than you can adapt to them. You need to learn how to manipulate your own abilities within a dream, so you can keep up with any dreamer."

"I'm open to suggestions." I barely understood how to manipulate dreams. Manipulating *myself* and *my* capabilities sounded even more complicated.

"It is no different from changing a dream. You just have to focus inward instead of outward." The Wind Whisperer slowly circled the perimeter of the dream orb.

"Right." That wasn't very helpful. "Did you see anything that made you think that girl might be the one who is kidnapping people?"

The Wind Whisperer paused its rotation. "No, but like I said, dreams are not a reflection of the whole of a person's thoughts, feelings, and actions. Chances are, this is a fruitless search."

I crossed my arms. "Yeah. Maybe." But trying made me

feel a whole lot more useful. Wind Dreamed powers weren't nearly as helpful as I first hoped. I had started feeling other people's emotions. Great. But I couldn't connect them to concrete thoughts.

The Wind Whisperer hovered closer. "You still have something to be proud of tonight, Wren. This was your second successful dream in a row and a tricky one at that."

"Thanks." I brought a smile to my face but couldn't keep away that nagging feeling that I hadn't done enough. "Could I try another one?"

If the Wind Whisperer had eyebrows, it would have raised them. "Another one? You were exhausted a moment ago."

"I've caught my second wind. I want to try again."

"Hm." The Wind Whisperer surveyed the slithering dreams around us and gestured to a pale blue one. "That one will probably be short enough for you to wake up in time to get to your classes."

It took my hand and glided up to a new dream. I steeled myself with a deep breath, then plunged in.

<h1 style="text-align:center">21</h1>

<h1 style="text-align:center">Twenty-One</h1>

I bounced out of bed after dream walking through another mermaid dream—who knew those were so popular—and almost stepped on Frida on my way to the closet to get dressed. I'd completely forgotten she was there.

She groaned and rolled over to face me. "Morning, Wren."

I winced. "Morning, Frida. Sorry, I didn't mean to kick you."

"S'all good," she mumbled and burrowed back under the covers. "Come kick me again when breakfast is ready."

Huh. "Ok."

I was more careful about stepping around her as I got ready and quietly slipped out of the room, leaving the door halfway open. We weren't supposed to be alone, but people were awake now, so she should be fine if she kept dozing for a few more minutes, right? I certainly didn't want to have to watch her sleep until she decided to drag herself out of bed.

Keres was in the living room, lifting her shirt to reveal a set of holsters and sheathes strapped to her torso. I couldn't help stopping and staring as she fitted white daggers and needles and all sorts of other weapons into the harness.

She turned and caught me looking as she pulled down her shirt and tucked it into her pants. Her clothing hid her arsenal surprisingly well. If I hadn't just watched her cover herself in a layer of blades, I never would have guessed she had enough weaponry on her to take down a small army. How long had she been doing this to have perfected such a complicated system?

"Good morning." She gave me a smile as if she hadn't just been preparing for war.

"Are all of those made of bone?" I should really stop staring at her torso, trying to find the tell that she had so many deadly objects on her person.

"Yup." She rolled up the leg of her pants and picked up a set of straps from Frida's loveseat. "Gotta be prepared. You never know what parts of your body you will or won't be able to reach in a fight."

"I thought you could use your Bone Touched powers to move them with your mind." Wouldn't that mean it didn't matter where the weapons were as long as they were on her person?

"I was never that good at telekinetically controlling bones. I had to learn how to wield blades like a non-demigod, so I need them somewhere I can physically reach them with my hands."

"Isn't that something you could practice? Meaning no offense of course." I held up my hands in surrender once I realized how insensitive my words sounded.

She smiled at me. "It's ok. It's a shortcoming I learned to accept a long time ago. I practice regularly, but sometimes you're just not good at something. Magic can be like that. You can't beat yourself up about it though. You can only adapt and move on."

I couldn't imagine not being able to do what I was expected to do. Just the thought that I might not be cut out to be Wind Dreamed after failing to get my first couple of dreams right had wrecked me.

I cleared my throat. "Did you make those straps yourself?" The one she buckled around her calf fit too well to be store-bought.

"No. We have a person who's really good at making them. All he needs are measurements and a description of what all you want on them. The rest is up to you." She slid a saw-toothed dagger into the sheath on the inside of her leg. "That mostly just means not wearing anything too form-fitting."

I nodded. Her shirt was tight across the shoulders but loose around her stomach where most of the weapons hid. Her pants hugged her waist but flared out at the knee. Her thighs looked smooth under the fabric, but I wouldn't put it past her to have something hidden there too.

"Are you going to have breakfast with us?" I wasn't sure what I wanted her answer to be. The other Wind Dreamed seemed to have mixed feelings about her presence.

"I appreciate your hospitality, but I need to get an early start. The dead don't rest, so neither can I."

"You weren't out hunting last night?" That seemed like the time for ghosts to wander around. According to every movie I'd seen and book I'd read anyway.

"I was, but even the Bone Touched need a few hours of sleep. If I head out now, I might be able to catch a whiff of something before the morning mist burns off. Then it's investigation time." Keres cracked her knuckles.

"Will you be allowed to question people or get access to crime scenes?" I was under the impression that those kinds of things were kept locked down tight.

Keres tossed me a very convincing police badge. "We also have a person for that."

My eyebrows rose as I looked it over. "Wow. You guys really have a whole system in place to take care of everything."

Keres took it back and tucked it in her pocket. "We have to. With no birth certificates or forms of identification, someone has to get us documents less than legally so we can cross borders and go where we need to in order to get stuff done. A lot of us even have day jobs, and these days you have to go through so much paperwork just to get into those."

I wondered if the Wind Dreamed had anything like that. I had all my documents in order because my family had money and traveled a lot, but I didn't know about everyone else. "You don't have IDs?"

Keres rolled her pant leg down. "Whatever lives we had before the Boneman are erased from our memories along with any paperwork associated with us. We become someone else when we are delivered to Mortorous Academy. As far as the government is concerned, we don't exist."

I couldn't imagine not having any memory of who I was. "That sounds... lonely."

Was that why Sylvan was always so quiet and closed off? Was that why she hadn't seemed to know how some of the most basic things worked? She had been new to Mortorous Academy not that long ago. How many memories had she had when I'd met her, if any?

"Maybe at first, but there are enough of us that you find your people. Or you become a lone wolf if you want. That's always a choice." Keres shrugged.

I wasn't convinced. I'd rather keep my memories and the friends I had now. "Well, good luck. I hope you find the person responsible for all of this."

"Don't we all." Keres headed toward the elevator. "I wouldn't count on seeing much of me if I were you. I'm probably going to keep some strange hours. I'd appreciate it if your professional chef saved some leftovers though. Ghost hunting is hungry work."

I waved a little as she entered the elevator. "Sure thing."

"Thanks." She bowed her head as the doors slid closed. Her red ponytail swished as she straightened a moment before she was fully blocked from view.

I heaved a breath and made my way toward the kitchen. Lorien and Imena were talking in hushed voices at the table. Lorien sat in Almos's orange chair. Imena had Lorien's hands in her own. The air around them hummed with concern and fear. I walked by them as fast as I could. Whatever they were talking about, I had a feeling I wasn't supposed to hear it.

Reve sat on a barstool in front of the stove. With him all hunched over like he was with his hair ruffled and his purple pajamas still on, I was a little surprised to see his eyes open and focused on the pancakes cooking in the large skillet in front of him. He looked like he could fall asleep at any moment.

"Morning, Reve."

"Mm," he grunted, not taking his eyes off the pancakes.

I leaned forward to examine the little red chunks in the half-finished pancakes. "What's in the pancakes?"

"Strawberries and chocolate chips."

"Yum. Keres asked if we could save her a plate. She headed

out just a minute ago."

Reve's head turned slightly in my direction. "She isn't coming to breakfast?"

I couldn't tell whether he was happy or upset about that. His voice was too even. "She wanted to get an early start. I'm assuming she'll loop back to eat at some point during the day."

He nodded and turned back to flip the pancakes. "Go get Frida up if she isn't already."

"Is Almos awake?" He wasn't in the kitchen nearly as early as Reve, but I thought he was usually out of bed by this time.

Reve shrugged. "Get Frida."

"Yes, sir." I rolled my eyes as I turned and headed back the way I came. Hopefully, Frida had gotten whatever extra minutes of sleep she needed. She was still a lump on the air mattress when I opened my bedroom door.

"Frida," I said softly. She didn't respond. "Frida."

She groaned. "Ten more minutes."

"You'll be late to class if you don't get ready soon."

A hand emerged from her blankets and waved dismissively. "I think my class can manage without me for a few minutes."

I grinned. "Reve said to get up now."

She cracked an eye open. "Is breakfast ready?"

"Yes." More or less.

She popped up out of bed so fast I barely saw her move before she was on her feet. "Why didn't you start with that?" Her voice was no longer sleepy and reluctant, but bright and alert.

"Didn't know I needed to," I muttered as she darted out of the room, across the hall, and into her own room to get dressed. I knew she loved Reve's cooking, but I didn't know it had the power to get her up and moving so quickly.

I wandered back into the kitchen. Almos had appeared at the table with Imena and Lorien. Reve carried a big plate stacked high with fluffy pancakes and heaved it into the middle of the table between a butter dish and a dish of homemade whipped cream. All the seats had plates and silverware in front of them already.

"Where is Frida?" Reve asked me.

I gestured vaguely at the kitchen door. "Getting dressed, I think. She got up pretty fast when I told her breakfast was ready."

Almos shook his head with a smile as he reached for the plate of pancakes to serve himself. "You could get that girl to do anything for food."

"For *Reve's* food," Imena corrected. "She has standards and rightly so." She winked at Reve.

Reve plopped down next to me with a giant cup of coffee and a handful of pills. My eyes widened at the sight of them. There were so many. He grabbed a napkin from the center of the table and set his medication down on them. I couldn't seem to look away as he took his cup of coffee and sipped it in between popping the pills.

I jumped a little when Imena passed me the plate of pancakes. She gave me a pointed "mind your own business" look.

"It's fine," Reve said, catching our silent conversation. "Wren watching isn't going to suddenly make me self-conscious about how many drugs I have to take to stay sane."

Imena pursed her lips like she wanted to say something but didn't. Reve pulled the significantly shorter stack of pancakes between me and him and started piling food onto his plate. I did the same. Frida breezed in and flung herself into her seat. She reached for the pancakes before I fully got my first one off the stack.

Reve smacked her hands away. "Manners, you animal. Last one to the table is the last one served."

She stuck her tongue out at him. "If you didn't make such delicious food…"

"You would starve yourself in protest?" he finished.

She lifted her chin. "No. I would go in your room and mess up all of your stuff."

Reve sat up straight and looked her dead in the eyes. The waves of animosity rolling off of him made me tense. "If you *ever* do something like that—"

"Where is Keres?" Almos interjected before Reve could finish making his threat. "I thought she was going to eat with us."

"She wanted to get back out there," I said, wary of how Reve was still staring at Frida like he wanted to feed her to a pack of starving hyenas. "I'll fix her a plate though. She made it sound like she was going to circle back and get food later."

Almos smiled despite the staring contest between Reve and Frida. "I'm sure she will appreciate that, Wren. How was your dream walking last night?"

"Good. Kind of tiring, but good."

"How so?" Imena asked. "Dream walking usually rejuvenates me."

I settled everything on my plate and started cutting up my pancakes. My mouth watered at the way chocolate oozed out of them when I cut into a chip of it. "Maybe tiring isn't the word I'm looking for. It was just a lot. The first one was a really fast-paced dream. I had to keep running after the dreamer."

"The *first* one?" Frida asked, breaking her stare-down with Reve. "As in, you did more than one?"

"Yeah. There was a little bit of time left, and I wanted to try doing another dream, so I did." I stuck the first forkful of food in my mouth and sighed in bliss. However Reve cooked, the food kept turning out to be the most delicious thing I'd ever tasted. It had to be some family secret.

"So soon after you started dream walking?" Almos raised appreciative eyebrows. "How did you like it?"

I swallowed. "I don't think I did as well on the second one even though I had more time to think about what to do."

"Maybe the split-second decision-making did you some good," Reve said, finally letting Frida have the pancake plate. "You can't get in your own head too much if you barely have time to think."

"Maybe. It's so stressful though." I was terrified of messing up in a big way if a decision was made too hastily.

"I'm proud of you for trying anyway." Imena smiled. "I didn't start doing multiple dreams in one night until I had several weeks of successful dream walks under my belt. I think Lorien was the same." Imena reached over and squeezed Lorien's hand.

It was only then that I noticed how quiet Lorien had been so far. She kept her eyes on her plate, mechanically cutting and eating her food. She hadn't said a word since she'd had her private talk with Imena at the table when I first walked into the kitchen. I hadn't heard a word of whatever went on between them, but something was clearly bothering her.

"Figures you would be an overachiever," Frida mumbled

around a mouthful of food.

I leaned around Reve to look at her. "What is that supposed to mean?"

She shrugged. "Just that you seem like the type who wants to go above and beyond and get stuff right and do it all on your own."

"And you seem like the kind of person who talks while she stuffs her face with food," Reve shot back.

Frida grinned at him. A streak of chocolate stained her upper teeth. "You know you love me."

"If by 'love you', you mean 'have a strong desire to throw you off a bridge', then yes."

Frida stuck out her tongue.

My phone buzzed in my pocket. Abandoning the latest fight between Reve and Frida, I checked it. Rich had said good morning. I texted a quick good morning back.

You want to get breakfast with me and work on the project in the cafeteria in a few minutes?

I glanced at the half-eaten stack of pancakes on my plate. *I already ate. Sorry.*

Already? Someone's an early riser.

Force of habit. My parents always told me that in order to be productive in a day, you had to have as many hours of daylight as possible. That meant very little sleeping in. Or staying up late. I didn't always follow that unspoken rule very well though. Not when the books were calling me.

Do you still want to work on the project this morning? Practice got cancelled 'cause coach is sick.

I'm with friends. I'll be there tomorrow to work on it in the library though.

I felt a little bad for ditching him, but it didn't seem right to leave in the middle of breakfast after I had already ducked out early once this week for book club. Besides, I wasn't supposed to go anywhere by myself. There were too many alleys between buildings where I could get pulled behind a row of bushes and choked to death by a ghost without anyone hearing or seeing a thing.

No problem. I'll see you in class.

See you.

I smiled a little to myself. Maybe Rich wasn't one of those people who would blow off the work and leave me to do it all at the last minute.

"You're smiling." Reve's quiet comment made me jump.

I locked my phone screen and stuffed the device in my pocket. "Is there something wrong with that?"

His dark stare was expressionless, but a buzz of anxious emotions swirled tightly around him. "Who were you talking to?"

"A friend from one of my classes."

"Anyone I would know?"

"They're not in one of the classes we share." What was with the third degree? Was I not allowed to have friends outside of the Wind Dreamed the same way I apparently wasn't allowed to be friends with anyone who was Bone Touched unless the Wind Whisperer approved it ahead of time?

"Hm." Reve faced forward again.

I tried to read the feelings swirling around him, but he had withdrawn them like he had the night before. I rolled my eyes. If he wasn't going to say what he thought, I wouldn't waste my time trying to decipher whatever was going through his head.

After breakfast, I tucked foil over the plate of remaining

pancakes and stuck it in the fridge for Keres while Almos helped Reve wash the dishes.

They were pretty efficient. I hadn't really noticed before since I usually went straight to the bathroom to brush my teeth before it was time to head for class, but the two worked in tandem with one another well.

Years together would do that to people though. Everyone had lived with each other for so long before I got here. Even Frida had arrived at the beginning of the school year, so she'd had time to figure out her place in the Wind Dreamed family structure. I wished I had more than a year and a few months with them. I had no idea how things would be once I graduated.

Maybe I could at least stay in touch with Reve and Lorien since we were in the same grade. And Frida had a couple years in high school to go. Unlike a lot of the friends I'd made over my time in boarding schools, these people seemed worth keeping up with long after we stopped sharing classes and a living space.

The walk to history class was painfully quiet. I didn't expect Reve to say much—he never did. But Lorien was continuing her silent streak. The emotional haze around her was sluggish and sad. After history on the way to our next class, I finally decided to talk to her.

"Lorien, are you ok?"

She perked up a little, plastering a smile on her face, but there was still a dullness to her gaze. "Yeah, I'm fine. Just..." She waved a hand around. "A lot going on in my head."

"Is it school stuff? 'Cause that assignment we have for English is kind of kicking my butt too." I tried a smile to lighten the mood.

One of our English assignments was more straightforward than I'd come to expect of Animos Prep schoolwork. The analysis essay over the use of micro-symbolism required a creative approach, but it was still closer to the stuff I would have done at Mortorous Academy than anything else I'd done for that class. We still had the knitted book sleeve to appeal to everyone's artistic side though.

Lorien's gaze dropped to the floor. "No. It's a personal thing. I don't really want to talk about it."

"Oh, ok." I chewed my lip, then leaned over and gave her the world's most awkward side hug.

I felt her mood brighten a fraction as she looped an arm around me. "Thanks."

"I'm not very good at the whole being there for people stuff. In case you hadn't noticed, I'm kind of awkward and in my own head a lot. But I'll try if you feel like talking later."

"That means more than you think, Wren," Lorien murmured. "But it's nothing big, just a bit of high school drama that'll last for a couple days and fizzle out without consequence."

Based on how she had acted so far, I doubted there wouldn't be any consequences. Lorien's emotional state was already suffering them. Even if she got over it, it still mattered.

But I wasn't going to push it if she didn't want me to.

She mustered a little more energy by lunchtime but still didn't talk much. I tried to tell myself that she was probably fine because it had looked like she was talking to Imena about whatever was bothering her this morning before breakfast. That didn't stop me from feeling useless though.

"You seem a little stressed," Rich said when I sat down next to him in finance.

Well, learning how to dream walk and looking for a serial kidnapper while trying not to get killed by any ghosts that might or might not have resulted from those kidnappings in addition to dealing with the drama of my fellow Wind Dreamed took its toll.

"It's fine. I'm just tired." I wasn't. At least not physically. Being tired was the one thing I didn't have to worry about now that I was consistently dream walking with a moderate degree of success. I didn't really understand it, but my quality of sleep was directly related to the use of my powers in the dream realm.

He nodded. "Aren't we all? I got up early this morning to go to practice and forgot to check my email, so I missed the message about it getting cancelled. And naturally, I already drank an energy drink, so I couldn't go back to sleep. The caffeine has worn off now though. I'm so glad it's almost lunch time. Maybe I can sneak off to my room and take a nap."

"Sleep helps. So does meditating." I couldn't believe it, but I had started looking forward to sitting in the middle of a field and emptying my mind of everything that was going on in my life. There was just too much going on in my head.

He propped his chin in his hand. "I don't have the patience for meditation. It's just so boring."

I cringed inwardly. I'd been in his shoes not long ago, but now that it had grown on me, that mentality sounded… close-minded.

Rich twirled his pencil between his fingers. "What do you do after school? Besides homework. Like for fun and stuff."

I shrugged. He would probably think that doing a group meditation or reading for hours on end was weird. "Just watch TV and stuff. Hang out with friends. Those kind of things."

He grinned and my pulse stuttered. He really was that good looking. "I was hoping you would say something like that. Friday night, if the game goes well, I was planning to go with my teammates and some other friends to the movies. It's kind of a tradition to celebrate our wins. I was wondering if you would want to go with me."

The offer took me by surprise. So much so that I blurted the first thought that came to mind. "Why?"

He shrugged. "You seem kind of fun. I thought you'd make a nice addition to the group."

My mouth opened but no sound came out. Was this a date? A group date maybe, since he said there would be other people there.

Other people.

I managed to get my voice to work. "Who all is going?"

"Most of the baseball team, obviously. Their girlfriends, if they have them. Their friends if they don't. We like to bring plus-ones to celebrate with us. The more, the merrier, and all that."

I was still stuck on the "girlfriends" thing. "And you want *me* to be your plus-one?"

"Yeah." He said it so sincerely.

"We only just officially met a few days ago. Don't you have other friends?" I should really stop talking. A boy was inviting me out on the closest thing to a date that I'd ever been on, and I was sitting there interrogating him about why he would choose me. What happened to "don't look a gift horse in the mouth"?

He scrubbed a hand through his hair. "I do, but I don't

know. I've taken them to these kinds of things before, and they didn't seem to like it all that much. They started making excuses about why they couldn't come or just refusing."

I raised an eyebrow. "Is it that bad?"

He straightened. "No! That's the whole point. I mean, we can get a little rowdy sometimes if we go out to eat, but we're high school kids. Aren't we supposed to have fun and make some noise? Within reason of course."

"Yeah." My mom said similar things all the time. I usually rolled my eyes on the other side of the phone but... "It sounds like fun. I'll have to check my schedule though."

His smile could have lit the room. "Great. Let me know when you know so I can buy the tickets ahead of time and get us some good seats."

I smiled back, heart pounding in my chest. "I will."

I was right. Rich wasn't like the other guys who took advantage of my intelligence and just wanted an easy A. He wouldn't go through the trouble of inviting me out and paying for my movie ticket if he didn't want to be around me longer than it took to finish this project.

He also wouldn't have texted me good morning and offered to work on the project over breakfast. Maybe I should have just gone to meet him this morning. What if he started thinking *I* was the one using him since I hadn't been willing to step away from one breakfast with the other Wind Dreamed?

I could make up for it. I could work really hard on the project when we met up tomorrow and go with him to the movies on Friday. Surely, he wouldn't question my loyalty then. And we could become friends. Maybe more than friends. And I wouldn't have to rely on the Wind Dreamed so much.

They shouldn't have to worry about me, my late start, and the ridiculous reason I'd had to become Wind Dreamed in the first place as much as they did. And if I showed them that I could balance my life as a Wind Dreamed and school and have a social life with normal people, they wouldn't have to.

22

Twenty-Two

I hadn't thought I would ever get the hang of meditating when I'd started, but over the last few days, I'd found myself more and more relaxed and ready to take the time off I needed to recharge. Since I didn't have my own dreams when I slept anymore, this was the closest I could get, letting thoughts float through my mind with no particular rhyme or reason.

It made it better somehow that I was doing it next to the other Wind Dreamed, like we were feeding off of and sustaining each other with our calming energy in an endless ouroboros. So, that afternoon as we all soaked in the warm, spring temperatures and breathed in the fresh air that smelled faintly of wildflowers, I slowly unwound.

There was an undercurrent of tension. The threat of ghosts and the kidnapper who might actually be a murderer still loomed over us. But when we were together, it was like hitting all the right points during acupuncture. There was an invisible synergy.

I knew the Wind Dreamed were supposed to exude a

peaceful aura to those in their presence, but we hardly did it to each other unless we were all together. I hadn't felt it much until after I'd started dream walking successfully.

But that wasn't surprising. I hadn't gotten in touch with most of my other powers until I successfully dream walked, like I wasn't truly Wind Dreamed until I had, and I hadn't even known it. More and more, I could feel everything around me, all of the life. Not just other people, but squirrels in the trees, birds in the bushes, bees buzzing over flowers.

Was this what the Wind Whisperer perceived? It didn't have any eyes or ears or nose to experience the world the way humans did. But if it could sense everything like this with enough clarity, it would have a good enough view of the world that it wouldn't need any of those other senses.

A gentle breeze blew across my face as if in confirmation. I smiled and leaned into it. A hand brushed my shoulder. My eyes opened.

"Come on, chickpea. Time to go back home." Imena started back toward campus.

I scrambled up after her. "Hey, Imena?"

"Yeah?" She glanced at me over her shoulder.

"I'm not going to make it to meditation tomorrow." I caught up and walked next to her, watching her face for a reaction.

I figured she would be the best one to tell. She and Almos seemed to be the authority figures among the Wind Dreamed, but I didn't know enough about Almos to broach the subject with him. He checked on me after I returned from Mortorous Academy, but he still felt a little distant.

Imena was always very levelheaded and willing to help. Hopefully, that meant she would be understanding too. Reve hadn't reacted well to me befriending someone who wasn't

Wind Dreamed. So far, he had been the odd man out in every respect, but this didn't seem like the kind of issue I should test that theory on.

She raised her eyebrows. "Oh, are your parents coming into town? Or your other friends? We'd love to have them join us."

I wrung my hands. "No, no one else is coming. I just have to work on a project with a classmate, and he's really busy, so this is the only time we can get it done before it's due."

Imena nodded. "Ah, I see. Good luck."

"That's it? I can go?"

Imena laughed. "You don't need my permission to work on a project with someone. If your time is limited, then you need to go. Missing meditation once isn't going to make you a bad Wind Dreamed."

"Right." I chuckled nervously with her. "I just... Reve didn't seem happy about it."

Imena sighed. "Reve is Reve. He's very protective of his family and friends."

Because of whatever Keres's presence had brought up for him? Lorien had her baggage. It wouldn't be unreasonable for Reve to have his own, especially with his mental health problems.

Imena gripped my shoulder. "You're getting closer to him. I think that scares him a little bit. He just doesn't want to lose you."

I snorted. "I'm not going anywhere." Both the Wind Whisperer and the Boneman had made that very clear when I tried to escape being Wind Dreamed.

"Maybe not, but if you're splitting your time between our world and theirs..." She jerked her chin in the direction of campus. In the direction of all those normal people. "As long as you don't leave us behind, Reve will be fine. A little jealous maybe, but fine."

The idea of cold, stoic, talented Reve being jealous of anything was laughable, but I couldn't deny that I had felt something similar when Sylvan chose to spend time with Nicholas instead of me. It wasn't something I was proud of.

"I would advise caution around non-demigods though. It can be hard to connect with them. There's always going to be that division between us. They may not know that it is the power of the gods separating our two peoples, but they'll pick up on it subconsciously."

That was how it had been with Sylvan. She couldn't tell me the full story, and it had driven us apart. But being Wind Dreamed was different. I didn't have to spend my days and nights hunting ghosts. I didn't have to go anywhere for my god-given job except my bed. And the Wind Whisperer hadn't erased my memories. There shouldn't be anything in the way of befriending Rich.

"Ok," I said anyway. "I'll be careful."

Imena nodded. "Good. The last thing I want is to see you get hurt over a misunderstanding."

Now probably wouldn't be the best time to tell her I was planning to go out with Rich and his friends on Friday. It was probably best to take this slow with the Wind Dreamed and gradually introduce them to the idea that they might be wrong about normal people.

Keres trudged into the living room halfway through the evening. Her face and clothes were streaked with a dark substance that looked too liquid to be dirt. Despite the slight hunch to her posture, her eyes glittered.

"Hello, Keres," Almos called from where we were gathered on the living room floor in the middle of all the seating, working on various projects. It had been his idea to do them together while we talked instead of confining ourselves to our rooms. It covered the "don't be alone in case a ghost attacks" base too.

She summoned a smile. "Hey. Doing arts and crafts?"

"School projects." Frida waved the hot glue gun in the air. Lorien leaned away from her and the burning hot tool.

"Fun. Sorry about…" She gestured to her dirty clothes. "Body dumping locations don't search themselves. I'll go get cleaned up."

"Body dumping locations?" Frida asked as Keres started to turn away.

Keres flashed her a wicked grin. "Bodies of water, ditches, sewers, dumpsters."

Frida made an exaggerated gagging sound.

Imena straightened, setting down the crochet she'd been working on. "Did you find anything?"

"Not yet, but the city is big. I can't search the whole thing in a day. No sign of ghosts yet either."

"That's… good. Right?" Lorien's voice quivered.

"Maybe. Maybe not. We still don't know enough. The victims could be alive, but that doesn't necessarily mean they will be for long. Time is of the essence. But my body is still human and needs rest. If anyone needs me, I'll be in my room taking a power nap before heading back out later tonight."

"Sleep well," Imena called.

"You too." Keres waved. And disappeared down the hall.

"So, nothing new," Imena sighed, shoulders slumping.

"Nothing new," Almos echoed.

A blessing and a curse. It figured that as soon as I was getting the hang of being a demigod, a bigger supernatural problem came along to overshadow everything. And to make it worse, I had to wait for someone else to sort it out.

"Isn't there a way we can help?" I said, mostly to myself. I hated feeling useless.

"Our powers don't work like that," Lorien murmured. "Unless Reve interrogated every single person in the city and read their emotions."

Reve rolled his eyes. "Don't volunteer me for that. Being bombarded by the emotions of every teenager in this school is bad enough."

My eyebrows furrowed. "Is it really that bad?"

He shrugged and dipped his brush into a tiny plastic container of red paint. "You get used to it. But if the person sitting next to you starts having a quiet panic attack because they got a bad grade on a project or thinking about what they're going to do with their girlfriend later that night, it can get overwhelming."

I chewed my lip. When he put it that way, feeling what everyone else felt didn't sound all that great.

"I wish we could do something too," Imena said. "I don't like having to rely on other people to solve my problems either." Her tone gathered momentum. Her crochet stitching got faster. "I'd much rather go out and fight the ghosts myself or track down the kidnapper than have my fate tied to someone else's ability to take care of me. The Wind Whisperer knows I've been disappointed enough in that regard."

Anger and anxiety swirled around her. The rest of the room had gone dead quiet. All eyes were fixed on Imena. Lorien scooted closer to her and rested a hand on her knee.

Imena heaved a breath. "Sorry. The last time I trusted someone with something important, they really let me down."

"I'm sorry," I murmured. "Was it recent?"

"No." Imena smiled sadly. "It was a while ago. Before I was Wind Dreamed. Let's just say my parents weren't as accepting of my sexual orientation as everyone here has been."

I winced. "I'm sorry."

Imena waved a hand at me. "Stop apologizing. It's not your fault they kicked me out of the house, and I had to survive on the streets for a few months until the Wind Whisperer took me in, made me Wind Dreamed, and gave me a home here."

The blood drained out of my face. "Isn't that illegal? I mean, they can't just kick you out! They have to at least surrender you to the government, right?"

"They didn't care." Imena turned the patch of crocheted fabric over and attached the ends together. "And neither did the law enforcement. Not in my area anyway. They didn't want to deal with us."

"Us?"

"There were a handful of kids who would periodically run away and live in a spot in a wooded area behind the local car dealership until the police came looking for them to bring them back to their families. They knew we were there, but unless they were looking for a specific person, they left us alone. They were at least that understanding of our situation. And probably didn't want to have to go through the trouble of tracking us down if we moved."

I swallowed hard. "How many were there?"

"About fifteen total, but they would rotate out, so there were only ever four or five of us there at any point in time including me." She gave me the numbers like they didn't mean anything, like there weren't that many children, just in one small area, who didn't want to be around their parents or whose parents didn't want them around.

"You stayed there until the Wind Whisperer took you?" My voice broke.

"It wasn't that long." She gripped Lorien's hand on her knee. "Four years here is enough time to outgrow that pain and find a new family."

My chest felt too small for my heart. I would never deny that I had led a charmed life up to this point. I never wanted for anything or went without necessities. I could buy whatever frivolous comfort items I wanted, furnish my room with a small personal library. My parents loved me even if they were busy with work most of the time.

And sure, I'd heard things, seen movies, read books where this kind of thing happened to people. But it was different when you heard the stories of people it had actually happened to. So far, everyone who had told me about their life outside of this school had some horrible tragedy attached to it.

Lorien had lost her parents. Imena did too in a way. They had been through so much. I just wanted to wrap them in bubble wrap and stick them in boxes full of packing peanuts to keep them safe from this world that had already hurt them so much.

"Anyway," Imena said and turned to Frida. "Pass the plastic eyes, will you?"

And just like that, we continued to work like we hadn't just brought up one of the most traumatizing things that could happen to a child.

* * *

240

"You're ok, right?" Frida asked as we settled into bed that night. "It looked like Imena's story shook you up."

"A little," I admitted. "I just never really thought about those things happening to people I know."

"You always think you're the exception to the rule until it happens to you," Frida sighed.

"Please don't tell me all of the Wind Dreamed have terrible stories like that, and I'm the only one who's had a good life. Trauma isn't a requirement for being Wind Dreamed, is it?" I wouldn't know what to do with myself if that were the case.

"No," Frida laughed. "I've had a pretty good life too. My mom's a little uptight about me doing something with my life, but that's pretty normal."

"Yeah, parents do that."

"She wants me to be a doctor or a lawyer or something like that where I can make a bunch of money and be financially stable. I'm not sure if she understands how much money it takes to go through that much schooling though. I would be in debt for a *decade* after I graduate no matter how well my future job pays."

I rolled onto my side to face her in the dark. "What do *you* want to be?"

A shimmer of hope surrounded the place when she lay on the ground. "An actress." Her smile showed in her voice. "I want to be famous and sign autographs and walk down red carpets in gorgeous dresses and jewels that cost more than most people make in a year. I want to act and bring stories to life and meet other famous people."

I grinned. "Sounds like you want the glamorous life."

"I just want to do what I want, have my name remembered, and memorialize my face in movies and TV shows. I don't think that's too much to ask."

"I think you'd make a great actress, Frida. You already have the attitude."

It was quiet for a long minute. "What is that supposed to mean?"

"Just that you already act like you can do whatever you want." I rushed to clarify. "I mean that in a good way. You know who you are, and you don't have a problem letting other people know it. It's admirable."

The smile returned to her voice. "Even when I'm annoying Reve?"

"Maybe a little less so then."

Frida snorted. I giggled.

"I'm glad he's letting you get close to him," she murmured in a much more serious voice. "He needs someone he can open up to."

"I don't know if I'm a good person to open up to." I stumbled over my words and said the wrong things all the time. Like five seconds ago when I'd accused Frida of having an attitude.

"If Reve thinks you are, then you are. He doesn't connect with many people, not even among the Wind Dreamed. He's good at figuring people out. So, chances are, he's got you figured out. And if he's got you figured out and still wants to be open with you, then he has deemed you *worthy*." Her voice trembled with dramatic emphasis.

I smirked. "No wonder you want to be an actress."

A pillow flew up from the ground and connected with my shoulder. I laughed and caught it before it fell back on the floor.

"Now, give it back," Frida ordered.

I hugged the pillow to my chest. "Don't throw stuff unless

you don't want it back."

The air mattress squeaked as she got up. I sat up and waited until her padding footsteps reached the edge of the bed before I swung the pillow at her. She shrieked and grabbed for it. I laughed and yanked it away. Frida fell on my bed, and we wrestled, grabbing the pillows, and smacking each other with them until the door flew open.

"Frida!" We both sat up straight at the sound of Reve's voice. He stood in the doorway, silhouetted by the hallway light. His hair hadn't quite gotten to the same level of messiness that I was used to seeing in the mornings, but it wasn't exactly neat either. His sleeping shirt and pants hadn't acquired any wrinkles yet. "Knock it off. We're trying to sleep."

"She started it." Frida smacked me with my own pillow.

Annoyance simmered in a dense cloud around Reve as he stalked across the room, grabbed the pillow from Frida and hit her with it at just the right angle to make her fall off the bed. "I. Know. You. Started. This." He punctuated each word with a blow from the pillow.

Frida cowered on the floor with one arm thrown over her head. "No fair! I don't have a pillow! I'm defenseless."

"Go. To. Bed—" Reve cut off when I raised Frida's pillow and brought it down on his head.

He looked up slowly, his cloud of anger fizzling. I hit him again before he could react, making him stumble and fall onto the bed. It was chaos after that. The pillows flew, colliding with each other and our bodies. Somehow, Frida got ahold of another pillow and joined in.

A deep, throaty rumble came from Reve that I didn't recognize at first, but it was laughter. We were *all* laughing as we hit each other with the pillows and wrestled on my bed until Almos, Imena, and Lorien came to investigate.

"What is going on in here?" Imena called.

We all froze. "Hi." Frida grinned. "Don't mind us."

Almos leaned on the doorframe and grinned at Reve. "I thought you were coming over here to tell them to stop making so much noise. Not join in on the noisemaking."

"He got a little distracted," Frida replied.

Reve whirled and hit her with the pillow. She fell on top of me with a giggle.

Lorien crossed her arms. "I can't believe you guys were having a pillow fight and didn't invite me."

"It was a little unexpected," I said with a crooked grin.

Lorien huffed exaggeratedly. Imena smiled.

Almos tilted his head forward. "So, are you sleeping in here, Reve?"

Reve tossed his pillow at me, got up, and stalked out of the room without a word. The rest of us grinned at each other before Imena and Almos peeled off to go to their rooms. Lorien wandered in and sat at the foot of my bed. Before I could ask if she was actually upset about the pillow fight, she flopped against me and Frida.

"Cuddle pile," she declared.

Frida threw her arms around both of us. "Cuddle pile."

We stayed there for a minute before Lorien moved. "Ok, good night." She got up and trotted out of the room.

"Good night!" Frida called, waving.

"We should probably go to bed too." The dream realm was waiting and with it my only chance to contribute to the search for the kidnapper, no matter how long of a shot it might be.

Frida sighed. "I guess."

She heaved herself up and trudged over to her air mattress,

taking her pillow with her. At least I thought it was her pillow. It could have been mine. For someone who had struggled to get out of bed this morning, she sure was reluctant to go to sleep.

"Good night," I said as she settled down.

"Night, night. Don't let the ghosts bite," she twittered back.

I groaned and rolled away to face the wall as she laughed. I played with the string of bone beads around my neck. If a ghost bit me in the middle of the night, I had a feeling it would be too late to do anything about it.

23

Twenty-Three

The Wind Whisperer was waiting for me when I arrived in the dream realm. "Still want to try searching dreams for our criminal?"

"I have a question first."

The Wind Whisperer inclined its head. "I will do my best to answer it."

"Can you access the dreams of people who are Bone Touched?" All this talk of ghosts and having Keres show up had gotten me thinking. If Sylvan was physically unreachable, who was to say someone couldn't find her in her dreams?

The Wind Whisperer stiffened. The ribbons of color undulating through its body slowed. "The gods do not interfere with each other's children, Wren. And their children do not interfere with each other. Your magics do not work on one another." Its voice was the most serious I had ever heard it.

I lowered my gaze to the bottom of the dream orb. "Oh. Sorry."

The Wind Whisperer relaxed a bit. Its voice took on its

usual gentle tone. "Why do you ask?"

"I had a friend when I was at Mortorous Academy, the one I found out was Bone Touched. When I… visited this weekend, I heard she had been injured a few months ago, and no one had heard from her since."

"Ah." The colors started flowing through the Wind Whisperer at their normal pace. "You are concerned for her."

"Yeah. She was a really good friend, and no one knows anything about what happened to her." Nick hadn't known. Keres hadn't been any help. The Boneman had given vague hints but refused to tell me anything for certain.

"I understand, but I cannot help you. We gods made a pact a long time ago that we would never allow our magic to be used against our children. The Bone Touched cannot manipulate each other's bones the way they can with any other living or dead thing. The Wind Dreamed do not dream and therefore cannot enter each other's dreams. And the Time Bent…"

The Wind Whisperer paused. "I do not have much experience with the Time Bent, but Time does not usually openly threaten or attack any other demigods and neither do their children. The last thing any of us needs is a magical war. The Boneman would be overrun by the number of restless dead. The dream realm would be chaos. It would be terrible for everyone."

I frowned. "But I can sense the emotions of the other Wind Dreamed. Isn't that using my powers against them?"

"It is a passive power, so I allow it. However, you could not sense the emotions of a Bone Touched or Time Bent no matter how much you tried."

I hadn't sensed anything from Nick, but that could have been chalked up to my inability to use my powers. I thought back to the times I had been around Keres. I had never picked up on her emotions the way I had with the other Wind Dreamed or even regular students at school.

"So, you couldn't figure out if Sylvan is alive because you can't access her dreams?" I summarized.

The Wind Whisperer nodded. "Yes. The Boneman is her keeper now. I cannot reach her."

Of course. I had tried everything, and it still got me nowhere.

The Wind Whisperer bowed its head. "I am sorry. I realize how much you care for her."

I fought the feelings of uselessness. "It's ok. If you really can't do anything, then there's nothing else for me to do." I swept an arm at the array of dreams, trying to sweep away the disappointment and worry with it. "Where to tonight?"

I hoped it wasn't another mermaid dream. Moving in water was so hard without a tail, and I hadn't figured out how to manipulate my dream form to allow me to make one for myself. Maybe I could practice tonight if the dreams we visited were tame enough.

"Let us see." The Wind Whisperer took my hand and reached for the glowing orange thread of a dream.

* * *

The dreams were very strange, a hodgepodge of shifting settings and elements. So, once again it was hard to keep up with the dreamer through a giant building, around the first floor of a hotel.

And then the dream *reset*.

I was so confused when I blinked and suddenly, we were

back in the ballroom of the hotel, where we had been halfway through the dream.

"What…?" I trailed off as the dreamer started going through motions they had already gone through earlier in the dream.

"Dreams do this sometimes." The Wind Whisperer floated next to me. "They reset in order to replay what the dreamer has already dreamed. That usually means the they wants to relive their past when they need to keep moving forward."

"So, I should try to get them to go somewhere else?"

"Exactly. In a place like this, that can be as simple as closing one door and leaving another open."

Or maybe…

As the dreamer moved through the ballroom, I guided some of the dream characters in her direction. They swept her up with their momentum, and in seconds she joined them as they migrated out of the ballroom. The Wind Whisperer and I trailed them.

"This is a direction they have not gone before," mused the Wind Whisperer.

The group headed toward the bank of elevators. Abruptly, the dreamer broke off from everyone else with a hazy-edged man. They made their way to a service elevator with a metal gate that closed like a garage door instead of two horizontally sliding doors.

I started to get in with them, but the Wind Whisperer held me back. "Wait."

"We're going to lose them if we—" I stopped when I noticed the greying of the scene around us. "Oh."

"Precisely. The dream will end before they reach the top, and we would have been stuck in there with them. Let us go." It tugged me toward the front doors of the hotel, which opened into the dream sphere. "The endings of dreams can creep up on you like that. You have to be aware of more than just the dreamer."

I nodded. "Right." I'd been so focused on where the dream was going that I didn't notice it was ending. "What happens if we get stuck in a dream, and it turns into sleep paralysis?"

The Wind Whisperer laced its wispy fingers together in front of itself. "The dreamer would be able to see us or at least parts of us and maybe some elements of the dream they had until we figure out how get out of their head. There is usually only one way out of the waking mind, and it can be hard to find if you do not know where to look."

"Where do you look?" I couldn't help staring at the way the colors racing through the Wind Whisperer's fingers flowed over each other, maintaining their shape while creating a beautiful pattern. Maybe I could paint it sometime.

"Toward things that ground them in reality." The Wind Whisperer said it as if the answer was obvious. "Naturally, you will not always know what those things are, so it can take a few minutes to figure it out, but generally they will be things that matter a lot to the dreamer. Things they keep in their room or near their bed are your most likely suspects."

That wasn't very specific, but it was something.

"Hopefully, you will never get stuck in the mind of a dreamer like that. It is…disconcerting." The Wind Whisperer shook its head and dropped its arms to its sides. "Would you like to try another dream?"

"Unless you saw something that made you think that dreamer was the culprit." I raised my brows hopefully.

"Another dream it is."

Dang it.

24

Twenty-Four

Morning brought a low buzz of anxious energy. My mind kept darting to my plans to study with Rich this afternoon. It was stupid. We'd planned this days ago, and I hadn't been this anxious. But now that the day was here, I couldn't stop thinking about it.

It was too much to hope that the others wouldn't pick up on it. Even quietly moving around my room to get ready without bothering Frida didn't work.

She raised her head with a groan. "What's got you so tied up in knots? Dream walking not go so well?"

"It was fine." I had done another dream after the first one in the hotel, and that had gone perfectly well. "Just ready for today to start."

"You got a hot date or something?" she mumbled. "No amount of dream walking could give you that much energy." As if to prove her point, she buried her face in her pillow.

"There's just a lot to do today. I have a bunch of schoolwork to get done." It was the closest thing to the truth I could get without incurring her endless teasing. I'd never hear the end of it if she found out I was going out with a boy, even if it was only to do a school project. Just look at the way she poked fun at Reve for befriending me.

She grumbled something into her pillow that sounded unconvinced and pulled the blanket up over her head.

Frida wasn't the one I was most worried about though, especially when she was so sluggish in the mornings. I avoided the kitchen like the plague until Lorien came to get me for breakfast.

She tilted her head when she saw me. "Are you ok? You seem nervous."

"I'm fine, just got a lot on my mind." I hopped up from my chair in the living room where I'd been reading my book from book club. "Is breakfast ready?"

She nodded. "Yeah. I'd hurry if I were you. Reve seems especially impatient today."

I abandoned my book on my chair. "Do you think it was because of the pillow fight last night?"

She shrugged. "He doesn't really open up to me much, not when he's in this kind of mood anyway. Sometimes afterward, but not in the moment."

"Hm." Would his mood get better or worse once he saw me? Only one way to find out.

I managed to sit down at the table with the others while Reve was putting the finishing touches on a plate of crepes. The minute he turned around with it in his hands, his gaze found mine. I tried to smile, but his eyes just narrowed.

"Leave her alone, Reve," Frida ordered as she pushed through the swinging door. "Unless you're glaring at her because she hit you with a pillow last night. In which case, get over yourself. You were having fun too."

Reve turned his attention to Frida. "I am *not* glaring at her."

Frida plopped down in her chair. "You kinda were."

Reve snorted and practically tossed the crepes down on the table before slumping into his seat. Frida winked at me as everyone started eating. I smiled. She could be a real handful, but she came through when it counted.

We managed to make it all the way through breakfast without bringing up my mood again. But when I went to get my stuff out of my room, I picked up my bag and turned around to see Reve hovering in the doorway with his hands in the pockets of his pastel purple pants.

"Hi," I said tentatively as he stared at me with a deadpan expression.

Without a word, he grabbed my arms and pulled me into a hug.

"Oh. Ok." I hugged him back. "Now, I'm concerned. Are you alright? I thought you didn't like hugs."

"I like your hugs," he mumbled over the top of my head—curse my shortness.

I smiled into his shoulder. "Thanks, but if you ask me, Lorien gives the best hugs." Lorien had a way of hugging you that made you feel safe and loved like nothing else did. Maybe because she squeezed you a little bit during each one.

"Your opinion is incorrect."

I smirked. "Don't tell Lorien that. She might just hug you to prove you wrong."

He shuddered. "I would never."

I shifted on my feet. "Is there a reason for this or did you just want an impromptu hug?"

"You know the reason."

We were quiet for a moment. I appreciated this new kind

of acknowledgment. Reve had graduated from staring and interrogating to actually comforting. Or at least trying to.

My head rested against his shoulder. "Thanks, Reve."

"You're welcome, Wren."

We stood there for a moment until we heard someone coming out of the bathroom and down the hall.

Reve let go and simply said, "It's time for class."

"Right, let's go."

* * *

I was fidgety all day. My legs bounced under the desks. My fingers drummed against the wood. It was hard to focus on the lectures. I could sense the curiosity of the other Wind Dreamed as we sat together in classes and during lunch, but none of them pressed me about it until my pencil flew onto the floor because I lost my grip while drumming it against the desk.

Imena picked it up and handed it to me. "Does all of *this*"—she gestured at me—"have anything to do with the project you told me about yesterday?"

I gripped my pencil. "What makes you think that?"

She raised a dark brow at me.

I threw up my arms as far as I thought I could without drawing too much attention to myself, which wasn't very far at all. "Fine. Yes, it does."

Imena propped her chin on her fist. "Are you worried something is going to happen? I could go with you if you're not comfortable by yourself."

"It's not that." I chewed my lip. "I've never been the best at making friends, but he and I are kind of developing a friendship. So, I guess I'm worried he'll think I'm too weird or nerdy and not want to hang out with me anymore."

Imena reached across the space between our desks to put her hand over mine, stilling my restless fingers. I hadn't even realized I'd started tapping them on the desk. "If he can't see past your weirdness, it's because he wouldn't make a good friend in the first place. I hope that isn't the case, but if it is, you will *always* have us. That's the amazing thing about being Wind Dreamed. You're part of the family."

"I know, but I want to make friends, not just have them assigned to me." Imena's hand stiffened on mine. I grabbed it to reassure her. "You're right. All of you are great, but I need to know that I don't have to have some god pulling the strings to form meaningful relationships. Everyone else can go out and meet people and make friends, so I should be able to also."

Imena sighed. "While I see where you're coming from, don't feel like you have to do everything everyone else does. You don't have to prove anything to anyone, Wren."

"This is something I'm doing for *me*." I pressed a hand to my chest. "It's not about anyone else."

She nodded and pulled her hand back. "Ok, just don't mix up what you want with what everyone else wants. You'd be surprised how easily it can happen, chickpea."

I was still thinking about what Imena said when I walked into finance.

Rich smiled up at me from his desk. "Hey."

"Hi." I returned his smile as I took my seat.

"We're still on for after school, right?" he asked.

"Yeah. I can head to the library as soon as the bell rings."

He wrestled a folder out of his backpack. "Great. My

schedule is packed, so I was really hoping we didn't have to reschedule."

"Does that include the movie tomorrow night?" I wasn't sure what I wanted his answer to be. I didn't really want to have to try to explain it to the other Wind Dreamed, but I still wanted to go.

Rich whisked our latest packet of classwork out of the folder with more flair than necessary. Somehow the movement set me at ease. "Don't worry. That's still happening as long as you're free."

"I am." The Wind Dreamed would understand. They'd have to. This was part of being a teenager. I just wanted to live my life.

My last class was mostly a lecture, so I had to sit in silence and watch the clock for the next hour, waiting to be set free. I practically vaulted out of the door once the bell rang. Rich was waiting at the library doors. He gave a little wave and held the door open for me. I tried to calm my rapidly beating heart.

Walking through the library with Rich felt different than walking with the Wind Dreamed. The silence was loaded. I kept glancing at him, trying to decipher the emotions he might be feeling. All I could tell was that he was content, probably happy to be done with classes and moving on to something slightly less torturous.

We sat down at one of the couches that was next to an outlet, so Rich could charge his phone. I had no idea how he managed to run down his battery during the day. School kept us pretty busy. In a good way. We had to pay attention during lectures and work during free time. There was always lunch though. And maybe he hadn't charged his phone the night before.

I stopped that line of thought. Why did I care about his phone battery? It didn't matter. The only thing that mattered was this project. And making a good impression.

"How much have you gotten done already?" Rich asked.

I opened my laptop. "Just setting up a spreadsheet with the equations plugged in. I didn't make any big decisions or anything without you."

Rich scooted over to look at my work. "I wouldn't have minded that much if you did. I'm not sure where to start with this."

"Well, we should probably pick our companies we want to invest in and distribute our hypothetical money between them *before* looking at the last six months of their stock statistics."

Rich cocked his head to the side. "You don't want to have the most money at the end of the project?"

I shrugged. "I mean, that's not really the point of the project."

"I guess. It would be cool if we could brag about how much money we would have made though, right?"

"If it was real money that we could actually use, then maybe."

He grinned. "Always need more of that."

"I don't know. I think I'm good for now."

He raised an eyebrow. "You're all set for life then?"

I chewed my lip. "I'm not pressed for money."

He rolled his eyes. "That's what people who are rich say. And I should know. That's kind of my name." He chuckled at his own joke. "I guess paying for your ticket tomorrow isn't that big of a deal then."

"No, it is! I really appreciate it. My parents' money doesn't mean anything." This was why I hated telling people about my family's fortune. They always took it way too seriously.

He turned to his computer. "Well, nice to know the upper class can be humble."

I smiled but kept my focus on my computer. "I suppose, um. What companies should we do? There have to be at least five, right?"

"Yeah, I was thinking some pharmaceuticals. That's where all the money is, right? People are always getting sick."

We'd just talked about how the amount of money wasn't an issue, but… "Sure."

It got a lot quieter after that. The rest of our time together was spent concentrating on the project. An hour and a half later, Rich started packing up.

"Sorry I have to go before we're done. I'll finish up adding the totals later tonight though, and that will be it unless you want to put some extra decorations on the slideshow."

"Sounds good."

His voice softened as he turned to me. "If you still want to come to the movie tomorrow, we all meet outside the main building to carpool into town. It's pretty casual, so don't worry about wearing anything nice. It's just a thing with friends. I'd really love it if you joined us."

I stayed where I was, sunk deep in the couch. If I went, I might ruin it like I had by bringing up my financial situation. "Thanks, I'll have to see. Some other friends of mine might want to do something." Would it be worth bringing up to the Wind Dreamed?

He nodded as he stood. "That's cool. Hope to see you anyway. And thanks for working on the project with me. I know a lot of people these days just push it off on the person who's the smartest or most desperate for a good grade. So, I appreciate that you took the time to help instead of doing that."

I huffed a breath. "Yeah, I know. I'm usually the person people do that to."

His eyebrows rose. "Really? I thought that was just a me thing. Everyone here is so spoiled with these arts and crafts projects that when they get to a real classroom where they have to do real work, they just can't. But once they figure out that I know how to do this kind of thing..." He shrugged. "Part of me gets it, but if they're not willing to put in the work, then they don't deserve the grade."

I sat forward. "I could *not* have said it better myself. I mean, we have things we want to do with our time other than their portion of the work."

Rich shouldered his bag and shook his head at the floor. "Kids these days."

"Kids these days," I echoed with a smile.

"See you tomorrow. In class at the very least."

"See you."

I sat on the couch for a while after Rich was gone. After all this time in this strange environment full of strange people, it was nice to meet someone who understood me. The beginning of the study session might have been a bit rough, but we had saved it in the end. Going to that movie tomorrow sounded more and more enticing.

25

Twenty-Five

All was quiet when I returned to the Wind Dreamed penthouse. Faint dinner-making noises came from the kitchen, but no one was in the living room or the hall as I made my way to my room.

My luck ended there. Frida was camped out on her air mattress in the middle of the floor with a tablet laid in front of her, sketching with a stylus on some digital art app with one hand and playing with the green ends of her hair with the other. She was doing that foot kicking thing people did in movies while she lay on her stomach, but she rolled over and sat up as soon as I walked through the open door.

"So, how did your date go?" She batted her lashes at me. "Did you hold hands? Kiss? Lie down on one of the library couches and—"

I clapped my hands over my ears to drown out anything else she might say. "No! We didn't do any of that, because it wasn't a date! We were just at the library to work on a partner project. And how did you even know where I was?" Had Imena talked? She was the only one I told.

Frida pulled her tablet into her lap and kept drawing. "Your behavior this morning was more than enough to give you away. I've only ever seen that kind of nervousness and excitement from someone who's about to go out with their crush. I took a wild guess about the library since you're such a nerd."

I stormed across the room and tossed my bag on my desk. "Well, you were wrong. It wasn't a date, and I don't have a crush on him."

Frida looked up slowly with a malevolent grin. "Even if I couldn't read your emotions, you're still a terrible liar, Wren."

"I just wanted to make a good impression. That's all. Rich is the first person I've tried to be friends with since I got here who isn't Wind Dreamed."

Frida rolled her eyes. "And how boring is it to not be Wind Dreamed?"

I huffed and stalked out of the room to go see if Reve wanted any help with dinner. Keres had said we shouldn't be alone with the threat of ghosts looming so close, but honestly, I wouldn't mind if the ghosts ate Frida in between now and dinner.

To my surprise, when I walked into the kitchen, Keres sat in Imena's yellow chair at the kitchen table chopping vegetables with a speed and grace I'd only ever seen matched by Reve.

She looked up and said, without slowing her slicing, "Hey, Wren."

Behind her, Reve worked at the counter with his back to us, not turning around.

"Hi, um, shouldn't you watch what you're doing? Not that I think you don't know your way around a knife, but I imagine ghost hunting would be harder if you cut yourself." It would be quite unfortunate if the Bone Touched who was supposed to be hunting down the ghosts of murder victims that might come to kill all of us lost a finger during meal prep.

She smiled, still not looking at the carrots as her knife bit into them over and over centimeters from her fingertips. "Thanks for the concern, but it's made of bone. If I don't have control over it with my eyes, I can feel it with my powers. Even if moving it with my mind isn't my forte, my hands are completely safe."

"Oh, *cool*." For the millionth time, I was envious of the Bone Touched. I leaned on the back of my red painted chair across from where Keres sat. "How goes the search?"

She finished dicing the vegetables and sighed. "I have some news, but I think it's better to wait until we're all here to share it."

I nodded. "Understandable." Even though I wanted nothing more than to hear everything she'd learned over the last few days immediately.

She stood up and lifted the cutting board full of perfectly round slices. "How was school?"

I drifted after her as she made her way back to Reve. "Pretty good. I had to work on a partner project in the library, but we got most of it done."

Keres set the cutting board down a safe distance from where Reve was stirring a pot of dark brown liquid. "I always hated group projects, but I think that's how everyone feels."

"This one wasn't so bad, just tedious," I replied. My gaze strayed to Reve. "Hey, Reve."

He paused the stirring of his pot to take a long look at me. The kind that I'd come to recognize as him reading my emotions. Keres glanced between the two of us. While she couldn't read emotions, I had a feeling mine weren't that hard to figure out without Wind Dreamed magic.

"Do you need any help with dinner?" I asked in a desperate attempt to break the tension.

"Keres is helping," he answered in a flat voice.

"Actually, I should go clean this off." She picked up the knife from the cutting board, which now that I knew it was made of bone, seemed all that more threatening. "Bone will hold up pretty well, but it needs a lot of care. I usually use my knives on much more insubstantial things than vegetables. I'll see you two at dinner." She sauntered out of the kitchen like she had been meaning to the whole time instead of stepping out to give us a moment of privacy.

While I admired her tact and appreciated her thoughtfulness, without her there, nothing stood between me and Reve's judgement. He had gone back to stirring the pot.

I wrapped my hands tightly around each other. "Are you going to talk to me?"

"The vegetables need to be added to the broth," he said it without looking at me.

"I don't mean about that." But I washed my hands and started scooping up the tiny pieces of carrot, potato, and zucchini. "You're mad at me."

"No, I'm not."

I dumped a handful of veggies into the pot, flinching back when the hot water splashed up. "When someone is mad at you, they stop talking to and try to avoid you. That's exactly what you're doing."

He pressed his lips together. "I'm not mad at you," he said a bit softer.

I stepped close enough that his sleeve brushed my arm. He

stiffened a bit, but I continued. "Then what's going on? Is it Keres? Ever since I got here, you've been… weird about the Bone Touched, and it's gotten worse since one came to live with us. Don't get me wrong, I'm curious about them too, but you get really intense about it. Is something going on?"

One second, Reve was staring into the pot like it might answer for him. A second later, he wrapped me in a hug tight enough that my cheek pressed uncomfortably against his collarbone. I hugged him back and refused to let go until he did though. We both needed it.

"I think my older brother was taken by the Boneman," he said so softly I thought I might have misheard him.

My grip on him loosened. "What?"

"He got in a car accident a few years ago, right after I became Wind Dreamed. He was driving with a couple friends down the highway at night, and someone hit them hard. Both vehicles tumbled into a deep drainage area." His voice got even quieter. "There were no survivors."

"I'm so sorry," I whispered. "I can't imagine losing a sibling like that."

"No, that's the thing. His body wasn't in the wreckage. His phone was still there. That's how we knew where to find him since he hadn't come home that night. His blood was all over the passenger seat where he'd been sitting, but there was no body."

I frowned. "Maybe an animal got into the car and—"

"That's what the police said must have happened, but they didn't find any bones or anything within two miles of the wreck. And trust me, my parents paid for several private search parties to find his remains after the accident. It was like he'd just gotten up and walked away. Or been taken away."

I chewed my lower lip. "What makes you think the Boneman took him? Not that it doesn't sound possible that someone would, but why the Boneman?"

He sighed into my shoulder. "It was just a feeling. I developed my mental illnesses after the accident. As part of my healing journey, my therapist said I should visit the place where the accident happened. I wasn't very far into my training as a Wind Dreamed, but when I went, I felt something. It felt like a remnant of a feeling long since gone, but strong enough to remain, like an echo. It felt like fear. Like death was lurking nearby. I don't know how to explain it, but from everything I'd heard about the Boneman, it felt like him."

My cheek was starting to ache where it pressed into his collar. "So, you think the Boneman saved your brother's life?"

Reve's voice deepened and that angry feeling returned to the air. "No. If he had saved his life, we would have found him. I think the Boneman took him. Made him Bone Touched."

This reminded me of me and Sylvan. "Then you two could be demigods together."

His fingers dug into my back. "Except that the gods keep their children separated. I might never see him again. And Keres said the Boneman takes all of their memories when he turns them into demigods, so even if I found him, he wouldn't remember me." His voice broke on the last words.

No wonder he'd been so determined to learn about the Bone Touched. He just wanted his brother back. But if Keres spoke the truth, his brother wouldn't recognize him. That must have been why Reve left in the middle of dinner the first night Keres was here. I couldn't imagine holding out hope that a family member was still alive only to hear that if they were, they wouldn't remember me at all.

My fingers dug into Reve's back. "I'm so sorry."

He released me and turned back to the stove. "It's not your fault, and there's nothing you can do about it. There's nothing anyone can do about it."

I fished for something comforting to say, but I had nothing.

Reve glanced at me. "Don't worry about me, Wren. I'm fine."

I wasn't totally convinced, but he seemed to have calmed down. The others trickled in not long after that. Keres was last to reappear. That was probably a good thing. The minute she sat down with her bowl of noodle soup, everyone gave her their full attention.

"You said you had news," Almos said with enough gravity to weigh down the air itself.

Keres twirled her chopsticks around her bowl. "Yeah." She stuffed a bite of noodles in her mouth.

The room was deathly silent as she chewed. Only Frida was still eating—I shouldn't have expected anything less. The rest of us had pretty much forgotten about our food.

"I've searched the town as best I can without breaking into every single building and tearing them apart to look for clues." Keres focused on her bowl instead of us. "There's still nothing to indicate who might be committing these crimes. And worse, there's been two more abductions." She paused to eat. "Obviously, with no evidence neither I nor the police can link the disappearances to the same kidnapper, but that's the running theory."

"That's it?" Reve demanded. "You made it sound like you had made actual progress on this case."

Keres's rust-colored eyes locked on Reve. "The lack of any damning evidence points to one conclusion. The culprit is on school grounds."

The blood drained from my face. Someone's chopsticks clattered to the table, rolled off, and hit the floor. No one bothered looking to see whose they were or trying to pick them up. We were too focused on Keres, who was still eating.

"You're sure about this?" Imena's voice was hushed and quick.

"The school is the only place I haven't searched, having assumed—wrongfully perhaps—that everyone here is innocent." Keres shoveled more noodles in her mouth. I hadn't seen much of her since she came to stay with us, but when I did see her at mealtimes, she ate a bucketload. I assumed it had to do with how many calories she burned running around town. But now was absolutely not the time to keep us in suspense while she scarfed down her food.

"But it's been days since the disappearances," Reve cut in. "If the kidnapper has been on campus this whole time, wouldn't the ghosts of his victims have found us too?"

"That brings me to my second conclusion." Keres jabbed her chopsticks at Reve. "The victims are still alive and being held captive somewhere on school grounds."

"Who here would do that?" Lorien whispered so softly I barely heard her.

"Someone who is a part of the staff, most likely." Keres plucked up a chunk of potato. "They would be the ones most familiar with the campus, so they would know where to hide that many living captives."

Living. From what Keres was saying, we no longer had to fear being attacked by ghosts—which was nice because

I was already tired of waking up in the middle of the night with the bone necklace poking me—even rounded beads got uncomfortable. But if she was right and someone at Animos Prep had been behind this the whole time… I didn't want to think about one of my teachers or any of the other staff I'd met doing something like this.

She went on. "The problem with a school that is patronized by a god is that it has a lot of secrets. Sometimes secrets only the children of the god can find. Mortorous has many hidden places that no one but a Bone Touched has the ability to uncover. I would expect Animos is similar."

"So, you'll need our help," Almos concluded.

"Most likely. If you could contact the Wind Whisperer and ask it about any hidden places on or around campus, that would be a tremendous help. Otherwise, I might need one of you to come with me while I search the campus."

Both Almos and Imena turned to me.

Before they could say anything, Reve spoke up. "I'll go with you."

Keres raised her brows. "You sure? I can't promise you'll like what you see."

Reve held her gaze steadily. "I can handle it." Out of all of us, I believed Reve would be the most levelheaded should they encounter the captives.

"Wren should talk to the Wind Whisperer first," Imena asserted.

I reared back like I'd been struck. "Me?"

"It's still supervising you when you dream walk, right?"

"Yeah."

"So, you'll see it tonight. And you can ask it about any secret passages or stuff like that."

"Oh, yeah. I guess."

I would have rather gone exploring with Keres. It sounded like something the characters in *The Crimson Empress* would have done. I could finally make myself useful to both the Wind Dreamed and Keres. But my Wind Dreamed powers were still developing, so they probably didn't think I could do it. I was stuck being the emissary, hoping for good news instead of actively helping.

Keres was nodding at the other end of the table. "I'll take tonight to do an initial sweep of the campus while you consult your god. Then the real work can start in the morning. With any luck, it'll only take a couple days to find these poor people."

The others murmured their support. But I was still thinking about the whole thing when I sat at my desk after dinner, staring blankly at the homework I was supposed to be doing.

Everything that had happened to me since I woke up in the Wind Whisperer's field felt like it was plucked right out of a fantasy novel, like I might be the daring heroine who learned how to wield incredible magic and sword fight and defeated her enemies all while romancing an equally capable and extremely attractive man.

But none of it was turning out that way.

It took me forever to learn my magic, which wasn't that impressive when compared to what other demigods could do. The closest thing to a weapon I'd learned how to use were Reve's cooking knives. And now, I was being tasked with the most boring of jobs in this investigation into not only a serious set of crimes, but a potentially disastrous supernatural situation. Just because the kidnapper probably hadn't killed their victims yet didn't mean they wouldn't before Keres and Reve found and rescued them.

Wasn't it better to have as many people looking as possible? Shouldn't Keres have called for backup? Or shouldn't the Wind Whisperer have asked for more Bone Touched? Expecting a single Bone Touched to find a criminal and bring them to justice while protecting a bunch of helpless Wind Dreamed wasn't very realistic.

The Boneman should know better by now. He'd been around for who knew how many centuries, millennia, eons. The Wind Whisperer too.

I was so stuck in my head, I didn't realize Lorien had followed me back to my room after dinner until she cleared her throat. I jumped a little and turned to see her hovering in the doorway.

I cleared my throat. "Oh, hey."

"Hey." Lorien took a few steps in and closed the door behind her.

I raised my eyebrows. "What's going on? Is something wrong."

She took a deep breath and gripped her elbows. "Listen, I know you want to go with Reve and Keres to find the kidnapper. I know you don't think you'll be in danger because you'll have them with you, but it's more serious than you know."

My brow creased. "If you're here to make sure I don't follow them and get myself in trouble, I'm not *that* stupid."

Lorien shook her head and stepped forward until we were only a few feet apart. "Remember when I told you this isn't the first time I've been caught up in a Bone Touched hunt?"

I crossed my arms. "Yeah."

"The last time it happened was when my parents were still alive. I was five years old. Old enough to remember, but not old enough to grasp the gravity of the situation. I didn't know it at the time, but my parents were both Wind Dreamed."

My mouth dropped open. "That's why you're Wind Dreamed?" I hadn't considered the possibility before, but it made sense that magic would be hereditary once it was so deeply ingrained in you.

"Partially. If a Wind Dreamed has a child, the Wind Whisperer will usually make that child a demigod too. But that's not the point I'm trying to make."

"Sorry, keep going." I waved for her to continue.

"My family lived in a nice neighborhood with friendly neighbors and amenities and everything you could want. At least outwardly. One of our neighbors had taken up the horrendous hobby of serial murder."

This sounded almost exactly like what had brought Keres here in the first place.

"He would bury the bodies in the park that was behind the neighborhood. People who aren't Bone Touched can't see ghosts, but they can still be attacked by them. And in a public park, it happened a lot. Some were just shaken up, some had serious injuries, and some died. The ghosts kept piling up, so the Boneman sent one of his demigods to put a stop to it. He came by to warn us but said he didn't think we were in danger since the ghosts stayed in the park."

Lorien paused a took a deep breath as if fortifying herself for what came next. "The Bone Touched got to work, but when the ghosts realized they were being hunted, they fled the park. We thought we were far enough away that they wouldn't find us, but one night they got into our house."

I put a hand over my mouth. "Oh, Lorien."

"I was oblivious to the whole thing. The ghosts came, drained my parents of their magic, and left without touching me. I found them in the morning."

A tear slipped out of her eye. I reached to hug her, but she held up a hand and took a step back. "The Bone Touched came with the police, but it was a different person than the one who warned us. She told me that the ghosts had gotten her partner, the man we spoke to, and that his magic emboldened them to leave the park. She apologized so many times and held me when we both started crying."

Lorien's voice wobbled. She didn't push me away when I tried to hug her again. She just clung to me as tightly as I clung to her.

"I know it was a different set of circumstances, and we think all the missing people are still alive somewhere, but that doesn't mean this is any less dangerous. We Wind Dreamed aren't supposed to fight threats like this. We're supposed to whisper in people's subconsciouses, not battle ghosts and criminals. I don't like that Keres might take Reve out hunting with her, but that's not my decision. I know I can't make you stop wanting to help them, but you have to know that this is bigger than us, and I don't know what I would do if I lost any of you."

I swallowed hard. "You won't. None of us are going anywhere."

26

Twenty-Six

"You seem upset." The Wind Whisperer's voice came to me before the image of the dream orb came into focus.

No kidding. It had been a day for bad news and heavy stories. I ran my fingers through my hair. "Keres made some progress on her investigation."

The Wind Whisperer clasped its insubstantial hands together. "Does that not warrant celebration?"

"Not if she thinks someone on campus has been behind the disappearances this whole time."

The wisps of color and wind flowing through the Wind Whisperer's body stopped moving for a moment before resuming their flow. Its voice hushed. "She thinks such a thing is possible?"

"She thinks it's *probable*." I folded myself into a ball. "She wants me to ask you if there are any hidden places on campus where the victims might be kept."

The Wind Whisperer put a contemplative hand to what would have been its chin. "Well, there are the crystal caves under the lake half a mile east of the school, but they are not technically part of the campus. And the secret art hall beneath the library. Then, of course, there is the animal sanctuary a bit north and the places other Wind Dreamed have dubbed the 'dream rooms' that are all over the place in the walls and under staircases. Though it would take me some time to remember where all of them are. The Wind Dreamed like to make new ones every so often, and they do not always tell me their locations."

That was already a lot more than I had expected. Keres had been right. After generations of Wind Dreamed had passed through Animos Prep, it had more secrets than a mystery novel.

And Reve was going to get to explore them without me.

"Which one of those do you think would be best to hold four kidnapped people?" I asked. "Which one should Keres search first, I mean?"

"The crystal caves would be remote enough that someone would probably feel comfortable keeping their prisoners there. And close enough for relatively easy access." Made sense. A set of caves sounded like the perfect place for holding captives. Many of the books I'd read would agree.

"How do you get into the caves?"

"There is a hole in the ground mostly concealed by tall grasses and bushes right next to a tree with a squiggly trunk."

I narrowed my eyes. "A squiggly trunk?"

"It grew a little strange, so the trunk looks like a child tried to draw a snake's body." The Wind Whisperer twined its hand in a serpentine motion up and down. "Very wavy."

"Huh."

"Yes. It is on the south side of the lake. I fear that is the best instruction I can give without being able to lead you there myself."

"I'm sure they can find it." It wouldn't surprise me if Reve had a GPS built into his brain. The boy was good at just about everything else.

"They surely will. I have the utmost faith in the Boneman and his children." The Wind Whisperer clapped its hands together. "Now, if you are done with your questions, we should attend to the matter at hand. I have picked out a handful of dreamers—"

"We can narrow the search down to people at the school." I might not be allowed to go exploring with Keres and Reve, but I was still going to do what I could to help the case. If I could find the culprit tonight, there would be no need for the two of them to risk their lives running around in some underground cave, chasing a kidnapper. We could just apprehend the criminal and make them tell us exactly where they were keeping everyone.

"There is a much higher chance you will know the dreamers if we do students and staff," the Wind Whisperer warned.

"I'll let you know if I recognize them."

It eyed me for a moment then sighed. "Alright. I think I have someone for you."

* * *

Relaying everything to Keres and Reve the next morning felt like pulling teeth. Putting aside the whole "searching for kidnapping victims" thing, I really wanted to visit a place called the crystal caves. If magic could be found, it would be in a place like that.

My brain buzzed so loudly with thoughts about the kidnapper that morning that I drifted through my classes in a daze.

"Ready for tonight?" Rich asked when I sat down in finance.

I'd completely forgotten about the movie with the new development in the kidnapping case. "You guys won?" That had been their stipulation for going out to celebrate.

"We just barely pulled through at the end, but yeah. We won." His smile was infectious.

"Congratulations."

"Thanks. So, the plan is to meet at five outside the front office. We'll carpool into town and get dinner before heading to the theater. They've got this awesome new movie playing called *Soul Saver*. It's this action movie with lots of fights and a heist and a bunch of other cool stuff."

I smiled back at him. "I'll be there."

"Great. Can't wait." He turned to face forward as the teacher assigned the order in which we were supposed to present.

"You finished the calculations, right?" I asked. I'd been so distracted by Keres's theories and my desire to explore all the hidden places the Wind Whisperer told me about that I'd forgotten to check the slideshow. That wasn't like me. I needed to get my head in the game.

"Of course. Don't worry," Rich assured me. "I would never leave you hanging like that."

I smiled down at my desk.

Our presentation was flawless. Rich really had come through. I would even venture to say our presentation was the best in the whole class. We were definitely getting full marks.

"See you in a bit," Rich called as he darted off the second the bell rang at the end of class.

* * *

"I want to go with you," I told Reve while we sat at lunch. I may have had plans with Rich, but if I could choose, I would absolutely prefer to hunt with Keres and Reve.

Lorien had shown up only long enough to tell us she was going to the library to look for a book on lampworking—a form a glassblowing that used a sort of blowtorch instead of a whole furnace to make small objects—for one of her classes. Then she whisked herself out the door, leaving us by ourselves.

"No," Reve declared as he lifted a forkful of ravioli to his mouth.

"What do you mean no?" I demanded.

"Keres only needs one of us to go with her, and I'm the best at sensing emotions, so I'll be able to handle the victims and/or the kidnapper better when we find them."

I knew that already. "In case you hadn't noticed, I'm a lot better with people than you."

"I don't have to be good with people. Keres can handle that part. I just have to tell her if the criminal is going to be reasonable or try to attack us. She'll do the rest."

I leaned forward. "I want to help, Reve."

"It's dangerous, Wren."

I threw my hands up. "I know that!"

Reve's eyes darted to the people around us. If they took notice of my outburst, it wasn't for long.

I lowered my voice anyway. "I'm tired of being the useless

new girl. I want to get out there and do some good in the world."

"You want to prove your capable by running into danger?"

I waved my fork around. "Isn't that what always happens? The main character rushes in to save her friends. She might get a little bloody and bruised, but everything turns out ok in the end."

"You're assuming *you* are the main character in this hypothetical story. What if you're not? What if it's me or Keres?"

I rolled my eyes. "You know what I mean."

He scooped up another ravioli. "I do, and I think comparing real life to the events of a fantasy novel is foolish. We don't have plot armor. We aren't the exceptions. We have to live and die by the rules of this world, and there's nothing we can do to change them."

I poked at my food. "I know that, but we're living in a fantasy novel right now. We have magic, maybe not the most useful kind in this scenario, but still magic. The rules have already changed."

Reve set his fork down and splayed his hands on the table. "You've only been Wind Dreamed for a couple weeks, Wren. It took you half of that time to figure out how to dream walk. You're only just starting to interpret other people's emotions. And now you want to run off into the unknown to fight bad guys? Doesn't the hero in books usually go through months or even years of training before they try to tackle evil?"

I propped my cheek on my fist and grumbled. "Not always. Sometimes they just get thrown into things without being ready for it."

"That's different from recklessly *throwing yourself* into it before you're ready. That's the kind of thing that gets the main character in trouble at the beginning and makes them spend the rest of the story trying to right their wrongs."

He was good. Too good.

"I still want to go."

"No. It might not seem like it, but I care about you too much to let you do that."

I stabbed my ravioli with a vengeance even as a smile tugged itself across my face. "Killjoy."

He smirked and went back to his own food.

* * *

It didn't matter that Reve forbade me from going to the crystal caves with him and Keres. I had my own plans.

I usually took more time walking back to the penthouse to take in the scenery. The flowers on the bushes and trees had started falling already, creating a speckled carpet of blossoms across the walkways. But today, I rushed through them, leaving a whirlwind of petals in my wake.

There was only about an hour between the end of school and the time I had to meet up with Rich. That meant less than an hour to get ready for this big night before I had to be at the front office.

I tried to tell myself that was plenty of time, but I should probably do something different with my hair than its usual braid, maybe put on some makeup. If only I had the courage to wear contacts. I was willing to bet the kind of girls these boys hung out with didn't look like me if they could help it.

I spent too much time sifting through the contents of my closet, picking out something that I thought would fit the occasion—I settled on white cutoff shorts and a blue off-the-shoulder top that hugged my body. And spent even more time trying to get my eyeliner right. None of what I did looked the way I wanted it to.

I had finally gotten everything as close to perfect as I could make it when a knock sounded at my bedroom door. Expecting Frida, I opened it, ready to tell her to leave me alone.

Instead, Almos looked me up and down. "Got a hot date?"

"No, I'm just going out with friends." I wished it had been Frida. I could handle her teasing. Almos's quiet judgement on the other hand…

"When will you be back?"

"I'm not sure. Probably later, why?"

He chewed his lip. "Just wondering if I should tell Reve not to set a place for you at the table once he gets back with Keres."

"Tell him not to bother. I'm eating out tonight." He would be suspicious, but I could navigate those waters once I sailed into them. "I'll see you guys later." I grabbed my car keys and headed past him.

He put a hand on my shoulder to stop me. "Real quick, have you seen Lorien? She asked for my help on a project and she's usually back by now. But she's not in the penthouse and isn't answering her phone."

"She said something about going to the library to get a book during lunch. She might be there." The library was big enough and full of enough books on the arts that Lorien might not have found what she was looking for before she had to go to her next class. I didn't have any classes with her after lunch, so I hadn't seen her since then.

He nodded. "You're probably right. She might even be out

in the meditation field early. She's had a stressful week."

I frowned. I'd noticed her mood before and she told me about her parents, but she'd seemed to be acting more like herself lately. "Is she ok?" Was she stressing out about the ghosts again?

Almos nodded. "It's just some drama with a boy who can't take no or 'I'm not into boys' for an answer. I'm sure she'll be fine. She has some pretty healthy coping mechanisms as far as teenagers go. Just being there for her is the best we can do at this point."

"Yeah, of course." I stuck my hands in my pockets.

"Well, have fun." Almos released my shoulder and walked a little farther down the hall to Imena's room.

Poor Lorien. After everything she'd been through already, she didn't deserve the stresses of teenage life. She could probably use a night out as much as I could.

I checked the time on my phone and bolted for the elevator. Frida came out of the kitchen as I stepped inside.

"Where are you going?" she called.

"Hanging out with friends. Don't wait up."

She gave me a strange look as the doors closed between us but didn't make any of her usual comments, which I thanked the universe for. I didn't have time to deal with her. If I didn't hurry, I was going to be late, and that would make a horrible impression on everyone.

A remarkably small group lounged on the front steps of the main building when I burst out of the door. I wasn't that familiar with sports, but I was pretty sure an average baseball team consisted of more than five players. None of which were Rich.

I checked my phone again. I was barely on time. Where

was everyone?

"You here for the party?" one of the girls asked when she saw me looking around.

"I guess." I gave her a wobbly smile.

"Are you Rich's plus-one?" the boy next to her asked.

"Yeah." A weight lifted off my shoulders. They knew who I was. Rich had talked about me.

The boy gave me an appraising look. "I thought you were a little nervous-looking. He brings a new girl to these things every time. He's a great guy, but the man needs to learn how to commit."

I swallowed. "Maybe he just hasn't found the right person yet."

"If you ask me, he's found a lot of right people, but that's none of *my* business," called another boy.

"Are you trash-talking me when I'm not even here to defend myself?"

I turned and breathed a sigh of relief as Rich and a handful of other guys pushed through the doors to join us.

"Nah," the first boy said, grinning. "Just giving a feel for you and your habits."

Rich rolled his eyes as he stopped beside me. "Don't listen to anything Jacob says. He likes to lie to cause trouble."

Jacob rolled his eyes. "You're no fun."

Rich shoved him out of his way with a grin and gestured for me to follow as he said, "And you wonder why none of the girls in school were interested in dating you after our first year."

I gladly left the others behind to trail after Rich. "Does he really lie that much?" I didn't want to think of Rich as a player, but...

Rich leaned in so the others, who had started to follow, wouldn't hear. "All the time. He's just trying to get a rise out of everyone. He still has to learn that isn't something people like, but between you and me, I don't think he's ever going to learn. He's almost an adult already. You know, the older you get, the harder it is to change how you think and act."

I did know. At Mortorous Academy, there were plenty of people too set in their ways. I thought of my conversation with Nick when I'd run off to visit Mortorous. My fists clenched. If only there were a way to prove who had hurt Sylvan, they would *have* to atone for their crimes and maybe learn a thing or two.

I made sure to get a ride in Rich's car. Jacob, another boy named Yoshua, and his girlfriend, Ursula, hopped in the back seat. The other four kept up a steady stream of conversation, but I sat quietly, listening, trying to figure out the dynamics of the group.

As far as I could tell, there was no order to them, not the way the Wind Dreamed operated. They were like a jar full of marbles that someone poured down the stairs, racing toward the same place, but they bounced off every conversation topic and rocketed in different directions.

They asked me a few questions when the conversation lulled, but otherwise, they were perfectly happy chattering amongst themselves. I supposed it was nice to not be under scrutiny. Sometimes the attention I got from the Wind Dreamed was a little much.

We arrived at a restaurant where we had to wait for half an hour for a table big enough to fit all eighteen of us. The staff had to join a bunch of tables so we could sit together.

Once we sat down, the roar of conversation was overwhelming. I had no idea how people could hear each other. Rich kept up with almost everyone on our half of the table, while I watched and listened as best I could.

He finally noticed me when we were halfway through our meal. "You've been pretty quiet. Are you alright?"

I tried to muster up a smile. "I'm fine. It's just kind of loud in here."

"Yeah, that'll happen when you're with like twenty other people. But you're having fun, right? That was the goal of all of this, so if you're not enjoying yourself—"

"No, this is nice. I'm just trying to get a feel for everything. I don't usually hang out with this many people at the same time." It was hard to know when to join a conversation and when to sit it out and just listen. It didn't help that these weren't the kind of people I usually hung out with either.

"Ok, well, if you get overwhelmed, we can step outside for a while. It should be better in the movie. There won't be nearly this much talking. Don't want to get kicked out again."

My eyebrows rose. "Again?"

"It was Jacob's fault, but most of us got kicked out too since we were with him. After that, we learned to sit in smaller groups separated by other people, so we're harder to lump together in case *one of us decides to start throwing popcorn at someone else.*" He raised his voice and looked directly at Jacob.

Jacob threw up his hands with a look of surprised innocence plastered across his face. "How was I supposed to know someone else would care about us throwing stuff at each other? It's not like they were caught in the crossfire."

"You made a mess all over the theatre. Of course they were going to get upset. Especially when you stood up to throw it," Ursula interjected. "You were being very distracting, and

I for one am glad you got thrown out."

"Says the person who was making out with her boyfriend in the back row and not paying attention to the movie at all," Jacob accused.

She crossed her arms. "At least it was quiet and didn't disturb anyone else."

They continued to snipe at each other, but their banter reminded me so much of Reve and Frida that I couldn't help my smile. Maybe this group wasn't so different from the Wind Dreamed after all. It was just bigger and consequently louder. That happened when you added more people to a group.

Unless they were people like me who didn't know how to act in big groups.

I wanted to bang my head against the table. *Just say something.*

I never got my opening. We finished our meals, paid, and left. In the car, I still had no idea how to interact with these people beyond answering questions that were specifically directed at me. They just talked so fast. One had barely finished their sentence before another started talking. Sometimes they talked over one another until someone backed down.

I could barely keep up with them, so it was a relief when we arrived at the theatre. I let everyone else debate what to watch. I enjoyed most movie genres. Any kind of story was worth investing time in. Unless it sucked, but this didn't look like the kind of theatre that showed those movies.

Rich managed to convince everyone to go to *Soul Saver* even though there was barely enough room for all of us. Some people had to sit by themselves between clusters of strangers.

Rich and I managed to get seats next to each other though. At least there was that.

The movie provided a much-needed reprieve from the tension of not having contributed to any conversations. I lost myself between the dialogue and the action sequences. This was what I loved. It was a science fiction heist story, so it was easy to get absorbed in. But the plotlines were a little shallow. Clearly, the filmmakers were relying on the fight scenes to hold the audience's attention.

It was completely dark outside when the movie ended. The bright lights of the theater signs cast crazy shadows across the ground as we poured out the door. The boys laughed at each other as they took turns mimicking the different characters from the movie. The girls clustered together and chatted amongst themselves.

I hovered near the door, unsure what I was supposed to do.

"You didn't have fun, did you?" Rich asked as he leaned against the wall next to me.

I wrung my hands. "Sorry you wasted money on my ticket. I'm just useless in big groups."

"Hey." He nudged me with his shoulder. "It wasn't a waste. And it's not your fault. I should have known putting you into a big group of strangers might throw you off. Next time we can do something with just the two of us."

I looked up sharply. "Next time?"

"If you want there to be a next time." He turned to face me, his shoulder leaning into the wall. "This may not be your crowd, but I like spending time with you. We have more in common than first appearances suggest."

Warm bubbles fizzed in my stomach. "I like spending time with you too, Rich."

He straightened. "It's settled then. Next time, it's just you and me."

I didn't stop smiling the whole way back to campus. Or as I walked to the dormitory and took the elevator up to the penthouse.

I didn't expect anyone to be in the living room. The other Wind Dreamed should have all been in bed or at least heading there by now. But when the elevator doors opened, Almos, Imena, Reve, and Frida were huddled together on Frida's green loveseat. They all looked up, startling a little like I'd scared them.

Imena leapt from the couch and ran to me. I had barely enough time to register her puffy red eyes and runny nose before she collided with me so hard we both staggered back against the elevator wall.

"Thank the Wind Whisperer you're alright," she sobbed into my shoulder.

I hugged her back. "Not that I don't appreciate this, but what do you mean? Of course I'm alright." I'd just gone out with some friends. I'd told Almos where I was going. More or less. This seemed like a bit of an overreaction.

"Let her get inside, Imena." Almos approached and put one hand on Imena's shoulder while he held the elevator doors open with the other.

She held onto me a second longer before letting go. We all stepped out of the elevator.

Reve hovered by the wall. "You weren't answering your phone." His voice lacked a level of accusation or suspicion. He just sounded tired and relieved.

"I was out with friends at a movie." I dug my phone out of my pocket and turned it on. A dozen notifications of missed calls and text messages from all four of them popped up on my screen.

For the first time, I registered the atmosphere in the room. Each of them carried it differently. Frida was a quiet ball of anxious energy. Reve seethed with silent anger, determination, and… guilt? Almos was a grim wall of dread. And Imena…

"What's going on?" I croaked as I took in the jagged sorrow surrounding her.

Tears welled in Imena's eyes. She tried to speak, but only strangled sobs came out.

Almos tucked her into a hug but turned his head to speak to me. "Lorien has been taken."

Twenty-Seven

"Taken? By who?"

I knew the answer, but I prayed for something else. Maybe the Wind Whisperer needed her for something, maybe some government agency had to talk to her since they had legal custody of her until she became an adult, someone, anyone other than—

"The same person who's been taking people all week," Reve growled.

"She didn't come back after school," Frida whispered. "She hasn't answered her phone, and no one can find her anywhere on campus."

My heart beat frantically in my chest. "Did someone tell admin?"

"Yes, they scoured the whole school. They're conducting a search of the surrounding area first thing tomorrow morning," Reve scoffed. "I've never seen them mobilize faster than when one of their precious Wind Dreamed is missing."

"What can we do?" I glanced around. "Where is Keres?"

"Out hunting," Almos replied as he led a shaking Imena

back to the loveseat. It seemed to swallow her as she curled into a ball on her side. Almos sat with her but turned around to speak with the rest of us. "She left as soon as I raised concerns about how long Lorien was taking to get back from school."

"Shouldn't we go look too?" The anxious energy of the room had infected me. How could we be sitting here doing nothing when Lorien could be getting farther and farther away from us?

Frida answered softly, "Keres told us to stay here—"

"Screw what Keres says! Lorien is our friend. We should be doing everything in our power to find her, right? *Come on, guys.*" Who knew how much time they had already wasted here? If I had known Lorien was missing, I would have demanded Rich take me back to school, so I could start looking immediately.

"Do you have any idea where to start?" Reve asked.

"We retrace her steps, right? There has to be some clue about where she went or who took her. We know for sure that it was someone on campus now. If nothing else, we can start breaking down doors and interrogating people."

"We can't do that, Wren," Reve replied in a maddeningly level voice.

I threw up my hands. "Then what *can* we do, smart guy? Cause I'll tell you what we *can't* do. We *can't* stand around doing nothing while her trail gets colder and colder. At least, *I* can't."

"Keres knows what she's doing, Wren. We have to trust her," Almos said from the couch.

I whirled on him. "We trusted her to keep us safe before and look what happened! Lorien is—" My voice broke. I inhaled deeply, my body trembling.

Frida was hugging me before I could calm myself down. "We all want to find her, Wren."

"Then we should go find her." My voice wobbled as the tears started coming. "All this time—All this wasted time..."

Reve gently pushed Frida aside and took her place hugging me. I gripped him tightly.

"I should have been here. I should have known." I wasn't sure how much he could hear around the tears that choked my voice.

He rubbed my back. "It's not your fault, Wren. No one could have seen this coming."

I didn't want to believe him. I hadn't even enjoyed going out all that much. I should have been here with everyone when they figured it out. I should have gone with Keres or comforted Imena or *something*.

Useless. I was so useless.

* * *

The five of us migrated to Reve's sectional, which had the most space, and tucked into a pile. At some point we fell asleep all jumbled together.

I was ready for the Wind Whisperer in the tangled dream orb.

"Where is she?" I demanded the moment it emerged from that wall of color. "You have to know where Lorien is." I frowned. "And why are you so small?"

The Wind Whisperer hadn't fully coalesced before the words were out of my mouth, but the wispy, humanoid shape of the god of life was no bigger than a toddler.

"I am trying to find her." Even its voice sounded high and childish. "I have split myself between the sleeping and waking worlds. It is… strenuous."

"How can you not know where she is?" I cried. "Isn't she asleep? Can't you go talk to her?"

"In order to enter the dream realm, a Wind Dreamed has to be deeply asleep. If Lorien is unable to sleep properly, I am not able to reach her." The Wind Whisperer's voice quivered. "I have never… I am doing everything I can to find her. I swear."

This was the first time I'd seen a crack in the Wind Whisperer's calm demeanor. I could yell at it, break down in tears in front of it, and it stayed strong. But this broke it. This made it tear itself in two, so it could go looking for its lost child.

"Please," I whispered. "Tell me there's something I can do to help."

The tiny Wind Whisperer put its hands to its face. "I do not know. I am searching every waking and sleeping mind in the city for a clue as to where she might be. Just… You have to dream walk. I cannot stay long in any one dream, so you will have to go on your own."

My hands fisted at my sides. "I want to stick to the people on campus still. Keres has to be right. It has to be one of them doing all of this."

The Wind Whisperer grabbed two of my fingers—its little hand couldn't hold much more—and pulled me over to the wall. "This one. And if you finish and want to keep going, try this one." It indicated a red thread and a purple thread very close to one another.

I nodded. I hadn't tried finding dreams on my own yet, but

I would certainly try. "Go find Lorien."

The Wind Whisperer didn't waste time saying goodbye to me before it whizzed to another dream and disappeared inside of it.

* * *

I darted from dream to dream, impatient to the point of rushing through them. I finished the two the Wind Whisperer had indicated and moved on to a third, doing my best to feel out the location of each colorful thread before I touched them. I wasn't sure if the boy whose dream I entered was a student, but I hoped so. Once I was done with his, I moved on to another, and another.

I was only pulled from the whirlwind of sleeping subconsciouses when the elevator dinged at Keres's return. Imena jumped up, throwing Frida halfway onto Almos. But when a very tired-looking Keres walked out and shook her head, Imena's sobs returned.

"I'm so sorry." Keres's voice was no more than a hoarse whisper. The look she gave us broke our hearts all over again. "I couldn't find anything. It's like they vanished."

My head fell back against the cushion. So much for the mighty Bone Touched and their powerful magic. They had failed Lorien again. Keres hadn't been any more help than any of the rest of us. She hadn't been able to stop the kidnappings, find the culprit, or keep us safe. What was the point of being the child of a god if you couldn't do anything to protect or help anyone?

Reve heaved himself up from the couch and shuffled into the kitchen as Imena returned to our cuddle pile on his couch.

Keres mumbled more apologies and something about trying to get some sleep before she disappeared down the bedroom hall. Reve returned a few minutes later with a large, steaming Tupperware container of breakfast leftovers from yesterday and a handful of forks. We scooted into some semblance of order so we could eat.

"What now?" Frida asked, voice rough from sleep.

"We keep going, I guess," Almos replied tiredly. "We help Keres when she needs it, and we hope for the best. The admin are invested now. The police have been involved the whole time, but a kid going missing from the school is bound to motivate them to look harder. Eventually, someone will find something."

Eventually.

What a terrible answer. It didn't promise anything like "soon" did. It didn't carry the same lightness as "hopefully." All it promised was that something would happen at some point in time. In days, weeks, years, someone would find something.

Would the hostages be alive by the time they *eventually* found their "something"?

I doubted it. If we relied on "eventually," all hope was lost.

28

Twenty-Eight

We spent the weekend in the living room huddled together on one couch or another. We shifted around to work on school projects and play board games, trying to keep each other engaged. Everyone was quiet even when we tried to make conversation. It always petered out and fell into silence again.

Keres was taking it hard too. We barely saw her all weekend. She left to search for Lorien early in the morning when it was still dark and the rest of us were asleep, was gone until midnight, came back to get a few hours of rest, then went and did it all over again. It couldn't be healthy. She wasn't there for meals anymore. I would just go to the fridge, and a significant portion of the leftovers would be gone.

She looked horrible too. Gone were the energy and confidence, the straight back and gleam in her eye, replaced by slumped shoulders and dark circles. The only thing that seemed to keep her going was grim resolve.

But she continued to find nothing. Racing through dreams didn't yield any results. The police search of the land surrounding Animos Prep didn't find anything either. It was nothing after nothing after nothing.

I was so tired of waiting, so tired of not doing anything.

Monday morning, we went our separate ways to class. Minus one.

Sitting down in history class felt wrong without Lorien next to me. So did every other class that I usually shared with her.

* * *

"Is something wrong?" Rich asked when he walked into class and saw me sitting at my desk.

I sighed. "It was a long weekend." I really didn't feel like explaining the whole situation to him right now. Or ever. He was the part of my life that was separate from all the Wind Dreamed stuff. He was my distraction. He didn't need to be bogged down with all my problems. If I couldn't do anything, he certainly couldn't.

He sat down, brows furrowed. "Sorry about that. Did it have anything to do with the movie disaster?"

"No, of course not. And it wasn't a disaster. This is all…" I waved my hand, trying to find the right words. "It's something else. I'd rather not talk about it."

"Ok." He laced his fingers on the desk. "Well, it's clearly bothering you. What do you usually do to cheer yourself up when you're upset?"

"I lock myself in my room and read until it feels like my eyes are about to pop out of my head." I'd done a lot of that over the weekend. Even drowning myself in fantasy worlds hadn't completely numbed the despair.

He laughed loud enough that a few people in the room turned to look at us. "You like to read that much?"

I wished I could stuff the words back in my mouth. Of course he would laugh about my reading habits. That was why I'd avoided telling him about them in the first place.

Rich regained control of himself. "I'm sorry. I'm not laughing at you. It was just funny how bluntly you said it. I've heard there's a book club here. Are you part of it?"

"Yeah. They meet tomorrow." I had almost forgotten about book club after the chaos of the last few days.

"What if we went together?"

My heart stuttered in my chest. "Are you sure? They meet before school, and I know you don't like getting up early."

Rich shrugged. "I'm not that into reading, but if it would make you feel better, I can make an exception. Where does book club meet?"

"In one of the library meeting rooms an hour before classes start. They have food and stuff, so you don't have to worry about trying to cram breakfast in before going."

"Great. I'll see you then."

"See you then." If I couldn't go out and look for Lorien, I could at least try to keep myself from going stir-crazy.

* * *

The happiness of having Rich with me at book club faded when I sat down at lunch. Lorien's empty spot felt even more empty knowing what had happened to her.

Reve and I picked at our food. He'd been going out to help Keres during the daylight hours in the hope that his heightened perception could pick up Lorien's distress or the malicious thoughts of the kidnapper. Wind Dreamed could sense each other better than they could sense normal people, and Reve was the best we had. But even he hadn't found her.

His guilt clung to him as much as his determination did.

"Where have you looked?" I asked.

"The caves mostly." He picked a pepperoni off his pizza and folded it in half. "They're big. Really big. Keres thinks we've covered enough ground in them though. We're going to try searching the school grounds soon."

"You think someone could hide that many people here without getting noticed?"

He shrugged and folded his pepperoni even smaller. "I'm willing to try anything at this point. The auditorium doesn't get used much during this time of the year, so they might be able to hide people in the orchestra pit or something." He tossed the pepperoni in his mouth.

I heaved a sigh. "I guess it's as good of a guess as any we can make at this point."

Reve peeled another pepperoni off his pizza. "I miss her. She was better for my depression than my meds."

Despite the circumstances, I smiled. "That's one of the sweetest things I've ever heard you say."

He rolled his eyes as he folded the pepperoni again. "It's a psychological fact that socializing with people you trust increases emotional stability. Don't read too much into it."

"So, you trust us?" My smile grew.

He leveled his most annoyed stare, one he usually reserved for Frida, at me.

I laughed for the first time since Lorien's disappearance. "You act all aloof, but you care enough to be out there looking for her in conditions you seem determined to keep me away from."

He shook his head. "I just know you wouldn't survive it."

I reared back. "What is *that* supposed to mean?"

"There aren't any books in the crystal caves. You wouldn't make it an hour." He said it with such a straight face it took me a moment to realize he'd made a joke.

"That's all you know about me, huh?" I challenged with a grin.

He shrugged, a faint smile curving his lips. "Is there more to know?"

"No, that's most of it. Unless you count how smart and talented and helpful I am."

He picked up his now pepperoni-less pizza slice and took a bite. "I guess you're good at following my expert cooking instructions."

"The best," I declared.

"The best," he echoed.

As we fell silent, the rush of reality caught us in its current. "I feel useless."

"There is a line between selfishness and selflessness called self-respect," Reve mused as he chewed on his pizza. "You're something of a people pleaser, so you don't know how to stay in the self-respect zone. So, when a situation like this arises, you feel guilty about doing nothing even though there's nothing you could do in the first place."

I raised an eyebrow. "I could come with you and Keres."

"But you wouldn't be contributing anything we don't already have. That's not your fault, obviously. There's not much that *anyone,* even a couple of demigods, can do in this scenario. We aren't omniscient. We can't read minds. We just have to keep looking and hope we find something. Yes, it's frustrating beyond belief. But it's out of our control. And sometimes that's the hardest thing to accept. That we don't have control over everything." He polished off his pizza.

"But shouldn't the gods themselves be able to do something? Maybe the Wind Whisperer and the Boneman are a little limited in what they can do, but what about Time?"

Reve looked at me sharply. "We don't talk about Time."

"Why not? If they have some kind of power that relates to the passage of time, couldn't they go back, find Lorien, and prevent her from being kidnapped, find out who has been taking these people, and rescue them?"

Reve gritted his teeth. "Time doesn't work like that. They aren't very… cooperative."

The Boneman had said something about that when I'd visited Mortorous Academy. The Wind Whisperer had said Time was very chaotic and that I should stay away from them as much as possible. But Time had helped when I messed things up with that DNA test. Shouldn't they help again if they could?

The bell to end lunch rang.

"Time operates by their own rules, and they don't have any rules." Reve stood and picked up his tray. "The Wind Whisperer may have asked for their help in the past or maybe even with this, but we can't count on them for anything. We're on our own."

29

Twenty-Nine

I clutched the book I'd gotten last week to my chest as I walked into the library the next morning. I had finished it in two days. Books about people with life-altering medical conditions weren't usually my thing, but after reading this book, I might have to explore the subgenre in depth. Yes, it had been sad, but it was hopeful too.

Rich had said he would meet me here, but when I walked into the meeting room where the other members of the club gathered, he wasn't there. I sat and did my best to calm myself down. I was here early, and Rich had said before that he had a hard time getting up in the mornings.

Dr. Scribira wasn't there yet either, but Professor Midrid stood in a huddle of other students. I wondered if I should go talk to him. He'd been friendly in the past, but I didn't know any of the kids he talked to, and I wouldn't want to impose on their conversation.

I grabbed the new book we would read this week, took a seat in the back, and fished out my phone to text Rich. After sending a quick "where are you" text, I set my phone down on the table and waited.

The other students milled about, grabbing food and talking to each other. After a while, Professor Midrid called for everyone to sit down so we could get started. Rich was still absent.

I tried not to be disappointed. He'd said he wasn't that into reading. Maybe he'd decided he didn't want to come after all. But everything had been going so well between us. To have him not show up and not even message me about it stung. Maybe I'd been misreading the situation. Maybe Rich didn't like me the way I thought he did.

I did my best to focus on what Professor Midrid was saying about the love interest in the book and not think about my own doomed love life.

Halfway through book club, the door opened, and Rich slipped as quietly as possible into the room. A few students glanced back at him but quickly turned back around to keep listening to Professor Midrid. I beamed when Rich spotted me. He managed a smile of his own as he walked over and sat next to me, even though he was panting and a little red in the face like he'd run all the way here.

"Sorry I'm late, I slept through my alarm," he whispered.

"It's ok." I was just glad he had come at all. "It's not like you read the book anyway. I was a little lost during my first meeting too."

"Oh good. I thought they were going to call on me to talk about metaphors in the book or something." He chuckled.

I shook my head. "No one is going to force you to participate."

The person in front of us turned around. "Shh."

My face heated. "Sorry." I'd never thought I'd be the person to get shushed in a book club.

The student turned back around. I glanced at Rich and had to do a double take. He was glaring at the kid like he'd punched him in the face instead of trying to get him to be quiet. Did he know them?

I cleared my throat. Rich stopped glaring long enough to look at me. I raised my eyebrows. He shook his head and muttered something I didn't catch because the person who shushed us asked a question at the same time.

That was weird.

But it wasn't my business. If Rich and that student had some kind of history, it was probably best if I stayed out of it.

I paid attention to the discussion for the rest of the meeting and even threw in my own observations at some points. It felt good to be back in the book world. Everything that had happened with the kidnappings and now Lorien's disappearance had me twisted up in increasingly tighter knots for weeks. It reassured me that stories could still help me unwind some of that tension.

Some. But not all.

As soon as book club was over, the dread started trickling back in.

Rich noticed and pulled me to the side after we walked out of the room. "Hey, is that thing from yesterday still bothering you?"

I nodded, still afraid that telling someone outside the Wind Dreamed would make Lorien's kidnapping all too real.

He tilted his head. "You seemed ok during the meeting."

"Reading and talking about books calms me down."

He smirked a little. "You really like books that much?"

My hands fisted, preparing to defend my favorite hobby.

"Yes."

"Then how about we meet here this evening. There's something I want to show you."

My fists unclenched. "What do you want to show me?"

Rich waved a hand about vaguely. "Words don't really do it justice. Just meet me here after dinner."

"Ok." My curiosity was piqued. I wanted to see cool things in the library.

Professor Midrid paused near us on his way out. "Don't linger too long, Wren, or I'll have to count you late to my class."

"Let's not go that far, Professor." I'd never been late to class without a valid excuse before.

"That's all up to you." He pointed a menacing finger at me as he strode out of the library.

"You have history with Professor Midrid first thing in the morning?" Rich asked. "Poor you."

I rolled my eyes. "It's not that bad." Except that I would have to sit next to Lorien's empty seat again. Maybe it *would* be as bad as Rich implied.

Rich must have noticed my face drop. "You could always skip."

I looked at him sharply. "Now you're the one who's going too far. I'm not about to ruin my perfect attendance record just because…"

Just because one of my newest and closest friends had been kidnapped and maybe even killed, and I had to sit through a class we were supposed to share and pay attention to the lesson instead of thinking about all the places she could be or the terrible things that could be happening to her.

Did Professor Midrid know that she wasn't there because

she'd been taken away against her will? Or did he just mark her absent and move on? He hadn't said anything yesterday. But if the admin was expending as much energy as it sounded like they were to find her, maybe all the teachers knew and they just didn't want to say anything to upset anyone.

The Wind Whisperer only knew what kind of panic it would cause among the students if they knew someone had been kidnapped right here on campus. They would start suspecting everyone. Honestly, they should. Keres had said the kidnapper was someone at Animos Prep.

It could be any of the staff. All the students were probably in great danger.

But they couldn't prove it was someone at Animos, so classes had to keep on schedule. That was one thing that Mortorous Academy and Animos Prep had in common. They didn't want to cancel school unless absolutely necessary.

Back at Mortorous, they had only stopped classes during the winter if a snowstorm got bad enough to knock the power out. It usually happened at least once a year, and only the dorms and staff apartments had backup generators to keep people from freezing to death.

As far as I knew, Mortorous had never had to deal with a serial kidnapper.

"Hey, Wren!"

I blinked in surprise as Frida strode up to me and Rich. "Hey, what are you doing here?"

"I thought I'd check on you considering…" She glanced at Rich. "Everything that's happened lately."

"I'm ok, thanks. Book club just finished up."

"Nice. Who's this?" Frida's gaze hadn't left Rich.

"This is my friend, Rich. We share a class right before lunch.

He joined me for book club today."

I bit my tongue to make myself stop babbling, but I couldn't push away how much I wanted Frida to approve of my friendship with Rich. Reve didn't like that I was making friends outside of the Wind Dreamed. Imena seemed a little cautious about it too. I didn't know where Almos stood on the matter, and I couldn't ask Lorien what she thought. But out of all of them, Frida seemed like she would be the most accepting.

"Nice to meet you." Rich held out a hand. "I don't think we've met before."

Frida took his hand. "No, you would remember meeting me."

Rich raised his eyebrows. "Clearly." He tried to take his hand back.

Frida held on, frowning at him. "Maybe we have met before. You look kind of familiar."

Rich cleared his throat and glanced at her hand, but she was staring too intently at him to notice. "Maybe we share a class. Are you a third-year?"

"No. First."

"Then maybe you've seen me in the halls between classes." Rich tugged on his hand again.

"Frida, let go of him," I hissed.

She blinked out of her trance and released Rich's hand. "Sorry. I'm a little out of sorts lately."

Frida's apology was almost as surprising as her behavior toward Rich. I wasn't sure I'd ever heard her truly apologize for anything. Lorien's kidnapping must have really bent her out of shape. Honestly, there wasn't a single one of us Wind Dreamed who wasn't shaken to the core by her disappearance, but Frida was usually so unflappable. Seeing her act so differently was even more distressing.

"It's alright." Rich glanced from Frida to me and back again. Had he connected the dots and figured out that we were both struggling with the same thing? "I should get to class. I'll see you in finance and don't forget about this evening." He winked at me before walking away.

Frida turned on me the moment he was out of earshot. "Is that the guy you were 'doing a project' with the other day?" She made air quotes when she said "doing a project."

I rolled my eyes. "Yes."

"And the one you were with on Friday night when we thought you'd been kidnapped along with—" Her voice broke, and she swallowed hard.

"Yeah," I said much more gently.

She shook her head to snap herself out of whatever spiral she'd sent herself into at the memory of Lorien. "So, you're dating him."

She didn't phrase it like a question, but I still answered with an exasperated sigh. "I don't really know. It kind of seems like things are moving in that direction, but he hasn't committed to anything yet."

Frida leveled a look at me. "Have you tried to get him to?"

"No, I don't want to push him into anything or come across as desperate or—"

"Wren," Frida interrupted me. "You would be half of any relationship you had with someone else. If you want something or even if you just want to clarify what's going on, you have to *communicate* that."

I sighed. "Yeah, you're probably right."

Frida started toward the library door. "It's probably for the best anyway. There was something… weird about him."

"You're one to talk about people being weird," I scoffed.

Frida gave me a shove. "I don't mean the way he was acting. I mean his emotions."

I side eyed her. "Is that why you were staring so hard at him? You were reading his emotions?"

"Yeah, couldn't you? I thought Reve was helping you learn how to do that."

"It's been a slow process." Even slower than learning how to dream walk.

I could see people's emotions like a halo around their bodies, but I had to really focus to see more than surface-level flashes. And doing that felt kind of invasive. I only practiced with Reve when we cooked together. He knew what I was doing and consented to it, but scrutinizing other people's feelings without them knowing I could even do such a thing didn't sit right with me. And doing that to someone I had befriended and might end up being more than friends with felt even more wrong.

"Well, there was something strange about them. It's hard to put my finger on." Frida's face scrunched in concentration. "It was almost like they were stagnant."

"Stagnant?"

"Stagnant, stationary, unmoving, take your pick. He had plenty of normal emotions on the surface, but underneath any superficial flashes of annoyance or confusion there was this thick layer of… something else. Something I've never seen before. I don't even know how to describe it!" Frida threw up her hands in frustration.

"So, you think there's something wrong with him?" I demanded.

"I'm not saying that. I'm just saying I think it's weird."

"Weird in a 'that's kind of funny' way or weird in an 'I should stay away from him' kind of way?"

Frida shook her head. "I don't know. Like I said, I haven't seen anything like this before. It could be completely normal for all I know. I haven't read the emotions of every single person in the world, so I couldn't say for certain. It just looks different. It's not something I'm used to seeing."

I frowned. "Ok."

I had never seen what Frida was talking about either, but I doubted I was able to look deep enough into people's emotions to see that kind of thing.

Reve was waiting on the other side of the walkway from the library when we stepped out. I didn't like that he was by himself. Now that I thought about it, I didn't like that Frida had come into the library by herself either. I probably shouldn't have gone to book club alone. If someone was on campus snatching up students and taking them who knew where, none of us should go anywhere without at least one other person to make sure we were safe.

Then again, there were students up and walking around campus, heading to their classes. The chances of a kidnapper stealing one away without someone else noticing had to be small.

I tried to take a deep breath and calm down. We were going to be ok.

Reve met us halfway and we walked together under the trees, which were rapidly losing their flowers.

"You were taking so long, I was starting to think you went to history without me," Reve said.

"Wren was introducing me to a friend of hers," Frida

replied.

Reve glanced at me. "I see." I could almost feel him reading my emotions. Sometimes I really hated that he could see through me so thoroughly with just a glance.

I tried to read his emotions in turn. I only caught the faint glow of caution, but that could have been about anything. There was a lot to be cautious about.

I felt it as I went through my day. Any one of the teachers or students I passed in the halls or sat near in the classroom could be responsible for Lorien's disappearance. The only class I managed to relax in was finance.

Maybe "relax" wasn't the right word. But having Rich there helped keep my mind off everything. And when he winked at me as we parted ways to our next classes, my heavy heart fluttered.

30

Thirty

I returned to the Wind Dreamed penthouse feeling a little lighter. Lorien's disappearance still loomed over me, but if I couldn't help her, I couldn't waste my time moping around. It was sapping the energy out of everything. If I couldn't help find her, I would do something else. That's what I'd always done.

You couldn't be good at everything, so what was the point in trying when you knew you were going to fail? Or when you'd already failed? Or when people didn't even let you try?

Seeing the living room empty after having all of us spend the entire weekend there was strange. I went to my room to drop my stuff off and found Frida sitting on the air mattress that was still parked on my floor with her tablet in her lap.

"Hey," she murmured without looking up. Ever since Lorien had gone missing, she seemed to have lost most of her usual teasing, snarky nature and shrunk in on herself. Her air quotes when she talked to me about Rich this morning was the extent of it. She didn't even goad Reve anymore.

"Hi." I tossed my stuff on the desk. "Is everyone back?"

"Almos and Imena got back a few minutes ago. Reve is still out."

I resisted the urge to worry. Reve would never get himself kidnapped. He was too observant. He would feel it if someone meant him harm. Besides, he usually got back a little later than me. I still decided to take my book to the living room and sit in my chair, so I would see when Reve returned on time or if we had cause for concern.

Reve wasn't the first person I saw, though. Keres came darting out of the bedroom hallway, muttering curses as she shoved bone weapons into sheaths on her forearms.

I sat up straight. "What's wrong?"

She shook her head. "Nothing. I just forgot to set an alarm when I got back this morning and overslept."

If she was just now waking up from returning to the penthouse in the dark hours of the morning, she must have slept for almost twelve hours.

"Did you eat yet?" I asked.

"There's no time." She leaned against the wall to roll up her pant sleeve and secure a wicked-looking dagger to her calf. "I've already lost so much of it. Is Reve back yet?"

"No."

She sighed and came to sit on Imena's chair. "I guess I should just wait for him. He'll be back soon, right?"

I nodded. "He should be." *Unless he got kidnapped too.*

She raked her fingers through her hair, pulling it back into a tight bun at the base of her skull. "Even though we haven't found anything, he's been a lot of help. Keeps me going when it's been a long day, and I'm tired."

"Thank you for looking for her." I wished she had something to show for her efforts, but at least she was allowed to do something.

Unlike some of us.

She braced her elbows on her knees and stared at the floor. "Don't thank me. This happened on my watch. I was foolish enough to think that just because there was no evidence of ghosts that all of you would be safe." Her toes tapped an irritated beat on the ground. "I'm so used to the dead being the only threat that I forget humans can be just as bad, *worse* even."

My gaze lowered to my book without really seeing any of the words, thinking of Imena's story about her parents. "Yeah, they can be monsters too."

The elevator beeped and the doors opened to reveal Reve. He raised an eyebrow at me as he came to join us. I lifted my book and waved it at him as if it were an extension of my hand. He rolled his eyes and tossed his backpack onto his couch.

"Ready to go?" he asked Keres.

She stood and gave him a grim smile. "Now that I don't have to wait on you."

"Then let's—" Reve halted and turned toward the bedroom hall a moment before Imena came stomping out.

I shrank back into the couch at the anger and determination radiating from her.

"I'm coming with you," she declared.

Keres pressed her lips together. "I wouldn't recommend that."

Imena's hands fisted at her sides. "I don't care what you recommend. I'm going to find my girlfriend. Besides, the more eyes you have looking the better the chances are we'll find her, right?"

"Not if those eyes are clouded by a desire for revenge."

"I'm fine," Imena growled. "And I'm tired of sitting around while someone is doing who knows what to Lorien."

Keres raised her brows at me and Reve as if we were supposed to handle Imena.

Reve shrugged. "I don't think we could stop her unless we tied her to a chair."

Imena lifted her chin. "I would still drag myself after you. But we should wait for the others."

"Others?" I asked. Almos and Frida marched out of the bedroom hall as if on cue.

"We're coming too," Almos announced.

A satisfied smile curled across Reve's lips. "Sounds good to me."

"So, you're *all* coming?" Keres asked. "You're sure you want to do this?"

"Imena and I discussed it." Almos put a hand on Imena's shoulder. "I think we're all tired of not doing anything." He glanced at me when he said it.

I swallowed the lump in my throat. They *listened* to me.

"Great, let's go then." Keres started toward the elevator. Reve, Frida, and Imena followed.

"Wait for me!" I leaped up. "Just let me put my book in my room real quick."

The others turned as if remembering I was still there.

"Actually, Wren." My hackles rose at Almos's careful tone. "You should stay here."

My grip tightened on my book. "What do you mean?"

Almos walked toward me. "Someone needs to stay back and look through the dream realm for Lorien."

"Really?" I demanded. "I spend all weekend complaining

about how I want to do something, and as soon as you all *finally* decide we're going to look for Lorien, I have to be the one who doesn't go?"

Almos frowned. "We were in shock, Wren. And listening to Keres's advice. But we're ready now and we need to burn the candle at both ends. You've been looking through multiple dreams in a night despite only being Wind Dreamed for a couple weeks. You're suited for this job."

I wasn't about to be put off by his flattery. "*We* weren't in shock. I was ready to join the search as soon as we figured out the kidnapper was someone on campus. *You*"—I pointed at all of them—"wouldn't let me. You were too scared. Then you froze up when Lorien got taken. I was the only one prepared to do what it took."

"Not the *only* one." Reve narrowed his eyes at me.

I jabbed a finger at him. "You don't get to talk. I begged you to let me come with you, and you refused to let me. But you're fine with everyone else going?" They wanted to preach about how all of us were equal, but they didn't take me seriously enough to listen to me. It was only once someone in charge made an executive decision that the rest of the Wind Dreamed supported them.

Anger poured off Reve. "This was a unanimous decision, not you running off to fulfill your fantasies. If I could keep all of them here, I would. I don't want any of them to get hurt any more than I want you to get hurt, but if we stand together like Wind Dreamed are supposed to, there's safety in numbers."

"Safety in numbers unless the number is one and that one is me?"

Almos stepped between me and Reve. "You need to stay

because you're not ready for this. You may be excelling at dream walking, but you're still so new. You can't sense emotions that well yet. You need to use what you're good at, and what you're good at makes you better for staying behind than going with us."

Almos was complimenting me, but I could tell it was just to dress up what he really meant to say. They didn't want me to go with them, because I wasn't good enough. I would always be the late bloomer to them, the one they needed to protect because I couldn't do what they did.

My fists clenched so hard, my nails bit into my palm and my book creaked in protest. "You don't think I can handle myself? Fine. But don't even try to pretend like you didn't change your minds just because Imena wants to play knight in shining armor for her lost princess."

Imena stormed up to me. "This isn't about me. And it sure isn't about you. This is about all of us sticking together and finding Lorien. If you were really Wind Dreamed, really chosen by the Wind Whisperer instead of some charity case, you would know that."

Her words hit me like a punch to the gut.

"*Imena,*" Almos hissed.

Imena held my gaze for a second longer. "If she wants to throw a temper tantrum and run off again, let her. We'll do fine without her just like we did before she got here." With that, she turned and stormed toward the elevator.

Almos stepped toward me. "She's just in pain. She doesn't mean that."

I shook my head, a tear trailing down my cheek. "Yes, she does." I whirled before anyone else could try to comfort me, before I could see the pity in their eyes, and bolted down the bedroom hallway.

I slammed my door and sank to the ground, trying to stifle my sobs.

The things Imena said weren't any different from the ones I thought about by myself, but it was so much more devastating to hear them from the mouth of someone you thought cared about you. Maybe Imena *was* in pain. Maybe she *was* angry and desperate to find Lorien, but this was the first time she'd ever said anything against me. She'd been so welcoming and understanding, almost motherly. At least, that's how it had seemed. Maybe from the moment I'd told them about how I became Wind Dreamed she'd started having these thoughts.

Maybe they all had.

"Wren." Reve's deep voice drifted gently through the door.

I didn't answer.

"Wren." His voice came a little harder.

I reached up and locked the door. I wouldn't put it past him to try to open it whether I responded or not.

He sighed. "We'll be back late, and Frida will sleep in her own room. So, don't worry about us waking you up. Leftovers are in the fridge."

His footsteps shuffled down the hallway until I couldn't hear them anymore.

No one else came to try to talk to me. When I emerged from my room half an hour later, they were gone, and I was all alone in the penthouse.

31

Thirty-One

Eating dinner at the table by myself felt like living in the zombie apocalypse, alone and depressing. We'd had leftovers before when Reve didn't feel like cooking or if he'd gone out with Keres, but these leftovers tasted worse than usual. Objectively I knew it was psychological, but I couldn't help feeling like I should stop eating and curl into a ball on my bed and never get back up.

Maybe it was this place. I needed to get out and luckily, I had something lined up already. And the sun wasn't even down yet, so it wasn't like I would be able to find Lorien in the dream realm yet, if she was even able to sleep deeply enough to get there.

I didn't bother getting all dressed up this time, just threw on a red hoodie over my uniform. It was a casual meeting at the library. Besides, after crying about what happened with Imena and the others, I didn't have enough energy to care. I just wanted to get out of here and forget about all of it for a few hours.

Rich was lying out on the grass lawn in front of the library looking up at the sunset when I got myself out there. I flopped down next to him and stared up.

The clouds were all wispy, providing the perfect canvas on which the setting sun could paint its rays. Thin blankets of orange and red and pink made the sky look as bloody and gutted as I felt.

Rich turned his head toward me. "Hey."

"Hi," I replied without taking my eyes from the sky.

"You look upset."

I sighed. "Have you ever told someone something you're insecure about, and they use it against you the moment you don't want to do what they want?"

He looked back up at the sky. "Not really, but that's mostly 'cause I don't tell people the things I'm insecure about."

"Good. It sucks. You think someone is your friend until suddenly they're not."

"Is this what you were upset about the last couple days?"

I sighed. "No. That was something else. But it kind of caused *this*. It's complicated. There's a lot going on. All of my friends are really tense right now."

"Not *all* of them. I'm not tense." A smile snuck its way into his voice.

A faint smile of my own curled my lips. "No, you're not. I'm glad you can be the one normal thing in my life."

"I'm glad you're my friend too, Wren. I think you're the piece I've been missing."

I turned my head to look at him, heart pounding. "What do you mean?"

He sat up. "The stuff that Jacob said about me dating around a lot wasn't exactly false. I've been through my share of girlfriends at this school. Almost all of the girls in our class actually."

I sat up, instantly on edge. "So, you *are* a player?"

"No, I just want to find the right girl and none of them have been right yet. But I think you have the thing that the others were missing."

My heart skipped a beat. Was this going where I thought it was going? "What were they missing?"

He chewed his lip. "It's hard to describe. Can I show you something?"

"What?" This was getting a little weird.

He stood up. "In here." He jerked his head at the library.

I got to my feet. "I guess."

I had no idea where this was going, but I was intrigued. It didn't hurt that he was talking about romance. Maybe my first boyfriend wasn't as far out of reach as I thought.

The sun was almost all the way down when we slipped into the library. A lot of the main lights were off too, giving the usual light and open, gallery-style layout a much more haunted appearance. The circulation desk that Dr. Scribira usually occupied was empty and dark.

"Come on." Rich waved me over to it.

"I'm pretty sure we're not supposed to be back here. I'm surprised the door was unlocked." I said as he ducked under the desk and started poking at the carpet. "What are you even doing?"

"This school is really old, so it has a lot of passages and rooms that have been boarded up but not torn down. A while ago, some kids ran across this one place in the library—Aha!" Rich pulled up a portion of the carpet. Underneath hid a little hatch that he opened. Inside was a big black button. "Would you care to do the honors?"

I crouched under the desk next to him. "What does it do?"

He grinned. "It opens the door to one of those hidden spaces. Some students found it several years ago and spruced it up. It looks incredible. Hurry up and hit the button."

"It's not going to trigger an ancient trap that will kill us with spikes and giant stones, will it?" I asked.

He rolled his eyes. "You watch too much TV. Just press it."

I pressed the button. For a moment, there was silence, and I wondered if Rich was playing some kind of practical joke on me. A hiss of air blasted from the wall next to the desk. I jumped to my feet and stumbled back while the wall cracked open in the rough shape of a door.

Rich got up and walked over to it. He shoved a shoulder into the door and pushed with as much force as he could muster. Whatever hinges the door had squealed relentlessly as it swung open painfully slowly.

I peered around Rich into the dark hallway beyond. The dimmed lights of the library didn't do much to illuminate the passage, but the switch from carpet to cement was clear enough.

Rich stepped inside, groping along the walls until he hit a switch and an old set of bulbs flickered to life, showing a short hall made of brick that turned into a set of stone stairs. I wandered in to look down. The bottom of the stairs was in complete darkness.

"There's another light at the bottom." Rich grunted as he swung the door closed again. "We'll have to find it when we get down there."

"Why are you closing the door?" If he had struggled to push it open, I couldn't imagine having to pull it open.

"Campus security searches the library before they lock it

up for the night. Can't have them finding this and following us. We'd get in so much trouble. Not to mention, it would ruin the secret of its existence." The door shut with a click. "Besides, there's a knob on this side, so it's easier to open."

It seemed like one of those things you yelled at a movie character for doing, but Rich had been down here before, so he probably knew what worked best.

I followed him down the brick stairs, running my hand along the rough wall. Finding the right footing was treacherous. Rich made it sound like whatever students had discovered this place had refurbished it, but he didn't say how well they did it. There was only so much a handful of high school kids could do without hiring a professional crew to take care of everything. And if these renovations had been done in secret without alerting the administrators, getting professionals was out of the question.

When we reached the bottom of the stairs, Rich felt along the walls for the light switch.

"This"—he flicked the switch— "is what I wanted to show you."

The lights popped on much brighter and quicker than the lights in the stairway. That wasn't the only thing that was nicer.

Rich leaned against the wall as I stepped out into the room. "I know the stairs didn't set the tone right, but this is how it really is down here."

I could only gape at the expanse of the massive hall we'd just walked into. It was a real art gallery. Like someone had taken the library above and moved it down here. But instead of bookshelves, little plinths and cabinets with glass cases displayed all kinds of pieces. Paintings and drawings hung on the walls, so many that they crowded together, jostling for space. Larger-than-life sculptures lurked in the corners. Even the ceiling was painted with an elaborate mural.

"You like it?" Rich asked, eyes fixed on me as I took everything in.

"What is all of this? How did they—" I ran my fingers over the frame of the nearest painting. It was easily taller than me and wider than my arm span. "How did they get all of this stuff down here?" I glanced at one of the sculptures. There was no way anyone could get that thing down those stairs. It was way too big and must have weighed a ton.

Rich shrugged. "Honestly, I'm not sure. I haven't found any entrance besides the stairs from the library, but they had to have a different way of bringing everything in here."

"Where did they get all these pieces?" I eyed a glazed vase that looked like it could be hundreds of years old.

Rich shrugged again. "I have no idea. I don't know who brought what or why or where those people might be now. As far as I know, I'm the only one who knows about this place. Or at least the only one who visits it regularly."

"It's incredible," I breathed, moving on to a tiny model of an old town rendered in perfect detail. "Is that Animos Prep?" I pointed through the glass box covering it to a building that looked suspiciously like the front office. None of the rest of the campus buildings surrounded it though.

Rich nodded at a metal plaque that read *Luxem 1784*. "It's what the city looked like back when Animos was first built. Do you know the story?"

"What story?"

"The story of the school and how the Wind Whisperer supposedly saved it." At my blank look he said, "I'll take that as a no. Usually they tell you on the tour, but I guess they skipped that when you came in."

The Wind Dreamed had given me a tour of the school when I'd first arrived. They'd shown me everything on campus, but they hadn't mentioned anything about how the Wind Whisperer had saved it. That seemed like a relevant detail given that we were the children of the Wind Whisperer. But it sounded similar to the story of Mortorous Academy and the Boneman.

Mortorous had been on the verge of shutting down, because no one wanted to send their kids to a school that looked haunted. The Boneman came and said he would provide the academy with a steady stream of new students as long as they took in his Bone Touched when he brought them in. Whoever had been in charge of the school at the time had agreed and thus saved Mortorous Academy from ruin.

When I'd been a normal student there, I hadn't thought much of the story. It was just a piece of lore that the admin played up to get us into the school spirit. I'd had fun poking my proverbial fingers through the plot holes in the tale. How did the Boneman get new students to come if he supposedly only showed himself to the Bone Touched? How had the Boneman known the school was on the verge of collapse? There were too many loose ends.

Now that I knew the Boneman and other gods existed, I didn't know what to think.

"Tell me the story," I said to Rich.

"It goes a little something like this. Back in the early days of Animos Prep, some famous politician or rich guy or someone like that wanted to enroll his kid at the school. But the headmaster took one look at the records from the kid's previous school and rejected him."

Rich frowned. "I can't remember if it was because his grades were so bad or because he behaved terribly. I've heard both versions, I think. The point being, no school in their right mind would admit him. But the kid's dad had the money to try to bribe the administration to let the kid in. The headmaster found out, got mad about it, and said his school would never allow such a horrible child to attend.

"Obviously, that didn't sit well with the dad. So, he cooked up a story, bribed some people to be witnesses, and went to the governing authorities to report the headmaster. Again, I don't really remember what the accusations were, but they were bad enough that the authorities went to Animos Prep and said they had to close the school or completely get rid of all the existing staff and let the government take charge of hiring new people."

Rich waved a hand. "You know, it was a different time. And despite the protests of many of the school staff, they couldn't do anything to change anyone's mind or convince them of their innocence. Everyone at the school had just about given up hope when the Wind Whisperer appeared to the headmaster in a dream."

Well, that part at least sounded right. Dreams were the Wind Whisperer's thing.

"It told him that it could change the mind of the man who made all those false accusations against him as long as he vowed that this school would forever be a home for its children, the Wind Dreamed."

"Let me guess," I said as I stared at the tiny replica of the old school. "The headmaster said yes."

"Obviously. The school is still here, isn't it? And the Wind

Whisperer is our mascot. I don't know if I believe that's how it would have happened, but it's a fun story either way."

I regarded Rich. "How did the Wind Whisperer make sure all the headmasters that came after that first one honored the original agreement? It didn't have any impending doom to save them from, did it?"

He shrugged. "Not that I've heard. But it's more of a fairytale than an actual story. One of those 'happily ever after' moments that doesn't show you how the prince and princess live with each other and interact after they get married. Not very realistic."

"The Wind Whisperer is a god. I'm sure it can pull whatever strings it wants." Unless it involved finding a lost Wind Dreamed, apparently.

"I guess." Rich wandered around in the gallery. "For a god it doesn't do much."

I bit my lip. It did plenty. It just didn't do the kinds of things you read about gods doing, which was annoying and frustrating at times, but the Wind Whisperer wasn't useless.

"That's assuming it even exists in the first place. It might just be an urban legend. Goodness knows we don't get any help from any other gods. We have to do everything ourselves."

I kept my mouth shut. The gods weren't the most benevolent beings, but they sure did exist. I was living proof of that for better or worse.

"I think you understand that."

I blinked. "Understand what?"

"That we can't rely on others to get things done. We have to do everything ourselves, take everything for ourselves. It's a lesson I only recently learned."

I frowned. "What do you mean?" I was all for being independent, but that didn't sound like what he meant.

He wandered between the aisles of displays. "Think of life like a group project. Ideally everyone helps out, and we all have a good time and get a perfect grade. But that's not how it works. Everyone is selfish and lazy, and they only work toward what *they* want instead of helping achieve a happy world for everyone."

"I wish I could argue with that," I grumbled. All my life, I'd been pushed to the side by people I thought cared about me and people who just wanted to take advantage of what I could give them. My own parents could hardly stay in one place long enough to spend time with me.

Even with the Wind Dreamed, I wasn't listened to or respected. Maybe it was because I was so new, but that wasn't an excuse. They'd refused to let me help look for Lorien and the other captives until they were ready to go too. We'd lost all that time because they couldn't bring themselves to do something about it. And then got mad at me when I took their advice and moved on.

Rich spun and pointed a triumphant finger at me. "Exactly. I was right about you. You *do* understand. This is what I was talking about before." He threw his hands to the ceiling. "No one understands that you can't just rely on everyone else, so you have to start taking things for yourself."

I was pretty sure that wasn't what I had said. "I'm all for getting stuff done yourself—"

"Good, because you were the one who taught me that I should."

I blinked. "I did?"

"Well, maybe it wasn't you, but I had a dream a week or so

ago that you appeared in. At first it was a terrible dream. I was reliving the moment my brother was taken away by our father. My parents got divorced and my father took main custody of my brother." He paused and blinked hard to banish the tears. "It was the worst day of my life. In the dream, I kept trying to run after them, but they just kept getting farther and farther away. And then you appeared."

My heart dropped. He remembered the dream I'd screwed up. And he had *seen* me. Dreamers weren't supposed to see Wind Dreamed unless they showed themselves on purpose. Had I accidentally let Rich see me?

He continued. "You were saying all these things that made me realize that I'd gone about the whole situation wrong. I shouldn't have just stood there when my family got ripped apart. I should have taken him back at all costs. I hardly see him more than once a year. We used to be so close. Now we barely talk."

"I'm sorry," I murmured.

"No, *I'm* sorry. I should have stopped it from happening in the first place." He sighed. "But every sunrise brings a new day and a new chance to fix old mistakes."

I chuckled. "You should write that in a book."

He grinned. "Maybe I will. But after I had that dream, I had to find out if you truly felt the same way that I had come to feel. And it seems like you do."

"I mean, I guess to a certain extent I do. What happened to your brother wasn't fair, and you should fight for him." I wasn't sure about the whole "take what you want" rhetoric though.

"I don't just mean about the big things, Wren." Rich wandered toward the back wall. "We have to fight for the little things too. Otherwise, no one will respect us, and they'll think they can push us around when it comes to more important things."

I trailed after him, unsure about where this was going.

"That means sticking it to all of the disrespectful drunks, annoying children, entitled adults, and everyone else who has the audacity to inconvenience us and not even realize what they're doing."

We stopped at a small door that looked like the kind of storage closet where cleaning supplies were kept. The paint on it blended so well with the wall that it was hard to tell there was actually a door there. It was only noticeable because it was the biggest space on a wall that lacked artwork. There was also the doorknob sticking out of it, but for all I knew, someone considered putting a doorknob on a wall art.

Maybe the door was a work of art in and of itself. It just looked like a doorknob stuck on the wall until you got close. The paint job was done in such a way that the shadows of the doorframe were counteracted by lighter paint and the whole thing was textured like the rest of the walls.

"That means taking things into our own hands and taking care of those who need to be taught a lesson." He reached for the doorknob. "People like these."

The door swung open. My jaw dropped. The closet was bigger than I thought it would be, almost the size of a small bedroom. All the shelves and supplies had been removed to make room for five people, who sat hunkered in the back, gagged and tied to the metal framework where shelves would go.

One was an elderly man. One was a woman who looked like she was in her thirties. One was a little boy who couldn't

be more than ten. One was a middle-aged man.
And one...
Was Lorien.

32

Thirty-Two

She looked nothing like the Lorien I'd gotten used to seeing during my time at Animos Prep. That Lorien was bright and bubbly. She bounced around with a smile and a cheerful tone.

This Lorien raised her head slowly as the door opened and glared out. Her eyes were bloodshot and ferocious like a caged animal's. Her blue hair was a greasy mess hanging around her shoulders. She tucked herself up in a defensive crouch.

And then her eyes found mine.

They widened. A pervasive aura of fear choked the air around her. She lunged for the door. The ropes strained but held firm. She screamed as best she could around the gag.

I took a step forward to help her. Rich's hand landed on my shoulder, clamped tight.

I whirled on him. "What's going on? Why do you have these people tied up?"

"I just explained it to you, Wren." Rich sighed. "Society might not care enough to do anything about the 'little' inconveniences that its members inflict on others. So, it's up to us to pick up the slack."

"What did they do that could possibly warrant tying them up in a closet?" I screeched.

"All sorts of things." Rich glanced disdainfully at the huddled group. "They thought they were special enough to withhold the respect that I—that *everyone* deserves. Once they realize how wrong they were, they can go, but none of them have yet." His eyes fixed on Lorien. "Especially that one."

Lorien still struggled to get to us. The ties at her wrists dug into her flesh, rubbing it raw. Her feet—bare feet—scrabbled on the smooth concrete floor, slipping and sliding all over the place as her bonds refused to budge. The other captives were trying to calm her down, but she shook off their gentle elbow touches and kept fighting.

They'd been here this whole time. All the people who had been kidnapped from the city were here in this closet. And Rich...

I swallowed hard. Before I could act, I had to think. He was right there next to me, showing off his evil deeds. Which meant he had a backup plan in case I reacted poorly to this new information. I kind of already had. He might have a knife in his pocket, or a rag soaked in chloroform, or any number of things he could use to incapacitate or kill me.

The other Wind Dreamed were searching the campus with Keres. They didn't know where I was or who I was with. They might eventually find this hidden gallery with its closet full of hostages, but who knew how long that would take. Reve was good at detecting emotions, but could he feel them from all the way down here? We'd climbed down a *long* staircase to get to the gallery.

Supposedly no one else knew about this place. So, I couldn't rely on anyone to stumble across and save us.

I was on my own. It was up to me to get myself and all these people out of here without getting myself caught. No pressure.

Rich put his hands on my shoulders and turned my back to the closet, making me face him. "Wren, you have to understand that this is the only way people learn. It's punishment versus reward. I understand that the law can't take care of such petty matters, but I can. *We* can."

I took a deep breath and spoke in as level a voice as I could manage. "What did they do?"

Rich turned me around to face the prisoners again and kept his hands on my shoulders as he leaned close to speak directly into my ear. I resisted the urge to shiver. "That old man there cleaned out the entire supply of one of the few types of cereal that I can eat because of my dietary restrictions. I even had my hand on the last box when he grabbed it away from me and told me he deserved it because he was older than I was. All the life he'd lived had earned him all that food. When I tried to tell him that I needed it for health reasons, he told me that it was all in my head and I needed to toughen up."

I frowned at the man as he cringed away from my gaze. It was certainly very rude of him, but not enough to warrant being locked in a closet for a week.

"See that little boy there? I was practicing baseball at a diamond in the city one afternoon about a year ago when he threw his frisbee into the middle of my way as I was running for a base. I stepped right on the thing, my leg flew out from under me, and I broke my ankle. He just ran off without any kind of apology."

I cringed at the image that story put in my head. But that had been an accident, and he was a *child*.

"And then while I was recovering, I had to go to the pharmacy to pick up my pain medication. *This* woman"—he jabbed a finger at the woman in her thirties who shrunk back behind Lorien— "pulled in front of me to take the only available handicapped parking space when she wasn't handicapped at all.

"Again, I tried to explain to her how much I needed that spot since the lot was crowded and I would have to park all the way in the back of the lot and walk up to the store. She said she was only parking for a minute, and I could wait or tough it out and walk. But when I parked in the back of the lot and got inside, she was taking her time browsing through the makeup section. I left before she did, and I had to wait twenty minutes for my medication to be ready."

"You didn't report her?" That would have been much more reasonable than kidnapping her.

"I tried. But apparently, her husband works at the local police department, so he cleared her of the charges. She can't hide behind him now." Rich sneered. "And him…" Rich glared at the middle-aged man. "He was my neighbor when I lived in Luxem. Has a nasty drinking habit. One night, my dad was walking our dog. They went to cross the street, and this idiot comes racing around the corner, hits my dog, and keeps driving."

Rich grew quiet. "Poor Tracy didn't make it. But since he hadn't killed a person, the charges were much less severe than they should have been."

The man was barely conscious, which could be attributed

to withdrawal, but he looked somewhat ashamed. That was a tragedy, and it was terrible that it happened because of an addiction. But Rich had locked him in a closet and let him go through withdrawal while tied to the wall. A person could die from quitting alcohol cold turkey.

"And what about her?" I nodded at Lorien, trying to be as impersonal as possible. It would be better if Rich didn't think we were friends.

She had finally stopped struggling but hovered in a defensive stance above where all the others sat, glaring at Rich and panting around her gag. If Rich was telling the truth about all these other people, I could see why he might want to get revenge on them. But I couldn't imagine Lorien doing anything like that. She was always so nice to everyone.

So, what was she doing here?

Rich took one hand off my shoulder and circled around to stand next to me. "She led me on for months, making me think we might have a chance to get together. She was playing hard to get, being coy. But when I finally confronted her about it, she said she had a *girlfriend.*" He spat the word like it was the worst possible outcome of that conversation, like Lorien was dirty for liking girls. "All that wasted effort, and she acted like I was imagining it the whole time, said she'd never been interested in me or any boy. So beautiful and so disappointing."

Lorien jerked on her restraints again and growled something that no one could have understood with the gag in her mouth. Her message was clear enough though.

My blood boiled. It took everything in me not to tackle him right then and there. He would have overpowered me in a second if I'd tried. He was an athlete who worked out and actually had muscles, after all. And I was just a bookworm who liked to shut myself in my room and read in bed all day. There was no comparison. If I was going to incapacitate him, I'd have to be able to do it in one blow. I doubted I could do it with just my bare hands.

He was still standing behind me, so pushing him into the closet wasn't an option. It hadn't looked like there was a lock on the door, and I'd rather not leave him in there with all those people he hated while they were tied up and helpless anyway.

That left the gallery.

I turned my back on the closet and eyed Rich. "So, what? We just kidnap everyone who pisses us off? That seems like a lot of work. I mean, clearly you have to feed them and give them water and a place to go to the bathroom. And eventually you're going to run out of space. What then? Start letting people go? They've seen your face. Some of them actually know your name. They're going to run straight to the police, and it'll be all over then."

Rich shrugged. "I've got time to find a new hiding spot for them, and if nothing else, we can make sure they never breathe a word about any of this to anyone. There is more than one way to *free* someone." A malicious grin spread across his face.

One of the people behind me sobbed. It sounded like the woman. I had to stick my hands in my pockets to keep them from shaking.

"But won't someone find the bodies? They've got some pretty advanced methods of figuring that kind of thing out."

Rich rolled his eyes. "They haven't found out who kidnapped them or where they're being kept yet. Besides, this campus has all kinds of pockets to hide things you don't want found. We could plant a new flower bed and bury the bodies under the blooms. We could throw them in the lake that's a couple miles south of campus. There are plenty of options."

I put a hand to my chin and started pacing around the gallery, searching for anything I could use as a weapon while I went. "The best way to get rid of a body is to cut off the hands and head and dispose of those separately, so they can't use fingerprints or dental records to identify the bodies. Then you have to get ahold of enough acid to completely dissolve the flesh *and* bones. But then you have to get rid of the acid."

All the art pieces that I might be able to use, the heavy-duty vases and sculptures, were trapped under glass. I wasn't sure I could break it, get one of the pieces free, and take Rich out with it before he realized what I was doing. And that was only if I could get to them. If this was the kind of glass they put over museum pieces to protect them from thieves, breaking it wouldn't be as easy as punching or kicking it.

That left the paintings—some of which were too big to maneuver—and the statues—which were all enormous. Enormous enough to pin someone to the ground if they were trapped under one of them when they fell. But Rich wasn't going to just stand still while I pushed a giant statue on top of him.

"Given this a lot of thought, have you?" His voice was too close for comfort. His footsteps followed me as I paced.

"I just read a lot." I stopped by the statue that would be my best bet: an androgynous figure holding a massive hourglass above its head. It had a square base, so it would fall in one direction when pushed or pulled. It was also top-heavy, so it wouldn't take much to unbalance it. I wasn't sure what it was made of, but hopefully, whatever it was wasn't heavy enough to kill Rich when it landed on him. I wanted him to pay for what he'd done by living through whatever punishment the law exacted.

But this was the hard part. How did I get him to stand still while I toppled the statue on him?

"It was really me who inspired you to do all of this?" I gestured back at the open closet door, where a few of the people inside were straining to keep us in sight.

He nodded. "Just like when the Wind Whisperer appeared in the first headmaster's dream and convinced him to take in the Wind Dreamed."

I channeled the heroines from all the dark romance books I'd read. "That's pretty romantic."

Rich leaned forward. "What can I say? You've got some great ideas. I can hardly take credit for any of it if it was just my subconscious conjuring you."

"What if I told you it wasn't just your subconscious?"

His brows furrowed. "What else would it be?"

"Magic."

He snorted and rocked back on his heels. "Magic doesn't exist. This isn't a fairy tale."

"But it does." I took a step closer to him and lowered my voice as if I were telling him a secret. "The gods exist. Their demigods exist. I'm one of them. I'm Wind Dreamed."

He stared at me. "I can't tell if you're trying to be serious or not."

"I'm very serious. We Wind Dreamed have the power to go into people's dreams and manipulate them to send those people certain messages they need to hear. You know, life lessons they need to learn." It felt strangely good to watch the surprise spread across his face as I told him the truth.

"So, that was really you in my dream?" I nodded. "Prove it."

"In the dream, you and some friends were playing in an office when that man, your father I suppose, came and took your brother away. You tried to run after them, but no matter how fast you ran, it was always too slow. The office morphed into a field, and your dad and brother disappeared on the horizon while you were still trying to catch them. And then I started telling you all the things that made you do all this." I gestured around the gallery.

His eyes were so wide they could have popped out of his sockets to roll across the floor. Slowly, a grin split his face. "And you used your powers to send me the message I needed to hear most."

My smile felt brittle.

This was all my fault. It was my mistake that led to all these people getting kidnapped. I'd lost my cool with the Wind Whisperer when I'd repeatedly failed to dream walk and set loose a serial kidnapper who might turn into a serial murderer if I didn't stop him quick.

I hadn't thought much of my powers as a Wind Dreamed. I hadn't known very many people who remembered and thought about their dreams once they woke up. How were we supposed to influence their train of thought if they didn't take their dreams seriously?

But here was someone who took his way too seriously. Or maybe I had more power than I thought. Frida said there was something weird about his emotions. What if it was because I'd accidentally used my magic to manipulate his thoughts and feelings and turn him into *this*?

Rich grabbed my hands. "So, all of the stories about the

Wind Whisperer are true?"

"Well, I don't know *all* of the stories, but it does exist."

"Amazing. And now I have you on my side." His eyes practically glowed with excitement. "What other powers do you have?"

I opened my mouth to tell him that my powers weren't all that impressive. I was still learning, and even if I wasn't, I didn't have anything in my repertoire that would be particularly useful to him or his cause.

But maybe this was my chance.

I freed my hands from his and stepped back. "I can show you, but you have to close your eyes. That's how Wind Dreamed powers work. You can't look, you have to feel."

He frowned. "But isn't the Wind Whisperer the god of life? How does closing your eyes have anything to do with life?"

"Well, what is life but a collection of feelings and perceptions we gather and clutch to our chests before our hearts stop beating? Life isn't just about breathing and eating and keeping warm. That's surviving. Not living. Living is about dreaming and making those dreams come true, moving forward, making progress, forming relationships, getting hobbies, making art, and enjoying yourself. That's life. And how can we truly feel all those things until we let go and allow ourselves to absorb them?"

Wow. I sounded like Imena.

Rich smiled. "Ok. Show me." And he closed his eyes.

I didn't have long. He would expect something grand to happen, and when it didn't, he would know I'd tricked him, and it would be me trapped in here for who knew how long.

"Now, relax," I coached as I took off my red Animos Prep hoodie. "Take a minute to breathe and feel the air around you."

I threw one end of the jacket up at the statue's head. It slipped off and I bit my lip to keep from cursing out loud as Rich took a handful of deep breaths.

"Clear your mind. Really ground yourself in the moment and let go of everything else." I gathered the hoodie and threw it again. The sleeve wrapped around the statue's neck. I reached up to grab the end.

Rich started to open his eyes. "Is your power to guide me through a meditation? 'Cause, no offense, but that's kind of lame."

I slapped a hand over his eyes, gripping the sleeves of the hoodie in a death grip with the other. "You have to trust me, Rich. I'm a little new at this so it might take a minute. Just listen to my voice." It didn't matter that he was right. I was just reciting things the other Wind Dreamed had told me when I was first struggling to get through our group meditations in the meadow.

"Ok, ok. I'll keep my eyes shut."

"Good."

I let go of his face to wrap both hands around the sleeves of my hoodie and pulled as hard as I could. The statue tottered and fell with a slow groan. I darted out of the way as it came smashing down.

Rich opened his eyes at the noise but couldn't move fast enough to avoid the hunk of stone bearing down on him. He screamed as it crashed into his back.

I circled the wreckage to get as far away from him as possible. Chunks of stone had broken off and lay scattered around what remained of the main body of the statue.

I ran to the closet. I had to get everyone out of there and

call the police. I had no idea how well Rich had taken care of them, but if their haggard looks were anything to go off of, he hadn't put that much effort into it. They probably needed food and water and comfort. Lots of comfort. I couldn't imagine what they had gone through, what they were feeling right now. I had to get them out.

A hand grabbed my braid and yanked me back. I cried out as my feet flew from under me and I went down hard on the tiled floor.

"That was clever," Rich panted above me. "But next time, make sure I can't get up."

I glanced back at the statue. The figure that held the hourglass was twisted at just the right angle to make a gap large enough for a person to wriggle through. It must have hit Rich in that spot, knocking him down, but not holding him there.

"I can't believe I thought you were like me," Rich growled as he wrapped a hand around my throat and dragged me across the floor.

I grabbed his wrist and kicked out, struggling to breathe and trying to alleviate the pressure and land a good blow. The magic of the Wind Dreamed was in their lungs. If we couldn't draw breath, we could die.

"The Wind Whisperer doesn't exist. Neither do the Wind Dreamed. My dream was wrong. You're just like everyone else who thinks they can take advantage of my moments of weakness." Rich walked with a strange gait. The statue must have hit him pretty hard. If I could just get him off balance, we might be on a more level playing field.

I managed to swing around and kick the back of one of his knees. He shouted as it buckled, and he fell. He instinctively let go of me to brace himself for the fall.

I scrambled to my feet and raced for the statue, gasping and coughing. I needed to get something sizable between us, and those chunks of stone that had cracked off would make good enough weapons. Rich's feet pounded after me a moment later.

I crouched, grabbed a piece of stone, and spun, throwing at him for all I was worth. He ducked. It sailed past his shoulder. I threw another, which he also evaded.

His grin was feral. "If only you played baseball."

I slipped behind the statue with my back to the wall and searched for more stones to throw. Something hit me in the side of the head. Hard. I fell against the wall. A muffled scream came from the closet. My vision blurred. Warm blood trickled down the side of my face. Beside me lay one of the rocks I'd thrown at Rich. It was red with my blood.

I barely managed to duck out of the way as another rock sailed straight for me. It exploded against the wall, shrapnel slicing into my arms.

"You can't escape, Wren. It's just you and me, and no one is coming to help you. You'll join your friends in the closet whether you keep fighting or not!" Rich stood over the statue, barely four feet from where I clutched my bleeding head.

My hoodie lay a few inches from my feet. "That's another thing about life." I grabbed it and threw it at him.

He caught it easily and threw it to the side at the same time I launched myself up, bloody stone in hand, and brought it down on his head. My momentum toppled us both over. I landed on top of Rich. His head bounced against the tiles. Whether it was from my blow or from hitting his head against the floor, Rich didn't get up when I staggered to my feet. His chest still rose and fell, but he was out cold.

"It always fights."

My head throbbed. The cut on my forehead was still bleeding, blood dripping down the side of my face. The scratches on my arms weren't as deep, but they stung as I trudged over to the closet.

Lorien's brows pinched, and she made a concerned noise around her gag when she saw me.

"It's fine," I mumbled. "Head wounds bleed a lot because your brain needs a lot of blood flow, so there are a lot of blood vessels in your head and when you cut it, it bleeds a lot 'cause there are so many, and they carry a lot of blood to your brain."

Part of me was aware of how much I babbled. Most of me didn't care.

The hostages started grunting once they realized I was there to free them, but I went to Lorien first and removed her gag. "Are you ok?"

"We're fine. He didn't feed us very well, but he didn't hurt any of us. You on the other hand…"

"It's just some scratches." I tugged at the knot tying Lorien to the wall, but all her struggling had tightened it. There was no way I could get it undone without cutting it. "Give me a minute."

I stumbled out of the closet to the groaned protests of all the others. Searching through the statue's wreckage, I managed to find a piece of stone that looked sharp enough to get the job done. The other prisoners tried to plead with me when I came back. I ignored them and went straight to Lorien. It took some time, but the sharp edge of the rock cut through her bonds. Her wrists were bruised and bleeding from yanking on them so much.

If only I'd dealt with Rich sooner…

I dug in my pocket and handed Lorien my phone and the sharp rock. "Call the Wind Dreamed and the police. Get everyone out."

She gripped the phone like a lifeline. "What will you be doing?"

"You heard what Rich said. This is my fault. I have to try and fix it." I made my way to the doorway and leaned heavily on it.

Lorien came up behind me and peered over my shoulder at where Rich lay on the ground. Blood leaked from his head where I'd hit him with the rock. It was up farther into his hair than mine, but I couldn't help reaching to touch the wound on my own head.

Would it scar? Would I always have this piece of Rich even if I managed to change his mind?

"You're going to go into his dream again?" Lorien asked.

"I have to try. I started this in a dream. I have to finish it in a dream." Whatever magic I'd accidentally used to convince Rich to kidnap the people who inconvenienced him was dream magic. So, it stood to reason that it could only be undone by dream magic.

Lorien's brow furrowed. "Are you sure? Aren't you supposed to stay awake when you have a head wound?"

"It's not as bad as it looks." I lowered my hand from my head, fingers slick with blood. "Will you watch over me?"

Lorien's face softened. "Of course."

"Thanks. Get them out of here and tell the others we're ok. Keres should know what to do."

I took a step toward Rich's unconscious body. Lorien

grabbed my arm and pulled me into a tight hug. "Thank you for freeing us."

I hugged her back. "We aren't free yet."

We let go of each other. She dialed on my phone. I went to Rich.

I lay down on the ground beside him, grabbed my hoodie, and balled it up under my head. Rich's limp hand rested on the ground a few inches away. I stared at it for a moment, trying to relax. Adrenaline still flooded my veins. I didn't want to have to get Lorien to knock me out. My head already hurt. But I needed to sleep to get to the dream realm. I had to fix my mistake.

And what would the other prisoners think? Had they heard what I said about being Wind Dreamed? Would they take it seriously?

They would already be confused by the fact that I was taking a nap on the floor next to their captor. I wasn't supposed to let anyone know about being Wind Dreamed or the Wind Whisperer or the existence of the supernatural world.

But I couldn't worry about that right now. Lorien would call Keres and she could run damage control. I had to fix my mistake. My eyes closed. I had to finish this.

33

Thirty-Three

The Wind Whisperer was nowhere to be seen, but I didn't need it. I needed one dream, and I knew where to find it. It was the same golden color as before, but dimmer, like it was dying.

I touched it.

The scenery bent in on itself and changed into the same dream. I stood alone in the entryway. This time, I didn't have to wait for the children to run by. I went to the office as the children barreled down the hall, laughing and shoving each other. They whipped the office door open and darted in, slamming it behind them.

I opened it back up and slipped inside.

The kids built their pillow trenches. I watched them crouch down and shush each other. Rich had his brother tucked close to his side, their hands clasped tight. They grinned at each other like they shared some kind of secret.

"What do you want?" I whispered to them.

Rich's head lifted, looking for the source of the question. He couldn't see me yet.

The door opened. Everyone went quiet, but the man, Rich's father, still summoned his little brother, who went the same way he had last time.

Had Rich been having this dream ever since I messed up the first one? Reliving the same nightmare over and over when he shut his eyes? No wonder he'd gone a little mad and his emotions were stagnant.

Rich got up and started moving toward the two, devastation written all over his face.

"Tell them what you want," I ordered him. "Tell them why."

His father and brother were almost at the office door. Rich stepped forward, hands shaking.

"Please don't take him."

I willed his father to pause and turn toward Rich. His brother still held his hand, but he looked back too, a confused expression on his face.

"We want to stay together." Rich looked at his little brother. "Right, Memphis?"

I took control of the little boy's body. Memphis looked between his father and brother. "We *all* stay together."

His father looked down at him. "We aren't all staying together. I'm leaving. You come with me, and your brother stays with Mom. Understand?"

That line hadn't come from me. The edges of the dream started to ripple. It morphed slowly into that field from the first time Rich had this dream. Was he fighting me somehow?

In the blink of an eye, Memphis and Rich's father disappeared, leaving me and Rich alone in the field. He dropped to his knees, put his hands to his face, and screamed into them. I flinched at the ragged, painful sound.

I crouched beside him and put a tentative hand on his

shoulder. I wasn't sure how to make myself visible to him except to will it to happen just like when I manipulated dreams.

"It's not that simple," he sobbed. "It's never that simple."

"But you tried," I said.

He smacked my hand away and shot to his feet. He was no longer a preteen boy, but his current high school age. "You would know, would you? You don't understand any of what I've been through."

I straightened. "I understand not being able to reach your family. I can't keep my parents from prioritizing their business over spending time with me. And I can't keep friends unless they're assigned to me by a literal god. Even then, it's like everything I do pushes them away. I'm a walking social disaster. Completely useless."

"That's not the same thing," he growled. "You still have no idea what it's like to have to see your sibling ripped away from you just because your parents don't love each other anymore."

"No. I don't. So, why don't you make me understand?"

He turned away. "You wouldn't even if I tried. And it's not like you're really here in the first place. The Wind Whisperer doesn't exist. Neither do the Wind Dreamed. You just said those things to trick me, because you're just like everyone else who keeps me from being happy."

I bit my tongue, but what did it matter what I told him? Chances were he wouldn't take me seriously anyway. Or maybe he would. Maybe this would turn into a giant disaster like when I'd found out about Sylvan. Maybe he would have to become a demigod. I wasn't sure how to feel about that, but all I could focus on was the present moment.

"I'm really here, Rich. I didn't lie to you. I *am* Wind Dreamed. It *was* me in that first dream. I was new to all of… this." I waved a hand around at the empty field we stood in. "And I messed it all up. I am so sorry that I can *never* make up for that. But I can tell you that it gets better."

He rolled his eyes. "My brother and I were separated five years ago. If it was going to get better, it would have by now."

"It won't get better if you just let it fester."

He faced me with his arms folded over his chest. "Why are you here, Wren? You've ruined everything. I'm sure the police are on their way while we're stuck in here. So, what's the point? Are you here to gloat?"

I was there to try to fix my mistake. But it didn't seem like anything I was saying was getting through to him. There was only so much I could do, but I couldn't leave him the way he was, the way I'd made him, without trying to do something about it.

It wasn't just about the kidnappings, though that was a big part of it. It was about the damage I'd done to his psyche. It might have already been damaged, but the things I said in that dream had done something to him, something I would regret for the rest of my life if I just turned him over to the police and didn't give him another moment of thought.

I sat down on the grass and stared out at the horizon. This reminded me way too much of the field I woke up in when I first met the Wind Whisperer, when all of this started.

"I'm here because I don't know what else to do." I sighed. "It's my fault this happened. But I don't really know how to fix it."

"You can't fix it." He huffed as he sank down into the grass across from me. "This was always how I was."

"Maybe. But I think—I *hope* you'll be more, that you'll learn how to grow around and past this." I hoped I did too.

He glared out at the gently waving strands of grass. "Is this it then? Your big motivational speech about how I should change my life sucks."

"I know. I'm not very good at this kind of thing. You deserve better." Hopefully, I'd get better. The other Wind Dreamed dropped nuggets of wisdom and life lessons on me so casually that I was starting to think it was a hallmark of being a child of the Wind Whisperer.

"I'm sorry I hit you with those rocks," Rich blurted.

I raised an eyebrow. "I'm sorry I had to hit you with one too."

"And drop a statue on me?"

"And drop a statue on you."

We sat quietly for a long moment.

Finally, I stood. "I wish you luck, Rich."

He tucked his knees to his chest and rested his chin on them. "I'm going to need a lot more than luck where I'm going. They don't accept that kind of currency in jail."

"You won't go to jail. You'll go to juvenile detention." Hopefully. I wasn't sure if he could be tried as an adult for this.

He snorted. "Like that's going to be any better."

"At least you'll be with people your own age."

He shook his head. "I'm screwed either way unless I can bulk up enough to scare people away, so they don't mess with me."

"I think you'll do ok."

"I hope so."

"Goodbye, Rich."

"Goodbye, Wren."

I walked off toward the distant horizon. The dream world would have some kind of end somewhere. I found it at one of the trees that stood at a crooked angle in the field. Behind it was the way back to the dream orb.

I paused with my hand on the trunk to look back at Rich. He sat with his hands propped against the ground behind him, face tilted up, basking in the sunlight. I smiled. I had no idea if any of the things I'd said to him had gotten through, but I'd given it my best shot. And he didn't look too unhappy. It was probably too much to hope for, but I did anyway.

34

Thirty-Four

The faces of the other Wind Dreamed swam into view as I opened my eyes.

Lorien put a hand to her chest. "Oh, thank the Wind Whisperer you're awake."

Frida threw herself down on top of me to hug me. I grunted as the fabric of her clothes rubbed against the raw cuts on my arms. My head still throbbed. Dried blood from the cut on my head cracked and flaked off my face as I moved.

"Get off of her." Reve yanked Frida back. "Can't you see she's in pain?"

"Can you sit up, chickpea?" Imena took my hands and gently pulled me into a sitting position.

Almos pulled a first aid box into his lap and sorted through its contents. "How is your head? Did you get a concussion?"

"I don't know," I mumbled. "I don't think so." The fuzziness had gone away. It just hurt.

I peered around them. The other four kidnapping victims were huddled together against one wall, talking to each other and watching our reunion. Keres was crouched over Rich's still unconscious body. I watched her take what looked like the femur of some animal out of her jacket and lay it across his wrists. With a twist of her hands, the bone curved around Rich's wrists, the ends melding into the middle of the bone to trap his hands behind his back.

Bone handcuffs. Cool.

I hissed as Almos rubbed an alcohol pad over the cut on my forehead. My fists clenched as he applied ointment and taped a wad of gauze over it. The others fussed over me as he wiped down the cuts on my arms too. Reve took another pad and carefully cleaned the blood off my face where it had run from my head wound. Imena clutched Lorien's hand the whole time, but their focus was on me. Everyone's anxious but relieved emotions swirled through the air.

Finally, Keres approached. "It's nice to see you're alright, Wren, but we need to get everyone out of here. I've contacted the admin." Her jaw clenched. "The clean-up crew is coming."

"Clean-up crew?" Lorien asked.

Keres's expression would have been more appropriate at a funeral than here. "Time."

Our eyes widened.

"Time is going to deal with this?" Almos demanded, glancing between Rich and the freed captives.

"Since it was caused by the power of the gods, it is the gods' mess to clean up. Time has agreed to take care of things," Keres replied.

"What does that mean, exactly?" Imena asked.

Keres shook her head. "There's no telling with Time. They requested we bring everyone involved to one of the classrooms in the main building."

I was the first to get to my feet, holding onto Reve's shoulder to steady myself. "Then let's go."

The Wind Dreamed huddled close to me as we made our way up the stairs, through the library, and to the main building. The hostages followed us, also sticking close together. Keres brought up the rear. We were met by a handful of administrators, who ushered us into a large classroom. They darted out almost as soon as we entered, but they left the door halfway open as we sat at the desks.

"When are the police coming?" the woman asked once we were alone and settled in the desks.

"They're on their way," Keres told her as she paced in front of the doorway. "Don't worry, we're going to get everyone out and back home as soon as possible."

"The police aren't really coming, are they?" I whispered to Reve.

"No. This is too delicate of a situation to bring in law enforcement. Involving Time is always a double-edged sword, but they keep this from being a legal problem." He slipped his hand into mine. "Just stay close to us. The gods don't usually mess with each other's children, but Time doesn't always play by the rules."

I took a shaky breath. Plenty of others had said things about Time. The more I heard, the more I dreaded meeting them. The god of time seemed more like a natural disaster than a god.

"They aren't going to hurt those people, are they?" Frida murmured.

"They wouldn't," Almos answered. "Not physically anyway. Further than that, all bets are off."

"What about Lorien?" Frida glanced at her. "She was one of the victims."

Imena, who perched on the desk attached to the chair where Lorien sat, put a hand on Lorien's shoulder. "Time will have to go through us to get to her."

A rhythmic knocking sounded on the half-open door. All eyes turned toward it as a figure slowly made their way around the door. The person continued their drumming beat until they stopped in the middle of the doorway.

We all stared at the tall woman. Her dark hair was pulled back in a high ponytail on top of her head. Her sharp, uptilted eyes offset the roundness of her face.

She frowned at the door. "No, that wasn't right." She turned and redid the beat a little faster, adding and subtracting a few knocks and ending with a drumroll. "That's better." She turned back to us. "Hello, everyone."

There was a moment of tense silence.

The woman in her thirties, the wife of the police officer, scowled. "Who are you? Where are the police?"

The woman in the doorway flickered, disappeared, and reappeared in front of the disgruntled woman. Everyone jumped back.

The tall woman took the other woman's hand and kissed the back of it. "To answer your first question, I am Time, god of time, watcher of worlds, and general agent of chaos. As for your second, there are no police. There never were, and there never will be. You are at *my* mercy, my dear."

The woman yanked her hand away from Time. "How *dare* you! I will have you know that—"

Time snapped their fingers. The woman's mouth kept moving but no sound came out. The woman stopped, frowned, tried again. Her eyes widened in panic. She clawed at her throat. Time morphed into a perfect likeness of the woman. If I hadn't watched it happen, I wouldn't be able to tell the difference between the two.

"I will have you know," said Time in a perfect imitation of the woman's voice, "that I get to decide your fate from here on out, so I'd be *extra* nice if you ever want to speak again." Time patted the woman's cheek.

"Time," Keres said. Her voice held a slight tremor.

Time turned to her and gave her a smile sharp enough to cut steel. "Hello, little bone bride. So nice of you to give me something to do. I've been looking for an extracurricular to liven up my monotonous days."

Keres smiled tightly. "What do you need?"

"For starters, I need your hair." Time's hair turned the same shade of red as Keres's. They twirled a lock of it around their finger. "Now that that's settled, I need you out."

Keres stiffened. "Out?"

"I told you I needed everyone involved in this debacle in one room. You weren't involved." Time waved a dismissive hand at Keres. "So, get out."

Keres glanced at us Wind Dreamed.

Time followed her gaze and grinned that blade-like smile. "Aw, how cute." They flickered out of existence and appeared in front of us. They put their hands on their thighs and leaned toward us like we were a bunch of little kids. "Did Old Windy put you in charge of all these baby breezes?"

Reve wrapped protective fingers around my arm. Almos tucked Frida behind him. Imena angled herself between Lorien and Time. We huddled in a cluster, cringing away from the god.

"Skittish little things, aren't they?" Time said. Their eyes paused on me. Their head tilted to the side, reminding me too much of how hawks looked at their prey before they struck.

Reve stood up, getting between me and Time.

Time gave him that slashing grin and changed shape again to look exactly like Reve. "You Wind Dreamed were always so close. What would you do if I touched her, I wonder?" Reve's voice coming out of Time's mouth made all the hairs on my arms stand on end. I'd never heard him use that teasing tone. It sounded wrong.

Reve lifted his chin. "Try it and we'll all find out."

I gripped the back of his shirt. It didn't seem like a good idea to goad such an unhinged god.

Time laughed, a jagged, half-crazed sound that also shouldn't be coming out of Reve. "Oh, I like you. Such a shame the old windbag got to you first."

"Time." Keres stood in the open doorway. "We don't exactly have time to waste."

Time raised a brow. "Darling, I know *exactly* how much time we have." They glanced back at us and nodded toward the door. "You lot can join your keeper out in the hall. My business is with these." Time fixed their eyes on the four victims. The woman was still clutching her neck and opening her mouth, trying to speak.

Reve turned and helped me stand. We huddled together, making our way out of the door.

"Don't go far, little dreamers," Time called after us. "It would be so much work to track you down if you run away, and I'm not finished with you yet."

I hated that they still wore Reve's skin and spoke in his voice, but at least we didn't have to stay in the same room anymore.

Reve's hand was still in mine when we came to a stop in the

hallway outside the classroom. Imena held one of Lorien's hands, but Lorien took my free hand in hers and gave it a squeeze. Almos and Frida joined the chain, so we all held hands with our backs to the wall.

Keres closed the door and sagged against the doorframe. "That's why we don't like getting Time involved in the business of other gods, especially where new demigods are concerned."

"Do they always do that? Change into other people?" Frida asked.

Keres nodded. "They can't seem to stay in one body for long."

I eyed the door, thinking about how easily Time had taken Reve's form. "What do they really look like?"

Keres shrugged. "Who knows? If they've shown their true form to anyone, no one has been able to distinguish it from any of the other ones they've taken."

"What is Time doing in there?" Lorien murmured, craning her neck but not moving from our line against the wall.

"Rewriting their memories," I answered.

They all looked at me.

"How do you know that?" Keres asked.

I squeezed Reve and Lorien's hands. "Let's just say I didn't become Wind Dreamed the conventional way."

Keres frowned but didn't press for details.

"What about Rich?" I asked after a long moment of silence.

"He's in there." Keres jerked a thumb at the classroom door across the hall. "Tied up and still unconscious."

"Time is going to do something with him, right? He knows what I am."

Keres compressed her lips. "Hopefully. If not, the other

gods will have to find something to do with him, and the options would be very limited."

Exile or becoming Wind Dreamed. Those were the options the Wind Whisperer had presented to me when I'd been in a similar situation. Rich *could not* become Wind Dreamed. I hoped that I'd repaired the damage I'd dealt, but that didn't mean I wanted him near me. I *definitely* didn't want him anywhere near Lorien.

I wasn't sure I was ok with him being exiled either. This predicament was at least partially my fault. Sure, Rich had taken things way too far, but it was because of my magic whether I knew it at the time or not. I shared at least some of the responsibility.

"We'll see when Time is finished with the others." Keres crossed her arms and took up a spot on the wall between us and the door where Time was doing… whatever they were doing with the victims.

We were all quiet, listening for any indication of what might be happening in the room. It was dead silent for several minutes before a little boy opened the door and walked out. It wasn't the same one who'd been held captive by Rich.

The boy, Time I assumed, looked up at Keres. "They should be good to go. They all believe that justice was served, and the boy is behind bars, but their memories of what he looks like are a bit fuzzy, so should they run into him again, they won't remember him."

"Thank you." Keres sighed.

Time cracked their knuckles and grinned the kind of grin that didn't belong on such a young kid. "Now, where is the little troublemaker?"

"In there." Keres pointed at the room across the hall.

"Excellent." Time skipped to the door, opened it, and slipped inside.

"I guess Time is going to handle everything," Keres said.

"Good," Imena breathed and rested her head on Lorien's shoulder.

I relaxed too. This would all be over soon.

The door opened a long moment later. A dark-skinned, stick-thin man emerged with his hand on Rich's shoulder, pulling him along. Rich kept his eyes on the ground, lips pressed together.

"Come on now. We're going to have so much fun together." There came a grin I was beginning to associate with Time no matter what form they took.

Keres straightened. "Where are you taking him?"

Time paused in front of all of us, bringing Rich to a stop too. Time propped their boney elbow on Rich's shoulder. "I'm taking him with me, of course."

"With you where?" Keres pressed.

Time waved a hand vaguely in the air. "Here, there, wherever I want to. He's mine now."

"Yours? You mean…"

"I've made him Time Bent. He is now under my jurisdiction and neither you nor any of the other gods can do anything to him without my *explicit* permission." There was a difference in the smile Time gave Keres. It was too smug, too satisfied. It dared her to protest.

Keres stood so still she might as well be one of the statues from the gallery under the library. "This job fell under the Wind Whisperer's jurisdiction."

Time propped their free hand on their hip. "And the Wind Whisperer asked for my help, so I get to decide what to do with him."

"This isn't how things work, Time," Keres tried again. "Since I was invited to investigate this case, the Boneman has more say in what happens to this boy than you do. You can't just do whatever you want with him. Order must be kept."

Time straightened and sauntered over to stand directly in front of Keres. "Do not think that just because you are Bone Touched you have any say in this world, girl." Their voice dropped and echoed as if there were more than one person speaking. The lights in the hall flickered. "I do these jobs because I want to. I do not take orders, instructions, or even suggestions from your master or theirs."

Time's eyes flicked to us. They had changed from a warm brown to a shifting, grainy gold and black pattern that flowed across Time's eyes like sand in an hourglass. We pressed back away from them, hands grasping each other.

But Time turned back to Keres, uninterested in us. "I am, was, and always will be. You are nothing but a walking corpse, breathing borrowed air that is spoon-fed to you by your creator. Do not tell me how things work. Do not pretend like you serve any purpose other than taming the dead. You know nothing of this world, and you never will." Keres seemed to shrink with every word.

I stepped out of the line of Wind Dreamed. "Leave her alone."

Time's head snapped in my direction. The shifting sands of their eyes slowed. "Ah, Wren Mentis." That smile curved across their face. Their voice went from sounding like many people speaking to just one. "This is not the first time I've had to clean up one of your messes."

Reve and Lorien pressed close as Time stalked toward me.

"I suppose thanks are in order for my new friend here." They patted Rich's cheek, ignoring how he cringed away from them. "At least they would be if I hadn't refused to wipe your memories, thus forcing dear old Wispy to take you in. So, really, I should be thanking me and my impeccable planning."

I gritted my teeth. "You knew this would happen?"

Time laughed. "Of course I did. Or at least I hoped it would. I can't control everything, but I've gotten *very* good at figuring out which rocks to throw into the stream of time to make the waves I want."

"All those people in there were kidnapped and held prisoner for days just so you could get a new Time Bent?" I demanded, letting go of Reve and Lorien to step up and face Time.

Time smiled the kind of smile you gave a child when they were throwing a tantrum about something trivial. "You're young. Not to mention new to all of this. And slightly concussed. So, I'm going to ignore your ignorance." They tapped a spindly finger to the bandage on my head.

Reve's hand darted out and smacked Time away. The sound of the blow echoed in the hall. The other Wind Dreamed gasped. Keres took a step forward. Time quirked an eyebrow.

Reve glared. "I guess we found out what I'd do if you touched her."

Time grinned, their eyes returning to brown. "I guess we did. Now, I've got things to do. And time is a-ticking." Time turned back to a rather pale Keres still with that placating smile. "Release my client immediately."

Keres watched Time out of the corner of her eye as she removed the bone handcuffs from Rich's wrists and backed away to join us by the wall.

"Thank you kindly." Time bowed their head to her. "It was so nice meeting all of you." Their gaze swept over us painfully slowly. "We will meet again."

Time glanced at me before morphing into a tall girl with pale skin, long, wavy white hair, and sharp cheekbones and jawline in a long-sleeved white button-up shirt and black slacks. My mouth dropped open. Time winked a silvery white eye at me before turning away.

"Wait!" I started after Time and Rich.

They flickered and disappeared before I could ask how Time knew what Sylvan looked like.

Reve put a hand on my shoulder. "They were just baiting you, Wren."

"But what if they weren't?" What if Time knew where Sylvan was, if she was still alive?

"They were," Keres breathed. "Even if they knew something about Sylvan, they wouldn't tell you unless it served their purposes. It's best not to tempt fate."

Lorien drifted over to me. "Let's just go home."

My jaw clenched as I stared at the spot where Rich and Time had stood a moment before. "Ok." It wasn't like I could go after them. No matter how much I wanted to.

35

Thirty-Five

We made our way back to the penthouse with our hands clasped. Keres followed, giving us space to just be with each other. And maybe giving herself space too. I hoped she hadn't taken to heart all those things Time said to her.

The god had been just as bad as everyone had said.

I had been willing to give them the benefit of the doubt before, but there was no excuse for what they did. Letting Rich torture all those people just to have the chance to make him Time Bent was inexcusable. If Time wanted Rich, they should have just come and taken him. All of this could have been avoided.

If they had just erased my memories of the whole DNA test debacle, everything that I'd been through never would have happened either. I would still be at Mortorous Academy. Maybe Sylvan would never have gotten hurt and had to return to the Boneman. Maybe she would have been the first friend I managed to keep for more than a year. I never would have known this magical part of the world existed. I would never have had my ignorant bliss shattered.

And I never would have met the other Wind Dreamed.

They were the one part of this that I did not and could not regret. They were a colorful group of people I never would have thought could get along. Despite them butting heads sometimes, they did. If rainbows could have so many different colors in them, why couldn't a group of friends have as many different personalities?

I squeezed Reve and Lorien's hands as we rode the elevator up. They glanced at me out of the corner of their eyes and squeezed back.

Lorien had stayed with us instead of running up the stairs. Whether it was because she was physically weakened from her time locked in that closet or because she didn't want to be separated from us after we were just reunited, I was glad we were all together. Even if it made the elevator incredibly cramped.

We spilled out into the penthouse once the doors opened. The others gravitated toward Reve's sectional sofa, where we'd spent that horrible weekend without Lorien when we hadn't wanted to separate long enough to sleep in our own beds.

I broke away from the pack. "I'll join you guys in a minute. I could really use a shower right now."

Dust from the broken statue and flying rocks had settled on my skin. Blood crusted on my shirt and pants. I wasn't sure which patches of it were mine and which were Rich's. At this point, it didn't really matter. I wanted to get rid of all of it as soon as possible now that we were out of danger and things were calming down.

"Do you need any help?" Imena asked.

I smiled wearily. "I didn't hit my head *that* hard. I should be fine."

"If you're gone for more than thirty minutes, we're going to come looking for you." Reve said it almost like a threat.

I nodded, watching the aura of protective concern undulate around him. "It shouldn't take me long."

Lorien probably wanted to shower too. There hadn't exactly been showers in the closet she and the others were held in. But she had attached herself to Imena, and I doubted any of the three gods could separate them.

I grabbed a change of clothes from my room and headed to the bathroom, where I got my first look at myself in the mirror since everything had happened.

Reve had wiped most of the blood from my face, but there were still flakes of it on the bridge of my nose near my eye and under my chin. With my sagging shoulders and the tired little wrinkles under my eyes, I looked weary in a way a seventeen-year-old shouldn't.

The wound on my head was close enough to my hairline that Almos had had to put some of the tape he'd used to secure the gauze pad in my hair. But that was a problem for tomorrow.

I shucked off my bloody clothes and jumped in the shower. The hot water stung the cuts on my arms, but once I got over that, it felt good. I took my time, careful to keep the bandage on my head from getting wet. By the time I turned off the water, despite having turned on the ventilation, the mirror was clouded, and the air was so thick with steam it was hard to breathe.

When I opened the door, I wasn't that surprised to find Reve sitting against the wall beside it.

"It's only been twenty-five minutes," I told him as I gathered up my bloody clothes.

He got to his feet and followed me. "You don't get the extra time it would have taken me to walk down the hall from the living room."

I tossed my clothes in the little trash bin next to my desk. I wasn't going to deal with cleaning them. I never wanted to see that set of clothes again, much less wear them.

"How sweet of you."

Reve leaned against the doorframe. "Sweetness doesn't have anything to do with it. If you fell in the shower—"

I grabbed him and hugged him tight. "You can be real with me, Reve. I'm not going to turn it against you."

His arms snaked around me. His chin rested on my head. "We walked into that gallery, and you were passed out on the floor with blood all over your face. How am I not supposed to worry?"

"I don't expect you not to worry. I just expect you to be realistic. I can walk. I can talk. I'm not seeing double. Unless you *don't* have an identical twin brother."

"Not funny."

I giggled. "It's a little funny."

"You have the worst sense of humor."

"I know."

His dark eyes scanned my face. "Are you hungry?"

"Starving."

He let go of me and stepped back. "Good. The others are pulling together some leftovers. Lorien's stomach wouldn't stop growling the whole time you were showering."

I chuckled, but it was strained. Lorien had been through a lot. She'd been harassed, kidnapped, held captive, half-starved, and those were only the parts I knew about. There had been four days between her disappearance and when I found her. A lot could happen in four days.

I tried not to think about it too much. She'd still had a lot of fight left in her when Rich opened that closet door. I would cling to that, instead of the horrible places my imagination went when I remembered that Rich took her because she refused to be romantically involved with him.

"Let's go get dinner." I frowned. "Or is it breakfast now?"

Reve shrugged. "Considering it's two in the morning, probably breakfast. But who cares about labels?"

"Good point." Food was food. And we were all home. That was what mattered.

36

Thirty-Six

The Wind Whisperer was waiting for me when I fell asleep that night in a pile with the others on Reve's couch. But it wasn't in the dream orb.

I stood in a meadow. One that looked incredibly familiar.

"You found her." The Wind Whisperer's soft voice reached me before its physical form took shape. It coalesced in wisps and fragments, pulling itself together from the nothingness of the air around us.

I chewed my lip. "I almost landed myself in the same situation as her."

"But you did not. You got them all out. I am so proud of you." The light twining through its body brightened as it wrapped its arms around me. It felt like getting hugged by a cool spring day.

My arms folded around my chest. "I caused this."

The Wind Whisperer withdrew far enough to look at my face. "What do you mean?"

"You were there when it happened. I guess you didn't realize what was going on at the time because you were so busy trying to deal with my little temper tantrum, but I did that. I'm the reason they got kidnapped. I made Rich do… whatever it was he did to them while he had them locked in that closet." The conditions hadn't been humane, and I still didn't want to think about all the time those people, especially Lorien, were at his mercy.

"Wren, you made him do nothing," the Wind Whisperer sighed.

I flung out an arm. "He said so himself! I didn't put a gun to his head or anything, but it was what I said in that dream that drove him to do those things. It's still my fault. And Lorien—" My voice broke.

The Wind Whisperer cupped my face in its breezy hands. "You cannot change people. People change themselves. At the end of the day, dreams are dreams, Wren. They only have as much power as a dreamer gives them. We do our best to send messages based on what we think people are missing in their lives, but whether they listen and do something about it is entirely up to them. You *do not* take responsibility for their actions."

My brow furrowed. "I'm not taking responsibility for his actions. I'm taking responsibility for mine."

"As admirable as that might be, it is misplaced. You already apologized for your behavior that night. Do not apologize for his after that."

I looked away. "They're linked. One caused the other."

The Wind Whisperer reared back. "Wren Mentis, your patron god has forgiven you and told you not to worry about it. Why do you insist on persecuting yourself?"

"Because all of this can be traced back to my decision to send in that DNA test, which shoved me into all of this, and I was bad at it, which caused the whole situation with Rich." I appreciated that the Wind Whisperer didn't hold me fully accountable for Rich's actions, but someone had to, even if that someone was me.

"By that method of thinking, it was the Boneman's fault for making your friend Bone Touched in the first place and allowing her to come to you for help. It is a circular logic that goes nowhere. No one is truly at fault for any of this except Richard himself."

My jaw tightened. "What about Time? They openly admitted that they refused to erase my memories of Sylvan's DNA test because they knew something like this would happen, and they wanted to make the criminal Time Bent."

The Wind Whisperer's colors dimmed. "Time does not operate by the same rules as the rest of the gods. They fail to hold even themselves accountable for the things they do. I am sorry you had to deal with them."

The image of Time turning away in Sylvan's body burned in my mind. "Can't you do something about them?"

The Wind Whisperer lowered its head. "It is hard to control a being that has power over time and space. We have tried, but Time is slippery. The one time we attempted to contain them…" The Wind Whisperer wrapped its arms around itself. "It did not end well. We learned a lesson that day. Life and death are the forces that drive the world, but they are nothing in the face of what connects them."

"Time," I breathed.

"Stay away from them if at all possible. They have been known to disregard our rule about not interfering with each other's children. If you cannot avoid them, play nice. Being a part of their game is better than what they could do to you if you angered them."

The memory of the shifting sand in Time's eyes when they faced off with Keres surfaced in my mind. They had taken that woman's voice, rewritten the memories of all Rich's victims, and assumed Reve's and Sylvan's forms.

Their power was time itself.

What else could that entail? What else could they do to people? What had they done to retaliate when the other gods tried to put a leash on them?

I shivered. "And you can't do anything about it?"

"Nothing permanent. Nothing they will not come back from with a massive grudge. I know it is not ideal. It goes against my nature as a god to bow down before them. But as long as we leave Time alone, they leave us alone. Mostly."

"There's always a bigger fish, isn't there?"

The Wind Whisperer straightened and shook its head. "That is not the point of this meeting. The point is that you have graduated."

I frowned. "I haven't even finished the school year." And I had a whole other year until I was done with school.

The Wind Whisperer chuckled. "I am talking about your powers. You no longer have to have my supervision to dream walk. You have proven yourself. In rather remarkable time too. I will pop in every once in a while, to see how you are doing, but you do not have to wait for me anymore. You can start doing things on your own."

My eyes widened. "Oh, wow. Thank you." There wouldn't be a safety net anymore.

"You do not sound very excited."

I chewed my lip. "What if I mess up again?"

"You will not. Not like you did before. You might still be

learning, but you have come a long way." A smile appeared in its voice. "You have done a great job, Wren."

I wouldn't say I'd done a *great* job. Adequate maybe, but not great. I thanked the Wind Whisperer again anyway. Maybe I hadn't done a great job, but I could. Couldn't I?

This whole Wind Dreamed thing hadn't gone the way I thought it would the first time I was in this meadow, but wasn't that what life was about? Finding a way to ride out the twists and turns you didn't see coming? If the Wind Whisperer was willing to forgive me for what happened with Rich, that meant it was giving me more chances to prove myself worthy of being a demigod.

"You can rest for tonight," the Wind Whisperer continued. "You have had a busy enough day."

I smiled. "Thanks." I hadn't really wanted to dream walk tonight. Traveling into Rich's dream had been more than enough. "And thanks for not giving up on me."

"Wren, you are my child. I would never give up on you."

37

Thirty-Seven

Despite everything we'd been through, there was still school in the morning. Reve still extricated himself from our sleep pile on his couch to make breakfast before anyone else was up. I woke as he wriggled out from between me and Almos. I waited until he got into the kitchen before I gathered my wits and pushed Frida off me to follow him.

She groaned and rolled over onto Lorien's lap, mumbling something about dolphins.

"Go back to sleep, Wren," Reve rasped in his rough morning voice as I pushed through the kitchen door.

"As welcoming as ever," I replied. "What are we making for breakfast?"

He pulled bowls and measuring cups out of a cabinet. "*You* aren't making anything. You're going back to bed. I don't want you around the stove and handling knives when you have a head injury."

I opened the drawer in front of me where all the teaspoon and tablespoon measurements lay nestled neatly inside of one another. It was probably his culinary background, but Reve kept the drawers and cabinets organized with military precision. "I'm fine, Reve. I want to help."

"No." He smacked my hand away from the measuring spoons and grabbed them himself.

I jumped up and sat on the counter. "Well, I'm not leaving."

He finally looked up at me with his patented exasperated expression. "Fine." He opened another cabinet and pulled out a caramel-colored bag. "Then you can make my morning coffee. I'm sure we'll all need some after the night we had." He pushed it into my lap.

I grinned as I jumped down from the counter. "No problem, Reve." I walked over to the coffee machine. "So… how do I work this thing?"

I'd never really cared for the taste of coffee. There wasn't enough creamer and sugar in the world to sweeten it up to my liking.

Reve sighed and came over to walk me through the process.

* * *

Going to classes where no one knew what happened the night before and we had to act normal felt surreal.

Not everyone acted as if *nothing* happened, though. Plenty of people asked about the bandage on my head. The other Wind Dreamed had helped me cook up a story about how I was running around in the lightly wooded area that surrounded campus and fell in a ditch where I knocked my head against a rock and got scratched up by some brambles on my way out.

It was a sufficiently "teenager" answer that no one asked any questions other than the occasional "Where did it happen?" I gestured off in some random direction and said I didn't quite remember. The story was that Lorien and Imena had found me fighting my way through the brambles and helped get me out and to the nurse.

The tale was received mostly with pity from the students and a little exasperation from the teachers that I'd been messing around out in the middle of nowhere by myself. No one looked too closely.

My hardest class came right before lunch. The Rich's seat was conspicuously empty. The whole time the teacher lectured and wrote equations on the board, I kept stealing glances at the vacant desk.

Where was Rich now? What had Time done with him?

He hadn't seemed entirely happy about the arrangement when he and Time had emerged from that classroom the night before. I wished I could have been in the room with them when Time woke him up and offered him a way out. Maybe I could have warned him against making a deal with the crazy god.

What had they said exactly? Had they toyed with him the same way they toyed with the rest of us?

I hoped they hadn't. His head had been messed with enough by powers out of his control. And even if he had kidnapped and held all those people prisoner of his own accord and not because of my lack of control over my magic the way the Wind Whisperer seemed to think, no one deserved to be left at the mercy of a loose cannon like Time.

But he had agreed to become Time Bent, which meant he would never be rid of them. Just like I would never be rid of the Wind Whisperer. Hopefully, he didn't regret it. Hopefully, he could turn his life around in some way.

What did the Time Bent even do?

"I have no idea," Lorien said from behind me that evening as I sat in front of the vanity in the bathroom. "I'm not sure anyone but the gods and the Time Bent themselves do. No one likes to talk about Time. 'Speak of the devil and they shall appear' and all that."

I winced as she pulled a little too hard on my hair. "So, no one knows anything about what Time or the Time Bent do? Surely the god of something so important has to have some big job like the Boneman and the Wind Whisperer do. They're equals, more or less, right?"

I would have thought so before. Life, death, and time. Those were the three big powers that ran our world in a crooked little trinity. But the Wind Whisperer made it sound like that wasn't the case.

Frida snorted as she looked up from reading the hair dye instructions. "I don't know if I would say they're equal. If the Boneman and the Wind Whisperer are as afraid of Time as it seems like they are, I'd say it's a pretty safe bet Time is the most powerful."

"I'm just glad they left us alone," Lorien murmured. "Ready for foil."

Frida jumped off the counter where she'd been sitting and ripped a strip of foil from the roll by the sink. Reve had shouted at her when he'd seen her taking it until she said it was for me. Lorien held out a lock of my hair, covered in red dye, for Frida to wrap it up.

I'd decided that if I couldn't tell people I was Wind Dreamed, I could show it off in a more subtle way. Lorien and Frida both wore their respective colors in their hair, so I thought I would give it a try too. By try, I meant letting the two girls dye a thin red stripe in my hair. I could always do more if I decided I liked it.

"I don't know if I'd call wearing Reve's skin and almost starting a fight with Keres leaving us alone," I grumbled as I carefully adjusted the foil-wrapped bit of hair.

"I can't believe they got away with that guy!" Frida threw her hands in the air. "Isn't there some rule about that? Doesn't Time have standards or any semblance of morality?"

I leaned against the counter. "No. I think that's their whole thing. That they don't care about anything or anyone besides themselves."

"Do you think we'll ever see either of them again?" Lorien asked softly.

Frida and I glanced at each other. Lorien hadn't said anything to either of us about her time stuck in that closet, but even if Rich had left them all alone in there, only feeding them occasionally, she and the other victims would have psychological scars for the rest of their lives.

"If we do," Frida said, gripping the roll of foil so tight her knuckles turned white, "we'll be the last thing they ever see."

Lorien gave us a shaky smile. She'd been pretty quiet since we escaped Rich, but she'd been far from alone. Imena usually stuck close to her, but the rest of us were rarely far.

"I'm gonna go see how Reve is doing with dinner," Frida declared. "I'm starving. You've still got twenty minutes on that hair, Wren." She pointed a warning finger at me.

I gave her a thumbs-up. "Got it."

"Don't let her overprocess, Lorien," Frida called over her shoulder as she headed off down the hall.

"What would happen if I overprocessed?" I asked Lorien.

"Your hair gets really dry and damaged," she replied as she peeled off her rubber gloves. "You're putting harsh chemicals on it after all. You have to be careful."

I turned toward the mirror and poked at the bundle of foil wrapped around my dyed lock of hair. When she put it that way, the whole process seemed so much more serious.

"Thank you for saving me," Lorien said.

I glanced at her out of the corner of my eye. "It was the least I could do." No matter what the Wind Whisperer or anyone else said, it was still partially my fault.

Lorien shook her head. "I don't think you get it. Being locked up in there was terrible. We got small meals twice a day, a bucket to use as our bathroom every once in a while, and we weren't allowed to talk to each other. We weren't always gagged, but Rich had a camera in there he used to watch and listen to us.

"We couldn't escape. We didn't even know where we were. He knocked us out and carried us down there when he captured us. I had no idea we were on school grounds until you freed us. We didn't know if he was going to kill or torture us. I couldn't even sleep deeply enough to contact the Wind Whisperer."

That was what the god of life said when I raged about it being as helpless as us Wind Dreamed when it came to finding Lorien.

"I'm so sorry, Lorien. If I hadn't messed up Rich's dream—"

Lorien grabbed me in a tight hug. "It's not your fault he's a psychopath. He did all that of his own free will. Not because you altered his mind in a dream. That's not how dream walking works."

So I'd been told.

I hugged her back. "I'm still sorry."
Lorien chuckled. "I forgive you."
I smiled into her shoulder. "Thanks."

38

Thirty-Eight

Keres's door was open when Lorien and I emerged from the bathroom. Inside, Keres was shoving clothes into a red duffel bag. She turned and glanced up at us. Her eyes combed over me.

She straightened with a grin. "Nice hair. Are you trying to steal my look?"

"No." I crossed my arms as she came to lean against the doorframe. "I'm inventing my own look."

"It's nice."

"Thanks." I peered behind her at the bag sitting at the foot of her bed. "Are you leaving?"

She nodded. "The case has been cracked, so it's time for me to move on."

"Where are you going?" Lorien asked softly.

Keres shrugged. "I don't know yet. But there's no shortage of places that could use an extra Bone Touched. People just can't seem to figure out how to stop dying."

I resisted the impulse to laugh.

Keres's face grew serious. "I'll keep an ear out for news

about Sylvan." She held out a folded piece of paper. "My number."

I took it. "Thank you."

All my questions about Sylvan's disappearance had resurfaced when Time shifted into her. No matter what the others said about Time, I couldn't help feeling like I'd missed the last opportunity I had to find out anything about her when they'd vanished with Rich last night.

Keres crossed her arms. "If you hear anything before me, let me know. Sylvan had a lot of potential as a Bone Touched and a lot of good as a person. A little lost in the world, but good."

I nodded as I unfolded the slip of paper and read the number. "She did—*does*." We shouldn't have been talking about her in the past tense when we were still unsure if she had died.

Keres smiled and turned back to her packing. Lorien headed for the kitchen. I was about to follow her when Keres called to me over her shoulder.

"You do too, Wren. I may not know all the nuances of being Wind Dreamed, but I know how to judge a person's character. Don't ever give up on what you want."

"I won't." I glanced at the floor with a faint smile and turned toward the kitchen.

Keres joined us for one last dinner before she left. We gave her the warmest goodbye possible. We thanked her for everything she'd done to help us and watched the elevator doors close. She held her head high, her hair falling around her shoulders like spilled blood, holding her duffel bag in one hand.

It was the same way I'd seen her when we first met, so

cool and collected. I wished I had her level of confidence. I hovered by the window in the living room, watching Keres's tiny form walking across campus toward the parking lot from six stories up.

What was it like to wander the world fighting ghosts instead of traveling through dreams every night?

"Wren."

I jumped a little at the sound of Imena's voice. "Hey, sorry. I was lost in thought."

She followed my gaze out the window. "Yeah, I could tell."

We stared out at the setting sun for a silent moment. From this high up, it was even more magnificent than on the ground. Since this was the tallest building on campus, nothing blocked the view.

"I'm sorry," Imena murmured.

I glanced at her out of the corner of my eye. "What?"

"I shouldn't have said those things to you last night. I don't really believe any of them. I was… desperate. And angry. And I know that's not a good excuse, but I couldn't leave things the way they were between us."

I turned back to the window. "I understand. I've said things in anger that I regretted. I mean, that's what started this whole thing."

Imena faced me. "Lorien told me something about that."

I winced.

"She told me you blamed yourself for getting her kidnapped."

If she was going to tell me it wasn't my fault, I was going to walk away and lock myself in my room.

"I get it. It's not my fault. I didn't make him kidnap Lorien. I just told him to be selfish, and he took it too far. I was the catalyst, but he committed the crime. But that's not how the human brain works. We hold our shame the way we hold a grudge. So, as much as I appreciate that you all keep trying to make me feel better about it, it's not going to work. You don't have to keep telling me."

Imena raised her eyebrows. "I was going to say you should go to therapy. Reve and I have a good therapist that both of us see in town. She's Wind Dreamed, so you don't have to worry about keeping our secret. We can hook you up."

"You know… that sounds like a good idea." I never would have tried it before. My parents would have lost their minds with worry if I told them I thought I needed mental help. But it was about time I stopped worrying about how much they would worry.

Imena grinned. "Great, you can go with Reve on Friday when he has his appointment. I'm sure he'll be thrilled to share another activity with you."

I rolled my eyes. "Sometimes I still have no idea what to think of him."

Imena shrugged. "No one does, but that's what we love about him."

I laughed. "That's what I love about all of you."

They all loved each other in their own way. Imena was the cool, calm older sister type, but she could do a full 180 when the people she cared about were in danger. Frida was the playful little cousin who got into trouble sometimes but knew how to get out of it and stay out of it when necessary. Almos was the big brother who held everyone together without being too clingy. Lorien was the little sister who looked at the world through rose-colored glasses but also knew how dark it could get. Reve was the grumpy but loving middle child.

And I...

I didn't quite know where I fit yet, but I knew I fit. Somewhere in this chaotic, caring family, there was a place for me. That was all I wanted. To have a place to come home to with people who would hug me, laugh with me, cry with me, *live* with me.

The start we had was rocky to say the least, but what family didn't have its flaws?

We could work past it, grow around it, live with it, as long as we had each other. I think that's what being Wind Dreamed is about. Whatever complications arose in our lives or from being the children of a literal god, we always had each other. I might not have become Wind Dreamed under the best of circumstances, but being Wind Dreamed was a pretty great thing to be.

"One more thing." Imena straightened, her tone grave.

I turned to face her, bracing for whatever else she might say. But she just threw her arms around me and held me tight. I hugged her back.

"Thank you for saving her," she breathed. "It turns out the one person who didn't go looking for her, the person I yelled at and criticized, was the person who found and rescued her."

I huffed a laugh into her shoulder. "I shouldn't have gotten so mad at all of you. I don't know why I was so—"

"It doesn't matter." Imena let go of me and took a step back. "You better not be trying to take my place as her knight in shining armor though."

I winced. "I'm sorry I said that."

She shook her head. "You were right. We should have gone looking for her that first night. We probably would have found her days ago if we had, and you wouldn't have gotten all..." She gestured at my injuries.

"They're not as bad as they look. Over-the-counter painkillers can work wonders."

Imena crossed her arms. "That head wound might scar though. You should change the bandage daily and make sure you put ointment on it."

I brushed my fingers over the bandage on my head. "Depending on how it looks, it might be a really cool battle scar. One of the characters in a book I read a while ago had a scar like this."

Imena rolled her eyes, but a smile curled her lips. "You *would* think like that, wouldn't you?"

I raised my brows. "Am I wrong, though?"

"Like you said, it depends on the shape of the scar. Though, personally, I'd prefer you didn't have any at all. No matter how cool they might look or how invisible they might be." She leveled a serious look at me.

I nodded. "That would be nice, but life rarely works that way."

She sighed and gazed out at the last fading light in the sky. "I know."

"Thanks for putting up with me and my..." I waved a hand around, searching for the right word. "Eccentricities. I know I haven't been the model Wind Dreamed."

"None of us were. I was so full of rage when I first came to Animos Prep. Lorien was pretty withdrawn, not wanting to participate in group activities. Frida is still working on growing out of her antagonistic phase. Reve was so out of it after what happened to his brother. And Almos was even more of a brat than you."

I snorted. "I doubt that."

"You should ask him about it sometime before we graduate. He's got some pretty embarrassing stories."

"What happens after you graduate?" I asked. I was just getting used to having them all here, and Imena and Almos were about to leave the school forever.

"We go out into the world, get jobs, make friends, live our lives, and when we sleep, we dream walk. Just like we do now. We'll just be adults out on our own."

"I mean, what happens with us? You're going to come visit, right?"

She smiled so broadly, it looked like it hurt. "Of course we will. We're going to miss you as much as you miss us. But you're only a year behind. And you'll have new Wind Dreamed come in next year."

I blinked. "We will?"

She smirked. "Yeah, with me and Almos leaving, the Wind Whisperer will send you at least one new demigod. It likes to have us together in groups of five to eight. Keeps the family dynamic intact. You'll have to introduce me to the new Wind Dreamed when we visit."

I chewed my lip. "Does the Wind Whisperer already have someone picked out?"

Imena shrugged. "Maybe. It might have its eye on a couple people, but it won't decide until summer. That way it'll have plenty of time to make them Wind Dreamed before sending them to you."

It felt so important and intimate when she said it like that. The Wind Whisperer didn't send us to Animos Prep. It sent us to each other.

"You'll do great with them. I can feel it." Imena glanced

over my shoulder.

I turned to see Lorien standing a little behind me. "Hey, can I borrow Imena for a minute?"

"Yeah, of course." I couldn't imagine what the kidnapping had done to their relationship. They probably wanted to spend all their time together.

"Thanks." Lorien held out her hand to Imena.

Imena took it, pulled her close, and kissed her. The kiss lasted a second too long for my comfort.

I cleared my throat and slowly walked backward toward the bedroom hall. "I'm going to go shower and take care of my head. Good night." I darted off. Their soft chuckles followed me down the hall.

The bathroom was thankfully empty. With this many people living together, it was more likely to have at least one other person in it. We had two showers and two bathroom stalls for just such an occasion, but there were plenty of times where at least one person had to wait.

I'd caught a lucky break. No one was in either of the showers or the stalls or messing around in front of the vanity. I'd rather address my head injury without anyone fussing over me. There had been quite enough of that since I'd gotten all the kidnapping victims out of the underground gallery last night.

What would happen to the gallery?

A lot more people knew about it now, and it didn't exactly have the best memories attached to it. Plus, there was the wreckage of that statue all over the back corner of the floor. Anyone who wanted to use it as a gallery would have to clean all of that up first. And the blood too. Between me and Rich, there was probably a decent amount of it on the floor.

Maybe if someone tidied it up and aired it out, it could be a nice place again, but it didn't stand a chance the way we'd left it.

I wriggled my nails under the adhesive near my hairline. It pulled painfully on my hair. Untangling it without ripping all that hair out took a while and left a long strip of my hair sticky.

It hurt to pull the bandage off my skin too, but I couldn't bring myself to just rip it off in one go. Pulling slowly, tears in my eyes, I removed it. The inside where it had been pressed to my head was spotted with blood, but at least it hadn't gotten stuck to the clot itself and ripped off the scab.

I tossed the bloody bandage in the trash and looked in the mirror.

My breath caught in my throat. I leaned as close to the mirror as I could. This couldn't be right.

I ran my hand over the place the bandage had covered. Instead of a jagged, scabbed-over cut, there was the thin squiggly line of a scar. I rubbed my hand over it. It didn't hurt at all. There was no blood, no perforation in the skin. It was like a year had passed and it was almost completely healed. If I leaned back, I could barely see it.

Footsteps padded in the hallway.

I slapped a hand over my scar and turned to see Reve stop in the bathroom doorway with a handful of clean clothes on his way to shower. He raised his eyebrows in that silent, unimpressed, questioning way of his.

"Reve, do the Wind Dreamed have some kind of healing ability?" I asked in a voice that was too high for my liking.

His eyes strayed to where my hand covered my head. "Not any more than a normal person."

"You're sure?"

He leveled a mildly annoyed stare at me. "Yes. I'm sure."

"Then how did this happen?" I dropped my hand.

Reve stalked forward, his face expressionless as he examined the scar. "This isn't possible."

I crossed my arms as he poked at it. "Well, it happened."

"Did Keres heal it for you? I think the Bone Touched have healing powers."

Of course they did. The Bone Touched got all the cool powers. "I don't think she did anything to it. And if she did, wouldn't she have said something about it? Told me that I didn't have to walk around all day with a giant bandage on my face?"

"You would think." He frowned, tossed his clothes on the counter, and scratched at the scar.

I swatted him. "It's not a prosthetic. It's not going to come off and start bleeding again."

"Then why does it look like so much time has passed since—" He stopped, went white.

"What? Why are you looking at me like that?" My heart rate picked up.

"Accelerated time," he breathed. "Who do we know who has power over time?"

The blood drained from my face. "No way."

"Time touched your bandage in the hall right before they left with that boy." He took a step back.

I rubbed my fingers over the scar. "You think they did this when they touched me?"

"If they can rewrite people's memories, take away someone's ability to speak, shift bodies at will, and turn someone into their demigod in a matter of minutes, I'd say there's a pretty good chance they can speed up the healing factors in your body to turn an hour-old injury into a year-old injury."

"But why? Aren't the gods not allowed to mess with each other's children?"

Reve clenched his jaw. "Time isn't good at following the rules."

I braced a hand against the counter. Time wasn't a benevolent god. They didn't dish out favors from the goodness of their heart. Did they even have a heart?

What was their purpose in healing my injury and not even telling me that's what they had done? Were they trying to send a message that I wasn't untouchable just because I belonged to the Wind Whisperer?

I had stood up to Time when they were belittling Keres. Had they not liked that and wanted to give me a subtle warning?

"I think they were trying to thank you," Reve whispered.

My brow furrowed. "What could they possibly have to thank me for?"

"They said they let you become Wind Dreamed so that all of this could happen, and they could make a new Time Bent. What if healing your head wound was their way of thanking you for helping all of that happen?"

"If they wanted to be the good guy, wouldn't they have told me that's what they were doing?" There had to be something sinister at work here.

Reve leaned against the counter next to me. "I'm not going to try to pretend I know what goes on in Time's mind. The important thing is that they left. We don't have to worry about them anymore. The only reason they were able to make it on campus was because the Wind Whisperer allowed it, just like it allowed Keres to come and hunt that kidnapper."

I hoped so. But even if that were the case, Imena and Almos were graduating in a couple months. Reve, Lorien, and I would follow a year later. We'd be out in the world after that, at the mercy of whatever forces wanted to mess with us, including Time and the Time Bent. Staying at Animos Prep was a temporary solution.

Reve snapped his fingers in front of my face, bringing me out of my doom spiral. "Focus on what's right in front of you, Wren."

I raised an eyebrow. "Like you?"

He gestured at the vanity. "I meant the first aid supplies you've scattered over every inch of the counter so no one else can use it. But I guess technically, I am *right* in front of you. That stuff is more to your side."

"Oh, oops."

"Uh-huh." He started picking things up and tucking them away.

I jumped in to help. "Thanks for being my friend, Reve."

"What else would I be?"

"A pain in the butt."

He snorted. "I guess you're lucky for having dodged that bullet then."

Yeah. I smiled. I was pretty lucky.

39

The Wind Whisperer

The Wind Whisperer glided over the field where the Wind Dreamed meditated. They sat in rainbow order today. That was a big deal. Ever since Lorien had returned from her ordeal with that boy, she hardly separated from Imena. That she allowed Frida to sit between the two of them showed how far she had come in the last two months.

The Wind Whisperer glowed a bit brighter with pride as its gaze found Wren on the end next to Almos. It hadn't entirely known how Wren would fit into the dynamic the other five demigods had.

Usually, when it hunted for a new Wind Dreamed, it observed the waking and sleeping lives of a few candidates for several months before choosing one or two to send to Animos Prep. It weighed their dreams and ambitions against their initiative and tenacity. The process had never steered the god of life wrong.

But Wren was a special case.

There had been no preparing for her, no grace period

to make a decision. The Boneman had come to the Wind Whisperer, and they had known their options were limited. The Wind Whisperer could have rejected the idea of making an exception to its carefully thought-out process.

The Boneman chose his children based on instinct and his first impression when he met their ghosts. But that was not the way of the Wind Whisperer. Tending the dreams of others required a certain touch that had become increasingly rare. It wasn't something you could throw someone into and expect them to know what they were doing.

The Wind Whisperer could have held to its convictions and let the Boneman deal with the girl. But she was a dreamer. A powerful dreamer so full of stories they practically oozed out of her pores. She just needed to be given permission to let herself go and tap into her creative side.

Animos had done wonders for her in that regard. Already, the Wind Whisperer could see the dream of writing stories of her own forming in her head. And with that history professor and the librarian to guide her, she could really make some literary magic.

Sure, she had fought it at first. She was so used to the rigid right or wrong way of the world. But she had gotten there.

It was due in part to the demigods surrounding her. It was a testament to the Wind Whisperer's process of picking its Wind Dreamed that they had stuck by her from the beginning. They had helped make her into the person she was now almost as much as she had herself.

The six of them had become more than the Wind Whisperer could have hoped for.

A sudden awareness tugged the Wind Whisperer's attention away from its children. It was the awareness of something powerful, something eternal, something unstoppable.

Something. Or someone.

The Wind Whisperer scanned the meadow from above. There, nestled in the boughs of one of the larger trees, sat Time. They had taken the shape of one of the Animos Prep students and watched the Wind Dreamed sit in the breezy quiet with their eyes closed, completely at ease and completely unaware of the danger that lurked so close to them.

The Wind Whisperer swooped down to hover beside the god of Time.

"Your newest baby sits at the head of the group," Time mused without taking their eyes off the demigods. "I wondered if she senses she will become one of their most integral members before she graduates. She's taken to her role quicker than expected. But *oh*, the havoc she wreaked. It was more magnificent than I could have hoped." Time giggled.

"Tell me you lied to her." The Wind Whisperer didn't often have trouble with controlling its emotions, but when someone messed with its children, all bets were off. Especially if that someone was Time.

Time's head lolled to the side to look at the windy apparition. "You're going to have to be *a lot* more specific, Breezy. Who and what are we talking about?"

The colors pulsing through the Wind Whisperer's body brightened in anger. "My *child*. Wren. She said you saw all this coming, that you set it in motion all because you wanted to force that poor boy into a deal with you."

Time stretched out their legs and folded their arms behind their head. "My dear Whisperer, I don't *force* anyone into anything, unlike you and Bones."

"You engineered a situation where the boy had no choice but to agree to become your underling or be incarcerated. That is no different. Stop pretending you are better than us."

"Only when you stop pretending you're better than me." Time reclined against the tree and closed their eyes.

A sharp wind sent the tree swaying and knocked Time from their branch. Their eyes flashed open as they plummeted from the tree. And stopped. Two feet off the ground. Time rewound itself, tossing the god back up onto the branch.

"That wasn't very nice," Time chided with a smirk.

The Wind Whisperer's shape pulsed with fury. "Tell me it is untrue. Tell me you did not put my children through those unspeakable horrors just to get a Time Bent out of it."

Time rolled their eyes and sighed. "I didn't put your children through those unspeakable horrors just to get a Time Bent out of it."

The Wind Whisperer sagged with relief. Time was a destructive god but never had the Wind Whisperer known them to lie. They had no need. With the kind of power they wielded, they didn't need to cover up the truth to keep themself safe.

Time glanced at the Wind Whisperer sidelong. "I did it for character development too."

"TIME!" The Wind Whisperer's voice rolled across the field like a hurricane wind, bending trees, snapping branches, whipping leaves and grass and flower petals into the air in a frenzy.

The gusts broke around the little knot of Wind Dreamed, creating a pocket of calm like the eye of a storm. Their eyes stayed closed in meditative concentration, none the wiser to their god's wrath. Time held their own bubble of protection, suspended in the moment before the raging wind rushed through the trees. It infuriated the Wind Whisperer how untouchable they were.

Time shook their head sadly. "All these years and you still haven't learned how to control your temper even in the presence of your demigods. For shame."

"How could you let them go through all of that? How could you *make* them go through all of that?" the Wind Whisperer seethed.

Time cast an annoyed glance at the Wind Whisperer out of the corner of their eye. "Again, I didn't *make* anyone do anything. They did all that stuff on their own."

"But you knew! You knew what would happen—"

"Not with one hundred percent certainty. The future is hazier than you might think."

What pathetic excuses. Time was all bluster and bravado with a response to everything.

"You let it happen anyway. You kick-started this whole thing when you refused to wipe her memory." The Wind Whisperer jabbed a wispy finger at Time. "I hold you personally responsible for the trauma they endured."

Time scratched at their neck, completely unconcerned.

"And you used your powers on her," the Wind Whisperer accused.

Time slid stolen green eyes toward the god of life. "Did I?"

"Do not play dumb with me. You are insane, not stupid."

Time grinned their feral grin. "Insane, am I?"

The Wind Whisperer's fists clenched. "Our one rule is that we leave each other's children alone, a rule we *thought* you followed as long as we left you alone."

Time picked at their long, acrylic nails. "I'd hardly call sending me to clean up your messes leaving me alone."

"We had an agreement after The Massacre that we would abide by your rules as long as you abided by ours."

"Agreements that are unspoken are meaningless."

"You would know about meaninglessness."

"Let me get this straight." Time sat up and swung to face the Wind Whisperer, eyes flashing their strange sandy pattern. It was the only true feature of theirs that the Wind Whisperer saw them show anymore. "You accuse me of making this mess, yell at me for it, knock me out of a tree for it, and then get mad at me because I cleaned most of it up."

The Wind Whisperer huffed and spluttered, searching for the right words, its shape growing and shrinking and distorting. Time was the only being in the world that could produce such a reaction in it. They seemed to know exactly how to get under the Wind Whisperer's nonexistent skin and used every opportunity to do so.

Time's eyes settled back to solid green. "Now, if you don't have any more grievances to air, I've got a new Time Bent that needs some training." Time's eyes glazed over as if they were watching something far away. "And another one who's about to find out exactly what she signed up for when she became my demigod. Toodeloo."

Time fell backward, warping time and space as they fell to teleport themselves elsewhere.

The Wind Whisperer was left alone at the edge of the meadow where the Wind Dreamed still sat in meditation. It took several moments to calm itself down before it turned to look at them. Time was a problem but it had been centuries since they had directly harmed any Wind Dreamed or Bone

Touched. They just wanted to get a rise out of the Wind Whisperer.

The six demigods were what really mattered.

The creators. The wishers. The ones that whispered in the minds of others. The ones that held the power of life in their lungs. They were the ones who would ensure that the world never stopped living.

The Wind Whisperer sent a calming breeze through the meadow with a whispered "keep dreaming" before it dissipated into the air.

Acknowledgments

I have often heard that the second book in a series is harder to write than the first. In some ways that was true for *Wind Dreamed*. It started when I decided to release this book only six months after *Bone Touched* and continued when I ran into repeated delays due to the holidays and a massive family vacation.

This is, of course, mostly my own fault. But I want to thank everyone who helped me keep somewhat on track for this release.

Sarah Hemmi, my wonderful aunt and beta reader/editor, I'm so glad that we could have those meetings and talk about this book both professionally and as its first fans. Thank you for not charging me thousands of dollars to edit my manuscript even though you are a professional editor.

Thank you to my sister who worked some magic and finished my cover within a week of getting the photos for it while I panicked about the tight scheduling.

To all my family and friends who have supported me through my writing career, it means a lot. To all the kids I was supposed to be substitute teaching while I wrote and edited this book, some of y'all were a handful, but you make it possible for me to write and have a day job.

Appreciation is in order for everyone who bought a copy of *Bone Touched* and loved it as much as I do. *Wind Dreamed* probably wasn't exactly what you expected, but I hope you liked it anyway.

And to anyone who struggles with "gifted kid syndrome" or wanting to live in a world other than this one, never stop dreaming and making your dreams come true.

About the Author

F. R. E. (Rita) Kinney grew up and lives in Texas and is the author of *Bone Touched* and *Wind Dreamed*, the first and second books in the *Crooked Trinity* series. When she isn't writing books inspired by weird dreams, she is taking long walks with her dog, crocheting, knitting, or lurking around her local Catholic church.

You can connect with me on:
🌐 https://frekinney.org

Also by F. R. E. Kinney

Bone Touched

Sylvan never asked the Boneman, the god of death, to kidnap her, erase her memories, and reform her body to make her one of his demigods. So, she was more than happy when he placed her in the care of a boarding school where she could leave the traumatic experience in the past.

Unfortunately, getting rid of a god isn't so easy, and Sylvan must learn how to find her own path in life while using her new magic to fulfill a divine purpose: capturing the lost souls of the dead.

www.ingramcontent.com/pod-product-compliance
Lightning Source LLC
Chambersburg PA
CBHW031109160726
47991CB00004B/1295